The Obergon Chronicles

Rayelan Allan

Contents

Part IV. Gunther's Story 291

Part V. A Message from Odon 415

Prologue

The story that is told in this book is so unbelievable that even I—the one who wrote it and lived it—have trouble believing it actually happened. The first part of this story began over 25 years ago. The second part began 16 years ago.

Over the ensuing years, many people have encouraged me to write a book to tell the story. Most people who encouraged me only knew part of the story. They knew me as the wife of Gunther Russbacher, The October Surprise Pilot. I was a political prisoner's wife. They heard me tell our story on radio, television and at conferences.

Our love was something I had only known from books and movies. I didn't believe it was possible to love with the power and intensity that I loved Gunther. From the moment I met him, I knew I wanted to spend the rest of my life by his side. He was equally surprised and maybe a little terrified by the sudden and instant love he felt for me.

Do people really fall in love instantly? We did. After you read this story, you will have to decide if the instant love we felt was genuine or if it had a dark side that was created in a CIA laboratory. Gunther and I decided within hours of meeting that we wanted to marry and spend every minute together for the rest of our lives.

Gunther told me that due to his CIA security clearance we would have to request permission to marry. Having been previously married to a government scientist who had to request permission even to travel, I was used to this kind of thing. I had gone through many background clearances, as my first husband was promoted to higher positions that required higher clearances for both of us. Furthermore, I had just been asked to go to work for a United States Senator, and as a result, I was right in the middle of a background check of my own for a security clearance.

It never occurred to me that our request to marry would be denied. But it was.

Had we not been in the middle of a passion that neither of us had ever felt before, maybe we would not have acted so foolishly. There was no way we were going to agree to be parted. We loved each other too much to do what they wanted us to do. And so we violated CIA protocol and married even though we had been ordered to separate for two years and have no contact with each other.

As a result of our forbidden marriage, powerful forces swept in immediately to "clean up" the mess. Part of "cleaning up" the mess involved keeping Gunther in prison while these powerful forces monitored our every phone call, letter, and visit.

People within our government needed to know what Gunther was telling me. They needed to know if he had violated national security secrets. They needed to know if he had told me about what he had done during his 28 years with the CIA. But most of all they needed to know what he had told me about President George H. W. Bush's involvement in the Reagan campaign's treasonous deal with Iran, a deal that has become known as The October Surprise.

Moreover, these powerful people knew things about us that Gunther and I didn't know about each other. I didn't know Gunther was the man who had flown George H.W. Bush to Paris to conclude the October Surprise. Gunther didn't know that I was the best friend of the woman who had just published the first book entitled *The October Surprise*.

Had we known these things, I think we would have been smart enough to realize the danger we were in, though I don't think it would have stopped us. I think the only change in our plans would have been to use the Lear jet we flew to Reno to marry to instead fly us out of the country.

Most people who urged me to write a book only knew the story that started in 1989 when I married Gunther. Our exploits were scenes out of a spy novel. The secret Lear jet flights, the meetings with the Director of the CIA, high level Admirals, Navy SEALS, and covert CIA operatives could have been scripted by Hollywood writers. The attempts on our lives involved beatings, ambushes, cars being blown up with rocket launchers, and assassins being murdered in front of me.

I didn't have to make up things to make our story interesting enough for Hollywood, in fact, I have had to omit many parts if our story just to make it believable.

The truth of what really happened the night we met was beyond comprehension. I quickly realized I couldn't tell anyone about it. If I did, they would never believe another thing I said. For years I kept this part of our story secret.

Then, in 1996, Gunther and I made the decision to break our silence about the untold part of our story. We agreed to tell the whole story at a conference in Florida. We also planned to expose our government's Manchurian Candidate programs, as well as the mind-control technology that is used to put "messages" into the minds of New Age Channels. Then, as we were making plans to meet in Florida, Gunther disappeared.

I was so angry at our government that I decided to go ahead with the conference even if it meant losing Gunther forever. For the first time, I told the story you will read in this book. At the time, I didn't know if Gunther was dead or alive.

After the conference, Gunther reappeared, but he was not the same man. In fact, he didn't remember ever being married to me. Someone had erased his memory of me.

The pain of losing Gunther was so devastating to me that I crawled in a hole for several years. When I finally emerged, I buried the memory of what we had gone through during the decade we were married. I buried the memory of our love because it was too painful to remember it.

Gunther died in August of 2005 without ever talking to me again. He died the day the Sirian Lion Gate opened. The fact that he died on this date told me that I had to tell our story the way it actually unfolded. Not only did I have to tell our story, but I had to tell it side by side with a story that began hundreds of thousands of years ago in the Sirian Tri-star system.

As you read this book, you will learn that Gunther was "The Lion of Salzburg." You will discover that his mother was descended from a Hungarian royal family who believed they came from Sirius. You will read a letter from Gunther to me in which he talks about the prophetic green gate that we will walk through together.

The story of Gunther and Rayelan is wrapped around another story—a story about Atalon and Raelon, two halves of a Supersoul from Sirius. It's this other story that began over 25 years ago when I began writing a series of short stories about the soul families that settled Earth.

When I decided to write this book, I realized that what will be presented will be extremely difficult to believe. It will also be extremely difficult for me to tell because I am too personally involved. In other words, I am right in the middle of the story, and I can't see the forest for the trees. Knowing this, I thought long and hard about how to present the information in this book.

The first part of the book reads like a science fiction novel. The second part reads like "channeled" messages from ascended masters. Part One and Part Two are easy to read and should be read in order. Many people who have read these parts have had personal awakenings.

The rest of the book is presented as a series of self-contained articles. I decided to include these articles as they were originally written for several reasons—one reason being that most of the articles were written many years ago, and I didn't have to slice open old wounds and reexperience the pain.

The articles that make up parts three and four can be read in any order. They were edited to "stand alone."

Most people don't read books like this in order. They pick up a book, open it, and start reading. Because I knew this, I decided that each article had to stand on its own. As a result of structuring the book this way, there are times that parts of the story are repeated. In some articles only a small piece of the story had to be told, while in others, the entire story had to be told to complete the puzzle. I don't think I have ever read a book that was structured the way this one is, and I apologize if the repetition is too jarring.

Part Four tells Gunther's part of the story. This had to be included so people can know who this man was. Gunther Russbacher was not some New Age space cadet. When you read the articles that he wrote and the articles that were written about him, please remember, that Gunther firmly believed he was from Sirius and that he *was* Atalon, my other half!

The Chronicles of Obergon are presented in order. Each one builds on the one that came before. It may seem as if some of the stories have nothing to do with the theme of this book, but each story teaches an important lesson, and these lessons have to be learned in order. Each story or lesson gives additional pieces of the puzzle that you need in order to understand what these stories are about.

By the time you have read all the Obergon Chronicles, the Lessons for the Children of Obergon, and the Awakening Prose, you will realize that the book you have been reading has turned into a different thing altogether. Just when you are beginning to feel comfortable with the information that is being presented, the book makes a light-speed change and begins connecting the stories from ancient times to the present day. This is done to help you understand that the characters in the Chronicles may *very* well be walking the earth today. In fact... *you* may *be* one of the Children of Obergon!

The information about me and my CIA husband, Gunther, is included so you can make up your own mind as to where the Obergon Chronicles came from. Did they really come from a hermetically sealed library under King Solomon's Temple? This is what I was told by a Templar I met in Salzburg. Were these Chronicles excavated by the Knights Templars, brought back to Europe and then stored in salt mines near Salzburg, Austria? Was Gunther's Austrian family privy to these stories? Was I chosen to be his wife because of my own royal blood, or because I really am Raelon? Were these stories put into my head by some form of government "mind control" technology? Were Gunther and I both being programmed to believe that we are beings from Sirius. Were we pawns in some kind of convoluted government mind control operation. Or... are we Atalon and Raelon?

I sincerely hope you enjoy the journey on which you are about to embark. This book speaks to different people in different ways. Be forewarned, if you are one of the Children of Obergon, you may never be the same!

Rayelan

Introduction

This book will never be sold in mainstream bookstores!

This will be true as long as the legitimate inhabitants of earth are enslaved by the financial yoke and media programming of their "illegal alien," self-proclaimed masters. These "masters" were trapped on Earth, aka Terra, when the Planetary Council closed Terra to all trade and interference from other planets. To the evolving race of humans, the technology, mind-control and other tricks used by the alien "masters," made the aliens appear as gods!

Presently, these so-called "gods" control earth through inter-connected corporations that are owned by the same 300 inter-married families. Some of these families have alien blood, others are "willing slaves" who have sold out their own kind for power, money, fame, fortune or the promise of eternal life.

The "illegal alien" corporations got their start-up money in this century by hijacking the money of the United States. They created the Federal Reserve Banking System. Most people assume the FED is owned by the United States government. It isn't. It is owned by the many corporations that these illegal aliens created. The FED start up money gave the extra-terrestrial trespassers everything they needed to stretch their tentacles to every inch of the planet. The illegal aliens and their corporations are involved in every aspect of human life. The illegal aliens use every aspect of human life as a means of controlling humans.

For a moment, consider the phrase, "television programming." There is a spiritual law that says that freewill cannot be messed with. In other words, these alien "masters" can't "program" you without your permission. So they created "television programs" with which to program you. You turn on the TV and select the "program"; therefore you give your permission to be programmed. The same goes for radio, music, videos, films and even books, magazines, newspapers and web pages. The gigantic "entertainment industry" is just one cog in the "alien control" of humanity.

They control everything.

- They control health care. They control it in such a way that humans are always sick or under the influence of prescription drugs. Their drugs cut you off from your spiritual nature and make you easier to control. Their drugs also make them very rich.

- They control education. They "educate" children to become good little cogs in their machinery. They print the text books used in schools. They write the history that is taught in school. They fill children's heads with "politically correct" thinking. They turn children against their parents, against their countries, against their religions, and even against their own sex.

- They control our food. Food is being genetically altered. No one knows what this will do to human bodies 50 to 100 years down the road. Our alien masters don't care, because they know they will be long gone when the problems start showing up.

- They control our water. They put fluoride in our water because it makes people docile and therefore easier to handle. Adolph Hitler knew this, so did the Soviet Union. Fluoride was used in Germany and Russia to render people docile so they would not try to fight back. Many pharmaceuticals, such as Prozac, enhance the mind numbing effect of fluoride.

  Water is also becoming a scarce commodity due to the pollution from these alien owned corporations. Soon water will be more valuable than oil and these same corporations will control the water. Without water, countries cannot grow their own food. A country with no food will cease to exist.

- They control our weather. Rain is also being controlled through new weather weapons. These "alien masters" have developed machines that control the weather. Blistering hot weather can force a country into submission by causing droughts or tens of thousands... possibly millions, of heat-related deaths. Weather machines can also create hurricanes and tornados. They can create Tsunamis, floods and blizzards.

- The alien "masters" can create earthquakes and volcanic eruptions.

- The alien "masters" can cause pandemics to kill off humanity. They do this every so often when the world is filling up with "useless eaters."

- The alien "masters" also control almost all of the financial centers of the world. They created credit cards to replace "the company store." The unions broke the backs of the companies and the company stores. To get even with the unions, the alien "masters" took over the unions. To replace the "company store," they created credit cards. People are now like squirrels running on a wheel. The more they charge on their credit cards, the faster they have to work to keep paying the bills. Not only do the aliens control the financial centers that ordinary people use, the aliens control all of the central banks in every country.

I could continue talking about the things that the aliens control on earth, but if I did, the introduction to this book would become a separate book.

There are a few hopeful things that need to be mentioned...

- There are not very many of these alien "masters." There are only 300 inter-married families.

- Their rule will not last much longer. They are dying out. In order to survive and rule all countries, they had to mate with humans. The inter-breeding with humans has diluted the alien gene pool. Alien souls can only incarnate in bodies that have a certain percentage of alien DNA. Soon there will not be enough alien DNA in a Terran body to accommodate an alien soul. When this happens, the alien souls will have to return to their home worlds or face total and complete death!

  This is known to the aliens, and they are planning their escape from Earth. They are building huge ships capable of space travel. They are planning to take a very large number of human slaves with them. Let's hope YOU won't be one of those slaves.

- Unknown to the aliens is that highly evolved souls have been incarnating into their family bloodlines. These souls are so evolved it is not possible for the "alien masters" to discover who they are or what they are doing. I do not know what these "highly evolved souls" are planning, but my guess is that it is good for humans.

Another message hidden in this book is graduation. Graduation is close at hand. Not for the "alien masters," but for the souls who are on this planet legitimately. These souls have learned what they came to learn and it's time for them to graduate and go to work or go to school elsewhere.

Another of the many messages of this book is, "Things aren't always what they appear to be."

This is probably the most important thing you can remember as you are reading this book. When you finish a "Story" or chapter, don't expect the next chapter to have anything to do with what you have just read. Sometimes it will appear connected, other times it will seem like you've started an entirely different book.

Don't expect things to stay the same. Once you have read something and believe it to be true, don't be surprised if you find out in later chapters that it isn't true. One chapter may explain things in ways that make you comfortable. They next chapter may make you face things that are very uncomfortable. Don't be too quick to judge anything, even the spelling and grammar! The "poems" were "dictated" as is —I was told *not* to change one word. The actual Chronicles and the Lessons are different. I was told I could change the archaic writing to make it more understandable. I changed very little.

Don't expect to understand what this book is about, until you have read it to the very end. And even then don't expect to fully understand everything. If I don't understand some of the things that are written about… and I'm the one who compiled all of this… how can anyone else expect to fully understand everything that is presented here!

In the past, I've told people that reading this book will be like "peeling an onion." But that really doesn't begin to describe this book. When you peel off a layer of an onion, what you have left is another layer of onion. When you peel off that layer, you find another layer of onion. No matter now many layers you peel, when you reach the center, you still have an onion.

The only way that reading this book could be compared to peeling an onion would be if the onion was a "magical onion" and each time a layer was peeled away, something new and wondrous would appear. Reading this book is like peeling a "magical onion" with a thousand faces. Just as soon as you think you have figured things out, you will be flipped a hundred and eighty degrees and suspended upside down in an alternate universe with a totally different face staring back at you.

Just as you think you are beginning to understand where you are and what is going on, you will be flipped again. You will watch as your mind tries to find your "sea legs" in a boat out of water on a world without seas.

Where did the stories in this book come from? Only the people who gave me the information know for sure. They said the information came from the "Historical Records of the Planetary Council." I never had the opportunity to ask, "What is the Planetary Council?" or "Where do you keep these records?" or "Is this the same as the Akashic Records?"

Thirteen years after I was given the first story in this book, I sat in a hunting lodge at the foot of the Untersberg near Salzburg, Austria. A young man, who was my "tutor", told me the origins of these stories, where they were found, and how they were translated. What he failed to tell me was why I was the one who was chosen to receive these stories.

The first story was 'given' to me in 1981. I copied and shared it with a few close friends and clients. By 1989, when my safe and secure world was turned upside, not more than 1000 people even knew of these stories.

In 1989, I entered a world that few outsiders ever see. I married a deep cover, covert CIA operative. I had known this man for many years. I knew him as a Naval officer. I first met him in the late 70s, when I was married to Dr. John Dyer, a nuclear physicist who was the Dean of Science and Engineering at the Naval Postgraduate School in Monterey, California.

When we met again in 1989, I thought I remembered his name was Bob, but he introduced himself to me as Gunther Russbacher. We chit chatted a bit and then decided to move from the dining room of the hotel where we met, to the bar, to continue our conversation. He went on ahead of me.

When I returned, I stood outside the bar and looked through the window. I saw Gunther sitting with some men. All at once I heard a voice so loud that I turned to see if someone was standing next to me.

The voice said, "If you go through this door, your life will change forever. Are you strong enough?"

I thought back over the year I had just survived—the sudden death of my husband, John... a quick and impulsive move to Uptown New York City, from tranquil and quiet Carmel Valley, California... surviving pneumonia with no insurance... hemorrhaging so badly in Virginia Beach that I almost bled to death. My mind went over the last year and I thought to myself... "Nothing could be worse than what I have just survived. I'm strong enough for anything!" Little did I know just how strong I would need to be to survive the next decade of my life.

I opened the door. The loud noise stopped and everyone looked at me. Gunther stood up and directed me to a table that was on the other side of the room from where he had been sitting. Some of the men he had been sitting with began throwing things at him. He turned around and said, "I'll get you for this!"

We sat down. The woman who took our orders was a tall blonde woman who literally "grilled" me. She wanted to know my entire life history. At that time I thought she was just being friendly, I would later find out her name was Marilyn, and even though she appeared to be an "old" cocktail waitress, she was in fact a Colonel in the Air Force who was attached to Gunther's Special Operations Team.

Marilyn brought our drinks and left. Within 5 seconds of her leaving, and an old Templar toast, Gunther began to change appearance. The thin, dark haired man who reminded me of Sean Connery, suddenly "morphed" into a young curly haired golden Adonis with bulging muscles and beautiful blue eyes. He placed his hands on the table and moved his face close to mine. He whispered so low I could barely hear.

He said, "My name is Atalon. You are my other half. I have searched the combined universes for you for millions of years. Now that I have found you, *no one will ever be able to separate us!*"

I couldn't believe what this "stranger" had just said to me. He had quoted almost word for word some of the lines from the first story in the Obergon Chronicles. The first story is about Atalon, the young prince of Obergon. At that time, I believed Atalon was the soul I was destined to meet, marry and eventually merge with, to accomplish some great mission.

I could *not* believe what I had just heard. Gunther could *not* believe what had just happened to him. We sat there staring at each other.

I finally changed the subject to the October Surprise because when Gunther and I were eating in the dining room, he told me that he was a United States Attorney working out of Denver. One of my friends, a CIA contract agent, was being tried for perjury by the U.S. Attorney out of Denver. Without taking my eyes off Gunther, I said, "If you're a U.S. Attorney from Denver, then you must know Richard Brenneke." Richard was on trial for stating that George Bush made a deal with the Iranians to hold the Embassy hostages until after the November election. This "deal" became known as the October Surprise, and insured that Ronald Reagan beat Jimmy Carter.

I had been investigating the October Surprise along with my friend Barbara Honegger since 1984. When I mentioned the name Richard Brenneke, I thought Gunther was going to pass out. Tears spurted from his eyes. I had never seen tears spurt from eyes before. I could *only* imagine what was going on in his mind.

After an amazing first night of coincidence after coincidence, Gunther asked me to marry him. I said yes with no second thoughts. Two days later we took his small Lear jet and flew to Reno. Two days after that he was arrested and I was told he was a small time con man who was on a crime spree marrying and defrauding wealthy widows.

As I began walking in this unfamiliar "shadow world", I soon discovered that most new people I met, turned out to be a spies, liars or worse. The FBI lied to me, the judges lied to me, and even his step-father lied to me. The only ones who told me the truth were the pilots who flew us to Reno and one of his cousins, who was also CIA. Members of my own family were turned into FBI informants. They headed off everything Gunther tried to do to free up money and get himself out of jail.

For a very short time I believed the FBI. I believed he was nothing more than a con man. Then I remembered what he had said in the bar...

"I am Atalon..., and you are my other half."

I truly believed Gunther Russbacher was my other half. No matter what he was... he was my "other half." Knowing I had found my "other half," I was able to summon the strength I needed, to do battle with some of the most powerful men and institutions in the world.

The only safe harbor I had in those days were the messages contained in The Obergon Chronicles. If all else was a lie... if Gunther really wasn't a Navy Captain attached to the CIA; if he really wasn't a Habsburg Baron; if he really was nothing more than a small time con man, at least I had these stories and the comfort they gave me knowing that at least Gunther and I shared the same soul and past.

Many people search their entire lives for their soulmate. These stories told me who mine was. In 1989, when I finally met him, these stories let me recognize him instantly. When everyone who knew him denounced him, these stories gave me the strength to stand by his side and fight the CIA, the President and the United States government to free him.

This book is far more than a few stories about a family from Obergon... a planet in the Sirius tri-star system. This book is about humans who were smashed and destroyed by powerful forces... forces that live in the shadows and carry out the bidding of the alien "masters."

It is also a book of hope because it teaches you that there are those who understand what is going on, and who are working "in the shadows" to make sure the alien "masters" leave at the appointed time... with *no* human slaves.

This book gives no absolute answers. It only tells stories and personal experiences. When you finish reading it you will be left with more questions than you had when you started reading it.

All I can do is share these stories, tell the story of how they came to be and how I learned the *truth* about them. I can also share my personal story of the long hard journey that finally ended on August 8th, 2005, when the Sirian Lion Gate opened.

On his father's side, Gunther Russbacher was from an old and noble Austrian family. The ranking male was called, "The Lion of Salzburg." On his mother's side he was descended from the Hungarian Esterházy family. As a child, he was told his mother's family came to earth from Sirius. He was taught that the Esterházys were descended from "the star," and "the star" was Sirius.

Gunther and Rayelan's Wedding Rings

Notice the 8-Pointed Star. Gunther's mother was an Esterházy. According to Gunther, Esterházy translates as "House of the Star" or "Descended from the Star." Gunther says the star is Sirius.

Gunther Russbacher died on August 8th, 2005, the same day the Sirian Lion Gate opened. I think it opened to bring him home. The last time I saw Gunther was October of 2004.

When Gunther died, he was married to Jane Ryder. To the best of my knowledge, he married Jane without ever divorcing me. At one time Jane was my friend. After she read, Atalon and Shalma, the first story in the Obergon Chronicles, she put down the manuscript and said to me, "I am Shalma!"

Lady Shalma was the woman that Lord Atalon believed was his other half. He kidnapped her from earth and took her to his palace on his burned out planet, Obergon. There she waited in lonely isolation while Atalon continued his search throughout all the combined universes for his other half. Shalma had a soul mate and her soul mate spent eons learning the skills he needed to rescue Shalma and restore her to earth.

The fact that Gunther died on the very day the Sirian Lion Gate opened is what finally convinced me to share The Obergon Chronicles, and the story of how my own life has been woven over, around and through them. My journey has been long and hard, but mystical and miraculous at the same time.

Everyone comes to earth to learn. I have recently learned that it is *not* necessary to learn *all* your lessons by living through them yourself. You *are* allowed to learn vicariously. Now that you know this, let's hope that you can learn from my life and you don't ever have to live one like mine or like Gunther's!

Part One

The Chronicles of Obergon

Story 1
Atalon and Shalma

Our story begins in the days before the Planetary Council had forbidden interplanetary trade with the small blue planet called Terra. Our first actor is Atalon, who came from one of the small planets circling the triple star, Sirius. His home planet was Obergon, the ruling planet of the Obergon solar system. From the planet Obergon, the court of his father, Lord Odon, ruled the smaller planets; (Felgon, Argon, and Trigon) that orbited the star Obergon. Obergon, Atreus and Sirius were the three stars that made up the Sirian Triple Star System. Obergon, the planet on which Atalon had learned the lessons of the physical world, bore a great similarity to Terra. Because of this similarity, Atalon yearned to rule Terra as he yearned to rule his home world, Obergon.

The young prince had learned the skill of interplanetary travel while still in his creation process, and thus was able to visit Terra whenever he desired. He would "think" himself wherever he wished to be and then materialize an appropriate body out of the local surroundings.

The blue gem called Terra spoke to Atalon in many subtle ways. On Obergon he was second to his sister, who was placed on the throne when their Father left. On Terra, he could make himself first with anyone, but especially with women. Atalon loved women because of the deep unacknowledged love he had for his sister. But he also felt mixed emotions of resentment and anger toward women because of jealously and hurt pride.

The story of how Atalon tricked his sister into going to Terra, and how he trapped her there, will be told later. Our present story tells how Atalon misused his power and consequently forced the Planetary Council to close the small blue planet to trade from other planets. An order of non-interference was issued. The punishment for disobeying the order was complete assimilation. Simply put, the offending entity would cease to exist as a separate being with a will of its own and would become one with the greater intelligence that rules the combined universes. Atalon was not the only space traveler who took advantage of the beauty and innocence of the planet Terra. There were many, but Lord Atalon is the one with whom we are concerned now. The story of his early visits to the planet Terra holds a special power for the human who bears the soul of Atalon. Somewhere on the small blue planet, a man looks up into the night sky and sees a bright blue star he feels is home. He has no idea why the star called Sirius speaks so sweetly to him. His memory of his life near that star is not yet fully awakened. And therein lies the reason for this tale.

It is now time for the sleeping memory of Atalon to awaken. Much has been learned from his stay on Terra, but it is now time for him and his family to leave, taking with them the knowledge and wisdom they learned in the Terran School. Atalon and his brothers and sisters are needed elsewhere in the universes where the special type of love that can only be learned on Terra is greatly needed.

Children of Obergon!

These biographical records are dedicated to you!

Allow them to awaken the secret knowledge that sleeps within you...

And let the journey begin!

Atalon made a fine looking human. His hair was the color of the Star Sol, and his eyes were as blue as the oceans of Terra. Compared to Terrans, he was tall. His skin was golden while theirs was white or dark brown. The raiments he wore bespoke his noble lineage. His retinue of faithful servants showed his great power.

Atalon was a master metaphysician. In his studies, he had transcended alchemy and learned matter transmogrification. This skill is not uncommon on the planets of the universe where the nature of material illusion is understood, but on Terra, where a young group of souls was being schooled, these skills made Atalon appear as if he were a god.

Not only could Atalon change physical matter; he also had learned to alter the most private thoughts of Terrans. He could make Terrans do whatever he wanted. He did not have to force or coerce them. He could make them serve him willingly and happily. He could erase their minds, change their memories, program them to serve him, or even to love him. Atalon loved having this kind of power. He played with the humans of Terra as children play with toys.

Lady Shalma, eldest daughter of King Phylos of Atalontis and betrothed to King Xanos of Egypta, was in the garden caring for her plants when to the gate a handsome young man approached. Shalma had heard stories about the great god Atalon, but he had not appeared in Atalontis since the time of her birth. Eighteen years was a lifetime to Shalma, but to Atalon it had been only long enough for a quick trip back to his home world to attend his sister's betrothal celebration.

Atalon stood at the gate, momentarily mesmerized by the beauty he saw before him. Never on Terra had he encountered such physical perfection. The features, the texture, the color... everything was so perfectly flawless he wondered if this was one the many beings he had created. The quickening feeling in his breast assured him that Shalma was not one of his creations. He had never felt love for his own creations. As he gazed at Shalma, he felt something he had never felt before. He felt as if he was falling in love.

His eyes had never before drunk in such beauty, such grace, such poise, such love. Here before him, in the garden of his old friend Phylos stood a creature so rare and so fine that only she could be his soul mate. Atalon had fallen deeply in love for the first time. It didn't matter if Shalma loved him. He would make her love him, even if it meant altering her thought patterns and memories.

Atalon truly believed Shalma was the soul created to be his other half, therefore he felt that anything he had to do to make her feel this also, was appropriate. If he had to erase the memory of her true soul mate, he would do it. If he had to change her thoughts so that she would love him, he would do it. If he had to program her to believe that their souls were destined to become one, he would do that also. He would do anything to possess the rare and lovely woman who stood in his friend's garden.

Vowing to leave with Shalma as his wife, Atalon quickly pushed open the gate and entered the private garden. He frightened Shalma and she summoned her guards. The guards quickly rushed toward the intruder. Shortly before they reached him, Atalon put into their minds the picture of the God Atalon. The guards quickly prostrated themselves on the ground in front of him. Shalma was too astonished to speak. Her guards were the bravest and best trained in the land. They feared no one. They bowed to no one but her or her father. "Who is this brash young man?" Her thoughts held disdain and fear, as well as wonder.

Arise and tell your Master of my return." Atalon commanded the guards. They quickly left the garden. He was alone with Shalma. Atalon rapidly scanned her mind to learn as much about her as possible. Shalma was totally oblivious to what Atalon was doing. As he was scanning her memories, he was changing the ones that did not suit his plans for her.

Shalma's higher self, a part of her soul that had never incarnated in the material, understood the peril. Her higher self pleaded on her behalf and told Lord Atalon of the great mission that Shalma and her soul mate, Xanos had been chosen to perform. She told Atalon about the breeding experiment taking place upon the planet Terra. She reminded him that Terra had been chosen as the planet on which the developing souls from Atalon's home world would incarnate to finish their lessons on the material plane. She reminded him that the sun from his home had become a red giant and his planet could no longer support life. She told Atalon that if that if he proceeded with his selfish desires he would set back the breeding experiment by ten thousand years. She also added that this delay could imperil the combined universes.

Shalma's higher self could not comprehend that Young Lord Atalon didn't care about the breeding experiment. He had heard about it, but he wasn't interested in it. That was his Father and Sister's project. He couldn't have cared less about it.

Therefore, taking Shalma from Terra, and installing her as his first consort back on his home planet, would cause him no guilt at all. It did not matter that his selfish actions would set back the evolutionary progression for millions of souls in his own soul family.

Shalma's higher self sadly realized that she was dealing with a soul that had no compassion for other life forms, not even those who were part of his own soul group. She saw that he understood romantic love, and she made one final effort to save from erasure the love that Shalma bore for Xanos. Atalon was told that Xanos and Shalma were the two halves of a soul that had been split in two for a planetary purpose. Somewhere, deep inside of him, the truth of this rang a chord. He listened as he was told that the two halves had been preparing for lifetimes to perform the great mission that had been assigned to them. If Atalon removed Shalma from Terra not only could she never fulfill her life plan, but also she would forever be separated from Xanos, her other half.

Shalma's higher self saw into the future and knew that one day Atalon would tire of Shalma and leave her on an empty world, served only by creatures that were created and programmed by Atalon. Shalma's higher self pleaded for Atalon to leave the memory of Xanos in tact. Atalon also saw into the future. Atalon knew the pain of separation. In this moment of pure new love, he vowed he would never do that to Shalma. Even though he would not permanently erase the memory of Xanos, he would conceal it so deeply, that by herself, Shalma could never find it.

Atalon listened carefully to the pleadings of Shalma's higher self. The conversation lasted about an hour of Terran time, but to Shalma only seconds had passed before she heard Lord Atalon laugh. As he laughed he sent back the silent reply to Shalma's higher self, "Before this day is gone, the love she bears for Xanos will not even be a memory. I, Lord Atalon, will be the only love of her life!"

Shalma's conscious mind had been totally unaware of the communication taking place between her soul and Atalon. She knew nothing of the pleadings to leave her and her soul mate alone so they could carry out the mission for which they had been created. The soul of Shalma begged Atalon once again to forget his own selfish desires and think about the other souls who were involved; the younger children of his Father, the Great Lord Odon. Atalon laughed once more, and ended forever all communication with Shalma's higher self. Henceforth Shalma's soul would never be able to reach her or Atalon.

Shalma now belonged to Atalon alone. She looked up at the handsome and arrogant young man who was standing before her. At first she had wanted him thrown out of her garden, but now she was feeling something for him that she had never felt for anyone but Xanos. Unknown to her, Atalon was busy changing her thoughts and memories. Soon she would have difficulty remembering the name of her beloved mate, let alone the loveliness of his face and the gentleness of his touch.

It was easy for Atalon to have his way with Shalma for hers was a young soul group not yet skilled in dealing with the thought-changers. Given time, the newly incarnated souls would grow wise in the ways of the material plane and develop skills equal to those of Atalon. But for now the conscious mind of Shalma was swept away by the overwhelming love she suddenly felt for Atalon.

She loved him with her body, mind and soul. However, each time she swore the oath upon her soul, another presence would grip her and she would fleetingly remember sweeter days and a different presence. She was not and would never be free of her love for Xanos. He was her other half, the masculine part of her eternal soul, the north pole to her south pole. He was the mate with whom she would reunite once her journeys were complete. Her mind and her body may love Lord Atalon, but her eternal soul would forever bear the pain and humiliation wrought upon her by the young Lord from Obergon.

After consulting with his old friend Phylos, a quick wedding celebration was performed, after which, Atalon physically removed Shalma from Terra. He installed her in his palace back on Obergon. Shalma's soul knew that Atalon had no more love for her than he would have for a fine animal. He would soon tire of her and be off again on another adventure. But after Shalma, Atalon's adventures would never be the same.

While scanning Shalma's mind, Atalon felt something he had never known before. The love between Shalma and her soul mate was mysterious and desirable. He vowed he would feel that kind of love. As the weeks and months wore on, Atalon slowly realized he did not love Shalma as she loved her soul mate, Xanos. While life with her was pleasant, Atalon now had a mission in life, a mission that would keep him traveling to every planet in the combined universes, looking for the one soul that could make him feel the kind of love that Shalma felt for Xanos. He vowed he would find his other half, even if it meant he had to meet every feminine soul in the combined universes.

The intensity of Shalma's love for Xanos had changed Atalon. He would never be the same. Shalma's love had opened a deep wound in Atalon. The pain was so intense he could not bear to look at it; therefore he never knew what was causing the pain. Without realizing that the secret of his own soul mate was hidden behind his pain, Atalon set off on his universal travels.

This time his journey had a purpose... a purpose other than playing with lower life forms. This time Atalon set out to search the stars for the kind of love he saw between Shalma and Xanos. It was a love that Atalon could never experience until he was forced to stop long enough to look within. Until Atalon was strong enough to face his own pain, he would never find the soul who had been created to join with him and become the other half of a new super-soul.

Because Shalma had a soul mate, Atalon assumed that everyone must have one. But this was not the case for Atalon. Even though it appeared that he and his other half were split souls like Shalma and Xanos, this was not the case. Atalon and his soul mate had burst forth from the womb of creation at exactly the same instant. The two souls were an experiment that had been sanctioned by the Universal Council. Atalon and his intended mate were created for the purpose of saving the Combined Universes. Whatever they did with their lives did not matter to the Universal Council. All that mattered was that they evolved, learned their lessons and accomplished their mission, before it was too late.

Atalon and his mate were created as two whole souls who will become geometrically more powerful than they were created, once their lessons are complete and they are permitted to join as one.

Shalma and Xanos were once one soul. They are now one soul in two bodies. After XanoShalma had matured to a certain level, their soul volunteered for a planetary mission, which required that they split into two halves. One half was the positive pole, or masculine side; one half became the feminine or negative pole. Because Shalma was a feminine pole, and Xanos was the masculine pole, they attracted each other like magnets.

Atalon could not attract his other half. He was created with the positive and negative poles within his own being. He was created whole, and could have felt whole, if the pain of his creation had not caused an open and festering wound. A wound so painful that he could not bring himself to look at it and discover what had caused it. Because of this, he doomed himself forever to walk the stars on a hopeless quest for a non-existent ideal.

Atalon chose to travel throughout the universe, while the other soul, (his sister, Raelon) the soul which was created to eventually unite with his, returned to the womb to help nurture the younger souls. Atalon developed his masculine nature, while the other soul developed the nurturing or feminine side of the soul. Atalon felt pain at being deserted. Because of this, he built a steel chamber to hide his pain. Until he opened the steel chamber and discovered what he had hidden in it, he was doomed to wander the universe like a blind man seeking sight. All he needed to do to become whole was to stop long enough to look within, but this truth was too simple and too painful for Atalon to understand.

*   *   *   *   *

The soul of Shalma, in great despair, brought her case before the Planetary Council. She set forth in detail the transgressions and manipulations perpetrated on the developing Terran souls by Lord Atalon of Obergon. She told how he had conducted his own breeding experiments creating women so beautiful that men from other worlds came to Terra to satisfy their own lustful desires. She told how Atalon enslaved some of the little Terran people, to work in his gold mines. Shalma spoke to the Council about Atalon's lack of compassion and how he influenced other souls until they became just like him.

Because Atalon was the powerful first son of the Great Lord Odon, the other souls felt that everything he did was correct and sanctioned by the Planetary Council. Many souls looked upon him as their Lord, their teacher and patterned their life plans after Atalon. If Atalon was selfish and heartless, these souls believed that this must be a desirable trait to possess.

Shalma's soul barely mentioned her own misery, choosing first to protect her family and friends. However, just as Atalon could read the minds of humans, the members of the Council could read the thoughts of Shalma's soul. Her true plea was heard. The Council immediately understood the grave situation that existed as a result of Atalon's selfish and hedonistic actions. The Council acted without pause.

The Planetary Council was in charge of the breeding experiment, which was taking place on Terra. They knew about the traders and travelers from other planets who had met and bred with the daughters of Terra. They even knew about Atalon's own creations. But since the resulting offspring were so few, the Council had decided not to take action. In the case of Shalma, things were different.

A being from Terra had been physically removed against the desires of its soul and the plans of the Planetary Council. The being that was removed was not just an ordinary soul. It was a soul that had been groomed and prepared for a planetary mission. By removing this soul, Atalon had not only altered the evolutionary plan for that soul, but he had altered the Planetary Plan.

Shalma was an ordinary soul. The mission she and Xanos had agreed to do would be critical to the creation of the lighter and finer bodies that were needed for the next evolutionary stage of soul development. As souls mature, they need bodies that are capable of handling more of the soul energy. Denser physical bodies keep a soul at the primitive level of survival and reproduction. As souls mature, they require physical bodies that are capable of intellectual reasoning and philosophical discovery. These advanced bodies pave the way for an enlightening or awakening response which signals that the soul is ready to graduate from the Terran school.

When Atalon removed Shalma from Terra he removed her gene pool. This gene pool had taken thousands of years to create. Shalma was one of the most genetically advanced beings upon Terra. Her offspring from Xanos would produce the DNA necessary for humankind to reach the pinnacle of creation upon Terra. Without Shalma's genes, the higher and finer bodies would not be created for tens of thousands of years. This meant that the Obergon souls, who were waiting for these bodies, would be delayed by that same amount of time. These souls were needed by Great Lord Atalon. Would he and his brothers be able to contain the threat at the border until his children were strong enough to join him?

After the Council became aware of the facts presented by Shalma's soul, they closed Terra to all trade and visitation. Even though their breeding experiment had been irrevocably altered by Atalon's interference, the council decided that the experiment could be saved if they closed the planet. They needed to make sure outside influence would not interfere with the steps they needed to take to restore the Plan on Terra.

The Council ruled within moments of hearing Shalma's story. Terra was closed to all souls who are not officially assigned to Terra by the Planetary Governing Council. The punishment for disobeying the non-interference order was immediate absorption.

Their action was fair and of great importance to the humans of Terra, but for Shalma, the decision came too late. Even though Shalma's soul had acted within seconds, the difference in time between Terra and Universal Headquarters saw the passing of a thousand Terran years.

During this time, Atalon had transported Shalma to his home planet of Obergon and set her up in his palace as first consort. Shalma's soul had been right in predicting that soon Atalon would tire of her and continue his wanderings. They had hardly settled on Obergon before Atalon was off again. This time Atalon did not leave seeking adventure, riches or new toys. This time he went seeking for the one woman who would fill the emptiness within him...the one woman who would love him the way Shalma loved Xanos. This time he went in search of his other half.

While Shalma's soul was with the Council she was given a glimpse of the soul evolution of Atalon. She was given this insight because the Council knew the part she would eventually play in the joining of Atalon with the soul that had been created to join with his. Shalma was told that part of the growth pattern Atalon's father had developed for his children was for them to become whole within themselves before being told of their mission. They would never be told that while they were created whole, they were intended to join with another soul to create one super soul, with powers far beyond any soul in the universe.

No wonder Atalon's search would be in vain. His soul was not like Shalma's. Had he spent more time on Obergon, instead of wandering throughout the combined universes, he would have known this. But he refused to subjugate himself to teachers on Obergon who could have taught him all the mysteries surrounding his creation. He refused to have anything to do with the mystery schools of Obergon because his sister, Raelon was in charge of them. Because he refused to become a student, he never learned the secrets of Obergon's mystery schools. These schools were the only ones that could tell him the secret of his birth. There he would have learned that his destiny was different. But since he would not consent to study the secret mysteries in a school run by his sister, he would never know he was different and could not find love as others did.

Because he did not understand that his creation was an experiment, he did not understand the tremendous sadness and desperation that filled him. It was a sadness created from separation, a separation that occurred when souls were ejected from the womb of creation at the exact instant. It was a separation that was required in order for growth to take place. It was a separation that required a circular journey back to wholeness.

In the beginning he was whole; in the end he would be whole. But at the moment, he was in the middle of the journey, with no understanding of the beginning, no belief in an end, and no comprehension of how to complete the journey.

In his ignorance, he longed for the simple joys of Terran love. He desired the wholeness that he felt when he probed Shalma's mind and felt her closeness to Xanos. Atalon felt separated from all things. The kind of love he experienced in Shalma's mind was the only thing that could make him whole. He needed to be whole, and he would become whole, even if it meant spending eternity searching for it.

Atalon had acquired great material riches. Desiring them no more, he gave everything to Shalma. She wanted for nothing. Her palace on Obergon was far more resplendent than her father's home on Terra. But all the riches in the universe could not soothe her troubled soul.

Shalma spent most of her years alone because Atalon's relentless quest kept him traveling throughout the combined universes. It was from one of these travels that Atalon brought home to Shalma a most precious gift. He brought her a companion in the form of a teacher. A man from her home planet Terra who had studied with the greatest metaphysicians in the universe and had learned the subtle arts they had to teach. Atalon had been doubly impressed with the man. Along with his vast knowledge, the teacher possessed great humility and deference...especially to Lord Atalon.

The man was called Phraedros, and the soul of Shalma leaped with joy when it beheld him. There before her, in the body of Phraedros, was the mate she had left so long ago on Terra. There stood Xanos, her one true love. The soul of Xanos had never forgotten his love for Shalma, and even though it had taken him many lifetimes of study to learn the skills necessary to accomplish her rescue, he had remained true to her memory.

As Xanos stood before Shalma and drank in her rare beauty, he felt his soul cry out in despair. Shalma's conscious memory was still controlled by Lord Atalon. Xanos would have to bide his time and play the game carefully if he were ever to regain his love.

One of the skills Xanos had acquired was the art of future-think. This was a technique that Atalon had been too busy to learn and it was this skill that would eventually lead Shalma to her rightful mate. Xanos had the ability to look into the future and see the forming thoughts of Atalon. Xanos would then change his own thoughts to conform to every wish or command. By doing so, Xanos always remained one step ahead of Atalon.

Now that Atalon himself had opened the door to Shalma's rescue by bringing Xanos to Obergon, all that remained was for Xanos to awaken the love Shalma had for him. This was easily accomplished because of the loneliness Shalma knew, but it did not happen as rapidly as Xanos had hoped.

To awaken Shalma, Xanos had to spark her memory. As he taught his beloved the skills she needed to take her place among the star travelers, he also taught her about a young woman and a young man from the planet Terra. The two Terrans had been very much in love until a man who possessed the ability to change thoughts came between them.

Shalma felt the old memories stirring deep inside her, but it would be many years before her full memory returned. Until it did, Xanos had to remain only the tutor of his beloved. His arms ached to hold her and his heart cried out in pain whenever Atalon returned and casually used the woman Xanos worshiped.

Atalon could not love Shalma the way Xanos did. She was not of his world or of his father's creation. Her evolution did not follow the same path as his. Shalma had been created with a mate and Atalon was not it. Atalon knew this and even though his love for Shalma was not the same love he would give to his own mate, he did love her. This was the reason he brought Phraedros/Xanos to Obergon.

Possibly Atalon even knew who Phraedros really was; this is not known for sure. What is known is that Atalon wanted Shalma to have the same skills he had acquired. These skills would free her from Obergon and eventually take her back into the arms of the mate for whom she was intended.

Atalon knew he had kept Xanos and Shalma separated far too long, but a part of him still was jealous of them for sharing a love he had never known. He was despondent whenever he thought of their love. There was nothing he could do but continue his long and heart breaking quest for that perfect ideal. He felt he had to experience their kind of love, but this quest for love was truly an impossible dream for Atalon. Until he found his other half within his own heart, he would never be able to find the mate with whom he could experience the outward fulfillment of this love.

But by now Atalon was too driven to look within. His quest focused outward. Only a major blow could force him to turn away from his chosen futile path and look within his own being for the secrets which had been there since the moment of his creation.

And so, his famous quest continued. Legends sprang up here and there throughout the universe. Some told of the noble young lord who had given up everything he owned and walked the stars seeking his one true love. As the years passed, this legend changed from seeking his one true love, to simply seeking the One Truth.

Hordes of people, who had heard the legends, formed groups and joined the quest. The search for Truth became the main religion on many developing planets.

On Markos II the quest took the name of "The Search for the Perfect Bosom." On Phylon III it had become "The Movement for Inner Peace and Tranquility." On Terra it was called "The Search for the Holy Grail." Had Atalon known of these movements he would have been amused, but he was too driven by his own obsession to be even aware of such things.

The more obsessed Atalon became, the more time he spent away from Obergon. His absences stretched into millennia; and Shalma, the beautiful Terran Flower, began to blossom and open during these absences.

For a thought-changer to have permanent success, it is necessary for him to totally obliterate all memories. Atalon respected the love Shalma had for Xanos too much to actually destroy the memory of it. What he had chosen to do instead was to throw a heavy blanket of illusion over it. This illusion was reinforced each time Atalon returned to Obergon. Probably the illusion would have held, even in spite of his long absences, had not Xanos in the guise of Phraedros been present.

Atalon was busy on yet another developing planet when Xanos was finally successful in igniting the spark in Shalma's memory that soon burst into the full reality of her love for Xanos. At first Shalma was so filled with joy she could think of nothing else. But when she remembered Lord Atalon and realized that he was the one responsible for her years of separation from Xanos, she felt great anger, an anger which almost overshadowed her love for Xanos.

In that moment, her only desire was to punish Atalon for the years of joy he had stolen from her. She wanted to make Atalon suffer the same loneliness that she had suffered. But as she listened to Xanos tell the story of Atalon's creation and his anguish, she began to weep. Compassion welled up within her and she vowed to do something to help him heal his pain.

Here was an entity in tremendous pain. Even though he was always surrounded by hoards of minions, he was alone and lonely. He was seeking his other half in order to be whole. But he could not find his other half because he did not know where to look. Shalma felt Atalon's despair and asked Xanos if there was any way they could help him find the hidden part of himself.

It was this decision on Shalma's part which signaled success for the Terran experiment. Instead of feeling hatred, Shalma felt compassion.

When the two Terran lovers stepped inside the solemn chamber where the Planetary Council held Court, the members of the Council could barely contain the joy that filled their hearts. The council and three judges, who sat upon the bench, had the ability to read minds. The moment Shalma and Xanos set foot within their chamber, the Council Judges knew they had come not to demand punishment for their tormentor, they had come to request help for him.

Xanos and Shalma stood before the bench and asked that Atalon not be punished, but be helped in his quest to find his other half.

The Judges looked at each other, and on a telepathic level celebrated their victory. The experiment on Terra was an overwhelming success! The planet was capable of producing souls with compassion!

The Judges and the rest of the council were so delighted by their achievement, that the request of Shalma and Xanos was temporarily obscured while the members patted each other on the back and congratulated themselves on the success of their Terran school.

Finally, the Judges and the Council Members focused their attention on the two Terrans. After a moment of pondering, the Council spoke, the High Judge delivered their combined statement. Their answer was no... they could not find Atalon's other half and show it to him.

Shalma and Xanos looked at each other with sadness. Even though Atalon had done them great wrong, they understood why he did it and they could not hate him. In fact, his treatment of them as individuals had been more than fair. If he had not been the one responsible for their separation, they could have even called him a friend. They grieved for their friend. They understood his sorrow because his sorrow, the sorrow of separation, had been theirs. They knew what kind of pain Atalon was feeling. The two Terrans looked back at the Judges, and were about to question the decision, when the High Judge spoke again:

"It is not possible to show Atalon his other half, because he simply would not believe that this being was his other half. He would feel that we were playing a cruel trick on him. There is only one way for Atalon to find his other half, and he has been shown this path repeatedly, however, the terror it holds for him prevents him from taking it."

The Judge telepathically shared much of Atalon's history. Shalma and Xanos realized that the only way Atalon could find his other half was to grow on an inner level. But to do that, he had to look within his own heart. Deep within him was the gentle nurturing part he had repressed for so long. It was the part of him that held his sadness and fear. It was the part of him that caused him pain. Because it gave him pain, he had erected a steel chamber around it. If he opened the door to his steel chamber, he was afraid the horror of his own personal hell would overwhelm him.

From the moment he was created he felt rejection and separation. Because he had these feelings he needed a reason for feeling them. He couldn't accept the fact that these feelings were normal. The feeling of separation is a normal process that the newly created soul goes through when it achieves individuation and is ejected from the womb of creation.

However, Atalon was different. Not only was he a powerful soul from a noble family, he was the First Born son of the Great Lord Odon. Atalon believed he was the First to individuate from Odon's line. He believed this because for quite a length of time, he was the only child of Odon in the combined universes.

However, because his pain of rejection was so strong, and his sense of family position was so great, Atalon refused to seek help from the older souls who had been trained to help new souls come into being. They were not from his Line, therefore, in his mind, they had nothing he wanted to learn. Because of his refusal to learn from those he termed "outsiders", he did not deal with the pain of his birth separation. Instead, he used the pain to fuel his universal wanderings. When he needed an explanation for the pain he told himself it was caused because his Father preferred his sister to him.

Whenever he was called back to Obergon he reinforced his feelings of parental rejection and sibling rivalry. Atalon's sister Raelon stood by her Father's side and took their Father's place when He was gone. Atalon believed his sister was not the first born. He believed the position she held should have been his.

In truth, all the brothers and sisters were created at the same time. Some achieved soul individuation sooner than others. Atalon and Raelon were the first to achieve it, and achieved it together, as one Supersoul. When they pulled their combined energy out of the Group Soul, the other children who were beginning to develop, or individuate, were set back in their process. It could have been labeled "fear", but since fear was not known to these developing souls, the feeling could only be described as a "disturbance" they did not understand, therefore they pulled back and waited until they understood what had just happened.

When Atalon and his sister individuated and were ejected from the Womb, Atalon burst forth and turned his attention to the Universe. Raelon turned her attention to the other souls who were still in the process of individuation. She sensed their trepidation and chose to return to the womb in order to calm their mixed energies, and help each one individuate in its own time.

Even though it appeared to Atalon that he was the first to achieve soul individuation and become a complete soul capable of being educated, this was not the case. Atalon and Raelon achieved soul individuation at the same time... because they are the *same* soul!

When Raelon chose to go back into the womb, this left Atalon alone in the universe. He did not know that he and Raelon had once been one soul. He thought that she was merely the eldest daughter of their Father. He also did not understand that she had chosen to serve the will of their Father by attending the younger children. She would have loved to have been by Atalon's side as he sailed throughout the Universe, but she knew that her duty to family came first. Because Raelon was the first born who chose to stay with the family, she was the one who was taught the duties of being the first in line to the Great Lord Odon.

If Atalon had not misinterpreted his own inner pain and turned his back on everything that reminded him of it, he could have sat beside her and co-ruled. But instead, every time he returned home he felt slighted and insulted and inferior. He felt this way because he saw the way their Father depended on Raelon and he interpreted this as meaning their Father preferred the company of his sister to the company of Atalon.

Atalon believed their Father had given her powers that should have rightly have been his. Because of his pain and his perceived humiliation, Atalon spent very little time on his home world. He returned time and time again to the stars where he found his own school and his own path to enlightenment.

The council members knew that in order to show Atalon the soul that was destined to join with him and become his other half, *and* make him truly believe it; it would first be necessary for Atalon to discover the secret of his birth. To do this, he would have to return to a painful time, the time of individuation; i.e., ejection from the womb. Lastly, he would have to deal with the inner turmoil and pain that was caused by the separation from the soul with whom he was destined to join as one. But before Atalon could actually see and believe he had another half, he would have to open the steel chamber where he imprisoned all his pain.

Hidden among his pain was the pattern of his complete soul. This pattern held all the attributes of both Atalon and of Raelon. Atalon had denied the existence of this part for eons. He blamed anything that resembled Raelon for causing ALL his problems. Therefore, he would never admit that he had a part of himself that was like Raelon. Without first finding and accepting the part of him that was like his other half, he would never be able to recognize her when he found her.

Without having foreknowledge of that which you are seeking, how will you recognize it when you find it? In other words, how could Atalon ever find his soul mate if he didn't know what he was looking for?

The only way Atalon could grow on a inner level, and thereby discover his hidden and imprisoned half, was for him consciously to give up his unbridled free will, the unprincipled use of his power and freedom, and to choose to study on a planet that teaches inner development and a reverence for all life; in other words: Compassion.

Neither the Council nor the High Judge and her cohorts, could force Atalon to make such a choice. The decision had to be his and his alone. And it would take a realization with the force of a supernova to make him choose to do this.

The Council further explained that although it would be difficult to help Atalon, it was not impossible. The solution had been with him since the time of his individuation. If Shalma and Xanos were willing to mold their futures around Atalon's, their request could be granted and Atalon could be helped to find his other half.

The Council gave Xanos and Shalma long and detailed instructions for carrying out the plan. Eventually the plan would bring the two inner halves of Atalon together. This wholeness would open him up to recognizing and receiving love from the soul which had been created at the same time his had been created, and was destined to reunite with him.

But to join with his other half, he had to develop both a positive node and a negative node. Both Atalon and Raelon were required to have two polar opposites in order to attract and hold the soul that was destined to become their other half. When Atalon could finally accept the negative pole he kept imprisoned inside his steel chamber, only then could he open up to meeting and recognizing the other half who was created to join with his eternal soul.

Once Atalon and Raelon were complete souls within themselves, they could join together to form a new and greater soul the likes of which the universe has never seen. There was a purpose for their creation, and their Father waited patiently for them to grow and develop and eventually carry out the destiny for which they had been created.

And so ends the story of Atalon and Shalma. Later we shall discover how Xanos, with the Council's advice, tricks Atalon into laying the seeds for his own undoing. In their father's absence Atalon convinces his sister, the Lady Raelon, to visit the planet Terra. There Atalon arranges events that trap her in the Terran cycle, making himself first in line to the throne of Obergon and acting ruler in his father's absence.

Epilogue

The players in this tale still walk the planet Earth. If the names and the presences have felt familiar, look into your own heart and discover the secrets that have been with you since the moment of your creation.

Story 2

Raelon's Secret

The Princess Raelon, first in line to the throne of Obergon, entered her father's private communications chamber. It was the chamber that was used for Command, Control and Communications. Or, as Odon referred to it, the C^3, (the C-Cubed) module. It was only the second time Raelon had entered the C-cubed room and the first since her father's departure. The voice of her father, Great Lord Odon, filled the chamber:

"The Evolutionary Plan on the planet Terra has gone awry. The responsibility lies with your other half, young Atalon. Atalon is presently on his way home. Before he arrives there are things you must know.

"The Planetary Council has decreed that he be confined to Obergon for the length of time it takes to reinstate the Evolutionary Plan on Terra."

Lord Odon scanned his daughter's thoughts and found her indifferent to the Terran Plan.

"Never lose sight of the importance of this Plan," he cautioned. "The future of all the combined universes depends on the successful functioning of the school which is being created upon the planet.

"A war is raging, my daughter, a war which my brothers and I are now fighting. The fate of the combined universes hinges upon our victory.

"The Terran school will train those who will join us at the frontiers, pushing back the Power which threatens to assimilate us and all that we have created."

The powerful voice of Great Lord Odon made the room vibrate. He continued his explanation to his daughter.

"The mystery schools on Obergon have taught you much, but the school on Terra is crucial for the development of the one quality which will act as your foundation... your launching pad to the stars.

"This one human trait, must be developed before further learning can be added. Without this one "human characteristic, the skills you learn could destroy all that we have worked to create.

"The planet Terra was designed as a school to teach compassion...

"Unconditional love for all things.

"Other mystery schools teach you to use your will to create whatever you desire. The mystery schools of Terra will teach you the Whole of the Law, as it was intended to be."

Great Lord Odon scanned his daughter's mind once again. He needed to be sure that she understood the full import of his words before he spoke again. When he was sure that his daughter had set aside her personal preoccupations and was fully present and intent on his words, he continued:

"Do what thou wilt is the whole of the Law.

"Love is the Law, Love under Will.

"Love and compassion must be the Foundation of Will.

"Without love, compassion,

"And reverence for all life,

"A powerful soul can damage,

"Or even destroy another soul… and in the case of the Invaders… the whole of our combined universes.

"Human love and compassion must be the foundation of all higher learning.

"Without Love, which itself is built upon compassion…

"Evil,

"Beyond description, Will be the Law."

"You and your brothers and sisters are the hope of the combined universes. My brothers and I need your strength to defend our homes from the Invaders. We grow weary. Your support is needed as soon as possible. The Forces with which we struggle are subtle and clever. If we brought you to the front without the training Terra can give you, you would be lost in the first wave of assimilation. Our Foe is an entity who was trained in Godhood long before any of us were brought into being. He is clever, cunning and wise in the ways of ordinary souls.

"Long ago in the early days of Creation he was known as XTron. He was the best and brightest. He was the shining star in our Creator's crown. He was the penultimate achievement… the crowning glory of our Creator's desire. Now his presence strikes terror into the hearts of the Brotherhood. His power and knowledge threatens to annihilate our very existence.

"The only thing that stands between our life and death… between existence and nonexistence is Terra. Terra will give you the knowledge you will need to join us and help us push back his invasion so the negotiations for a cease to his assault can forge on."

The voice of Odon took on a cautionary tone.

"Remember, my daughter, this information is not for all. This is why I have asked you to meet me in the C-cubed module, where all that is said in private remains so."

Odon continued, "Young Atalon, in his quest for adventure and pleasure, has disrupted the experiment."

Raelon felt her cheeks blush. She knew she was Atalon's other half. She had learned this in the mystery schools of Obergon. But her dislike and indifference to the young brash lord had kept her from telling him or anyone. In her guilt, she felt responsible for her brother and for the damage he had done to the Terran Plan.

To give Raelon the background information she would need in order to make educated decisions, her father continued,

"As you know, the material world of Obergon vanished eons ago when the neighboring sun became a red giant. Because of this, the final stage of Obergonian soul development was postponed until a suitable host planet was created.

"Terra was selected as this host planet by the Planetary Council. They monitored the evolution of Terran life forms for millions of years. After deciding that the Terran humans were at a stage where outside DNA could speed up the evolutionary process, Obergonian physical bodies were introduced. The Planetary Council transported these people from Obergon in a Mother ship that was constructed for just this purpose. Obergonian physical bodies were slightly more advanced than the human bodies produced by Terra. These more advanced bodies were needed in order for the Obergonian soul to complete its lessons in the material world.

"The Obergonian soul had advanced beyond the basic lessons, and to make sure time was not wasted by forcing souls to repeat lessons, the Council chose not to transport the full group of Obergonian souls to Terra until suitable bodies had been created for them.

"To complete the lessons they had started on Obergon, the souls needed bodies similar to the ones they had started with. To create these bodies, the Planetary Council set up an Evolutionary Plan on Terra. For their Plan to be carried into the advanced stage, they required physical bodies from Obergon to pass on the DNA to the humans of Terra.

"You have wondered about the strange pyramid-shaped structures on the material dead hulk of Obergon. These structures served to protect the physical bodies of these people until transportation could be arranged. With the help of the Council and neighboring star systems, those who chose to stay in physical body were eventually transported to Terra, where they mated with the smaller human life forms that were native to the planet.

"After tens of thousands of years, the first wave of Obergonians had seeded enough of their DNA to insure the Plan of success. Of course they had not counted on one of their own sabotaging the Plan for his own greedy and selfish purposes.

"Odon again scanned his daughter's thoughts. Was she truly understanding what he was telling her? Was he expecting too much of a daughter? Her basic nature was programmed to nurture and to serve. Yet he was asking her to carry out a mission that even the most highly trained of the warrior souls would find difficult. He had no choice.

Because of the Invasion at the edge of the universes, Odon had been called away before he had completed setting up the mystery schools on Obergon. He had completed the school that Raelon headed, but he had not been able to complete a program for the younger brothers of Atalon. Ideally, they would have had a role model in Atalon, but because Atalon had chosen to follow his own path, the younger souls who were just emerging from their individuation process had no male path to follow.

These souls should have been able to follow in the path of their father or an elder brother, but when Atalon chose to leave Obergon, before one of the younger brothers had been trained, there was no male soul model available to follow. Thus, the younger brothers had to follow Raelon's path. Raelon had to be both mother and father to her younger brothers and sisters.

Because of this, those souls who individuated during Raelon's rule became Androgynous. This added a wrinkle to the Plan that Odon had not foreseen, but it also created women who were exceptionally strong as well as nurturing, and men who were exceptionally sensitive as well as strong. However, it did create a separation in the soul evolution of the souls who came into being under Raelon's rule, as opposed to those who individuated later… after Atalon returned to head the school.

The sisters who evolved under Raelon's rule were stronger than the sister's who evolved under Atalon's rule. And the brother's of Raelon were kinder and gentler than the brothers of Atalon.

Odon wistfully wondered what things would have been like if his primary experiment had been carried out with no modifications. But he knew the universe is an open-ended experiment where anything can happen. Even the best-laid plans are subject to failure and/or modification. He was proud of his daughter. She had taken a difficult situation and found an answer that worked for everyone. Odon returned to his soliloquy:

"After the first wave of Obergonian souls had successfully completed their mission by seeding enough DNA to insure that stronger and finer bodies were created on Terra, they went home. They gave up their physical bodies and traveled back to Obergon in their light bodies.

"You too had a physical body, my daughter, you gave it up to stay on Obergon. When your physical body left, so too did the memory of your days in the material plane. It was decided that the half-finished lessons of the material world would cause you more harm than good, and so, a blanket of amnesia was created.

"Only I have the power to give you back your memory. Yes, my daughter, you once possessed a physical body, and it is now time for you to remember those days...

"Remember my child... remember..."

Odon's voice became soft and soothing. Raelon began to drift. Her powerful and structured mind seemed to be melting. There was nothing to hold onto. Her reality was shifting. She felt as though she were falling down a long tunnel. There was nothing she could do to stop the feelings. All she could do was let go and let Odon...

The power of Odon's words brought about strange and unfamiliar sensations. Fear, apprehension and wonder gripped her as his words penetrated her being. Memories of worlds she had never known began to flood into her mind. Countless lives, lived in countless bodies, streamed before her. Visions of beauty, visions of ugliness, feelings of love, feelings of hate all crowded her consciousness.

In one shattering second of soul-remembrance, all her false pride, vanity and ego lay exposed before her. There was no way she could continue to pretend to be the pure, pious, protectress of her younger brothers and sisters. Her own incomplete soul development hung before her like the dismal dregs from a once noble cask of amontillado.

Her unacknowledged and often denied ego raged to the forefront of her consciousness as the unfinished pattern from her previous lives struggled to live. Never again could she hide behind her veil of amnesia and feign her position of wise and holy priestess protectress. Her illusion had been stripped away in one fell swoop of truth.

Odon assessed his daughter's inner turmoil. He had hoped to wake her up more gently, but there wasn't time. Raelon was strong. Odon knew she could handle what he had done to her. Some of the younger souls were not yet advanced enough in soul individuation to be able to take such an assault to their perceived illusion. Raelon might be knocked off her center for a while, but she would recover quickly. Odon was sure of her. He continued:

"You have seen and you have remembered. Your development was not finished when we were forced to abandon the world we had created to teach the ways of material existence. Atalon chose to keep his physical body and make his own way. You chose to live in your light body and take over the instruction of the younger souls who are still struggling to individuate in the womb of consciousness.

"When you chose your path, it was decided by me and the Council that all that was ours in wisdom would go into your keeping. You became the protector and teacher of our truths. As such, you were allowed to create a fifth dimensional Obergon in the image of our old material world. As you have now realized, all this is merely illusion."

Odon watched as Raelon's thoughts tumbled and swirled and closed in on themselves. She was using every shred of logic known to her to make sense of all she had experienced in a millisecond of truth-shattering awakening.

Odon continued, "I can tell by your thoughts that you had truly forgotten your past. Your power of illusion is very impressive, my daughter. However, I can see that you have learned another valuable lesson:

A creator of illusion must never forget:

IT IS AN ILLUSION!

"However… just because you can now remember your past lives in physical bodies, don't feel that the memory of these times is crucial to your present position or to the mission you are about to perform. The only reason I chose to show you this is to make you understand that nothing is as it appears to be… all is illusion. Given more information any picture of reality can change. This is true no matter whose universe you are in."

"As you now remember, you and Atalon both had physical bodies at the time Obergon became uninhabitable."

As the memories came flooding back, Raelon remembered that she had been married to Atalon and had been very much in love with him. She now understood that her indifference to him was created because he had chosen to wander the universe rather than stay with her. She felt rejected. She had stifled the pain of rejection because she felt it beneath her. In its place she had put indifference.

Odon saw that his daughter finally understood. He continued,

"Atalon enjoyed his physical body more than you enjoyed yours. He was not ready to give it up in order to stay on Obergon and act as a mentor for his younger siblings. He would have preferred to go to Terra along with the souls who had offered to act as the DNA transmitters…but he did not want to give up his memory or his powers. When he realized that the energy fields of Terra would have caused him to eventually lose his powers, he chose a third alternative.

"Because Atalon had perfected the art of soul travel, he decided that he would visit Terra before he made his choice. While there, he discovered that he could use his power to materialize a superior Terran body, one that was capable of possessing all the powers he had learned throughout the universes.

"He knew that if he chose to go to Terra and be part of the physical Obergonians who were DNA transmitters, he would have to transport his physical body to Terra. Once it had been transported there, it would stay there until it died. In other words, he would be trapped there until we came for him. He would not be able to soul travel while his soul was on Terra. Terra is a quarantined planet. No one can enter or leave without permission and assistance from the Planetary Council. With the spirit of adventure that lived in Atalon's soul, he could not choose this way.

"He could not choose your way either. Instead Atalon decided to keep his physical body, but not be part of the Terran Plan. To keep a physical body on a planet that had been destroyed by a red giant, he built a special structure on Obergon. It was a fully contained biosphere. Within his biosphere he created his palace. Within his palace he created a room from which he could launch his soul to any point in the combined universes. After he arrives at his destination, he assesses the environment and then uses the skills he learned eons ago to materialize an appropriate body out of the native elements.

"That was his choice, all souls have free will. Atalon chose to retain his powers and all his memories. The original Obergonians who settled Terra also possessed these powers, but over the eons, their powers were lost or diminished due to the Terran environment. The first wave of Obergonians gave up their material bodies and were allowed to return to Obergon once their mission was successful.

"Their replacements on Terra were younger Obergonians who had not yet begun the individuation process on their home world. Their Group Soul had traveled to Terra along with the first wave of Obergonian settlers. As the original Obergonians bred with the Terrans, the resulting children required souls. These souls were individuated out of the Group Soul. Because these new souls were unskilled in the material planes, they quickly forgot their mission. Instead of carrying out their prime directive, they chose to immerse themselves wholly in physical sensation. Such is the draw and the temptation of the Terran world.

"However, I am afraid that again I have to look to young Atalon as the cause of this change of plans. When Atalon traveled to Terra in his soul body, he created a beautiful body for himself out of the native Terran elements. The second generation Obergonians wanted a body like Atalon's. His body was tall and light skinned, like his original Obergon body. The second generation Obergonian souls did not have the full understanding of the breeding experiment that was being conducted on Terra. They compared the offspring of Obergonians and Terrans and decided that they like the Obergonian body better. So they crossbred with themselves until they had produced a body that was tall and light, more similar to Atalon's. As a result of Atalon's first interference on Terra, the Obergonians stopped breeding with the Terran natives and started inter-breeding a superior race of their own.

"The Terran natives became little more than work animals for these Obergonian souls who had twisted their mission and as such became twisted individuals. But Atalon's negative interference did not stop with just putting an end to the breeding experiment. He needed gold to support the atmosphere for his biosphere on Obergon. This is where his physical Obergonian body stayed while was on Terra. To protect his physical body from the radioactive particles still coming from the collapsed red giant, he enslaved the Terran humans and sent them underground to mine gold for his biosphere. To transport his gold back to Obergon, he made alliances with rogue races that had learned how to get around the quarantine imposed by the Planetary Council.

"The Planetary Council was aware of what was happening and was subtly bringing about a new direction. Egypta was where Atalon had brought about this altered breeding plan. The King of Egypta, a human named Xanos, was noble of heart and spirit.

The other half of his soul, Shalma, and he had volunteered to be the two Terrans who returned the breeding experiment to its original course. Here is where young Atalon disrupted the Plan again and caused the Council to close Terra to all unauthorized visits... even those from the Rogue races. Any rogue who was found on Terra after the quarantine was imposed was subject to harsh punishment by the Planetary Council. This being known, the rogues used their superior technology to create underground cities where they could hide until the quarantine was lifted. Sadly for humans, the rogues did not stay in their underground cities, slowly, very slowly they began to creep to the surface of earth. They liked what they saw and vowed that one day they would control Terra.

"Atalon fell in love, or should we say lust, with the female half of the couple who had been chosen by the Planetary Council to "restore the plan" on Terra. He kidnapped her. He physically abducted a human with a human soul from the planet Terra. He brought her back to the long dead planet Obergon, and installed her in the palace he had created under his protective biosphere pyramid. The young woman you know as Shalma is the one of whom I speak.

"It is a pity you never took the time to probe the cloak of illusion Atalon placed over her. If you had taken the time to look into the mists of Obergon that still surround Atalon's Pyramid, you would have heard her soul cry out for help. Did your indifference to Atalon cloud your perception? Or could it be that you have not mastered compassion?"

Raelon felt the sharp edge of her father's rebuke, but she was given no chance to defend her actions. Odon continued:

"In spite of your other half, the Terran experiment has been successful. Shalma and her soul mate Xanos are evidence of this. They are the first souls to graduate from the Terran school. Now it is time to complete the breeding experiment so that appropriate bodies will be ready for the influx of young souls from Obergon.

"Because young Atalon caused the breeding experiment to go awry, it is up to you to set it right. If Atalon had not interfered, there would already be millions of bodies available for Obergonian souls. But because he fell in love with a soul he thought was his other half, he set back our Plan by about ten thousand years.

"It is now up to you to restore the Plan on Terra. You, Raelon, have been chosen to head the task force of your brothers and sisters who will accompany you to Terra to set things in order. Some souls have already gone on ahead and incarnated in Terran bodies. Others will accompany you and do as you will... materialize appropriate bodies out of the native surroundings.

"It was important for you to know the true nature of this mission. When Atalon returns with Xanos, Shalma, and his guards from the Planetary Council, the story he tells you will bear slight resemblance to the truth. Atalon has not yet been shown the whole truth. He is still immature. Had he completed his education on Obergon, he would now be the most powerful being in the universe. When I think of the soul evolution of XTron, the Invader, I shudder to think what could have been possible if Atalon had not been stopped now.

"Your Terran mission is twofold. The primary reason is to reinstate the Evolutionary Plan so the Obergonian souls will have appropriate vehicles to teach them the Terran lessons. But the other part is to trap Atalon on Obergon so that he will be forced to study in her mystery schools. Once he has studied here, he will be sent to Terra. Over the eons, he wanted to return to Obergon many times, but he would never return while you ruled, because he refused to be second to you.

"But now, you will be on Terra supervising the restoration of the Plan. Since you will not be present on Obergon, Atalon will be able to study the mysteries he has avoided and once he understands the secret of his origins and his purpose, he will join you on Terra."

The Great Lord Odon stopped transmitting for a moment and smiled. He thought to himself

"The amnesia produced by the Terran bodies will cause both of them to lose their memories. Only after their lessons are learned will they be able to recognize each other and join together as I have planned."

Odon checked Raelon's thoughts once more. Finding that she understood the overt part of her mission, and did not suspect that there was more in store for her than she had been told, Odon finished speaking:

"Go now, my daughter. Young Lord Atalon, your other half, awaits.

"Remember...tell no one of this communiqué. It is vital to the success of the Terran experiment that the true purpose, for the creation of Terra, be kept secret. Were the truth to be known, beings who seek the demise of all we know and have created, would set their priorities on the destruction of Terra. As it is... it is all we can do to contain the threat at the far end of our universes.

"We need help, and we need it soon. Only Terra can produce souls capable of giving us that help. Go now and know you are always guided, guarded and protected. You are first born of Odon. Remember that."

Odon's presence slipped from the chamber. Raelon stood alone for a moment. Her father's message had sobered her. Her life had seemed like a playland up until now. Now suddenly... in the space of a few moments, her perception of reality was transformed and her playland became a deadly reality where one wrong move could mean the end of everything she knew.

Raelon composed herself before leaving the chamber. Her telepathic powers already had informed her that Atalon and his entourage awaited her in the Great Hall. She entered the small foyer next to the throne dais and donned the ceremonial robes. "I must play my part well," she thought, "Atalon must not read my thoughts."

And so, with skills yet unknown to Atalon, she placed the memory of her father's words in a part of her being no one could reach... sometimes... not even her! Upon completing this, she strode from the foyer to the throne where she sat prepared to receive her brother, the other half of her immortal soul... the being whose fate it was to join with her to form the greatest soul the universes had ever beheld.

To Raelon, Atalon had been a cross she had to bear, the immature side of herself that she chose not to acknowledge. She knew full well that the two halves were created to join and become one. But she could not imagine herself being joined forever with Atalon. His arrogance, his immaturity, his selfishness were all too much for her to cope with. She loathed the thought of her pure thoughts blending with the selfish and gross thoughts of Atalon.

As much as Raelon was revulsed by the thought of joining with her other half, Atalon was enamored with the idea of finding his other half and joining with it. Atalon had woven a picture of romantic love around the eventual meeting and joining with his other half. He viewed it as the most desirable and wonderful thing that could happen to him. In his mind, his other half was seeking him just as desperately as he was seeking her. When they joined, love would surely fill the combined universes. In some ways Atalon was correct, love would fill the combined universes, but not before he and his other half had walked through lifetimes of death, destruction, pain, suffering and horror, the likes of which he could not begin to imagine.

Both of Odon's children would have to grow immeasurably before they understood the plan Odon set in motion with their creation. Atalon's hedonistic sensuality and Raelon's pious self-righteousness would both have to mellow before any joining was possible.

On Terra, they would meet each other on equal footing. On Terra, they would have an opportunity to learn to love before they found each other. They would learn real love... one based on compassion and reverence for all life. If all went well with their teachings, the love they learned would turn inward to the repressed half of themselves. Once they had learned to love all of themselves, and not just the part they felt was lovable, they would be whole while separated.

Once they were whole within their present separate consciousness, they would be able to recognize outside themselves the love they had within them. Once this happened, they could find each other. When they were whole in their Oneness, they would become like magnets attracting to themselves that which was like them... their other half... the soul that had been created at the exact moment of their own creation, the one created solely for the purpose of joining with them, to create a new supra-soul, the likes of which has never before been known in the Combined Universes.

* * * * *

And so ends Raelon's Secret.

In the upcoming, Raelon's Mission, we will journey with Raelon to the planet Terra.

We shall discover how Xanos, with the advice of the Planetary Council, tricks Atalon into laying the seeds for his own undoing.

In their father's absence Atalon convinces his sister, the Lady Raelon, to visit the planet Terra. Once there, Atalon arranges events that trap her in the Terran cycle, thereby making himself first in line to the throne of Obergon and acting ruler in his father's absence.

Atalon's pride prevented him from seeing that the plan he thought would make him ruler of Obergon, in actuality made him a student in the Mystery Schools of Obergon.

Epilogue

The players in this tale still walk the planet Earth. If the names and the presences have felt familiar, look into your own heart and discover the secrets that have been with you since the moment of your creation.

Story 3
Raelon's Mission

Raelon sat on her throne and surveyed the assembled throng. Her thoughts rested for a moment on the two Terrans. Xanos and Shalma had played their parts well. While before the Planetary Council, seeking help for the man who had disrupted the evolution of their home planet and irrevocably altered their own personal soul evolution, a discovery was made.

The discovery signaled hope for the struggling planet Terra. For those who knew the true secret of Terra, the discovery sent a ripple of joy throughout the combined universes. Terra was the school that would train the souls who would eventually save the combined universes. Shalma and Xanos, two souls who had only been taught in the Terran school, had stood before the Planetary Council, not to demand punishment for their tormentor, but to ask what they could do to unite him with his own soul mate... his other half. They did not seek to strike back with hate and anger. They chose compassion as their foundation and love as the way to heal themselves and their tormentor.

The joy which filled the hearts of the members of the Planetary Council was the joy of a scientist whose experiment was successful. The foundation for the supra-soul the council was creating and educating on Terra was compassion. Until the moment Xanos and Shalma came before them, the Planetary Council had been unsure if their Terran experiment was working. A planetary school capable of producing compassion in souls was vital to the creation of the supra-souls needed to battle the foreign invader. Once compassion was part of the soul's make-up, a whole new tempering and kneading process could begin on Terra. But was Terra capable of igniting compassion from the small seed that lived within every soul heart?

The Council had carefully chosen Xanos and Shalma and had prepared them for millennia, knowing that if compassion could be created in their less developed natures, then surely compassion could be created in the more highly evolved souls of Obergon. Obergonian souls had already undergone extensive evolutionary development both in the material world and in the spiritual world. Terran souls had only experienced the material evolutionary process of Terra.

Even though Terrans and Obergonians are equal in soul age, in soul-development Terrans have lagged behind, due to the relatively recent formation of their planet and solar system. Terra is a young and developing planet, and the souls assigned to it are newly separated from the womb of creation. Obergon was a burnt out hulk long before the primordial oceans of Terra had spewed forth their first one-celled life forms.

Yet even at this early stage of Terran development, Obergonian souls were present to map and chart the Terran specie. These early visitors from Obergon incarnated in every form of life, from one-celled plant life to insects, reptiles, and dinosaurs. These chronicler-souls are responsible for the recording of evolutionary history of Terra. Their stories will be told soon and as their collective memory is awakened, a whole new chapter of human evolution will be written.

Watch for the appearance of these men and women among you. Their skills will help you awaken the memories that lie sleeping within the very cells and atoms of your body. These people will teach you how to separate Terran memories, which are trapped in the physical matter which makes up the body; from the Obergonian soul memories, which lie in the spaces between the matter, the so-called electro-weak force present in atoms.

When Shalma and Xanos stood before the Council pleading for help for their tormentor, it was evident that compassion could be developed on Terra. The ripple of joy felt by the Planetary Council reached outward to all the universes. This signal was what brought part of Lord Odon's consciousness back to Obergon to speak with his daughter Raelon.

His daughter Raelon now sat ready to receive her brother and his entourage. Already she had scanned their minds to learn how much of the truth each had been told. Atalon had only been told he had disrupted a breeding experiment. She also learned that Xanos had tempted him with the throne of Obergon, and Atalon had become involved in a plot to send Raelon to Terra and trap her there. All was part of the Plan Odon and the Planetary Council had created.

Atalon knew that without his sister present on Obergon, he would be first in line to the throne of Obergon and ruler of all the planets revolving around the remaining double stars, Obergon-Sirius. Because of his jealousy for Raelon and his long-held desire to usurp her position and become number one in his father's eyes, Atalon chose to overlook certain signals which could have warned him of the plan to trap him first on Obergon and then on Terra.

Atalon felt he knew the law of Obergon, which was that the highest evolved soul, would rule. By rights, he should have been the highest evolved soul once Raelon was gone. But there was more in store for young Lord Atalon than he could ever imagine.

Raelon also scanned the minds of Shalma and Xanos and saw that they had only been told that the breeding experiment was designed to produce a superior vehicle for soul inhabitance. They were not told that the superior body was designed to house Obergonian souls. If by chance they should guess, a blanket of illusion would be placed upon them the moment they entered Terran space.

Raelon scanned the minds of the Council members who had escorted Atalon home. They greeted her with warm welcomes and assurances that all was on course. She silently thanked them for their help and support and turned her feigned wrath upon her brother.

As Atalon approached the throne, Raelon rose. She rose not out of courtesy or respect for him, but to remind him that she was the ruler of Obergon and only she possessed the power, strength and wisdom to hold on to that rule.

The last time Atalon had been with Raelon was for her betrothal ceremony to King Fan Ra of the solar system of Alcyone in the Pleiades. Atalon noticed the change in her immediately. Her being was far more radiant and powerful. He felt her consciousness could expand to fill every part of the universe, if she so desired. He was in awe of the change and secretly wondered if he was truly capable of deceiving such a powerful being. What he did not know was that this illusion of power came from the recent meeting with their father, and it would soon fade.

Raelon drew herself up to her most resplendent austerity. She reflected inwardly for a moment to make sure Atalon could not probe her secret. Then in a well prepared and well rehearsed lambaste, she proceed to castigate and chastise Atalon by reminding him of his birth and his duty to his father and his people.

"You have a position to uphold in the combined universes. You are not just a son of Lord Odon, you are his first-born son and as such you must be an example to the younger sons of Odon. Your little brothers look to you for their example and if they find out the mischief you cause in the universes, a full-scale chaotic invasion of young Lords from Obergon would result. There's no telling the damage a whole army of young Atalons could do.

"But there will be no chance of that. I am placing you permanently on Obergon and to insure that you do not leave, I am leaving you first in line to the throne and keeper of the power while our father is absent."

Atalon could not believe his good fortune. His plan was working and he had not even spoken his piece.

"I, in turn, will proceed to Terra, with certain of our people, and I will endeavor to correct the experiment you ruined when you stole Shalma. There are conditions to your stay on Obergon. The first is that no order shall be carried out without the authority of the Council, and second, you shall enter the mystery schools as a pupil, not an adept. And finally, a warning:

'Should you attempt to leave Obergon without permission while you are invested with "The Power," you will immediately be absorbed back into our Father's body and you will cease to exist as an individual soul with a will and destiny of you own."

A shudder ran through Raelon as she spoke. For the first time, she realized how connected she was to Atalon. If he failed his trust and tried to leave the planet, she too would cease to exist. They were a pair. One could not evolve to greatness without the other. If Atalon became absorbed, then Raelon too would lose her separateness and individual will.

She must not allow Atalon to fail. And so, in that moment of self-realization she decided to create a being to watch over Atalon and herself. She separated out of her soul a small part of herself and imbued it with very special powers. This being became her guardian, what we now call a Guardian Angel. Each soul that comes to Terra now has one!

At the same moment, she used the power of her own Will and the power of her newly created guardian to pull out of Atalon a similar guardian being, an angel to watch over him and see that his path proceeded safely and carried him to his final destination so that Raelon and Atalon could fulfill their common destiny.

"Now dear brother, I leave you to the Council and the mystery schools." Raelon knew full well the plan for Atalon's education. There was no one on Obergon who was capable of subduing Atalon long enough to teach him anything. His powers were so great that he could cajole and bamboozle anyone.

He would throw a blanket of illusion over the Council members and make them think that they were actually teaching him something while he would be off somewhere else figuring out how to break the rules without losing his individuality. Lord Odon knew his son well, this is why he arranged for a teacher from another universe to come to Obergon and take over Atalon's education.

Odon's elder brother had a son who was known throughout the combined universes for his power, his wisdom and his compassion. He was also known for his sense of humor. This young lord was called Anteb Trimagus. He had just assisted his father in the creation of the third universe.

Now that the universe was stable, Anteb was free to travel as the ambassador from the Third Universe. Raelon knew of her father's plan. She had met Anteb at the betrothal ceremony. She was suitably impressed by his advanced abilities. She laughed to herself because she knew full well what Atalon had in store for himself.

She smiled and embraced her brother, and then with a sweep of her royal robe, Raelon, Shalma and Xanos disappeared. Atalon was alone in the Great Hall, his guides or guards from the Planetary Council had become invisible to him. He sat down on his Father's throne.

Absolute glee filled his once-pained heart as he realized that at long last, he possessed one of the treasures he had coveted his entire life. Atalon's glee was to be short lived. Now that his father had successfully trapped his wayward son, it was time to set about educating Atalon as to the reason for his being and his destiny.

At the same time, in the Universal Headquarters of the Planetary Council, Raelon was receiving her instructions. Xanos and Shalma had already been processed and returned home to Terra. They incarnated as the twin son and daughter of their old friend and father, Phylos. The souls of Phylos and his mate Phylon were Obergonian chronicler souls. These Chronicler souls had never lost their ability to hear Odon's words and so, even before the birth of Shalma and Xanos, Phylos and Phylon were aware of the destiny that lay before them.

Phylos was now king of Egypta. It was 5,000 Terran years since Xanos had abdicated the throne of Egypta and turned to the stars to seek his soul mate. In that length of time there had been many upheavals on the planet Terra. The Island kingdom of Atalontis had sunk below the ocean's waters and various outposts were all that was left.

Egypta had been influenced mightily by Atalontis tradition, but the roots of Egypta were from Obergon. Egypta comprised what is now the upper half of the African continent. It was the people of Egypta to whom Raelon would appear. It was the people of Egypta who held the key to the future for Obergonian souls. It was the people of Egypta on whom the fate of the combined universes hung.

Here in this land were the descendants of the original Obergonians who had traveled to Terra by space ship in their material Obergonian bodies. It was these people who had carried the DNA from Obergon to Terra.

Raelon would appear before these people, in the temple they had built to worship their father, Lord Odon. In the temple, she would appeal to them to look into their hearts and remember the reason for their superior bodies. While it was true that most of the original Obergonian souls, which came in the material bodies from Obergon, had now in fact returned to Obergon, it was also true that the superior Terran bodies were now occupied by Obergonian souls.

These souls had been dispatched to Terra the moment Odon learned of Shalma and Xanos' presence before the Council. He had chosen a cadre of his younger children to travel to Obergon and help their older sister in rectifying the breeding experiment.

However, do not think that awakening the memory of home in these souls would be an easy task for Raelon. The amnesia brought on by the material body is powerful. Combine that amnesia with the body's own Terran memories which are carried both in the DNA and in the atoms; and you can begin to appreciate the task Raelon had before her.

Look to your own soul memory as an example. Of course you are from Obergon or you wouldn't be reading this. But even though this fact is truth, how much of your home planet and of your life there do you recall? Look to your own skepticism, cynicism or disbelief and you will understand the reason for Raelon's failure.

Her attempt to convince the newly incarnated Obergonian souls to continue the breeding experiment and breed with the lowly Terra creatures they used as slaves, was considered sacrilegious to the people of Egypta. They believed they were created in their Father's image and it would be a desecration of that sacred image to defile it by performing unholy and bestial acts with sub-humans.

When Raelon heard the small native Terrans called sub-humans, she laughed. These creatures were the real humans. They were the original inhabitants of this planet. They had more right to be there than did the haughty lofty lords who held them in slavery.

Unknown to Raelon, her twin-soul and betrothed, Fan Ra, of Alcyone, had chosen to come to Terra and assist her. He had been advised by the council to incarnate in the body of one of the native little people. This he did and with the help of the council he retained his memory so that when the time came, he and his beloved Raelon, could lead the little people out of slavery and into their destiny.

As Raelon spoke to the people gathered in her Father's temple, she knew they did not believe her and would not let the little people go without a show of power.

Raelon dematerialized her body briefly and returned to the mother ship from Universal Headquarters for a consultation. The Mother Ship came to Terra with the first Obergonian bodies. It has stayed in Terra's orbit ever since. The Representatives from

Universal Headquarters advised her to use a show of strength and force which would make her appear as a Goddess to the people.

She transported down from the ship and appeared in the middle of the temple. This time she spoke saying, "I am Raelon, first born of my father Odon. This is his temple and you are his children." The tone of voice and the power it projected sent a shiver of fear through those gathered in the temple.

Raelon continued in a voice so powerful that it vibrated the walls of the Temple. "You have shamed and degraded my Father's name by your ill-conceived and ignorant worship of a deity you no longer remember and therefore create in your own image. You would fall to the ground in fear were my father to appear before you in his natural form. It is only because I chose to walk among you as an equal that I come to you in this body."

At the back of the temple, some of the men, who had only just arrived, began shouting for the woman to be removed. Raelon had not realized that by choosing a body of the so-called weaker sex she was thereby prohibited from worshiping in the temple. The cry from the back of the temple was joined by more men who called for her to disappear as she had before.

"Out!" they cried, "Out, you witch; leave us to our worship of our Father. Take that devil you call a father and be gone to Hell with you both."

Again Raelon laughed at their ignorance and she raised her hands above her head. The ceiling and the floor of the temple began to vibrate.

'Earthquake!' the men screamed as they ran to the exits. One of the younger priests chose to stay. He was a young man named Brunan and even though there was skepticism in his mind, there was belief in his heart. Raelon motioned him near her and protected him with her power as the walls and ceilings began to crumble and disintegrate.

For dramatic effect, she caused the eternal flame of the holy alter to grow and engulf the entire temple in flames as the walls came crumbling down. Her sense of humor carried her away and her laughter rang out from the center of her burning theatrical display. Those outside, the ones who had not run away, prostrated themselves on the ground, as if awaiting their judgment. When the flames died down Raelon spoke. "Brunan, take me to the leader of Egypta!"

The leader of Egypta was Phylos, who had already heard of her feats from fleeing temple-goers. His two young children, Shalma and Xanos, had also heard of the strange witch-goddess, and eagerly waited with their father to meet her.

"Will she destroy our palace too?" they asked.

"No, dear children. She is the prophesied redeemer and you must go with her."

"Father," they cried "Won't we be afraid?"

"Not when you see her. You will recognize and love her. Now prepare, my children. The hour of which I have long spoken, approaches. Play you parts well for I shall not see you again in this life. Remember, until we meet again, I will always love you. Now and forever, you are my children."

The children began to protest, but their mother Phylon joined them and quieted their fears.

She spoke to her husband, sadness welling up in her voice. "The appointed day has arrived, my mate, and I am ill-prepared to leave your side. I love you and will await you when we pass out of human form. Even though I know that we are never really apart, it pains my human heart to leave you. I have loved you from the day we were created, but these lives we have lived on Terra have made me love you more than I love life itself. My husband, my mate..." Tears appeared in her eyes. Phylos approached her and took her in his arms. He laughed as he held her.

"You take this too seriously, my wife. This is the great day of celebration for which we have waited. Soon more of our people will join us on this planet and our Father's true work here can begin. Rejoice, my wife. This coming separation is only temporary. These bodies and these personalities are only ours for brief moments. Don't take any of this too seriously. Remember," he said with a sly wink, "The play's the thing!" He laughed and embraced his family. He was still laughing when Raelon and Brunan entered the palace.

Phylos quickly covered his laughter and turned to his family. "We have rehearsed this scene for years. All of you must play your parts well and remember... it's only a play." He winked at them all and then turned back to Raelon. Hundreds, maybe even thousands of Egyptans, had crowded into the palace behind Raelon and Brunan.

"You are King Phylos, the wise and just ruler of Egypta. I have come with a message from my Father, the Great Lord Odon. The breeding experiment he set in motion on Terra has gone awry and he orders you to amend it."

"How should I do this, child?" Phylos asked with a mocking and condescending tone.

"By breeding with the little people you use as slaves," Raelon replied.

Phylos began to laugh, and as he did, the others who had gathered in the palace took courage from his defiance and also began to laugh. Raelon was excitedly caught up in the moment and was enjoying the drama of the spectacle more than she had ever enjoyed anything.

She spoke again, but her words were drowned out by the laughter. She too was caught up in the moment and began to laugh. She quickly caught herself and raised her arms above her head. When she clapped her hands, peals of thunder and flashes of lightening crashed through the palace in a deafening roar. Absolute silence descended.

Raelon suppressed a giggle and spoke. "If you will not agree to breed with the little people, at least give them to me. They are not animals, they are humans and must be treated with dignity."

"Absurd nonsense!" responded Phylos. "They are animals. They are my property."

At this point Phylon rushed past her husband and to the front of the dais. With words she had rehearsed every day since she and her husband had married, she said,

"If they are animals then you have committed bestiality and your own children are beasts. I am one of the little people."

The assembled mass gasped in horror. Their Queen was an animal! No, it couldn't be. They looked to Phylos for guidance.

"What do you mean, my sister, my wife? Are you not from the same loins as I? Are you not of my mother?"

"Yes, I am from her loins, but my father was her servant Exlo."

"You... are an animal?" Phylos asked incredulously. Then he roared as he held his head in his hands: "And my children...my children have beast blood. My blood flows in a beast body?"

He cried a loud agonizing wail that seemed to raise the roof and rend the walls. Phylos was a better actor than he had ever thought himself to be. He was inwardly laughing at the performance he was giving for the benefit of the gathered crowd.

"Out! Get *out* of my sight! Take *all* of them with you! If one beast or half-beast is in the city by nightfall I shall kill it myself."

His children ran to his side crying, "Father, father, don't do this to us. Don't send us away." He threw them cruelly to the ground at the feet of Raelon and quickly turned to walk away. Only Xanos saw the wink he threw at them before he disappeared behind the curtains.

"To the slave quarters!" Raelon ordered, and she and her entourage exited.

* * * * *

This has been the story of Raelon's first triumphant visit to the planet Terra. Later, we will tell the story of her brief love-affair with

Fan Ra, the beast human, and how she creates the threads of karma which eventually trap her on Terra.

Raelon was brought into existence on Obergon, a sun in the Sirius Tri-star System. The planet on which Raelon and Atalon first walked was also named Obergon. The planet Obergon was destroyed when a neighboring sun became a red giant. A strong, hyper hot wind swept the atmosphere away.

For a short time, Raelon continued her studies of the material world on a planet in the Pleiades. This planet orbited the sun named Alcyone. The soul that held the energy of Alcyone was named Ra. The Ra's are solar souls. They hold the energy of suns. Once the sun is established, the "male" half of the soul can leave. The "female" half stays within the sun, holding the energy together. Suns can also be "incubators" for new souls. Not all suns act in this function, only the suns that have planets which can sustain certain types of material bodies.

Fan Ra was the solar soul of Alcyone. He and Raelon were betrothed back on Obergon. In Terran terms, they became twin souls. Twin souls are two souls whose paths have mirrored each other. Fan Ra and Raelon attended the same schools, were sent on the same missions, and followed the same developmental path. Fan Ra was Raelon's best friend. The one who was always true to her. The one who would help her no matter the cost.

In later stories, we will also introduce Raelon's sister Sharlon. Sharlon was an adept in the mystery schools of Obergon. It was Sharlon who was given the assignment of educating Atalon. Sharlon was very hurt that she was not allowed to go to Terra in the first wave of Obergonian souls. Raelon had passed her indifference to Atalon onto Sharlon; and as a result, Sharlon did not look forward to her assignment.

Sharlon did not want to be around Atalon. She considered him impure and felt he would corrupt her and the teachings in the Mystery Schools of Obergon. She was overjoyed when their cousin Anteb Trimagus appeared and agreed to take on Atalon's education. What Sharlon did not know was that her father Odon had asked his brother to send his first born to take over Atalon's education.

In the story, "Sharlon Meddles," we will see how an overzealous sister causes Raelon and Fan Ra to desert their destiny and create the karma that binds them to earth. Raelon and Fan Ra fall in love. They learn about the powerful sexual energies that Atalon had mastered eons ago. Raelon and Fan Ra spend thousands of years learning how to be human and how to master the feelings of love they feel for each other. Together they teach each other about all the different sides of love… love and loss, love and hate, love and betrayal, friendship, familial love, love of animals, flowers, and Mother herself!

Story 4
Chief White Eagle

The battle began at noon. The sun shone directly down on the small peaceful green valley. The hoards of armed and mounted invaders sat astride their fierce looking horses on the crest of the opposite hill. The small but mighty army of native warriors stood with clenched fists and spears raised high. Their battle cries filled the air. Before dusk would fall, not one of these brave warriors would be left standing.

It had been written in the stars and Grandfather had told the brave warriors who went to battle the insidious invader, that there was little hope for them. But he also told them that the battle had been prophesied many years ago, by the Great Spirit who lived in the sky.

Grandfather had told us the story many times; that in his youth, the Great Spirit told him he should leave the camp of our people and wander far to the east. Grandfather said the spirit told him to find a place so flat that all the surrounding mountains, on both sides of the big valley, could be seen. When he found that place he was to kill a deer, feast upon it, and offer its antlers to the Great White Spirit.

Grandfather said it was about mid afternoon when he crossed the last mountain and saw the huge expanse of flat land that stretched out before him. He had never been so far east before and the land looked like it went on forever. He strained his eyes eastward and there on the rim of the earth he could faintly make out the Mountain of God that the legends had told of. He squinted his eyes even harder, and tried to see the white top of the mountain, where it met the white cloud of heaven.

Grandfather walked farther that day, toward the Mountain of God. He walked until sundown, which came late that time of year. Grandfather sat down. He was tired and wished for nothing more than rest when suddenly a large buck came charging straight at him. He barely had the time to pull his knife from its leather sheath when the buck was on top of him. The weight of the buck falling upon the sharp stone knife drove the knife deep into the breast of the deer. It fell dead at Grandfather's feet.

Grandfather said that in the last few moments of the beast's life he heard it say to him, "Thank you dear brother for removing me from this yoke. You have set me free to wander the heavens and find my real home. Feast tonight upon the flesh that held me prisoner, and know that you are my beloved brother in whom I am well pleased."

Grandfather roasted the meat of the deer, and as the full moon rose in the sky to the midway point, he held the deer's antlers directly overhead and offered them to the Great Spirit. As he did this he said the hand of the Great Spirit reached down and accepted the gift that was offered. The hand then touched the head of Grandfather and he fell into a deep sleep.

It was in his sleep that the visions of the future were shown. Grandfather said he felt himself being lifted up far above the clouds… into the stars. He said it felt like he traveled many hours at great speed. All around him was black, but he knew all was well.

Finally he knew his journey was over and he opened his eyes. Before him was a light more powerful than the one in our sky. It's brilliance shown upon this place. All colors, like the ones in the bow after the rains, filled this place. There were structures all around. They were made of the most beautiful white stone Grandfather had ever seen.

Inside the structures Grandfather could see all manner of beings. Some he recognized as being old friends from his youth. Others he said he knew, but could not remember from where. He was greeted by his mother's brother, a young warrior named Lame Bull, who had died in a fall from a cliff. Grandfather knew that Lame Bull had been dead for many years. He thought he had also passed beyond the great divide which separates heaven from the earth. "Not so," he heard Lame bull say. It was as if Lame Bull had heard the thoughts inside Grandfather's mind.

"No my brother, you have not passed beyond the great divide. You are still very much a part of the world below. You have a great and important task to perform before it will be time for you to lay down that body and join us here. Come with me, my brother and meet the greatest warrior of them all He is called by many names, but the one we will use today is Great Lord Michael."

Grandfather told us that Lame Bull led him into one of the tall buildings. The light inside the building was just as bright as the light outside. At the far end of the building, in the most massive chair grandfather had ever seen, a being of great beauty was seated. Grandfather fell to his knees and bowed before the Being, but Lame Bull lifted him up saying, "Have no fear, Great Lord Michael wishes to speak with you and show you things from your future."

Grandfather trembled as Lame Bull led him closer and closer to the radiant being of light who was smiling down upon him.

"Are you the Great Spirit who lives in the sky?" Grandfather asked.

The being smiled and laughed, "No my brother, I am only one of the elder sons. I am here helping all my younger brothers to find their way."

Grandfather could not believe that a being so beautiful could wish to help him. The being continued,

"From this time forward you shall be known as Chief White Eagle. You shall live for many hundreds of years and you shall oversee the closing chapter of your people.

"You shall wander far in your journeys teaching your people that their lessons have come to an end and their school has been closed. You will meet with many who will not accept what you say and who will fight hard to preserve their old way of life. But nothing they can do will change the way things are. The time has come for the curriculum to change and to change the lessons we must change the classroom. Do you understand White Eagle?"

Grandfather stood before Great Lord Michael, with his eyes cast down, saying nothing. Michael stood up and walked down from his chair and placed an arm upon Grandfather's shoulder.

"Come with me to the Fountain of the Future and I will show you the way things are to be."

Great Lord Michael led grandfather to the most beautiful blue pool he had ever seen. In the middle of the pool he saw water bubbling up.

"Look into the pool White Eagle and see the events that will change your land forever."

Chief White Eagle stared into the blueness of the water and before his eyes all sorts of visions took place.

He found himself looking into a very dark and crowded room. Men were sitting around a large table. They were dressed in heavy clothing and papers were scattered over the table.

On one of the papers there were drawings that Grandfather knew were of the place he called home... Terra, the planet earth. An older man was speaking to a younger man.

"Cristobal, it is your destiny to be the man who opens up the rest of the world. Trust us to know that the time is now right. The souls who have lived on the opposite side of the world have now finished their lessons. Their soul group is leaving. The school that had been reserved for them, has now been passed to our soul group."

"For eons our Order has protected them from the less advanced souls in our world. We have created myths and monsters that have kept the small superstitious minds of our men from interfering in things they could not understand.

"We told our world that the land they live on was all there was and that if any man ventured to the edge of the water he would fall into the great abyss to be devoured by all manner of demons. It was our sacred trust, just as it is now yours to go forward and to open up this new land. We need a classroom that teaches men about freedom and the power and responsibility that goes with it.

"The old souls are being told of their coming departure from this world, and there will be little resistance. The people there are peaceful and friendly. By the time the great hordes from Europe descend upon them, they will know in their hearts that it is time for them to leave. However, the physical tribes of these people will remain, and many of our souls will incarnate in these bodies. There will be problems with the 'red race', but it will not come from the soul group who lives in the bodies at this time. The problems will come from members of our own soul group."

"But my friend, I do not understand how you know all of this." The Cristobal asked.

His friend replied. "There are truths that have been handed down from generation to generation. Secret Orders grow up, around these truths, to safeguard them. We have within our Order, books that tell us of the future and the part we are to play in it. Our Order of the Red Cross has been the keeper of the New World. We were given the job of seeing that no one interfered in the lessons the souls were studying there.

"It was from one of these books that we were told of you and your great mission. You will sail west in three small ships and you will discover a land that you shall name in honor of your old friend."

The older man laughed. Cristobal put his hand on the shoulder of his old friend and laughed also. "Amerigo, my friend, sometimes your words make me think that you are having fun with me."

"Cristobal, your father was my friend and my teacher. He is the one who gathered together all the ancient knowledge and brought it here to Florence. You are the child that was born for this task. No one but you has the knowledge and the inner site to bridge the two worlds and usher in the next era for mankind. Your father protected you, hid you and educated you for this."

Grandfather could feel that the younger man clearly did not believe the words of the older man.

Grandfather looked into the fountain again and this time saw the three small ships that Cristobal was to command. He saw the ships sailing across the oceans and then back again. Then he saw more ships and more men sailing off into the dark seas. The men with the lighter skins began landing on the shores of his land. At first all was peaceful, but then, as more white men came he saw his people being pushed back. He saw Rivers of blood as the new invaders slew his helpless people.

Somehow Grandfather knew that it was all part of the Great Spirit's Plan. He remembered the deer who thanked him for freeing him from his yoke of flesh so he could roam the heavens once again and return to his true home.

Grandfather saw that the red blood of his people added power and strength to his land. The new students would need this power and strength to complete their lessons.

Death was only the passageway from earth across the great divide into this beautiful land where he how stood. Grandfather watched, as the white people settled in the eastern part of the Land. He watched as they fought with themselves.

After they had finished fighting with themselves, they fought and killed Grandfather's people. Once the white people had driven the red people from the Eastern seaboard, they turned their anger and hatred on themselves and fought a huge and long battle. Many white people died. Once the great battle was over, the white people once again turned their hate and anger on the red people and began killing them. Grandfather felt the white people did not hate his people any more than they hated themselves.

He watched as the white people moved across his land. He saw good men… men he would know and help. He saw the part he played in helping establish a nation where this developing soul group would live and learn. He saw the nation he would help create begin to take form. To honor him for his help the Founders of the new nation would choose an Eagle as their symbol.

Grandfather then saw mother earth spinning below him. He saw sparks of light begin to shine. Most of the sparks were in his homeland. His homeland began to glow, and he knew this was good. There were also sparks in the country called Europe and the small islands to the west. Around the world he saw sparks begin to spread and grow. Soon the whole earth was a planet of light.

He saw that the souls he helped with their final lessons were ready to graduate and leave the material plane. As they began to move into new dimensions, they carried with them the entire planet and all the souls thereon.

Grandfather saw that this new and seemingly young soul group was as old as the universe. They were new to the ways of the earth plane, but they were masters in other realms. The power that lay sleeping while these souls were on earth, had never before been known on earth. Grandfather saw that the earth needed this soul group as much as this soul group needed the earth. The two were linked together. One could not develop without the other. One had to be nurtured and suckled like a baby. One had to be the mother, and suffer the pains of the child. But when the child matured, the child would open the door for the mother and usher her into a new form, in a new universe.

Such was the power that was contained in this new soul group... the power to transform Mother Earth, herself. Grandfather understood all he had seen, and yet understood nothing. All would unfold in its own time, and all was good. Deep within him a clear, still pool of knowing was created. From this pool Grandfather would pull the waters of truth and quench the hot thirst of the braves that rode into battle. Grandfather placed his hand over this pool and knew all was well.

At this moment Great Lord Michael placed a hand on Grandfather's shoulder and said, "You have seen enough, White Eagle. Return now to your home and know that all that will unfold is good. Know that your people have finished their studies and their graduation day is at hand. Know too, that you will live far beyond the normal years, and you will help all your people through these coming difficult times."

Michael removed his hand and Grandfather found himself back on the flat land of the big valley. He made the journey back to his home in less than half the time it took to make the original journey.

From that day forward, never a day went by without Grandfather telling his people the story of what he had seen while he was with the Great Lord Michael.

And so it was...

On the night before the great battle, Grandfather gathered together all the warriors from our camp and told them one more time of the great spirit and our elder brother who was waiting for them beyond the great divide. From that still pool of knowledge Grandfather brought back with him, he poured the waters of truth upon the hot flames of hate and anger. Our brave warriors left the earth knowing all was well and they had completed their lessons on time. Grandfather White Eagle had done his job well.

Epilogue

This tale was told because it is time to understand that when a new soul group comes to Earth to study, the curriculum usually changes. When the lessons change, the school sometimes changes. Sometimes the change is gradual and the souls from one group overlap with the souls from another group. Sometimes the different soul groups are part of the same soul family. Sometimes they are different soul families. Sometimes the new souls incarnate into the same bodies as the old races and nations. If the races and/or nations are fighting each other, the new souls continue the fight.

Some souls are assigned to Terra as teachers. They teach the lessons that Terra wants humans to learn. Terra is the name of the Mother. These souls have been on Terra from the beginning. They have lived in all countries and in all races. At the moment, many of these teachers have chosen to incarnate in certain blood lines. You will find these teachers in the aboriginal people around the world.

These teachers are Druids, Native American Medicine Men and Women, Australian Aborigines. These are the people who have been given the task of preparing their "students" for their graduation. These teachers may or may not accompany the students when they graduate. Some graduating students may stay on Terra and become "teachers."

When the student is prepared, there will be no fear and the soul can leave earth in joy and love. When a soul fully understands this, change can happen quickly. When there is no fear, the transition from the material world to other dimensions can happen as easily as changing clothes.

Story 5

The Sylph King's Story

This tale is being told because it is time to understand that sometimes enemies are not evil, sometimes they are merely unaware of the totality of the picture. Once a being is made aware of the whole story, it is hard for them to hate or condemn.

A BLACK HOLE RIPS APART A SUN

Two x-ray telescopes have caught a black hole in the act of ripping a star apart.

February 18, 2004: Thanks to two orbiting X-ray observatories, astronomers have the first strong evidence of a supermassive black hole ripping apart a star anconsuming a portion of it. The event, captured by NASA's Chandra and ESA's XMM-Newton X-ray Observatories, had long been predicted by theory, but never confirmed ... until now.

Astronomers believe a doomed star came too close to a giant black hole after being thrown off course by a close encounter with another star. As it neared the enormous gravity of the black hole, the star was stretched by tidal forces until it was torn apart. This discovery provides crucial information about how these black holes grow and affect surrounding stars and gas.

http://science.nasa.gov/headlines/y2004 18feb_mayhem.htm?aol3401

"Let us talk to you about a time in the distant past... long before the star you call Sol had come into being. In a far distant part of your universe, a small band of souls were valiantly defending their star, Folarius, from an invading force which had broken through the barrier that separates the universes. This force was trying to claim the energy of Folarius for its over lord. If the invading force was successful in capturing Folarius, the entire solar system would perish. The sun provided the light and the energy that allowed the beings upon the planets to live and learn. Without the sun, the school that had been established upon this world would be forced to close.

"I and a few beings like me had volunteered to help the developing planets by holding them in their orbits so they did not crash into their companions. These planets revolved around their sun in a circle. It was not like your solar system where different planets have different temperatures so that different schools can be established on each planet. On Folarius, the group soul was so large that many different worlds were needed to house all the bodies that were required for the learning experience.

"The people of the Folarian system were evolving at a more rapid rate than the people of Terra. The Folarian system was created to train a special group soul for a very important mission. The Folarians were being trained to protect their universe from the attacks of the neighboring universe and its invading force, until appropriate channels of communication had been established. It was hoped that once appropriate channels were established, the invading force would understand that it was interfering in the free will of another universe, thereby putting an end to the aggressions.

"The overlord that dominated the neighboring universe had been a cause for concern from the moment he had been given permission to create his own reality. His picture of reality was one that was not harmonious with other universes. All beings who reach the level of universal soul have the opportunity to engage in any type of experiment they wish, as long as they do not endanger the existence of neighboring universes.

"Overlord XTron was unaware that he was causing problems to his neighbors. XTron was one of the first sons of the creator. Your father Odon was a son that was created many sons after XTron. On earth you have a legend about the great knight Lancelot. If we were to compare XTron with anyone it would be with Lancelot. Just as Lancelot desired to be the best human and knight to ever live, so too did XTron strive to be the best son his father had ever produced.

"In the schools where XTron studied, he was taught that souls learn their lessons much quicker when they are put under pressure. To use earth language to explain this concept let me discuss diamonds. You know that a beautiful and rare stone is created because a common and not so pretty piece of coal is put under extreme pressure for millions of years.

"XTron decided he wanted to become the best and brightest creation of the Creator. And so, he created a universe that became similar to what you call a black hole. His reason for behaving in such a way was to sincerely see if he could expand and refine his powers under pressure. XTron's devotion to his Creator was all encompassing and his attempt to emulate the Creator was sincere. He was trying to become pure enough and wise enough to join as one with the Creator in perfect harmony thereby expanding geometrically the light of the combined universes. XTron was the brightest and most devoted of all his Father's sons. All he ever wished to do was please the Creator.

"XTron did not realize was that his power was so great that shards and threads of his powerful magnetic energy flew out to the frontiers of his universe and began sucking and pulling like huge suction snakes. These snakes eventually broke through the barriers that separate the universes. A small hole was rent in the fabric that creates the universal barriers, and the suction snakes began streaming through claiming everything in their path. They sucked it into their gigantic maws, thereby speeding it home to XTron.

This space tornado looks suspiciously like one of XTron's Suction Snakes.

Thanks to http://www.thunderbolts.info for finding this photo of the energetic stellar jet of HH (Herbig Haro) 49/50, as seen through the Spitzer Space Telescope.

"It was at this time that the planetary commission created the Folarian School. Folarius was a place that would teach a group soul how to combat the energy vampires until the mediators had successfully contacted XTron and told him how harmful to other universes his type of experiment was.

"What those in charge of the Folarian School had not bargained for was the powerful cunning intelligence that the suction snakes possessed. These suction snakes were only energy rays emanating from XTron, but they acted like living, thinking beings who had minds and wills of their own.

"They must have begun to sense that a growing danger to them was being created in the Folarian system, because one of the feelers of the sucking energy began to wend its way toward the Folarian system.

"This feeler sensed not only the purpose of the Folarian system and the danger the system posed to XTron, but it also sensed the presence of a great mind. Because it knew that XTron wanted to gain all knowledge rapidly so that he could more quickly join with his Creator, the suction snake knew that its job was twofold. First it had to neutralize the danger the solar system presented to XTron, and then it had to pull the power of Folarius into its maw and capture it for XTron. This powerful group soul intelligence would be a great addition to XTron's experiment.

"At this point, those of us who had been placed in the Folarian system to keep the planets in line sensed a growing danger. We sent out a distress call to the Universal Headquarters and that call was answered personally by a representative of Lord Odon. Lord Odon and several of his brothers had created a group experiment when they created their universe. It was their universe that was most in danger from XTron. Lord Odon was asked to head up the task force to protect the combined universes from XTron.

"Lord Odon, and other secondary sons of the Creator, began patrolling the barriers of the universes. They used their power and energy to shore up weak spots where the suction snakes could break through.

"His eldest daughter Raelon, Princess of Obergon came with her retinue, to protect the Folarian system. Princess Raelon quickly realized that it was the powerful group intelligence of the Folarians that the feeler was sensing and seeking. After consulting with her father on the most appropriate methods of handling this situation, it was decided that she and her retinue would transform themselves into a group mind more powerful than the Folarians and act as a decoy who would lead the feeler in harmless circles until the Folarians had finished their training and established themselves as guards of the universal barriers.

"It is for this reason that I and my kind will forever offer assistance to the Raelon energy and to all of her brothers and sisters who accompanied her to Folarius to protect us as we served our Lord.

"The Folarians completed their training and reinforced the rent in the fabric of the universe so that a plan could be devised that would enable representatives from Universal Headquarters to catch the attention of XTron and show him the damage he was doing to neighboring universes.

"Because of the type of experiment he had chosen, all his attention was turned inward. Attempts to contact him had proved fatal to more than one ambassador from HQ. But it was not the deaths of the ambassadors that worried Headquarters, it was the fact that their energies became one with the energy of XTron, and thereby increased his powers geometrically. The Ambassadors who were sent were powerful Second Sons. Now they were one with XTron and he became even more of a threat to the combined universes.

"Much thought had to be given as to how to contact XTron without giving him more power. The one lesson that XTron had not been taught because its use had not been foreseen was the concept of compassion, unconditional love, and respect for all life forms. After HQ had pondered the threat from XTron it was decided that the answer to the XTron problem was powerful ambassadors trained in unconditional love and compassion.

"These ambassadors first had to be trained in a school that was so powerful it could teach them to survive any assault, even one from XTron. In order to train these souls, it was first necessary to create a school to train them. This task fell to Odon because he had performed so well the first time. But it was also given to Odon because Universal Headquarters was well aware of Odon's experiment to create a super soul.

"HQ felt that if these supersouls were trained properly, then they could be used as ambassadors to XTron. But first Odon had to train them. This was not an easy task for Odon. He had spent much time away from home while attending to the XTron matter. Because of this, his powerful first born son and daughter had educated themselves. Both had become self absorbed and self important.

"Even though they felt in their hearts that they were serving their Father's wishes, their actions couldn't have been more disappointing for Odon. It was not until Odon was finally successful in getting both of his children to the school he had created on Terra that he finally felt his battle with the invading suction snakes would be won.

"Once his children had graduated from the Terran School, he would dispatch them as a powerful super soul to XTron. When XTron absorbed the new soul that had been created for just this purpose, he would also absorb the lessons the soul had learned.

Once the lessons of compassion and universal respect for all creation became part of him, he would no longer be able to conduct his experiment in the way he had been.

"Now, even though it appears as though Raelon and her brothers and sisters are still studying on the Terran school, it is known to me that their mission was successful. Time only exists on Terra. I live in no time, and so it is easy to see how all things turn out.

"The Children of Obergon completed their education on Terra and left on the mission Odon had volunteered them for. The moment they were absorbed into XTron he stopped his invasion of other universes. He quickly realized the error of his ways, and within an instant, had restored everything to its original place and position. The Children of Obergon were returned into their father's keeping.

"Odon has recently applied for permission to create his own universe."

Epilogue

This story was included to help you understand that the more you know about something, the more your perception, as to whether the thing is good or bad, is altered. It is also included as an effort to help you understand that time is not what you think it is. If you are in the stream, you understand time. If you are outside the stream, there is no time. Those who originally wrote these stories were/are outside the stream. For us, there is no time.

*   *   *   *   *

The Sylph King Speaks on Elementals and other things

"We are known to you as the Sylph Kingdom, and I am the Sylph King, SK for short. We are the beings who volunteered to come to the Terran School and hold the protective atmosphere while the souls attending school developed.

I and my kind have been in service to humanity since the moment the earth school was established. We are the guardians of the airways - we are the force behind the wind - we are the spirit of the wind - the carriers of the Holy Spirit - the transporters of the Christ Consciousness - the directors of the rays. We conduct the energy streams that flow to the earth from the celestial realm. We orchestrate and regulate the flow of energies to the planet and to individuals. In other words - We deliver the goods.

"SK"

* * * * *

The Sylph King on "Elementals"

"Time has no barriers and therefore cannot be measured if one is inside of it. And since this is the case for all of us who are concerned with this story, let us simply say that in the beginning, when it came time for our Creator to make the material and spiritual worlds, He also created a specie of beings that He called Protectors of Humankind.

These Protectors formed many different "subspecies" and each "subspecie" was assigned a different task. The "subspecie" that was assigned to Earth consisted of the Angelic Kingdom of World Servers.

"This kingdom was divided into five subkingdoms - one kingdom to rule over each of the elements and a proud umbrella of powerful angelic beings to work with each kingdom as the need arose. All humans fall within one or more of the kingdoms, and therefore have one or more of the "subspecies" of the Protectors of Humankind protecting them.

"The Sylphs rule over the kingdom of "air." Our domain starts where the earth and the ocean meet the sky. In addition to everything else we do, we protect those who travel in airships.

"The Salamanders are the spirits of fire and gasses. Pele is their ruler. They have the power to bring about great change and transformation. They are the patrons of the alchemists. They are the hardest task masters. Honor Salamanders, make them your friends.

"The Gnomes are the protectors of the Mother Planet, Terra. They nurture and care for Terra. They are like her ladies in waiting and her footmen. Gnomes work with certain humans who have an affinity for the preservation of balance within the Mother. To successfully work with the Kingdom of the Gnomes, a human must be able to sense energy fields, ley lines, weather patterns, crop cycles, animal migration and magnetic energy, both in the earth and the animal kingdom, including humans.

"The Undines are the spirits of the sea. Their ruler is Tritone, (Tritunny) and very strident is she. She is the second hardest of the taskmasters. Do not trifle with Tritone. Not only does she rule the seas, but she rules the emotions. She can turn you upon yourself just as the sea turns upon itself.

"Each human has an affinity with one or more of the elements. Usually the combination is one easy kingdom and one difficult one. But those who have chosen to walk a path of rapid awakening usually have the spirits of fire and water as their teachers....i.e.; two hard taskmasters to speed up the learning process.

"The kingdom that oversees all of these "subspecies" or "subkingdoms," is the gentle Angelic kingdom. This kingdom is made from the essences of the souls who are studying upon the earth. These essences are so fine and lovely that they seem to be a separate kingdom, totally removed from the crass beings that are upon the planet. But they are the best part of the humans who are attending the Terran school, and as such, they serve the humans and offer love, healing and help whenever they are called on.

Each human has his own Guardian angel, which is made from a piece of his own soul that has never incarnated in a material form.

However, all angels help all humans. If your Guardian Angel is unavailable, which has never been the case, but just to calm your questioning mind, know in your heart that you will be served just as well by the Angel on Duty (the AD).

"All the kingdoms are upon the planet to serve the planet and the humans in the Terran school. Call upon us when you need us.

SK

* * * * *

More Thoughts on Elementals from the Sylph King

"The elemental spirits of water are Undines.

"Their ruler is Tritone (TRI-tunney). Tritone is the mother of Athena and also the "Sacred Mother" of all Undines. She was the first of the elemental water spirits to travel to Terra. She and her two sisters formed the sacred lake Tritonis in what is now Libya. It was out of this lake that the first elemental life forms developed, hence, the Athena legend.

"The legend of Tritone, in regards to the sea, was stolen by the Greeks and Tritone became Triton, the male God of the Sea.

"The Undines are the spirits of the sea. Their ruler is Tritone...

A strident taskmaster is she. "She is the second hardest of the taskmasters. Do not trifle with Tritone. Not only does she rule the seas, she rules the emotions. She can turn you upon yourself just as the sea can turn upon itself.

The Sylph King Speaks about the Lessons of the "Elementals" and Ancient Initiations

"The ancient mystery schools taught the adepts to overcome their fear of Elementals through the various initiations, such as the initiation by fire, i.e., trial by fire. Most humans fear the Elementals and you can never get an elemental to work for you if you are afraid of it.

"People who fear water (Undines). fire (Salamanders), heights (Sylphs) or caves and small spaces (Gnomes) cannot successfully command the Elementals. Different human weaknesses fall under the rule of different elemental kingdoms.

"A person who cannot control his passions, whether they be sexual or substantive, (alcohol, food, drugs, etc.) is at the mercy of the Salamanders.

One who is driven by greed and the desire to acquire material wealth cannot control the Gnomes. Gnomes can only be controlled with cheerful generosity.

(Remember the lesson on "The Importance of Greed." If you haven't read it, please do so.)

"The Undines are ruled with firmness, the Salamanders with placidity, the Sylphs with constancy and the Gnomes with cheerful generosity. The opposite of these traits, in a human being, can be the undoing of that human.

"The elementals are here to assist the human in his lessons. If a human is in need of tutoring in a specific area, the Elemental becomes the harsh taskmaster who pushes the human through the lesson. It may appear as if the Elemental is evil or angry, but all that is needed to change the Elemental from your enemy to your friend is the knowledge of how to control him; i.e. firmness, placidity, constancy or generosity."

The Origin of the Sylph King's Information

The Sylph King's tale and his information came from The Obergon Chronicles. The "Tale" is one of five biographical stories and numerous writings received between 1981 and 1992 by Rayelan Allan. At the time Rayelan was receiving these stories, she believed she was in contact with ascended masters, angelic beings, or some other cosmic representative of our Lord and Creator.

After Rayelan married Navy Captain Gunther Russbacher, ONI and CIA; she was confronted with a reality she had not yet explored. Conversations with her husband and with his boss, a four star Admiral, made her realize that a lot of channeled information was not coming from representatives of God. She was told that through various techniques of mind control, human based organizations were trying to shape "the thought of the world" by tapping into a human longing to know the Truth.

She was told that certain groups had long understood how powerful religions of the past had successfully controlled human thought for ages. These groups realized that modern day religions could no longer be used by them to introduce new ideas and ways of controlling humanity. Religions of today have their holy books written down and preserved. Not only this, most followers of modern day religions can read the Holy Books and interpret the scriptures for themselves.

Even though it can be done, it is not easy to distort or misinterpret the Holy Books in today's world, especially in the advanced first world countries where everyone can own and read the religious texts by themselves.

Because of this, the groups who wish to use religion to control the masses realized that they needed to introduce *new* religious dogma to the world through modern day prophets, which they would create through new technologies that can make people "hear voices" in their heads.

The information that they would transmit, would be created in their think tanks. It would then be transmitted to their chosen receivers i.e. "Prophets" through various techniques that fall under the heading of "mind control."

Rayelan was told about several New Age channels who are receiving their information from New World Order think tanks. She was also told about a group of people who were working to oppose the New World Order. She was told that these people are also employing similar techniques to get their information to the public, but their intent is to raise the consciousness of humanity, **not** prepare humanity to be willing slaves and servants to a New World Order and new world religion.

Rayelan was never directly told that her information came from devices that can transmits words and voices into the human brain. However, knowing that she has been married to two high level government employees who were involved with Electronic Warfare and mind control, it is now her belief that The Obergon Chronicles were transmitted to her through a form of voice to skull electronic transmission.

Her husband, Gunther had owned a CIA proprietary business in Houston, close to NASA headquarters. His company was called "Space Based Designs." Its cover story was that it produced space saving office furniture, but in fact, it was engaged in research and development as well as the application of stolen NASA technology to meet earth and human needs.

One such NASA creation that has been adapted for use on earth is called "Space Based Telepathy." This is a means of putting words and thoughts directly into the heads of Astronauts. This is one of the devices that have been linked to the recent plethora of new age channels.

Rayelan's first husband, the late Dr. John Dyer, had been a professor of physics at the Naval Postgraduate School. In this capacity, he developed the Electronic Warfare program. One aspect of this program was the creation of electronic frequencies which can influence a human's mental or emotional state, making an enemy terrified, disoriented or hopeless and suicidal. During the Persian Gulf War, the newspapers reported that the Iraqi soldiers were surrendering in droves. Speculation has always been that these Iraqi soldiers were "beamed" with mind altering radio waves.

Knowing that she had been married to two men who had connections to electronic mind control techniques, Rayelan became certain that the messages she had received for years were a product of this technique rather than messages from ascended masters. When she confronted her husband, Gunther with her feelings, he responded that it didn't matter where the information came from if it was true.

She asked him how he knew it was true. He told her that there were "vast libraries" of information regarding the history of the earth and the universe that had not been released to humanity because the time wasn't right to do so. He went on to say that the group with whom he worked, used various New Age Channels to release the part of this work that they felt would not damage the psyche of the world. He said they only had a short amount of time to wake up humanity to the reality of what and who they are.

Rayelan tried to press him for more information. She was unable to do so. He fell asleep. She later was told that Gunther had built-in programs to control how much information he could release. If he came too close to releasing something that was still highly classified, he would begin to ramble nonsense and then fall asleep. She was never able to have him confirm the source for the information that is contained in the Obergon Chronicles.

While Gunther and Rayelan were in Austria, at a Templar Lodge, which had been in Gunther's family for over six hundred years, she was told that the Templars have huge underground libraries full of information that is slowly being released to the public.... as they are ready for it. Even though she was not told out right that these "vast libraries" were the source of the information contained in the Obergon Chronicles, she assumes that they are.

While Rayelan was at the lodge, she talked extensively with various men, who discussed the Templars, King Solomon's Temple, the hermetically sealed chambers below the temple, the original "settlers" from the Sirius Tri-Star system, and the Templar Library which was exhumed from the chambers below the Temple.

During the Crusades, the Templars built their stable over Solomon's Temple to hide what they were doing and to make it easy to transport the library, the gold and the birth records of the royal House of David, back to Europe without being detected.

The library was taken back to Europe, most of it was stored in the Cathar region of France, however, as the demise of the Templars was nearing, the library was moved to salt mines near Salzburg, Austria.

While Rayelan was talking with this man about the library, he told her that the Templar Library contained many of the manuscripts and scrolls that were in the Library of Alexandria when it burned. He also told her, that much of what is in the library is technology that was brought to the planet by the original "settlers." This technology has been hidden because the human spirit is not advanced enough to use it responsibly. This man also told her that the Obergon Chronicles were true historical records of some of the early "Settlers" and visitors to the planet earth.

> *2006 Note from Rayelan:*
>
> *Story 5, THE SYLPH KING'S STORY, was the last of the stories I received about the Children of Obergon. I know there are more stories. I was once told that ALL of the stories were "downloaded" into my brain and will be released at the appropriate time.*
>
> *I was also told that there are other people on Earth today who also have memories of Obergon. I was told that these people WANT to find their true family and share their stories. If YOU feel you are from Obergon or from the Pleiades, and have a story to tell, you can go to:*
>
> *http://www.obergonchronicles.com*
>
> *Click on the link that says Forum. You will need to choose a name and then you will be able to share your story with other people.* t

Afterthoughts

Was the Atalon and Shalma story the Prequel to "TAKEN?"

If you watched the Stephen Spielberg mini series, TAKEN, you will understand this article. If you did NOT see the miniseries, you will still understand this, but not quite as well! You might want to take a break from reading right now, and go out and rent the mini-series.

"the experiment on terra was an overwhelming success!"

(From The Obergon Chronicles, Story One, Atalon and Shalma, by Rayelan Allan)

"the experiment was an unqualified success"

(From TAKEN: The above sentence was uttered by the alien great-grandfather, of the little girl, who was the end-product of the successful alien breeding experiment.)

In 1981 I began to receive, as in channel, stories about beings from the triple star system Sirius. At the time, I truly believed that I was a "new age channel" and I was receiving information on the settlement on earth and the breeding experiment being conducted by our ancestors from Sirius.

It was this information that caused me to marry Gunther Russbacher, an ONI (Office of Naval Intelligence) officer who was attached to the CIA.

It was this story that gave me the strength to fight against the George Herbert Walker Bush Administration with a courage I did not know I had... to keep both of us alive.

In 1989, when I married Gunther, only a small number of people had read the story of Atalon and Shalma. I had only released it to family and friends, and to my mailing list which numbered about a thousand. At the time I met Gunther, I believed there was no way he could have had any knowledge of the Atalon and Shalma story... UNLESS, he was Atalon!

I ran into Gunther in Medford, Oregon. We had known each other from the Naval Postgraduate School in Monterey, California. We first met in 1976, and then over the years, we had brief encounters at cocktail parties, dinners, dances and other events. Each time I saw him, the energy that flowed between us was so thick you could actually see it. When we ran into each other in Medford, I felt God had arranged it. As the evening progressed, I became even *more* convinced that our meeting was divinely ordained.

After our initial meeting in the restaurant, I agreed to meet him in the cocktail lounge to continue our conversation. As I approached the door to the lounge, I could see him through a small window. He was sitting with a number of men. They were talking and laughing. Suddenly, I heard a voice. It sounded as if someone was standing behind me. The voice said. "If you walk through that door, your life will change forever. Are you sure you are strong enough?"

I thought about everything I had been through in the last year: Finding my first husband's body. Moving from tranquil Carmel Valley to New York City. Developing pneumonia in the dead of winter and discovering that not only didn't I have medical insurance, I didn't have any money either!

After recovering from pneumonia, I spent months being immobilized by panic attacks so severe, all I could do was curl up in the fetal position and silently rock myself while tears streamed down my face.

Shortly after conquering the panic attacks. Senator Claiborne Pell asked me to become his administrative assistant in charge of a "black project" that was covertly funded through his Senate Foreign Relations Committee. Pell told me that he no longer trusted the man who was overseeing these projects. He said he needed someone he could trust completely. In his mind, I was that person. I never asked him why he chose me.

I told him that I needed time to think things over. My career was extremely successful and getting more so everyday. My clients were made up from the Hollywood glitterati, the cream of New York's fashion, acting and diplomatic communities: as well as Washington D.C.'s Capital Hill. I was on top of the world, and I wasn't sure that I wanted to give it all up to go to work for the government.

I was staying in Georgetown with a girlfriend at the time. I went home, told my girlfriend what had just happened, and then I went to bed. About two o'clock in the morning, I felt a hand at my throat and the warm air of someone breathing on my neck. I opened my eyes and saw a man in a black hat bending over me. The first thing I thought of was a vampire. I knew the man in black was trying to suck out my energy and if he were successful, I would die.

I was frozen in fear. I knew that if I didn't do something, I was never going to wake up. The morning papers would say, "Visitor from California Dies in Sleep." I tried to move, but I was frozen. I knew the only thing that could save me was God. And so I prayed a prayer that I had learned several months before. The prayer is supposed to be one of the most powerful in the world, and is said to possess the power to protect you from evil forces that are out of body.

As I said the first word, "Kadoish," I sensed the man reel backwards, as if I had hit him with a baseball bat. In fact, the woman with whom I was staying told me she heard sounds coming from my bedroom that sounded like the crack of a baseball bat. Each time I prayed another line, the man backed further away from me until he finally disappeared into an open closet.

The next morning I called Senator Pell. I knew he had experience in out of body projection and I felt that he had been involved with what had happened to me the night before. I am sure the CIA was very amused by the telephone conversation between the two of us. We were yelling at each other. I accused him of being the visitor who tried to suck out my energy. The Senator assured me that he did not have the ability to do such things, but he told me he was certain he knew who had arranged to have my visitor pay me a visit. He believed the man whose place he wanted me to take, was behind the psychic attack. He told me he would have a talk with Mr. Jones.

I was planning to go to Virginia Beach that afternoon. My late husband's ashes had been scattered there. I was supposed to have gone there with his two daughters to scatter his ashes. But they lied to me about the date of the trip, and by the time I found out, they had already been to Virginia Beach and had returned.

Six months later, I planned my own trip to Virginia Beach to say goodbye. It was July and the weather was perfect. I rented a Mustang convertible and drove from Washington directly to Virginia Beach.

I checked into the Cavalier Hotel, put on my bathing suit and walked down to the beach. I had been there about an hour when I noticed two men on the catwalk to the left of me. They stood out like sore thumbs. They were wearing raincoats in the middle of summer. They were carrying a camera with a lens on it that was the longest camera lens I had ever seen. I found out years later that it wasn't a camera; it was a microwave beam weapon.

Suddenly I felt a stabbing pain in my abdomen. I felt as if I had been stabbed with a knife and slugged with a fist at the same time. I doubled over. I felt the blood begin to gush down my leg. I grabbed my towel and ran back to the hotel while trying to keep from leaving a trail of blood behind me.

I was hemorrhaging. Blood was everywhere. The room was beginning to look like someone had been murdered. At the time, I didn't connect the visitor from the previous night, who looked and acted like a vampire, with my sudden loss of blood.

I picked up the phone to call for help, and then I remembered WHY I had been in Washington, D.C. I had not gone on a vacation. I had gone to hand carry information to Senator Claiborne Pell that would implicate President George Bush in the treasonous deal the Reagan Campaign made with Iran to hold the 52 American hostages until after the November elections. This deal is now known as the October Surprise.

A thought flitted through my pain-numbed mind that the CIA could be responsible for what was happening to me. I was afraid to go into an emergency room, I was afraid of being murdered.

I didn't know what to do. My late husband had been raised in Virginia Beach, but there were no friends or family left there. He had told me stories about Edgar Cayce and his family. He had even dated one of Cayce's grand-daughters.

I called the Edgar Cayce Association. I explained my physical situation. Then I told the woman who answered the phone that I was the widow of a man whose family had been prominent in Virginia Beach, and who had known Edgar Cayce. As luck would have it, the woman who answered the telephone was a longtime resident of Virginia Beach who knew my late husband's family. She arranged for me to see the grandson of Edgar Cayce's personal doctor. This man put me back together long enough for me to drive back to Washington and get on a plane to California.

I barely made it back to the small town where I had grown up before the hemorrhaging started again. This time the doctor who helped me was the same doctor who took out my appendix when I was 11. He had been our family doctor for over 30 years. I was certain the he wouldn't kill me.

It took me six weeks to get my strength back. I had lost a great deal of blood, and had refused blood transfusions due to the AIDS contaminated blood supply. As a result of the hemorrhaging, I did not go to work for Senator Claiborne Pell, as he had wanted. While I was too ill to move, he called almost everyday to see if I was strong enough to accompany him on a trip to Pakistan. I was too was too weak to even get out of bed, let alone go to Pakistan.

A month late, I had begun to regain my strength. I could stay out of bed for several hours at a time. My mother asked me if I would drive her and my niece to Seattle, Washington. I told her okay, but we had to stop and rest the moment my strength ran out.

It was on that trip that I met Gunther and I heard the voice which asked me, "Are you sure you are strong enough?"

My mind went over all the things I had been through in the last year, and I thought to myself, "After what I've just been through, I'm strong enough for anything!"

It was as if the voice heard my reply, and was giving me fair warning. Once more it tried to dissuade me from entering the cocktail lounge.

"If you walk through that door, your life will change forever. Are you strong enough?"

"Of course I am," I thought to myself as I opened the door. Gunther stood up and walked to the door to meet me. He pointed to a table that was a few feet away from the men he had been sitting with. We had not been sitting there more than ten minutes when suddenly Gunther began to physically change. Gunther is tall and thin with dark brown eyes and hair. Suddenly, I was sitting with a man who was just as tall, but who was as muscular as a football player. His eyes were blue and his hair was golden and wavy.

The man leaned forward and whispered, "My name is Atalon. You are my other half. I have searched the combined universes for you for millions of years. Now that I have found you, *no one* will *ever* be able to separate us!"

As soon as the words came out of his mouth, the tall blonde man disappeared and Gunther came back. "What the hell just happened?" he asked. I was too stunned to answer. We made small talk for a while and then left the bar. The next day we decided to get married. When Gunther requested permission to marry me, he was told that we would have to separate for two years. If we still wanted to marry at the end of two years, he could retire from the Navy and we would leave the country.

We decided that we didn't want to wait two years. We used his private, government jet to fly to Reno where we got married. Two days later, Gunther was arrested by the FBI. They told me he was a conman on a crime spree marrying and defrauding wealthy widows. His stepfather told me that he was a "creature" built by the CIA. His "friends" in the CIA told me that he was an assassin and maybe worse. His enemies in the FBI told me that he was a terrorist who was wanted in every country around the world.

Because of what had happened in that cocktail lounge in Medford, Oregon, I knew this man was my other half. I knew he was Atalon, the husband/brother from whom I had been separated for eons. He was my other half, and I didn't care what else he was.

The first few days, weeks and months of Gunther's incarceration were the hardest days, weeks and months of my life. I had never known anyone personally who had been in jail. And never in a million years did I think that I would end up married to a man who was a prisoner.

If it had not been for the story of Atalon and Shalma, I would have believed the FBI, the CIA and his stepfather. I would have signed the annulment papers the FBI brought me. But because I had "channeled" the story of Atalon and Shalma myself, and because no one but a trusted handful of people had ever read it, I knew that Gunther could only have known these things if he really was Atalon!

Not only did I love him with my human heart! I loved him with my eternal soul. There was nothing the FBI or anyone else could tell me about him that would cause me to leave him or stop loving him!

And then came TAKEN!

Like many Americans, I watched the TAKEN 20 hour miniseries. While I watched it, I kept thinking about how much the story line in TAKEN was like the story line in Atalon and Shalma. TAKEN was about a breeding experiment being conducted by aliens. The Atalon and Shalma story, from The Obergon Chronicles; is about a breeding experiment on earth that was being conducted by aliens from the Sirius Tri-star system.

In my story, the breeding experiment goes awry because one half of the final pair, who were destined to marry and produce the "perfect" human container for the Sirian/Obergonian soul, was abducted by Atalon and TAKEN to his home planet.

According to the story, Atalon and Shalma, the interruption of the breeding experiment happened 10,000 years ago. When I heard the alien on TAKEN utter these words, "The experiment was an unqualified success." I remembered a line in Atalon and Shalma that sounded very similar, "The experiment on Terra was an overwhelming success!"

At the time I was "receiving" the stories that are part of this book, I truly believed I was receiving divinely dictated messages from God.

I had been married to Gunther about six years when I finally realized what had been done to me and HOW I was hearing those voices in my head.

Before marrying Gunther, I had been married to a high level DOD employee for 15 years. It is an unwritten government law that the families of government employees are "allowed" to be used, without their permission, in government experiments.

The experiment that I was unwittingly part of was one whose mission was to create New Age channels who would become leaders in the spiritual community. The type of technology that was used on me is called "voice to skull" telepathy. Voices are transmitted via micro waves into your brain. You "hear" them in exactly the same way you hear the voice of someone who is sitting in the same room with you.

It had taken years for my "handlers" to create me as what they called a "Clear Channel," meaning one who did not inject their personal beliefs into the work they were receiving. The path I took during this time included one of intense psychological and physical healing, all of which was directed by the "voices" I was hearing.

I was told to change my diet, my exercise regimen, and my spiritual beliefs. I began studying yoga, working out at a gym, running several miles each day. My diet changed. I only ate pure foods. I sought out a nutritionist who diagnosed my blood to see what I was missing. At the same time, I was healing many scars from past lives. I worked with a number of different "out of body" teachers for 5 years before the Atalon and Shalma story was dictated. The entire Atalon and Shalma story was written in less than half and hour, and... it was followed immediately by Chief White

Eagle. It took 10 years before the other stories were completed, and some are still not finished.

When Gunther and I were in Austria in 1994, I got the rest of the story of the Obergon Chronicles.

Gunther and I were staying at a lodge in Salzburg that had been in his family for six hundred years. At the lodge I was introduced to men who told me they were Knights Templars, descended from the Original Templars who were murdered at the end of the 12th century. One of these men told me that the Obergon Chronicles were ancient texts that had been found, during the Crusades, by the Knights Templars.

My Templar teacher told me that the Knights Templars were the descendants of the House of David. He told me that the history of their people had been passed down in oral history from the time the Romans put a price on the heads of all the descendants of King Solomon. I was told the Templars had created the crusades as a "cover story" under which they could excavate King Solomon's Temple. Why did they need to do this?

The Templars knew that a treasure beyond compare was hidden there. According to this man, the treasure they sought was a library comparable to the one at Alexandria. There was also more gold than existed in all of Europe. Even though the gold allowed the Templars to become the richest and most powerful force in Europe, it was secondary to the documents they excavated.

The man who gave me the history of the Obergon Chronicles believed the stories were true and that Gunther was Atalon. He also believed that I was Atalon's sister, Raelon.

He told me that he belonged to the same "group" that Gunther belonged to. He said that they also had tools to transmit information via microwaves directly into the brains of the people they intended to use as their "scribes." He said that in some cases, releasing information this way had to be done due to the importance of the mission, and the secrecy under which it had to be hidden. I didn't fully understand what he was telling me. I wish I had been smart enough to have recorded it all or made better notes.

The man told me that Shalma, the other character in the Atalon and Shalma Story, was the end product of centuries of selective breeding. She was the perfect human! She was created to mate with her own soul mate. The two of them were destined to produce a race of human bodies that were strong enough to carry the more powerful Sirian souls. But Atalon, due to his lack of compassion, put an end to the experiment because he fell in lust with Shalma and abducted her. He took her to his home world where she lived for eons until she was rescued by her soul mate.

In 1994, it never occurred to me that Shalma would eventually appear in our lives. The first time I met Gunther, he told me he was Atalon. The first time I met Gunther's present wife, Jane Ryder, I showed her the story, Atalon and Shalma. After she finished reading it, she turned to me and said, "I am Shalma!" If I had had any sense, I would have immediately cut off all ties with her. But I didn't.

In the story, *Atalon and Shalma*, Atalon used mind control to make Shalma forget about her one true love, the soul mate with whom she was to be united. In real life, just as Gunther was released from prison in Austria, and he and I were going to be re-united, he disappeared. When he showed up again, he had been subjected to some kind of mind control. Even though we had been married almost 10 years, he had no memory of ever being married to me. He thought his new wife, Jane Ryder, was the woman who had stood by him and fought for him during those deadly years when he was a political prisoner of George Herbert Walker Bush. He had no memory of me! Jane, aka Shalma, was the only wife he knew.

Some people who know us both believe he IS Atalon, and what happened to him was his karma. He was learning what it was like to be separated from his own soul mate, the one for whom he had searched for eons. It may have been HIS karma, but the devastation I felt was a nightmare of universal proportions.

Gunther married Jane without ever divorcing me. When I decided I wanted to remarry, I had to track him down to get a divorce. Before he signed the divorce papers, he called the office that issues marriage licenses in Reno, Nevada, and asked them to fax a copy of our marriage license to him. Our years of marriage had been completely wiped from his memory. Seeing the license was the only reason he agreed to sign the divorce papers.

Do I really believe that I am Raelon? Do I really believe that Gunther is Atalon and Jane is Shalma? Do I really believe that these stories were found in King Solomon's Temple and tell the real history of how this planet was settled?

Until I watched TAKEN, I believed that the CIA spent years getting me ready to be Gunther's wife. I did *not* believe that he was Atalon or I was Raelon. I believed that we were *supposed* to believe this in order to give us the strength to fight the Devil himself to stay together.

While I stopped believing that I carried the soul of Raelon and Gunther carried the soul of Atalon, I still believe these stories were found in King Solomon's Temple. After watching TAKEN, I am now *certain* that the story of Atalon and Shalma and the rest of the Children of Obergon is true. I believe the breeding experiment was designed to produce an end product... one similar to the little girl on TAKEN. Whether or not I am Raelon or Gunther was Atalon is *not* important. What is important is the history these stories give!

According to the story, Atalon and Shalma, the original breeding experiment was derailed 10,000 or more years ago. I now believe this breeding experiment has succeeded and there are people in government who want us to know this.

As the alien on TAKEN put it: "The experiment was an unqualified success."

I believe the story of Atalon and Shalma is the true prequel to TAKEN... a prequel set 10,000 to 50,000 years ago! I also believe that if the government leaked all the information it did to Stephen Spielberg, it must mean the experiment is finally successful. And if this is true, it means that Sirian souls are now capable of living in human bodies, without killing the body in a short period of time!

What this may mean is the return of the 900-year life span... along with a few other abilities like telepathy and teleportation! What it also means is the "souls" from Sirius, whose education in the material world had been interrupted when their world was destroyed by a red giant, can finally finish their lessons. I suspect this also means that these souls will soon be coming to earth.

Since I believe that much of the alien abduction stories had to do with creating "the perfect container" for these souls, I imagine that millions of these new souls will arrive in bodies that look very similar to ours.

The next question you should ask yourself, is how are they arriving? I was told over 20 years ago that they would be arriving in a Mother Ship that is as large as a planet. Could this Mother Ship be the mysterious Planet X that the internet is buzzing about?

Children Of Atalon

Applying the Lessons of Atalon to the Present Day
Posted on http://www.rumormillnews.com
By: oliverhaddo
Date: Monday, 23 December 2002, 4:26 a.m.

"I the LORD thy God am a jealous God, visiting the iniquity of the fathers upon the children unto the third and fourth generation of them that hate me."

Yahweh, whatever he was, understood the dynamic perfectly, how the self-loathing parents train the child in self-loathing, and the child passes it on to its own offspring.

Similarly, the gift of Atalon's incompleteness would be passed to his children on Earth, and to his children's children. And perhaps to his children elsewhere. Atalon's rejection of–then blind search for–his other half recapitulates itself like a leitmotif in every aspect of human civilization. Almost explicit in works like Yeats' "Song of the Wondering Aengus," it lurks implicitly in nearly every corridor of that great mythic castle we call our culture....

Her name, I found out later, was Sherry. She came in around midnight, head down, eyes averted and sporting fresh bruises on her face. I'd been a third shift convenience store clerk long enough to suss people out quickly, so I wasn't surprised when she quietly wandered through the aisles as if she were actually shopping. Somebody had just been real bad to her, and what she wanted most right now was a few moments in a clean well-lighted place. I went back to making sandwiches.

When she came to the counter with something (a pint of iced tea, maybe–this was years ago), her head still down but her whole being radiating a kind of strength, most of it committed to Keeping It All In, I asked quietly, "are you okay?"

She squeezed her eyes in a mostly successful stab at preventing tears, then took out a faint smile she'd learned as a little girl, put it on, and nodded. When I handed her the change I made a point to touch her palm. She made eye contact for the first time and I said, "be good to yourself." Sherry nodded and left

I felt several things. Compassion. A revulsion against my own gender. Other feelings that had no handy names. But I knew whatever small gift I'd offered her had been accepted, just as surely as I knew I'd given it as much to myself as to Sherry..

Yahweh's First Principle–or what I sometimes call Murphy's First Law of Culture–ensures the assembly-line production of masses of males like Sherry's husband, who reach nominal adulthood lacking contact with a core area of their psyches, and in denial about the loss. They come especially close to this loss when confronting women, since their missing component is feminine. To cover their denial about it,("I'm a man, therefore a whole entity") they often resort to dominance of, and violence against women.

(If you're imaging alpha male gorillas at this point, and thinking that a lot of this behavior comes from the animal kingdom, I think it's worse than animal. Atalon's lost soul mate is, on a lower level, our lost interior. What he did to this planet's dominant creature was to retard our evolution as a species just as his spiritual evolution was retarded. We growl UG! and GRR! and root for soccer and football teams with animal frenzy, while our governments destroy our rights and measure us for uniforms and our banks rip us off.)

And, yes, the culture factory stamps out enough women with low self esteem (plus, you could toss in an early fascination with Foxe's "Book of Martyrs") to furnish docile mates for these hollow men.

In her well-researched "Clan of the Cave Bear" series, Jean Auel constructs a detailed picture of social life during the interglacial period before this one. Goddess worship, symbolized by the prevalent Willendorf Venus figurines, led Auel to construct a fictional culture that was more advanced than most of us imagined. Guided by the Cult of the Great Mother, few of Auel's male characters have surprisingly little trouble acting "masculine." They hunt, they drink, and some of them are rogues or worse. But the majority fit naturally into a society governed by a few rules and a "consult" model that takes over for important group decisions.

We know more about the current Interglacial period, which kicked in 15,000 to 20,000 years ago. It would have begun with a rising sea level as ice melted, and with accessibility to new interior real estate as glaciers retreated. It would have begun like spring begins, with a burst of new life–flora and fauna. Cro Magnon, already experiencing its own baby boom, would have been forced to migrate as the shorelines changed and as the food supply moved. Humans would have outbred that food supply, and begun to experience overcrowding. It was about this time that agriculture appeared, and along with it, I suspect, organized warfare.

War, as some English poet wrote, is a game for kings which would not be played were their subjects educated. The Greeks noticed a tendency for opposing phalanxes to veer to the right (assume shield held in left hand, sword or spear in right); this was not entirely an outflanking or defensive strategy, but also a human attempt to avoid conflict. So they placed their fiercest warriors on the right, and literally rolled up their enemy's line. Sparta placed every first-rank warrior in front of his lover.

The principle these stratagems addressed never made it into Clausewitz because it was not a thing to be mentioned when writing on war: the innate revulsion of humans when asked to kill their own kind. I suspect war could only originate here because so many males repressed the feminine side of their souls. But the slogans of war weren't enough. In times of danger creatures reach into themselves, bypassing whatever blocks are there, and access all areas of the psyche for something that will help them survive the here and the now. (Been there. Not in combat but on a chill California night in Los Padres National Forest, lost & lying on the side of a hill without blankets & feeling September's heat leach away into the arid dark. It was a dream that saved me.)

Only 15 to 20% of US infantry forces ever fired on the enemy in WWII. Advances in training raised the fire rate to 50% in the Korean War, and operant conditioning took it to 95% in the Vietnam War. There were some failures, of course. Gerry Grossman, trained historian, psychologist, and a retired US Special Forces Major, writes of a "tunnel rat" armed with a .45 and flashlight crawling into an underground labyrinth and suddenly flicking his light on a Vietcong eating rice from a bowl. For several seconds neither man moved. Then the VC laid down his bowl and crawled away.

"Now I know why men go to war."

"Because the women are watching."

> — Fragment of dialog from a made-for-TV movie,
> circa 1980, caught while channel hopping.

In the wake of Civil War battles, men went out and found muzzle-loaders that had been charged eight, ten or twelve times. These were not the artifacts of cowardice. Those men would not desert the line, but also could not shoot at their own kind. So they waited till their neighbor in line fired, then aped him by reloading an already loaded gun...

Us, and them,

and after all

we're only ordinary men

> —Pink Floyd

Sherry came into the store two weeks later and told me she'd charged her husband with assault and rape. She still kept her head down, but not as far as before. And the practiced smile was there....

The Romans, experts at warfare, worshipped both male and female deities. They divided the soul into two halves, the "animus" or masculine soul, and its feminine counterpart, "anima." "Animus" has since evolved into a popular courtroom term meaning 'hostility' or 'antagonism'. Boy, howdy, ain't that curious?

Being Aristotilean enough to so succinctly dichotomize the soul doesn't mean the Romans had thoroughly grokked their souls. They didn't have to. They had the best armies of their era. And we all know how decadent they were.

Juggling archetypes as we are here is a dangerous pastime.

Misunderstanding is always just around the corner. Important to realize is that archetypes like animus and anima are archetypes precisely because they act unconsciously on multiple levels of experience. But when one gets into defining terms like "masculine" and "feminine," one is in quicksand. These qualities are experienced and expressed differently by individuals of both genders.

It's even hairier when we try to track the archetypes into the jungle of sexual preferences. Is a gay male automatically united with his anima? I don't think so. But studies show gay males have more connections between the left and right brains than the common population does. What does that mean? Maybe they're better at Dungeons and Dragons. (I read about this in San Francisco, so caveat lector.)

You could, however, make a case that homophobia is a symptom of the repressed anima–the denial that it's even there at all. Marcello Mota, an occultist of some repute, wrote years ago that Yahweh himself is a repressed homosexual personality.

Is one brain hemisphere Aristotelian and the other Platonic? Or are we just passing around shards of some beautiful jar that we cannot ever know in its fullness?

What does seem clear is the prevalence in history of males trained to deny their anima. Much of history can be seen as a blind groping of these half-humans as they hunt outside for something that's buried inside them, someplace they will not look. The institutions fabricated to distract us from this simple truth are legion. It is often the secret fulcrum of jokes, most of them dirty. These legitimized dodges grease the wheels of social intercourse, and rob us of the truth about ourselves and each other while we conceal our loss in song, in story, and in art.

Literature is full of this theme. Oedipus Rex. The Grail Legend. A cryptic little tale by Borges about two brothers running a gang of outlaws from a wilderness cabin, till one returns from the city with a bride, and when the husband rides out for a few days, the brother samples her wares, and this goes on till the gang starts to fragment, so the brothers have a confab after which the husband takes her out and shoots her; life must go on, you see. Hemingway: I left the hospital and walked back to the hotel in the rain. You take her and go while I hold them off here as long as I can with the machine gun. The good guy never gets the woman in the end.

Come back, Shane!

You can see that all that's changing now. Novels now have happier endings.

What's going on here is that Atalon's children inherited his sense of loss, but are just now aware of having mislaid something. And we are reassembling our whole selves again.

Come home, Atalon. It's about time. Some of us will open our arms to you, and others will shun you. The important thing is for you to fulfill your destiny. We are on the brink of fulfilling ours.

It's not happening uniformly to all of us, and it's a struggle of course. But great mysteries & magics are alive on this planet at this time.

....I used to see her around town. She'd always say hi and stop to chat. For three or four years she sent me a card each Christmas. Maybe she worked a positive arrangement with her yinless yang mate. But I'm not sure. Because she never again looked me in the eye.

oliverhaddo

August 5, 1986

A Momentous Day in the Development of Planet Earth

2006 Note from Rayelan:

As I was putting this book together, this message kept popping up in many different places and different ways. Sometimes it would pop up on my computer. Other times a hard copy of it would fall on my desk. Sometimes when I needed to find it, I couldn't... then suddenly it would miraculously reappear. At first, I had no intention of including it, because on the surface, it appears as if what was predicted, 20 years ago, did NOT come to pass.

However, the more I thought about this, the more I realized that this book is a book about exposing that which is hidden and/or false. If this piece is false, then it needs to be included as an example of "fake predictions."

Back in the 80s, many predictions were being made. I wonder how many of them have come to pass? However, we first must ask ourselves this question: How will we ever know if these predictions came to pass?

So much is hidden by governments, corporations, and the mainstream media (MSM), that it's possible that no one will ever know if these predictions, were fact based, and side-railed by people who did NOT want them to come to pass... or if they actually came to pass and no one told us about it.

In case you don't know this, the global mainstream media is owned and controlled by the same "illegal aliens" that have been trying to rule the planet from their "underground palaces" for eons. Worldwide control of the entire planet began in earnest in 1913 when these "illegal aliens"... using their "willing servants," created the United States Federal Reserve Banking System. Americans have been systematically "looted" by these people ever since.

These "illegal aliens" have controlled the British monarchy and banking since the late 1500s. The center of their "empire" is a separate "country" situated in London, called "The City of London" or Londinium. After gaining complete control of the United States money system, these "illegal aliens" went on to gain control of all the national banks in all countries... communist and capitalist alike.

However, while these "illegal aliens," aka Faction One, aka the New World Order were planning to take over the world and eliminate most humans... the ones they refer to as "useless eaters"; there has been another group at work.

Faction Two has been at work trying to make sure that Faction One is NOT successful in carrying out their plan for a one World Government.

One of the things I learned from Gunther is his group, aka Faction Two, works in 20 year cycles. In other words, what was set in motion 20 years ago, may *only* become visible this year.... 2006

For those who are not familiar with "Gunther's Group," aka Faction Two... It is a group of like-minded individuals, from all around the world, who state that they are working to "restore the original plan" for Earth and the legitimate earth dwellers.

Gunther referred to this group as Faction Two. The original Faction was referred to as Faction One, or the New World Order. It is made up of the "illegal aliens" who violated the "quarantine" of Planet Earth... aka Terra. These "illegal aliens" along with their "willing slaves" have worked to create a One World government, with *them* at the top of the pyramid, for eons.

These "illegal aliens" have used several methods to control their "willing slaves." The foremost method is the promise of eternal life, or a life that is greatly extended. The next favorite method is the promise of money and power that can be handed down through the family bloodline. There are other ways to create willing slaves. The promise of fame and adoration is one. Sex, in all its perverted forms, is another. The promise of drugs without fear of arrest is another. Still another is the promise of a secure job or a political office.

The "illegal aliens" have hundreds of millions of willing slaves working for them, and probably ten times that number of unwilling, coerced or mind-controlled slaves working for them.

When I chose to include the following article from August 5, 1986, I did a Google search for the date. I came up with two things that may or may NOT mean anything.

August 5, 1986 was the day that the Senate passed SDI. This was Ronald Reagan's famed "Star Wars." SDI was supposed to have been a device that could shoot down nuclear missiles and explode them in the air before they struck the United States. Many believe it was "Star Wars" that eventually "broke the bank" in the Soviet Union and caused the collapse.

(There are others who believe that the Soviet Union never collapsed, it's just playing possum and will soon be back to what it was. While I think it will become a powerful first world country, I do not believe that it will return to a repressive, communist country.)

In 1986, I was married to John Dyer, a nuclear physicist who was Dean of Science and Engineering at the Naval Postgraduate School. In this position, he was required to make frequent trips to Washington D. C.. One of these trips was to visit the SDI office and try to steer some of the research to the Naval Postgraduate School.

When he came home, he described his visit to the SDI office. Evidently he arrived before his appointment. When he stepped into the office, the first thing he noticed was there was no one there. There were tables, desks, chairs and computers... but there were no people. He said even the file cabinets were empty. In other words, it was just an office with a name on the door. From that moment on, he began to wonder where the SDI money was really going and what was being done with it. John didn't live long enough to find out. He died in his sleep from a heart attack in 1988.

One of my Sources for Rumor Mill News told me that the SDI money went into HAARP, the mysterious installation in Alaska that Nick Begich wrote about in his book, "Angels Don't Play this HAARP." HAARP is a method of heating the upper limits of our atmosphere. My Source believes if HAARP is deployed properly, it could explode warheads high above the earth. So maybe SDI funds were diverted to create HAARP.

However, my Source also believes that HAARP can be used for mind control, and he has recently stated that HAARP, in conjunction with chemtrails, could be creating a screen on which images can be projected.

In my book, Diana, Queen of Heaven, I talked about Operation Blue Beam. Canadian investigator, Serge Monast presented enough documentation to prove to me and many others, that some government was working on a device to project images in space. Monast believed that these images would be of religious leaders. He predicted that the New World Order would use these images to usher in a New World Religion. Serge didn't live long enough to find out if his theory was correct. He died of a sudden heart attack.

My Source has also wondered if HAARP and chemtrails are creating a "blue screen" which hides the approach of Planet X and/ or the Mother Ship that is coming to take the Graduates of the Earth School home, or to their next assignments.

There is one other thing that was going on in August of 1986. A group of Faction Two CIA operatives were working to expose the drug connection to what eventually came to be called, "The Iran/Contra Scandal." Gunther was one of the people who planted the "documents" in the airplane that crashed in Nicaragua. These documents implicated many people in the Reagan/Bush Administration and the Iran/Contra hearings effectively shutdown the White House for the last few years of Reagan's term.

Gunther went to prison in 1986. It was only for a few months, to get him out of the way. I didn't know Gunther in August of 1986, but when we married in August of 1989, the charges for which he was arrested in 1986 were the charges that eventually caused him to be sentenced to 28 years in Missouri State Prison. On the day we finally beat the charges and he was released, there was a throng of reporters with cameras. Not one of them wanted to know about the October Surprise, the scandal that made Gunther famous. The reporters wanted to know about his involvement in Iran Contra. He walked through dozens of reporters, to the Judge's chambers, saying, "No comment, no comment, no comment."

If Gunther and his group set something in motion in August of 1986, I don't know what it was. If he was right when he told me that his group works in 20 year cycles, then by early summer of this year... 2006; I think it's possible that we may see what it was that was set in motion 20 years ago.

While the political and governmental changes were not as evident as I would have like to have seen, it is evident that many governments around the world have changed radically. The most incredible change was the "fall" of the Soviet Union. The second change that I find most unbelievable is the "capitalization" of China. In 1986 I don't think any of us would have thought that China would allow its citizens to own gold, to start their own businesses, and to own computers.

> *Note from Rayelan (2006): The following message also talks about the changes that people will go through emotionally and spiritually. Every month I interface with hundreds of thousands of people on my webpage, Rumor Mill News. From what I can tell, by the responses I receive from my readers, the spiritual, mental and emotional changes that were predicted back in 1986 happened and are still happening.*

August 5, 1986

This is a very momentous day in the development of the planet earth. There are forces being set into motion right at this very time which will insure that all that has been worked for, for the past 18 million years, has finally come to pass.

Do not be mistaken as to the time and the mode of this message. It is the 5th of August, 1986 of which we speak. And events which occur today will have world reaching effects. Because of this, those who have been in power and have been corrupted by the power that was entrusted to them, will be removed to other ineffective posts.

The world is entering its final phase. Do not be concerned when we call it the final phase. The world as you know it will exist no more, but a better world will take its place.

What we have succeeded in doing is awakening enough people in high places, to the fact that there are people in power the world over, who only want what is good for them and a few of their friends. What has happened today is that the first such rat was exposed for what he is and it will start a house of cards toppling, which will be felt around the world.

There are many people who are living in their selfishness and greed nature. They are just slightly above the level of animal. When this type of person seeks power they usually get it, because others look to their greed and see it as a symbol of power. In this case, the people mistake power for right action and wisdom. People know what they want in a leader, but they are misled by a calculated plan to deceive them. Speeches and television commercials are designed to make people believe a selfish, greedy, power hungry man has their best interest at heart. People want leaders who are benevolent. Most world leaders, who enter politics, do so only because it allows them to acquire massive wealth and the power to do anything they wish.

What has happened today is that a hornet's nest has been opened up and this hornet's nest will point to many people around the world who have kept themselves in very powerful positions by the blatant misuse of the sacred duty entrusted to them. The hornet's nest will turn into a rat's nest when politician after politician resigns in disgrace. It will reach all levels.

Once this has been accomplished there will be a settling time and then the world will begin a new routine… but the new routine will be one of world cooperation and the righteous selection of those people who will govern. The seeds of a new government have been sown today. No more will the old way of doing things work. The government has to be by the people and for the people...all the people!

It is now time for the corrupted way of passing legislation through governments to come to an end. And it now has.

As for the spiritual change that has been manifested on the earth as a result of this change in government....

It is now time for each and every man and woman on the planet to realize that the small spark of God that rests in each of them has finally been brought to fruit bearing stage. It is time for the crop to be harvested. The souls have worked long and hard to fight their way out of the animal bodies in which they were trapped. They have successfully joined the world of evolved, sentient beings; and therefore have returned this planet to the Federation of Light Planets.

It is not clearly understood by all who read metaphysical journals that the earth was, at one time, a light planet. This is before the early travelers from other planets came. These early travelers from other planets had developed massive technology, but little compassion. They were still very deeply rooted in their animal natures, and because of this they enjoyed having power over the developing inhabitants of the planet earth.

These travelers of lower nature taught the earth people their bad habits; and those they did not physically enslave, they mentally enslaved. This was accomplished by very powerful mind to mind melds... techniques that resemble today's hypnotism but 100 times more powerful. Those who were enslaved by these perverted mind control techniques, have been held in slavery until this present day.

Many have worked themselves free with the help of souls who have loved them throughout time. But many more are still held in slavery and cannot be freed until certain truths are set forth onto the planet.

Technology is now available which will allow almost all the world to know of new discoveries within 24 hours. This technology is what was needed before the new revelation could be brought forward. A worldwide announcement will topple the control of the usurping travelers from other worlds.... the "illegal aliens" who have worked for eons to enslave the souls on earth.

One must not forget that, in this world of dualities, the usurping travelers had their counterparts. Their counterparts took the form of "settlers" who were sent by the ruling council of planets to see that the Plan was restored upon the earth. It is now time for all of these early "settlers" to awaken to their true nature and realize that the final chapter of their stay upon the planet is being read.

It is also time for them to understand that many of them came eons ago for the sole purpose of being prepared for their mission at this final time. These souls have spent lifetimes in training. And now the much-prepared-for lifetime has finally come.

Have a little more patience!

For some of you it still may not be time for the mission you chose to perform. So keep on educating yourselves and raising your vibrations, so that when your mission presents itself, you will *know* it and you will be prepared.

Your mind asks, "How will you know what to prepare for?"

Do what comes naturally to you. If you love to work with wood, become a carpenter. If you love history study all history. If you feel you need to be on television... then learn the tools of the trade... but remember... at all times in everything you do... you must keep the mission of God/Creator at the forefront.

You must not lose yourself in your career. You must keep preparing yourself to give the best possible performance when your time has come. So you just keep on keeping on and when God/Creator chooses you for one of his missions, He will select you by your background. But of course... please remember that your higher self will have already known that you had the possibility of being chosen for some great mission, and since it knew what the general parameters of the mission were, you came into this world predisposed to certain likes and dislikes.

In other words, God/Creator will never give you a mission to perform, for which you have not been prepared, from the day of your birth.

It is important that each one of you continue on your path and continue refining the skills with which you were born. That is why it is so important that you be able to throw off the negative programming of others who want something from you and force you to carry out their will. These people may be advertisers who want to sell you their product, whether it be a university degree or a soft drink. These people may be your own frustrated parents who are trying to live their unfulfilled lives through you.

It is important at this time that you learn to hear the small voice of God/Creator that lives within each and every one of you. It is your true self and your true beacon of light in this world.

Let your heart light shine.

Be true to yourself.

By learning to talk with your inner self and listen quietly to the answers, you will begin to empower yourself and shake off the negative programming of others. As you grow stronger in the light, more light beings will flock to you to give you aid and comfort in your journey into the light. Many of these beings exist in other dimensions. As the years go on, the dimensions will come closer together, to the point of bleed through.

Many light beings are walking the planet earth in a variety of bodies. Some are angels, unaware of their true identity... others

were powerful leaders of the world in ancient times, who have
come back to assist those who have chosen to lead in this life. These
people come to you, at all times, and in all kinds of disguises. As you
begin to let your light shine you will begin to attract these
wonderful beings to you. They will guide, guard and protect you
while you start to grow. As you get stronger they will step away to
see if you have become strong enough to handle yourself without
support.

In this sense they become like the parent who is helping a child
learn to walk. If they stayed to protect the child from every fall, they
child would never learn to walk. The same is true with your seen
and unseen protectors. If these protectors allowed you to continue
leaning on them, long after you had developed your own strength,
then it could be possible that you would stop developing your
strength and possibly even atrophy and stagnate. To keep this from
happening, your wonderful guides and guards begin to let you
venture out into the world on your own. But they will only let you
do this when they know you are strong enough to do so. Remember
that God will never give a person a load that is too heavy for them
to carry. Your guides and guards will never abandon you to a task
that is too difficult for you to perform. They will be by your side
every step of the way.

But there are warnings that must be set down at this time.

There are very powerful dark forces that want to consume every
new light that is beginning to grow. Many of these dark forces are
innocent beings who have had their minds altered through this
process of perverted mind melding. These beings want your light
because in their heart of hearts they know that your way it is the
right way, the one true way. However, because they are still in
bondage to the dark forces of power, lust and greed… to mention
but a few, they seek to steal and destroy, rather than merge through
osmosis with the light thereby becoming the light.

When this happens to a soul who has recently allowed its own
inner light to shine this soul sometimes feels overwhelmed by grief,
depression or other negative emotions. Sometimes their entire
world begins to shatter and fall apart. Sometimes accidents happen,
friends die, jobs are lost, spouses or partners leave… tragedy in
every form can sometimes appear. These tragedies are not necessarily all caused by the dark forces.

Many times the so-called tragedies are simply part of your own
internal growth process. In the case of a job or spouse being lost,
you may have simply outgrown these situations, and the only way
of getting you to move on is actually throwing you out. In some

cases, if the partner has refused to grow in anyway, the partner chooses to die.

As you can begin to see, even though there are many possible answers to every given situation, it really is impossible for us to know at any given time which answer applies to us at the moment. And so this is why we ask that all of you learn to pray only for the highest good for all concerned.

As the newly lighted soul begins to open up, there are very powerful invocations which will invoke the highest good for all concerned. These are rituals which have been used for so long that they have infused themselves into the collective threads that bind us all together.

When one soul puts out the message that all forces contrary to the will of God/Creator should leave its territory right now, those forces who have been sowing darkness and deceit know that if they do not respond immediately to this command, they run the chance of having their very consciousness absorbed back into the One. Being absorbed isn't really the correct word. The offending soul is stretched until its individual consciousness is so minute that virtually nothing exists of it at all. It is a painful process for a soul to endure when the soul is not ready. When the soul is ready and asks for such a thing to happen, then there is no pain or fear. But this topic will be the subject of another lesson.

Once the newly lighted soul is comfortable with the invocations to keep darkness at bay, it is time for that soul to venture forth into the world and test its wings. Of course what must be remembered is that the protective powers of light are never very far away and can be called upon at anytime… but the newly enlightened soul must follow its own heart light and know when the appropriate times are.

The Master Jesus is the perfect example of this. He could have called in his angels anytime he wanted to stop the process or change its direction, but he knew that certain things had to continue as God/Creator had ordered, even if it meant pain and suffering. Which is not to say that all pain and suffering must be endured in the name of God.

There were many during the Inquisition who understood the lie within the lie.

In other words, they knew that if they lied in the framework of another even more horrendous lie, that the larger lie canceled out their smaller one. In this way many people avoided long painful torture and died quick deaths. This form of lie has to be understood at a soul level, or it will continue to haunt the soul in lifetime after lifetime.

How do you discover if you have permission to lie? There is only one way to discover anything about yourself. This way is to get in touch with your own inner light and listen to it.

How can this be accomplished? There are as many ways as there are people. No one way is right for everyone. Again, you must trust your heart to lead you in the proper direction to even find the proper way of talking to your soul.

Meditation is one way, but there are many kinds meditation, and unfortunately some of the more popular methods have become cultish, with the student ending up by paying homage to some being in body who calls him or herself a guru. Or worse yet... being taught, by the guru, to send all prayers and energy directly to the guru. This effectively cuts OFF your connection to God/Creator. It cuts off your ability to ever KNOW your own inner light.

Beware that you don't get caught in such a cult. How do you do that? Just remember that at this time there is no one on the planet who is so far ahead of you that you are required to worship them as if THEY were GOD. There are wonderful teachers who can help you along your way, but when you have learned everything from them that you need to learn, you will know inside that it is time for you to leave. If you are afraid to leave, the good ones will throw you out when they know you are ready. False teachers will try to bind you to them for the rest of your life. You can recognize the false teachers by this trait. They will try to tie you to them for the rest of your life. They want you to follow in their footsteps even as they tell you to find your own path.

Just remember that God, the Creator is weaving a huge tapestry the size of hundreds of combined Universes. Each soul makes up one thread in God's tapestry. If thousands of souls abandon their personal paths... their own tapestry threads... then God's tapestry will not be woven perfectly, it will be full of holes.

Learn to hear your own inner voice, prepare for your mission, and then walk your path!

Part Two

Earth Lessons for the Children of Obergon

Lesson 1

Let's Deal With Money

June 1, 1991

L et's deal with money!
Rather shall we say... let's deal with abundance. In fact maybe we should state it differently still. Let's deal with having all you need when you need it.

How's that?

➤ What good is money if there is nothing there to buy with it?

➤ What good is abundance if it is the wrong kind?

The most important thing you can learn from this message is to direct your thoughts carefully or you will end up with lots of gold and no food or shelter.

In the world in which you currently live, money is the thing that buys you everything you need. Yes that is true... for now. But the earth and her people are getting ready for a major shift, and when this happens all the systems of money exchange will be gone for a while.

And so... if you are too tied-in to the concept of the green dollar bills, that bring you everything you need, then you will be in for a very rude shock.

Pay careful attention to this message and begin to read the messages that come into your mind as you are reading this.

Many times the purpose of this kind of writing is to awaken, within the reader, his or her own inner guidance system. As you begin to hear your own inner voice you will resonate to the confirmation of the truths that are being stated here.

If you do not resonate, do not feel that it is because you are too "un-advanced" for these teachings. It might very well be that you studied all of this lifetimes ago and you simply don't need to repeat these lessons, especially now when time is growing short for learning lessons.

It could also be that you are not ready to hear these truths. The shock of what you sense is coming might be so great that you are in denial. It's the old ostrich story. If you hide your head, it will all go away.

Another reason that these words may not resonate with you is that these messages need a foundation. You may be new to this phase of the lesson, and your foundation is still being built.

Whatever the reason might be, if you don't resonate with what is being said in these messages, that's all right. Please don't judge yourself, or the messages or the "reason"; because the truth is, you may never know the reason these lessons are not for you.

*   *   *   *   *

Money, prosperity, and survival are all coming to the surface in the coming decades. People in the first world countries have just gone through an unparalleled time of abundance and prosperity. But this abundance was built on a foundation which was rooted in the future. The future is not here, with us in the present, and, because the abundance of the future was borrowed and brought back... into the past, the future begins to look awfully bleak. Once we get to the end of this decade and the beginning of the next century, the effects of "our borrowed future" will be seen!

As the time continuum wends its way slowly into that drained future, the people... all those who are still living, will take up residence in this drained future, and they will begin to experience a profound lack.

And what will they do?
How will they act?
Will you be one
Who enters the Land of lack?

If you don't want to be one of these people, what steps do you take to prevent it?

Is there any place where you can put your money so that it will be there when you need it? Are banks going to continue to protect your money? Is the stock market going to be safe? What about insurance companies, retirement funds and your Social Security? What about all the plans you have made for your long and well deserved retirement and old age? Will any of the money you counted on be there when you need it?

Listen and feel the fear that arises as these questions are asked. Money causes fear because money and fear live in the same chakra. Fear arises as the body thinks it might cease to exist. Money in today's world buys the food, clothes and shelter needed to survive, therefore; money is equated with survival in today's society.

Survival energy comes to us from the base chakra. Fear is the energy within the base chakra that insures that the fight or flight response causes the body to behave in the appropriate manner to save itself.

Fear and survival are seated in the base chakra or the first center. That center is red in color, the color of blood. Abundance in money has been seen as green. Green is a very abundant color on the planet. Green is associated with all the growing plants that are consumed to feed and nourish us and give us life. Green and red are etheric opposites, you can use red to attract green and vice versa. The life force dissipates fear. There is much more information to be given on the colors green and red, but this is enough for this moment.

It has been said that soon all the green money that is currently used in the United States will be replaced by red money. Much panic and fear has gone through the hearts of the populace as a result of this information. But let me reassure you. When this does happen, it will signal that the United States has made a quantum leap in consciousness.

Ages ago, an abundance meditation was taught to those adepts who had completed the training in the mystery schools, or in the sacred secret orders that followed the mystery schools. One of these sacred orders was the Knights Templars.

The meditation used the red energy of the base chakra to draw in all the abundance that was needed. Remember, upon the planet earth, green represents abundance. The Founding Fathers of the united states of America gave their new country a monetary system that would insure that it became the most abundant country on the planet. And it did!

But the country was based on a principle of ownership on a continent that had existed for millennia with no ownership. In other words, the prime directive of the united states of America was at loggerheads with the energy of the land on which it was created.

So, what does this mean?

If all goes well, we will see a shift back to the very principles that were taught to the Founding Fathers by the original inhabitants of this land. These souls have been guiding the energy of the country throughout its turbulent history.

Of course there have been setbacks for these peoples, but this is to be expected. Living upon a planet that is based upon the duality principle, it seems that all learning or progress has to be made at considerable pain. For every cause there must be an effect, for every force there must be an equal and opposite force.

The spirit of the red race is rising up out of its unsettled slumber and embracing the whole of the united states of America, and much of Mexico. This spirit will cause much turbulence to take place, and out of the ashes of our old way of life a new life will rise.

And part of this new life will be red (pink) money. Can you begin to get a small glimmer of how right red money is at this point in our evolution? Green money activates the base chakra. At lower stages of evolution this is needed to keep the beings alive. But at higher stages of evolution if the base chakra is continually activated, the being tends to live in a schizophrenic state of fear and/or arrogance depending how strong and powerful the being is.

Red money activates the heart chakra. The heart chakra is the center of the being. It is where the earth body and the spirit body meet. Its color is green. By activating the heart energy and sending out green energy upon the planet, you will bless the planet upon which you live and you will attract red energy to you.

Remember that red is the energy of the base chakra, it keeps you alive. It is also the energy of courage and courage will be very important in the coming times.

As you can see, there is much in store for the peoples of this world in the coming years. There is very little that you can do to prevent the coming changes or to even prepare for them. All you can really do is know in your heart that all that is happening is part of the Great Plan that is being restored to the planet at this time.

Make sure that you prepare yourself internally.

This is the only way you can prepare. Look deep into your own heart and see the distortions that still lie there.

The coming times will be making diamonds out of those of you who are strong enough to survive the pressure. The pressure will squeeze out everything that is impure and you will be left with a polished diamond like brilliance.

Rejoice!

The awakening times are here...

And YOU are lucky enough to be alive to behold them!

Lesson 2
The Importance of Greed

The message for today is actually one that was written over twenty years ago. At that time such a message would not have been understood as well as it will be today. The decade of the eighties was one that was based on greed. When I received this message in late 1980, it had not yet dawned on Americans that they were embarking upon a journey that would teach them everything they needed to learn about greed. Now that we are out of the excesses of the eighties and the nineties, we have some distance to look back and evaluate our lessons; it is now time to really understand....

September 19, 1980: 9:25 A.M.

The lesson for today is on greed.

Greed can consume the human container, permeating it to such a degree that the soul dwelling within the container can become temporarily contaminated.

Greed, like all the other "deadly sins" is another way of teaching "strength of character." A soul can never become strong of heart, body and mind without working at it.

Every part of the soul is divided into positive and negative. The counterpart of greed is generosity. To be generous is a virtue; it is a manifestation of love. This is a state to be desired. However, metal that is not tempered properly can break under pressure.

In order to produce a strong sword it must undergo the change of flame. In order to produce a strong and pure soul, it must also undergo the purifying and transforming fires of change.

A soul can be created with generosity in bloom, but unless that virtue is put to the test, unless the soul experiences greed and after experiencing it, rejects it in favor of generosity, then the soul will forever have the possibility of slipping from its personal Garden of Eden.

Greed, as are all the seven deadly sins, is another learning tool on the way to perfection. Do not condemn a greedy person; just realize that they are still in school studying generosity.

You, yourself, are here studying something. The things you study may be perfectly obvious to those who have finished this particular course, but to you, they are hidden.

There will come a day when you have graduated. A day when you will be able to look back and understand all the lessons that you have mastered.

You may do this while still in this life, or it may require additional lives for the soul to learn the lessons properly.

Enough!

Today's lesson is a short one because the concepts contained herein are powerful ones. We suggest that you do no more reading for now. Put down the book and meditate on what we have said.

Then go on about your business... and come back later.

Lesson 3
The Coming Changes

Today's message is one concerning upcoming changes in the world and in the solar system. But to understand what we are about to impart, it is necessary for you to have some background.

Many of you have heard of the teacher Ramtha. While it was not necessary for most people in this life to learn the lessons he had to teach, it is necessary for everyone at some time in the earth cycle to understand the teachings of Ramtha.

Let us digress for a moment and address those of you who have had an aversion to the Master Ramtha. Those of you who were repelled by his teachings were repelled for one of two reasons. The first being you already studied them at some time in your past history, the second reason being, you didn't need to study these particular lessons in order to complete your mission successfully.

The lessons that Ramtha came back to Earth to teach this time were being taught to a particular group of advanced souls who were too busy in other lives serving humanity to bother keeping up with the lessons that humanity was learning.

There are souls who did not come to the earth plane to learn. These souls came to the earth plane to serve the developing human race. However, as these souls became immersed in the Maya of material incarnation, they began to lose their memory of why they came, and indeed they began to lose the remembrance of who they are.

Many of the former teachers have become students just long enough to have their memories jogged back to life.

Once this happens, the only way such a soul can regain its memory is by entering the earth school and graduating. And so, what we see at this juncture in history is many of the former teachers have become students. They have become students just long enough to have their memories jogged back to life. Once they have awakened their memory then they can take up their rightful places as the teachers and servers that they are.

However… this aside needs to be placed here, and it needs to be remembered throughout all that you read, whether in this book or in all others. There are dark lords, (aka "illegal aliens") upon this planet who wish to enslave all souls. These dark lords have perfected the art of mind control and brain washing. It must be known that many of the students who gather at the feet of the so-called "masters" have been "peeled" off from the teachings of light and perverted by the dark lords.

This said, let us continue:

We will continue using the Master Ramtha as our example for this day.

Over four thousand years ago upon this planet the class of souls that make up the first world countries entered a time of war. They had graduated from their sexual chakra to their power chakra. Each chakra contains many lessons.

The base chakra contains the lessons of survival on the earth plane. Souls who are new to the earth plane stay in this chakra for hundreds of thousands of years. Once the first chakra, also called the base chakra, has been mastered, it was time to master the second chakra.

The lessons of this chakra were overseen by a group of wise feminine souls. The wise feminine souls came to the earth specifically to assist developing souls by teaching them the skills they needed to master the art of staying alive and reproducing the species.

The skills taught by these wise feminine souls concerned all aspects of the physical world from planting to mastery of the elements. The healing arts were taught. Agriculture was taught. Plants were utilized for food and for healing abilities. Planting seasons were taught. Invocation of the devic kingdom was taught. All manner of survival skills were taught, even some that have been lost in today's world.

Once these skills were mastered it was time to move on to the lessons of the power chakra.

In some places on the planet the lessons of the power chakra came into play almost fifteen thousand years ago. Remember that in this book, we are talking only to those souls who are in one particular class. This class is made up of souls who entered the earth plane at various intervals starting about two million years ago and ending as recently as three thousand years ago. These souls make up a group soul... and it is this group soul that is getting ready to graduate.

Do not class these souls as slow learners and fast learners. The ones who came millions of years ago prepared the way for the ones who entered later. Do not think that the ones who entered later were lazy, childish or foolish. Many of these latecomers had duties on other worlds that were so important they needed to stay with their assignments until the very last moment.

Some of these latecomers are some of the wisest souls upon the planet because they have not been here long enough to forget who they are. Some of these late comers had to master all the lessons of the material plane in just a few thousand years. Learning at such an accelerated rate caused unforeseen problems. Some of the worst problems humanity has faced, has been during the last three to four thousand years. These problems were a direct result of this accelerated learning process.

All souls will eventually graduate...
or they will return to the One Mind.

The reason for digressing so much on the age and learning abilities of the various members of the soul group is so you can understand that it doesn't matter how old or young a soul is a this plane. All souls will eventually graduate, or they will be returned to the One Mind. Souls are only returned to the One Mind when they have become so damaged that they are incapable of future growth.

It must also be understood that not all souls here on the planet are of the same group family.

Also understand that some souls who are of the group family will need extra time to graduate and therefore another planet must be created for these souls as a sort of "remedial learning school."

These souls will be given a certain amount of time on this new planet to learn the lessons of the material plane. If, after an appropriate amount of time, it is judged that these souls have damaged themselves too greatly to ever catch up with the rest of the group family, then their souls will be absorbed into the One Mind that we call God.

Let us explain absorption.

It is simply returning to the godhead to become one with the Father/Mother Creator. This is a condition that causes enlightened beings to leap with joy, however, when the soul is still caught up in ego, absorption is considered a fate worse than death. Because it is true death. The death of the ego.

However, the memories and the lessons that were learned will live on forever as one with the Greater Knowing,

To lose all you have, to become One with greater Wisdom...

It sometimes is hard for us to understand how this concept can strike fear into the hearts of men.

Now that we have given you sufficient background to understand what we wanted to talk about today, we will begin.

The Master Ramtha was the high priest of the Age of Aries. The Master Jesus was the high priest of the Age of Pisces. Soon there will be a high Priest of the Age of Aquarius. Many names have been used for this person.... messiah, prophet, redeemer, teacher... We chose to use the word "high Priest" because it denotes a teacher who sets the lessons for a particular period of time.

Ramtha was teaching the lessons of the solar plexus or the power chakra. Jesus was teaching the lessons of the heart center or the lessons of love. Each chakra requires a different amount of time to successfully complete the lesson. The solar plexus took approximately five thousand years... on average. The heart center has taken about two thousand years... on average. Please also realize that biological changes in the human species were also going on during these periods. The human body is changing and adapting to the newer and finer vibrations that are required as the soul moves up the chakra ladder.

Another aside must be added here:

The dark lords are doing all they can to stop the biological changes from taking place. Foods are being engineered to rob the body of energy. Diseases are being engineered that keep the body in constant pain. Drugs have been introduced that numb the mind and prevent the spirit from developing. In order for your spiritual self to awaken, one must first learn to purify the body. To do this involves a total immersion in the physical, from knowing where and how the foods you eat are grown, to knowing what vitamins and minerals you need to supplement your food with. Also understanding the nature of prescription drugs and what they can do to your spirit body is very important. But there is no time for these things to be discussed in this book. That is something you will have to learn on your own.

Getting back to the lesson of the moment: Remember what we said about the feminine souls who led the way during the age of the base chakra and the sexual chakra? Many of these souls took a back seat during the age of the power chakra. These souls had already studied power somewhere else. But there were other feminine souls that joined the battles and fought with and against the rest of the souls who were learning the lessons of power.

Now that the planet, for the most part has learned the lessons of power, the two soul types, masculine and feminine can join together and co-create the Age of Love.

When we refer to the different soul types as masculine and feminine, do not think that we are talking about the two different sexes here on the planet earth. The concept of original "masculine souls" and "feminine souls" has nothing to do with male and female as you know it. These terms can best be described by comparing a whole soul to a developing solar system. There is a whirling central mass that will eventually become a sun. The pieces that are either brave, or foolish or unstable enough to break off and go their own way are referred to as the "masculine souls." The souls that choose to stay near the center of the group soul and learn from the group experience are referred to as the "feminine souls." When we refer in this way to masculine and feminine souls, we are referring to souls that are split souls... one soul that is now two souls.

Throughout this discourse we have referred to some souls who came, saw their missions, performed them and went their own way. These are souls who have remained whole throughout their journey, or are souls who have split to perform the job faster and then joined back together as one soul.

Sometimes it is far harder to be a complete soul upon the earth plane, because it is impossible for a whole soul to fully understand the longing a split soul has for its other half.

The romantic quest was created by split souls who search for their other half. But many whole souls have fallen prey to this addictive behavior and search hopelessly for their other half while all the time it is within their very Oneness. It is now time for these people to wake up and realize that they are already whole and they have no need to continue their fruitless search. In other words, it is fine for some people to be alone. They are whole and they are happy.

At this time upon the planet approximately forty per cent of the group soul are whole souls. These souls have no need for spouses or children. They are complete. They are also very, very busy, and as such, there would be little time for a normal family life.

As you can see, it is sometimes very hard to quickly communicate certain ideas. But suffice it to say, we will continue to try.

Upon the planet great change is taking place.

We are very quickly ending the Age of Pisces and beginning a whole new arena of learning. In the Age of Aquarius all the higher chakras will be instantly accessed and opened. Humankind will commune once again with the Gods... But before this takes place, something has to be done with the souls who are still learning the lessons of the power chakra.

The planet named after the God of War will teach peace

That is why a new planet is being terra-formed. The planet is Mars. Settlement on Mars has already begun. Humans from this world have already visited Mars and have begun setting up the resources that will be necessary to support human life. The same was done for your world hundreds of thousands of years ago. Mars is being prepared... once agaTho sustain human life. Trees and plants will be seeded upon the planet to create just the right amount of oxygen for humans to breathe. As soon as the proper climatic changes have been brought about, settlement will begin.

Isn't it interesting that the planet that is named after the God of War is the planet that will teach peace to the warring souls?

And what about the souls who have learned the lessons of love? Where will they go? Many who have developed their bodies to the point of light will go to Venus. Others will stay here on earth overseeing the next stage in the development of planet earth. Still others will leave this solar system.

What has just been described will take place in the next two hundred years.

But what about right now? What is happening on earth right now?

The planet is shifting from a consciousness that is centered in the power chakra to one that is centered in the heart chakra. Because of this we simply can't allow war any more. War has become incompatible with the lessons that are being taught. As the time for war comes to an end, more wars will erupt and these wars will be more dangerous than any we have seen before. Technology has advanced faster than morality.

One thing must be remembered. The earth is more important to us than the school upon her body or the students in that school. While we love all of you dearly, it is your soul essence that we love, not your physical bodies. We know that the physical is temporal and will eventually pass back into the atoms that make up the earth.

In the play that is being created in the universe as a whole, there are beings who have roles which are very important. These beings have been in training for eons and those of us who have agreed to be guardians of such beings have sworn to protect these beings no matter what the cost.

Mother Earth is such a being. You cannot understand her role in the Combined Universes at this time. But her role will allow the universe to continue its expansion until all the souls who wish to complete the training course in "Godhood" have finished their lessons.

Now can you understand why it is more important to save the earth than it is to save the humans on the earth? The souls in these bodies will eventually incarnate again. If they are reasonably advanced they will come back to earth. If not they will incarnate on Mars.

And so, earth is entering a very dangerous period. It will be marked by war, famine, pestilence, plague and changes in the earth plane. It will also be marked by economic collapse. Governments will shift. Countries that are powerful now will fall into third world status. Eastern Europe and the Soviet Union will rise as the great bastions of human freedom and democracy. (The reason for this is they have been learning the lessons of democracy for almost a century. Remember your lesson on greed and apply it to democracy.)

This region will become a great first world power. New enlightened souls from other dimensions will incarnate in this region. Physical changes in the gene pool will take place in this area and a new type of body will be created. It is already underway in the countries that made up the old Yugoslavia, especially the part that is nearest to Hungary. This new body will be able to work with the higher and finer energies that are surrounding mother earth and helping her planetary soul finish her mission.

The earth school has become secondary to the mission of the mother. The Mother is awakening and will be changing. She will first repair herself. The coming earth changes will be intended to clean the pollution from the land and seas, and repair damage to the higher layers of the body... those above the earth that we call the stratosphere and the ionosphere. These regions are also part of the earth's body. The Mother can heal herself without physical help from humans. Of course She appreciates the mental and spiritual help that humans give Her.

Mother Earth (aka Terra) will create the doorway to the new universe

The Mother Earth is very important to the current Soul Family that is studying upon her right now. There have been many soul families upon the Earth, but this soul family is approaching the end of their lessons. In a very short period of time... a few eons... the family will have learned all it needs to learn to complete its transition into a "God" capable of creating its own universe. Mother earth is being prepared to create the doorway to the new universe that will be created by this Soul Family.

These concepts are difficult to define and relate. We hope that you have been able to follow them. Everything is connected. Even the bank failures and the stock market crash are connected to Mother Earth's evolution. It is very difficult to make the tremendous jump that is necessary to follow this line of thought. But to understand the coming changes, it is necessary to keep in mind all aspects.

The reason it is necessary not to lose sight of the spiritual changes is because this knowledge will keep you free from fear. Fear is the great immobilizer. It is the "mind killer." It is also the energy that will bring chaos and destruction into your lives.

The economic system will change throughout the world. It will no longer be necessary to have the large separations between rich and poor. Most people who are in the first world countries have learned the lessons they came to earth to learn. These last few years for them will simply be the polish on the diamond. And for those who can't adapt quickly enough, these next few years will provide the exit they will need to allow them to take up residence on the other planet.

For those of you who are reading this and truly understanding it, we wish to say that you will be protected and provided for. Have no fear because your light will shine wherever you go and because of this you will attract to yourself the protection and the guidance to continue to perform your mission here on earth.

July 11, 1991 11:20PM

Lesson 4
Solar Eclipse

...the awakening times have begun

Today was the beginning of the reshuffling energies. All things will be reshuffled and many people will not be able to handle the reshuffling.

Where will you be when the new hand is dealt? If it is something you do not like, how will you deal with it? Will you want another deal or will you take a deep breath and learn to live with it?

The energies on the planet are changing and today marked the inauguration of the sweeping energies that will sweep away all that is not of the light and usher in the New Age of Peace and Prosperity and Light.

Everything sounds wonderful doesn't it? Well don't be fooled. As the old world crumbles, a lot of pain is going to be felt upon the planet. And this is what this note is about.

How will you deal with this pain? Even if it is not yours, how will you deal with it? Every time you watch television you see starving children or dying children. You know that in other parts of the world major changes are taking place and your heart goes out to the sick and dying and oppressed. But what are you doing about it?

Has the impact of their suffering touched you enough to cause an empathetic learning response? Have you vicariously learned any karmic lessons from the pain you see on the evening news?

Do you even watch the evening news? And if you watch but somehow blot out the parts that cause you pain, do you think you might have missed an easy way of learning a really painful lesson?

What am I talking about? What am I trying to get you to see? Well ... understand that these lessons are not just pretty poetry that is being spewed out in a feeble attempt to create an "Ah Ha" response in you. Understand that the wording and the syntax are carefully constructed to create an evoking response from deep within you. Your own inner voice is being called forward. Your own inner wisdom is being asked to shine.

Awaken and arise...

Like flour into bread dough...

In Thine, thy Father's eyes.

If you are one who chooses to blot out the suffering of others because you cannot bear to think of their pain, maybe you have missed a valuable way of learning lessons easily. If you refuse to watch television or read about the suffering of others because you don't believe the media, or don't want to pollute your "finer thoughts" with baser constructs, then maybe you are depriving yourself of a rapid way of learning. But then again, maybe you are preventing yourself from being programmed by the dark lords. Don't ever forget that there are souls upon this earth whose agenda is to keep you from awakening... therefore there are distortions and lies in much of the media, designed to keep you trapped. However... we can still use what is presented in the media as a means of personal growth if we know how to do it.

There are lessons that can be learned by examining the difficult conditions of others. This is the purpose for all good literature. The addition of television and films have taken this form of vicarious learning and refined it to a high art form.

However, if you cannot get beyond your own pain, you cannot fully examine the reasons behind another's painful lesson. If the suffering of children causes you so much pain that you turn off the television or look away, then you must understand that there are unresolved painful abscesses in your own soul. These must be dealt with before you can move on. If you don't deal with them, you may be forced to walk the same path. Think about this... you can learn vicariously, or you can learn by enduring these same horrors.

Which way would you rather learn?

Why would this be true?

If you can't even bear to watch suffering on television, then it is because there is unfinished business... in similar situations... in your own life plan.

This unfinished business could be the pain you carry within your own soul memory of a similar life where you starved to death as a child. Or it could be of a life where you watched your child starve and there was nothing you could do about it. Or you could be remembering a life where people were starving and dying all around you and you "fiddled while Rome burned."

In other words, you could be feeling guilty for not stopping a tragedy when you had the ability to do so. Or... you could be feeling the guilt for creating a tragedy that took millions of lives. Or you could be reliving a horror that happened to you!

Whatever the reason for your unfinished business, if you shrink from the television in horror or revulsion at the sight of these human tragedies, then it is obvious that you need to do something to clean up your remaining "unfinished business."

Cleaning up your own garden is vital to the Plan upon the earth and your own graduation. You can't properly fulfill your mission if you still have garbage cluttering up your own home. And you cannot graduate and take that garbage with you when you leave earth. Believe us, the rest of the universe doesn't want to be infected with your garbage.

We gave an example of how to test to see if you have garbage. We can't really tell you in this communiqué what the garbage is or how it got there. What we can tell you is that if you have the above-mentioned responses to the evening news, then it is important for you to look deeper within yourself and learn new tricks and techniques for healing the imbalances that lie within you.

The healing that works best for you is up to you. It could be participating in a "Save the Children" type organization... or sending money to help the oppressed... It could be finding a technique that will remove the negative patterns from your soul memory. Or it could involve taking the bull by the horns, finding the real reasons for what's causing the suffering, and changing it. There are souls upon the planet right now who have the power and ability to alter life for many suffering people. These souls simply KNOW what must be done, and have the connections and/or power to bring about change, with NO help from governments or organizations. Most governments and organizations have been taken over by the dark forces. Finding new roads for change is what must be done now. Depending on what lesson you need to learn, all avenues are open to you.

In other words, to heal these situations, all approaches can work, from hands on ... to sitting in the lotus position and visualizing perfection... All approaches can and will work. The trick to finding which one is right for you, is to actively follow through on the one that feels right to you... the one that pulls you through the knot hole and causes you to change!

> ♦ If you can use events of a distant land to help you finish your lessons here upon the planet...

> ♦ If you can learn vicariously ...

> ♦ If you can open your heart to learning from any and all directions ...

Then enlightenment will truly be yours.

The energies that entered the planet on July 11th, 1991 will stay with us until January 11th, 2011, transforming those who will be placed in positions of leadership. It is a grand time to be alive. You will be taking part in the enlightening of a planet, the evolution of a species and the graduation of Gods ... (maybe "godlets" is a better word. We certainly don't want any of you to start taking yourselves too seriously.)

But while we are talking about all this high and wonderful spiritual stuff, please don't forget that you are still very human with all the human frailties and foibles. There is going to be a time of trials and tribulation upon the planet. We can't say how long this time it will last... that is up to those of you upon the earth.

If you... as a group soul... get the message quickly and shape up, then the trials and tribulation will not last much longer than two years. But if the world is resistant to change and starts going backward, trying to hold on to the old and familiar, then "the trying times" will take much longer.

The light of the One God has begun to work its way into the darkest and deepest recesses of human garbage. Prepare yourselves for much uncovering in the next few months and years. Bacteria and fifth cannot live in the sunlight. Lies and deceit at a world level will be exposed.

History will be rewritten. It will be rewritten as it was lived, not as the victors of wars want you to believe. Great tombs of hidden information will be released and mankind will begin to understand his link to the stars.

The circles in England (Crop Circles) point the way to the first of these sacred vaults.

Prepare yourself!

For the awakening times have begun!

Awaken quickly and easily...

Spare yourself unnecessary pain.

Lesson 5

The Creation of

a New Matrix

Or how to Survive the Coming Shift

The earth is a school.

Students come to learn, once they have learned... they leave.

Some may choose to stay behind and teach.

Some may decide to take additional courses.

Some may be hired on as administrators or caretakers.

But for the most part... once the lessons have been mastered, the students leave.

When the ages come to a close, as has happened many times on earth, this signals that there is no further use for the classroom as it has existed. The reason for this is that every soul who needed to study the lessons being taught at the Terran School has already graduated. If there are no new or remedial students, then there is no reason for the Terran School to continue to teach the same curriculum.

Ages are like school years. Elementary school consists of grades K through 8. High school usually takes four years as does college. The Master's Degree usually takes two years and the PhD takes three. There are specific time periods set down by tradition that tell the student how long they have to study in a school before they graduate.

The Terran School is no different.

The elementary lessons on the Terran School take considerably longer than the advanced lessons. The elementary lessons teach the soul how to survive on a material plane. These lessons consist of basic survival, i.e.; food, clothing and shelter. After these lessons are mastered, the art of procreation is added to the curriculum. Once procreation was mastered, the lessons begin in earnest.

There are seven major learning steps or lessons. These seven steps correspond to the seven chakras. The beginning steps take souls longer to master and therefore the ages, or the time allotted to master each lesson, must be longer.

The time allotted to master the art of surviving in a physical body was somewhere between two and three million years.

Reproduction was divided into two categories. The first category, which we refer to as the unconscious period took approximately 250,000 years. The second stage of this period, which was the conscious and directed stage of reproduction, took 50,000 years. This latter phase of reproduction required outside help. The reason for the outside help was to insure that the bodies being created could adapt to the higher and finer vibrations that the soul would bring into it.

Denser bodies keep souls trapped at a lower level of development. These souls are never able to break free from the lower two chakras. They live life struggling to survive and procreate.

New physical bodies were needed on Terra. As the souls mastered their lessons and began to climb the ladder to enlightenment it was necessary to prepare bodies that could assist that leap.

The dense level of awareness of the early Terran students was about that of a tree sloth. Therefore, it was necessary to bring to the Terran School scientists from other worlds who understood the lessons being studied at the Terran School. These scientists introduced new DNA and developed a reproductive program that would insure that the appropriate bodies would eventually evolve.

Many of these scientists stayed on earth to watch over their experiments. They created myths and religions that would propagate correct behavior and insure the survival of the newly created beings. And then they sat back and watched while they waited for the long appointed time to finally come.

The first learning step on the Terran School took millions of years; the second step took hundreds of thousands of years. The third step, which corresponds to the third chakra or the power chakra, took tens of thousands of years. The fourth step took thousands of years.

The fifth, sixth and seventh steps all will seem to come about at one time. These steps will bring about the reintegration of the lower, or animal body; with the higher body or the Real Self... The SELF you really are, when you are not in material form. These steps will unlock abilities such as psychic and healing abilities, out of body journeys, mystic experiences, and finally, full Awakening, total recall and remembering or Enlightenment.

Once the Terran Student has fully awakened it means they have mastered all Terran lessons and they can choose to graduate and go onto other duties, or they can choose to stay and add their power to the energy that is working to bring about mass Awakening.... "the hundredth monkey" effect!

For the last five hundred years small pockets of awakening students have been popping awake all around the earth. Most of these pockets have been deemed to be a danger to the surrounding people and they were exterminated, ridiculed and scoffed, or banished. The Cathars in Southern France are but one example of a group awakening that was stopped through torture and extermination. However, it is good to note that the light of awakening is never extinguished, it merely cloaks itself for a time. If it appears to go out in one area, it is because the awakening soul group is migrating to another land and another time.

The United States of America was created by awakening souls to be The Awakening Beacon which would draw the soul group together once again. If the Plan works on schedule, the light of the United States will shine out, over the globe, and bring about the mass enlightenment that is needed for this age to finally end.

At the moment it appears as though the United States has failed in its mission, but do not believe everything you see. The degeneration of the American economy and the loss of everyday freedoms are needed to awaken the sleeping American people.

If the bed is too soft and the room is too comfortable sometimes a person oversleeps. This is what has happened to many souls who live in the United States. In a few years the United States will have lost its place as the economic leader of the world. The decline in the quality of life will cause many people to wake up and take notice. If enough people take notice in time, the United States can avert a totalitarian police state run by the ruling two percent for the benefit of the ruling two per cent.

The United States has served its purpose. It has served as a beacon of light to awaken the world.

However, a bright light shining in the dark will attract many bugs and moths. The United States is such a light, and it has attracted a large share of moths and other bugs. At the moment the mass of "bugs" striving to get to the light is blocking out and killing the light. Sometimes it seems as if the striving for the gold is killing the golden goose. The massive onslaught of immigrants from third world countries is taking a huge toll on the resources of the United States. Many of these immigrants take jobs from the people who were born in the United States. These people become angry and embittered.

This too must be. There are certain souls who are very sound sleepers. In order to wake these "comfortable souls" up, things must become difficult for them.

It should also be stated that some souls have become damaged while on the Terran School. They learned to adapt to their "damage," and as such, they prefer to stay where they feel most comfortable and secure. These souls have partially awakened, but they are afraid to move forward for fear of the pain they may have to go through.

They want to keep the status quo to avoid personal suffering, and because of this, they use powerful media manipulation to enslave the rest of humanity. Just as the powerful dark lords of Atlantis used drugs and hypnosis to control the minds of the people, so too do their modern day equivalents use the same techniques to create a slave society. These are the people who make up the group you refer to as the New World Order!

The masters of modern day manipulation have learned from their previous errors. In today's world the manipulators create the illusion of self determination and freedom, all the while enslaving the people through lack of education, media propaganda, control and lies, prejudice, economic position, credit cards, taxes, drugs, alcohol, sex and all the other addicting behaviors. The Masters of Manipulation have learned that the "best slave" thinks he is Free. "All the People" will only wake up to the truth when life becomes unbearable.

….and the difficult times are rapidly approaching!

Changing weather patterns, deliberately created by modern technology; combined with man-made earthquakes and volcanic action, will affect the food supply within the next ten years. Unequal distribution of the wealth and the food, combined with deliberate racial and gender incidents, will sow hatred and separation and cause open warfare. This warfare will be subdued by a police state action. This police state will lead to a revolution, and people will begin to wake up and reclaim their freedom.

The United States will eventually become a loose confederation of countries very much like what you see in the states that were once part of the old Soviet Union. When all countries are reduced to the same economic level, and the control of nuclear weapons has passed to a new and enlightened world body, then the full Awakening energies can be turned upon the planet. This will happen within the next quarter century.

Many students will awaken and realize that they have finished their lessons and they no longer need to study on the Terran School. Others will awaken and see the damage their class has done to the planet and will decide to remain as healers and caretakers. Others will stay to help the new students adjust to their new school.

When new schools are established, there is often a blending of the old students with the new students. This will take place for a hundred or so years. Once it is deemed that the new students are capable of surviving and learning, then, all the old students/teachers will leave because they are no longer needed.

Those of you for whom this message was written have a very special role to play in these Awakening Times. The Mother Body needs to create a new matrix, from which will come the new Earth School, that will accommodate and serve the new student souls. To do this gently requires help from souls already upon the planet. If it is done properly the earth will shift gradually and the living beings of all species will be given a chance to live out their life spans.

Climates will change, the poles will shift. What had been ice and snow will become tropical. What was the breadbasket of the world will no longer grow food. People, animals and plants will have to adapt, and migrate, but they will live and survive.

Without the help of awakening souls, the planet will shift on her axis rapidly and such a shift will mean the end of all life as we know it.

Since compassion is one of the most important lessons being taught upon the earth school, we know that you will willingly agree to be part of those who offer to help the earth shift gradually. And how do you agree to help? By agreeing to the creation of a new matrix for yourself. Once there are enough people upon the earth who have created new individual matrices, then the earth can begin to create the new matrix which will bring about a gradual but total and complete shift. The creation of the new individual matrix will be the subject of the next update.

However, it must be noted here that the masters of control have taken the word matrix and given it a different and false meaning. To understand your individual matrix; how to create it, refine it and activate it, you will have to learn to filter out truth from lies, and to do this, you must learn to listen to your heart mind, for within it dwells your connection to your true self. There are those who do not want the Terran school to end. They enjoy their positions of power and they are afraid to leave this material world because they know they will have to stand before the Universal Court and explain their actions.

The message of this update bears repeating.

Graduation time is near at hand. Not only are the current students graduating, but also…. there are no new students who need to study the old curriculum. Because the new students, i.e. souls who will come to Terra need different facilities, the classroom has to be repaired and/or remodeled. The remodeling can be done gradually and gently, or it can be done suddenly and violently. The outcome will be the same. It is only the individual experiences that will differ. One way will be easy, the other way will see much pain and suffering. But the results will be the same and the choice is yours.

Your school is closing, the Mother planet is getting ready to create a new school for new students.

Do you wish to help?

In the split second it took you to read that last sentence, you made your decision. There is no period of contemplation granted for this question. Either you agreed or you didn't. Your answer has been heard and recorded.

Lesson Six
Creating a New Matrix

A how-to manual for creating your light body

For years now spiritual teachers have been talking about the coming age of light bodies. Most people have envisioned the light body that Jesus had when the disciples met him on the road and Thomas put his hand through Jesus' body. People think a light body is very much like the etheric body or a spiritual body... a body that isn't quite material and isn't quite spiritual.

But let's look at light in another way.

When you go to the grocery store you see foods that are labeled "lite." What does this mean? It means that many of the heavy calories and carbohydrates have been removed and therefore the food is supposed to be better for you. "Lite" spelled in this way has come to mean, less calories. Fewer calories mean less fat, or bulk or density!

Maybe instead of talking about "light bodies" we should be talking about "lite bodies." When we refer to creating your lite body we are referring to a process that creates a new meridian system that no longer has a place for imbalances to hide.

The lite body we are referring to is one that has left behind all addictions and dis-eases and emotional imbalances. We are creating a lite body that is free from negative karma and is free to come or go on the wheel of incarnation.

Our lite body is light all right, but it is both kinds of light. It is light in the sense of not being weighted down with the heaviness of the earth experience. And it is light in the sense of having a new bright spiritual radiance. The masters of old seemed to shine with an inner light. So too will the newly created "masters" appear to shine from within.

How do you create your new lite, light body? What do you have to do?

The one thing you don't want to do is go to someone who has hung out a shingle that reads: Matrix shifter. At this time in the development of awakened souls, it is best *not* to go to others for help because a newly awakening soul is trusting and naïve. They can easily fall under the spell of the dark lords who wish to keep them enslaved upon a material plane.

Your higher self is in charge of your shifting matrix. It can and must only be accomplished on the higher level by your own soul. Whatever you do, do not.... repeat; do not go to someone who claims they can help you shift your matrix.

There are many clever servants of darkness upon the earth right now. They know that their very existence depends upon keeping you trapped in ignorance and darkness. You cannot risk being trapped using mind control, drugs, hypnosis or machines that accomplish the same end of enslavement.

These dark lords want the status quo to remain the same. With their new technologies they have developed subtle mind control techniques that can enslave you first on a physical level, and then on a spiritual level.

Claiming to shift a matrix is one way of gaining access to your unconscious where hypnotic blocks and suggestions can be placed.

In many cases, it only takes ONE visit to one of these dark lords. After these people have gained control of your mind, they easily gain control of your money, once your money is gone then they send your out to work for them, and you have become their slave.

You all have heard of Reverend Sun Moon and his Moonies. He is just one example of the dark brotherhood upon the planet. There are many spiritual teachers who appear to be taking their students to enlightenment through regular meditation; instead they are subtly putting in hypnotic suggestion and mind blocks.

Remember.... you are a child of God; you need *no* teacher but GOD! You need *no* third party to intercede for you! However, remember that God is always in control, and even the best-laid plans of these Dark Lords are subject to instant and total revision. Those who at first may appear to be total slaves of an evil master may in fact become front line warriors in the war of Awakening.

At this point in your development, it becomes extremely important to find your own center and become your own teacher. Do not give your power away to anyone. You have the same access to God, as does the next person. Use it. You don't need a priest, you don't need a guru, and you don't need a minister. You don't even need a prophet of old. You are a child of God and because of the fact that you were born on earth at this time, you are endowed with certain rights and privileges, one of which being... you have a direct line to your Father. It's time for you to remember this and start using it.

Listen to our words carefully.

You don't need intermediaries. You don't need Angels. You don't need master teachers of all religions. You don't even need the one that is called the Son of God. You are all Sons and Daughters of God, the

Great master Jesus knew this and taught this, but his words have been distorted and his teachings have been slightly altered, but altered in such a way that you are cut off from the Father that Jesus came to earth to teach you about.

All you have to do is start talking to your Father. Some people call this "prayer"… but all you really need to do is talk… and talk often, with all your heart, mind and soul. Do not think that any of your "talk" is unimportant to your Father. Everything you have to say is important.

Getting back to the creation of your new matrix…

All you have to do to initiate this process is to tell your Father you are ready.

Then relax, sit back, wait and watch.

Some of the signs you can watch for are feelings of overwhelming tiredness in the middle of the day. A feeling that if you don't lie down and sleep that you will pass out on the spot. When this happens, surrender to it. You aren't tired, you aren't sick… you are having a wake up call which will take you out of body to a place of learning on another plane. While you are out of your body, your body can be cleansed and returned to a perfect state of balance.

If you are in a regular job, you might consider finding a job where you can be your own boss. It would also be good if your job kept you in your own home. If you have children in school, it is a good idea to begin home schooling. If you are going through a "matrix shift" it is likely that your children will be experiencing it also. You must also understand that the drugs that are being forced upon your children by their schools are designed to keep them from awakening. For the sake of your children, rearrange your life so you and they can stay at home.

Many families are starting home businesses. There are many advantages to this beyond the control over your own life that you will have. Many younger souls are highly advanced and need the protective care of a loving and supportive home life. The dark lords are doing everything in their power to destroy these young souls before they have a chance to accomplish their missions. If you are a parent right now, you need to wake up quickly, because if you happen to have one or more of these powerful souls, you run the risk of having the dark lords who have taken over child protective services, interfere in your lives and try to extinguish the spark of light that your child brought to earth.

When you are born, a certain percent of your soul enters the body. As you walk your path closer toward enlightenment, more of the essence of your soul enters your physical body. This is what the dark lords want to prevent.

Because your soul does not want to pick up the imbalances that are present in your body, emotions and thoughts, it will NOT fully enter a body which has been damaged beyond repair in one lifetime.

At this time in history, many of you who will be the teachers and leaders, have at least eighty to ninety percent of your soul body incarnate. When that "soul body" decides to "take a vacation and go back to school," you cannot stay alert and operate on automatic pilot like you used to. There was a time when your physical body was running itself purely on its animal body. When your soul decided to take off for a few months, you barely noticed it was gone. But in the past few years your physical body has gotten used to running itself on your soul energy. Therefore, when your soul body leaves to prepare itself and your physical body for the next step... YOU will need to take measures to keep the physical body safe. The best way to do this is to lie down and take a nap, preferably in your own bed, in a safe and secure environment!

The presence of your soul body is one of the reasons many of you have gained weight in the last few years. Because your soul body provides your physical body with energy, you simply don't need to eat in the same amount you have been eating. Your physical body is receiving its nourishment from your higher body and not from the food you eat.

The world is coming closer to living on air... prana... the life force!

Now do you begin to understand why your eating patterns are shifting, and your weight is fluctuating?

Fresh live foods are the order of the day. Those of you who are still eating meat will experience a slower shift than those who eat only fruits and vegetables. For some people, giving up meat is a necessary part of the path, however, for other body types, you will need to continue eating small amounts of animal protein, until you know you no longer need it!

Those of you who grow your own foods and lovingly cultivate and talk to the energies in the plants will experience the shift faster than the others. But there is no race going on. Everyone will arrive at the same place. However, modifying your eating habits will make the trip easier for you.

Now... back to the shifting matrix.

After you tell God that you want to volunteer to become a matrix shifter, all you have to do for the next few weeks is be aware of the times you feel sleepy. Acknowledge those times and allow yourself the luxury of afternoon naps. What will happen at these times is that your higher body will exit your lower body for a while. On the higher levels your soul will experience a shifting of its energies so that when the soul reenters the lower body, the lower body will begin to change. Outside energies will also be focused on your sleeping body in order to bring it into its natural state of balance!

This will not occur overnight. When it starts to happen it may happen everyday to you for a week. Then you will be given an opportunity to assimilate the new energies that have come into play in your life.

After these new energies have been mastered, you will begin another series of out of body experiences.

Again you will need to assimilate the change and once you are comfortable with the change you will begin the process all over again until you have successfully created your new matrix. Some people will require months, others will require years!

Once your new matrix is in place you will be a different person. You will look back to your old self and wonder if you are a walk-in. You are not. You are simply one of the souls who have finished their own personal mission or karma and rather than dying, you have chosen to stay on the earth to help the planet go through her matrix shift in a gentle way.

Once enough people have experienced the individual shift in their matrices, then the hundredth monkey phenomena begins. People, animals, plants, rocks, and the earth Herself will begin the shift.

If you want to participate in this new experience, and can't because you work, then give yourself the freedom of an out of body experience when you get home from work. They take one to three hours. You will still be able to sleep a regular night's sleep once the experience is over.

You will have to plan your early evening so that you are not disturbed. Forget about your own dinner. If you have family always keep special dinners in reserve for these occasions.

When you feel the feeling coming on, go home directly after work and lie down. Some people need "white noise" to block out the world. Others need music. There is no *one* way of preparing for this. Some have even experienced the "shift" while having a television on in the background. When the time comes, all that is necessary is for a safe environment to surround you. This is why it is necessary to have your family involved in this, if at all possible.

If the experience is going to happen, it will happen within fifteen minutes. If you are still awake and conscious at the end of that time, then you are not going to have an out of body experience, matrix-shifting experience. So get up and go about your regular evening routine.

Make sure to tell God again that you are ready and willing, and try again the next time you feel one of these "overwhelming desires to sleep."

If you still can't seem to accomplish it, then look into your life and see what the problems might be that are tying your soul to the earth plane. Family problems, money worries, fear, young children, all of these may keep you tied to your body.

One by one, you can solve these problems. Once you have completed your self-examination and you see all the cords that are tying you to the earth plane, ask God to release these cords. Once this is done, try the out of body, matrix-shifting experience one more time.

If you are serious about the shift, it will happen. And it will happen under the guidance and direction of the teacher that knows you best, your own higher self.

On this we conclude...

Remember to direct your prayers to world leaders. They too must experience the shift and most of them are under the direct control of the dark lords, so they need your help to make the shift.

Before you direct your prayers at these leaders, surround yourself in a cloak of invisibility. Not all of you need to do this, but there are some who are extremely powerful prayer warriors, and the dark lords want to know about you.

There are many ways to create a cloak of invisibility. The best way is to imagine yourself as a mirror. Scientists will soon perfect an invisible aircraft. It will appear to be invisible due to mirrors. The same technique that will make this aircraft invisible can be applied at a soul level. Your soul mind will turn the concept of "mirrors" into the tools it needs to keep you safe.

Create your protective mirror, then talk to God and ask that He show you which world leader you need to work with! The one you choose may not be the one who leads your own country. You may be surprised at whom your prayers may be directed. Also know that some world leaders have passed over and are helping from the other side. These leaders also need your prayers and help.

* * * * *

The messages for the past two lessons have been brought to you by a traveling band of "lite workers." Sometimes we have been called magicians; sometimes we've been called saints. At the moment, as we sweep the earth from top to side, we're being called the cleaning crew.

Just remember...

You must earn your right to be a collector of garbage. In the new world, the garbage collector becomes the priest/healer.

Good day... Good bye...

God be with ye

Lesson Seven
Awakening Prose

The following two poems are written in the same type of "Awakening Prose" that Shakespeare used. Sir Francis Bacon also used this type of awakening-structured prose when he wrote the King James Version of the Bible. Both men learned to do this from the Bards, who learned it from the Druid priests, who learned it from the Egyptian priests, who learned it from our extra-terrestrial ancestors.

Words can be placed together in certain patterns and structures so that they create a firing mechanism in the human brain. This firing mechanism triggers responses in the brain that causes a human to tap into a higher consciousness. Even though the experience lasts only a minute or less, the person is given a glimpse of a larger reality. People have referred to these awakening experiences as "peak experiences," "ah haa" reactions, and reveries.

The art of writing in such a manner was one of the skills taught in the ancient mystery schools. It is an art that has been lost to most people upon the earth. This art teaches people how to awaken all knowledge within them. This tool is so powerful that it has been suppressed. The evil controllers of planet Earth do NOT want their human slaves understanding the true nature of the universe. If humans wake up, the illegal immigrants on planet earth, the ones who have plundered and raped the legitimate occupants, would no longer have slaves to wait on them and fulfill their every fantasy.

Awakening prose works to awaken the sleeping memory in the Children of God. It is time for it to once again be known and used upon the earth.

If a person remembers how to write this way and teaches other people to write this way, then many books, which are written using the "sacred key," can come onto the market. When other people read these books, their own inner truth will vibrate awake, and one more enlightened person will walk the earth. Once enough people have awakened, then the earth will return to the Sacred Plan that was laid down for Her eons ago.

An aligning process was seeded in 1983. It started its work in 1987. Because of this, people are waking up more rapidly than in past times. Each time a new person awakens to Universal Truth, the whole of humanity rises one notch. The higher humanity rises as a collective group soul, the more important it is to make sure that every aspect is in alignment.

Humans have seven chakras within the physical body. The chakras need to be in balance within themselves and each other for humans to operate at peak performance. Not only do humans have a chakra system in their physical bodies, they have a chakra system in their higher bodies.

Imagine seven chakras in the first higher body. Then imagine seven higher bodies, one beginning where the crown chakra of the lower body ended/began. There are seven levels in each body and there are seven higher bodies that stretch from the material plane, all the way back to the beginning of creation. Each body becomes higher and finer as we travel upward.

The time has come for humans to learn how to align these higher bodies. The process begins in the physical body. Humans must learn to balance the physical chakras first. Once this is accomplished, then the knowledge of how to balance and align with the higher bodies will be transmitted. All bodies will soon be brought into alignment. This means every one of your higher bodies, going all the way back to the powerful central sun at the center of the combined universes will be aligned.

When enough humans balance and put themselves into alignment with the Higher Will, the earth will be brought into alignment. At this time we will see a pole shift. Do not be frightened. Life on earth will NOT end.

The earth has seven chakras. Her base chakra is red and is at the center of the earth. Her second and third chakras lie below the surface of earth. The fourth chakra is green and is the surface of the planet. The fifth chakra is the air we breathe. The sixth is the stratosphere and the seventh is the ionosphere. As humans align their chakras, the planet aligns her chakras.

When this happens we will see a shift in the poles.

Again… don't be alarmed by this. The poles have shifted many times before. Some of the landmasses that now are peopled and prosperous will become deserts or ice caps. This of course is done for a reason. The earth needs to heal Herself and rid Herself of the toxins that have polluted Her body. She will simply be placing the polluted areas in the proper type of healing environment.

As humanity balances itself individually, so too will Mother Earth balance Herself. As she does, the axis will tilt ever so slightly until the Mother has brought Herself back into alignment with the Great Central Sun from which ALL has come. When this happens it will signal the arrival of a new and enlightened age upon planet earth.

These enlightened ages have happened many times before. They presage a graduation time.

Souls are not native to earth. They come to study. When they finish their lessons they graduate. As they prepare for graduation a time of quiet beauty and enlightened peace falls upon the earth.

Many of the souls upon the planet Earth are preparing for that time. The Awakening process for this graduating class began in August of 1987.

When a group of souls gets ready to graduate,

A gentle feminine energy comes to take the group soul to its next school.

A Divine Feminine power will soon be felt upon the earth. This feminine force is the true "other half" or feminine side of the Great Creative Spirit we call God. She will be soon be making Herself known upon earth. This power has not visited earth in many years. It is not Mother Earth. This gentle feminine energy is the true feminine creative power... the Great Mother from whose womb all of the universes sprang... the vesica pisces... vessel of the fish... the age old symbol of the feminine power!

The Mother's feminine presence is required whenever a soul group is getting ready to graduate. The Mother's presence signifies great creativity and a transition or birth into a new reality. The Mother energy will be entering for the next six months, and then there will be a transition period as the world becomes accustomed to the new changes that will be occurring. In some places a real backlash will occur because people will slip into fear. But realize that all is as it should be and what occurs in one part of the world is right and timely.

- ❥ Things are happening quickly now.
- ❥ There is no time to take twenty years to cure a person of their drug addictions.
- ❥ There is not time to spend a lifetime teaching a person about sexual addiction.

Young people don't have the luxury of spending twenty years in the romantic shopping market

The years of leisurely learning have ended. Those people who do not agree to wake up real fast and get on with it will probably be given another chance real quickly in their next life.

All the humans who are getting ready to graduate must be brought into balance within the few decades... and this means balance on *all* levels.

It's always easier for negative life patterns to be modified at an early age. Fortunately, as the world moves into enlightenment, methods of healing aberrations from past lives will be discovered and used correctly.

If you are dedicated to Awakening as quickly as possible so that you can get on with your mission, then ask yourself if you would like to take part in an Awakening Adventure.

The following poems that you will read will help you awaken your own power and latent talents. They are written in Awakening Prose.

When you read the first poem, please understand that it was written in its entirety in about forty minutes. Not one word has been changed even though the addition of a word or two would make the rhyme better. The poem is written the way it is because each and every word plays an important part. The message contained within the poem is less important than the effect of the words. Remember, the words are arranged in such a way that they create a "firing mechanism" in your brain. This "firing mechanism" is what signals the start of your own awakening process.

Be aware of the thoughts that rise as you read this poem. Each time you read the poem you will have new thoughts. Keep a journal of your thoughts. You will be amazed and in the future, this journal will serve to help others awaken.

The old ways of psychiatry, drugs and hypnosis have never worked to cure a person or bring them into a state of balance. The only way to balance a person on all levels is to put them in alignment with their own higher Will and allow each person to become their OWN teacher and healer.

To begin the healing and aligning process, we are going to introduce to you an example of Awakening Prose.

This example was transmitted to our contact on Earth many years ago. We asked that NOT one word be changed. When you read the Prose, you will see that some of the sentences don't make sense, and some words are misused... this is done on purpose.

As you begin to study the "poem" and read more deeply, you will discover that what at first appeared to be a mistake was indeed put there purposely, not just for the "firing mechanism" to react, but there is a timely message included.

Enjoy your Awakening Journey!

Part 1

Dear One,
For whom we've waited,

Patiently, we must add ...
Welcome!
All is well with the world.
God is in His Heaven
And in the hearts Of Man upon the Earth.

The long appointed time
For which the world has waited
Is drawing near the Earth.
The Angels sing,
The Harbingers bring
Sounds of joy for all to hear.

Join with us in exaltation,
For the time of joy is near.

Take fear and throw it to the wind,
For light is the way love will descend.
A light that fills the earth
And all the hearts thereon
With joy and understanding
And a pleasant evenin' song.

For now comes the Time,
The end's round the bend,
For all of you who've chosen
To leave... in love... ascend.

Great tidings of joy and comfort
Await you at your home.
Your summer camp is closed now.
The winter has set in.
The time to join with those back home
Has once more settled in.

Allow the settling to enter your core,
For the message there is lain.
Far centuries back you placed it there,
Before to earth you came.

Take heart, my loved ones

And feel the presence
That gathers 'round the Earth.
The Ancient Masters once again
Await the joyous birth.

All see for those who will
All hear for those who can.
Great joy descends from Heaven
And fills the hearts of Man.

The evenin' song is singing
The sounds are in the wind.
All movement hastens homeward
The chapter nears its end.

Take hearts and lift them upward,
To your Father in the sky
He brings your elder brother
To prove that none e'er die.

With joy around his presence
And love within his heart
He draws together all his clan
So none shall ever part.
With sounds of joy and gladness
His love surrounds the world
His love has gathered all of us,
And into his heart we hurl.

With joy and love abundant,
We dance in ecstasy,
With faith our Father knows our fate,
We meet out destiny.

Go softly now my young ones,
Through hill and dale and vale.
The time's not up.
The book's not writ,
The curtain's yet to fall.

The old order is rapidly changing,

The ways of man are done,
All the gentleness that's staying
Is the world to finally come.

Open up your hearts in gladness,
Allow your heart again to shine.
Focus it upon the Heavens,
And allow His love in thine.

Fill your hearts with joy and gladness
For the rays shall stretch to Him
And give Him the needed stairway
He can once more in love descend.

Here comes the called for Savior.
He shall descend on Earth,
Not into one man or woman,
But into His safe home berth.

And where, my friends, is it,
That Christ shall call His home?
Safe within the hearts of those
Where love has freely shone.

Now take this message far and wide,
For God has proclaimed it so.
The Christ in Man now can shine
As elder brothers know.

Take all your outworn wisdom,
Allow it to float away...
New days, New ways, New changes
Await the coming age.

New love,
New hope,
New beginnings...
For all who will accept.

The ancient road has led us well,
Don't feel the need to tred

Where feet of old have walked the path
And for Mankind have bled.

The road is new,
The wisdom too...
Allow it its own place.

The ancient myths foresaw this time
And directed Mankind's fate.
But allow the myths to nobly die
Once their purpose has been done.

For now the appointed time is nigh
But the ancient wisdom has not shone
Just how the act shall close.

It says Christ will lead us safely home,
But how and why and for what purpose
Never have been known.

So now its time to let go
Of ancient days and ways.
Take into your hearts
A new way
Of serving Man and God.

Allow yourself the freedom
To drop your heavy load,
Your burdens of guilt and failure...
For none of you have failed.

And here at last
We all have come ...
Safely, we must add.

Allow the tears of gladness
Down your cheeks to roll
For man has come at last to grace,
And Christ shall bless us all.

So in your heart of hearts,

Learn from this modern rime.
The clock's run out . . .
The ancient time shall mark the path no more.
Ancient ways and ancient days
Shall only hold you back,
Lay down your guilt and suffering
Lay down your shame and blame.

You failed him not...
 Your train arrived at the appointed time.

We all are gathered waiting
For Christ upon the Earth
To turn your hearts skyward
And release you from your berth.

He has entered and is helping
All those who lead the way.
The time has come,
The lesson's done ...
Come learn a whole new way!

Lay down your guilt and suffering
For Christ has come in you.
You all are saved,
You all are through ...
You all are now Christs too.

Turn not away, the prophecy's made ...
His Word will see you through.

Lay down your guilt
You failed Him not
The road is now arrived.

You led Him home
So now He too
Can lead His family home.

With sounds of joy and gladness
He leads you from the earth,

And overwhelms your senses
With the wonders of your mirth.

Great joy and gladness fill you
And carries you right away...
The appointed day,
The prophesied way,
Now descend to earth.
Miss not the train that's coming
For its stop is short and quick.
For all who must reach it ...
The heart now holds the trick.
Look deep within your own heart
Forget about all others.
The time has come.
The old way's done.
The Plan at last is come.

Within your heart the Christ is.
Seek Him out for He shall lead.
The station's ready
The train draws high
The Christ light now shall lead.

Open your hearts
All ye who hear,
To the joy to be received...

From God and love
In Heaven above...

Your tethers have been freed!
Enter softly in joy...
For you have been expected.

Part 2

Even though the prose which will follow was brought forth in 1985,
it was deemed necessary to withhold it until now.

Why? ... you ask.

A story was told about the farmer who was so anxious for his plants
to grow and bear fruit that every evening he went out into his field

and tugged at the little plants hoping to make them grow faster. One evening he pulled so hard that the little plant came up root and all. And of course, because the plant was no longer rooted in the earth ... it died.

Can you see the parallel?

The human is rooted to the planet through the first or base chakra. This is the chakra of survival and it is tied directly to the Mother body or planet earth. This is the first chakra to develop, and it must stay in good repair, actively open and working, or the body it is supporting will die.

Why is this knowledge connected with the parable we just imparted? Because there is a danger in opening up to the higher planes too quickly.

The danger lies in their beauty and peace... in the all-knowing Oneness that permeates them... in the tremendous sense of well-being and love that one finds here.

The danger lies in the fact that many who find their way to our shore never wish to leave.

The danger lies in the fact that if one sojourns too long in the higher realms, the lower bodies atrophy and eventually die.

The base chakra of many spiritual seekers is almost nonexistent. Because these people spend many hours in meditation, their consciousness is directed to higher levels. Therefore, they neglect to give the base chakra the energy and the needed attention which will allow it to supply that the grounding and connection to the earth that is needed to survive. The base chakra is the chakra of survival on the physical plane, therefore, it is the chakra that is connected with the creation of "the means to survive" ... and in the world of 20th century America, the means to survive is seen as money.

Many spiritual seekers experience problems with money. The reason for this is their desire to become enlightened has dis-empowered their survival chakra. If the lack of money becomes critical, then the being does not have the means to create food, shelter and clothing. This may lead to a downturn in the physical health of the body.

As more and more emphasis is placed upon spiritual advancement, more and more energy is taken away from the energy center (base chakra) that keeps the body alive. When this is the scenario, any rapid method of enlightenment can prove fatal to the physical body. And while we do not always find this condition undesirable, we do find it problematic at this time in the evolution of the Mother Body.

Let us continue this discourse by discussing the Oracles at Delphi. Delphi contained a mystery school, the most famous of which is remembered in the legends of the Oracles... the wise prophetic priestesses who helped people understand their lot in life.

In the early years of their rigorous training, many young priestesses died. Why was this? It was because they had not sufficiently built up their base chakra so that it could sustain them through their lengthy out-of-body sojourns.

During the "channeling" process used at Delphi, the higher self of the priestess would simply move out of the way to make room for the higher being who brought the message. The higher self of the priestess would be free to roam the planes where the Ascended Masters dwell. The higher self had the freedom to study or rest or frolic. Many times the higher self became so enamored by the beauty or wisdom of the higher realms that it would forget to leave at the appointed time. When this occurred, it was sometimes possible for one of the older and wiser priestesses to reach up into the higher realms and pull the soul back into body. But if the young priestess was not in close proximity to a wiser sister, then the priestess ran the risk of returning to a body that was either close to death or already dead.

If the soul stays out of body too long, the body forgets to eat, forgets to drink, and may even experience a shutdown of the autonomic responses such as breathing, heart beat and other organ functions.

Now let us return to our parable of the farmer who wanted his plants to grow so badly that he tugged at them hoping to stretch them into maturity. And stretch them he did ... until he broke their connection with the sustaining power of the Mother, and they died.

If we were to have allowed these poems to be released in 1985... to all beings, then we would have run the risk that some of you would have awakened too quickly. You would have been given the ability to climb the heights, and after seeing our world, some would have chosen to stay with us. This is all well and good in its time.

To everything there is a season.

A time for planting...

A time for harvesting...

And the in between time...

The time for growth.

Back in 1983, the Awakening energies were first seeded upon the planet. Many awakened at that time. These few started writing, lecturing or giving individual sessions to others who in turn awakened and began to share their gifts.

The next influx of energy came in 1987. More people awakened. And now we are in the most critical of all the awakening times. However, there are obstacles that must be surmounted.

There are people upon the planet who do not want to awaken. They are happy in their play and they wish to remain asleep. These people are usually ones who have achieved some manner of comfort and happiness.

The more comfortable you are, the less likely you are to want to rock the boat or wake up. Within this group of Happy Sleepers lies another more insidious group. It consists of a group of people who create their happiness at the expense of others. Within this group are people who have so thoroughly enjoyed the game being played on earth that they have thrown themselves totally into it. They play it with every fiber of their souls and as such they have become so consumed by the game that they have completely wiped out any way of reminding themselves that this is a game ... this is illusion.

The more comfortable you are,

The less you want to wake up.

These beings play the game to win, and it doesn't matter what they do to the planet or to their fellow humans. Their only purpose here on earth is to collect the most toys and if this means swindling retirees out of their life's savings, or destroying the rain forests, or killing every human on the planet, they will do it.

You don't have to look very far to see a few of these people. Look at the international bankers who control the money supply of nations. They make themselves rich at the expense of the natives. Look to those who are making money from the sale of drugs AND pharmaceuticals. Look to the trans-national corporations who (not which... corporations have the same status as humans!) foment war around the globe so they can make money by selling weapons and gain more control of the earth. Look at doctors and hospitals that are in the business of making money and so they never truly heal their patients.

The list goes on ... but we have made our point. These powerful Sleeping Warriors have personal greed, lust for power, and fear as their motivators. Any one of the factors would be powerful by itself, but put all three together and you create an almost unstoppable force.

Of the three driving forces, fear is the most powerful. This small group of Sleeping Warriors is afraid to wake up because they fear that God and their REAL Mother will hold them accountable for what they have done to the planet and to other souls. They fear they will have to pay the price, and they are afraid that the price will be more than they can bear; including the possibility of total annihilation at the soul level ... absorption is what we called it in past discourses.

While these souls are asleep, they can pretend that there is no God and that they are all powerful.

When these souls wake up, realize their mistakes and agree to fix them… and some are doing this right now… they discover that they are welcomed back into the soul family with open arms.

However... there are those who have awakened enough to see that what they are doing is not for the highest good of all concerned and yet they have still chosen to stay their course and continue their harmful practices. There are very few of these souls on the planet. But these few are some of the most dangerous.

These are the souls who genuinely feel they have become Gods-upon-Earth. (These are the black magicians of ancient lore.) They feel they are so powerful and important that nothing they do is wrong, and even if it were... who would dare stop them.

As the Awakening times approach, these people become agitated. Their agitation could cause them to panic and plunge the world into full-scale wars, which could end up in nuclear war.

As the time of peace draws closer…

We are entering the time

when world wide war

looms highest.

To protect themselves and their positions of power, these Gods-upon-the-Earth can and will cause mass destruction. You only have to look at the recent wars in the Middle East, as well as the small wars in Africa and elsewhere, to understand our meaning.

Do not feel that the leaders of the most powerful countries in the world have escaped our notice. The leaders of the United States, Great Britain, France, Germany and Japan have a great deal to lose if their people wake up and begin to make just demands. And so, the sleeping darkness continues and the masters of illusion who perpetuate the sleeping darkness believe they are allowed free reign.

Why have we chosen to release the Awakening prose now?

Because ... It *is* time.

The seeds have been sown ... they have been allowed to germinate and sprout ... and now they can be gently coaxed into blossom.

The flowering time is about to happen. And as each one of you begins to blossom and bloom, the beauty of your flowering will cause others to blossom.

When enough souls have blossomed or awakened, then the hundredth monkey syndrome will come into effect and a worldwide awakening will occur.

The flowering time

Is about to happen.

And so ... to say simply, we did not release our awakening prose earlier because if we had, many of you would have chosen to leave. You would have been like the young Oracles who became so enamored with our realms that they chose to stay with us until their Earth bodies withered. If you had become enlightened ahead of schedule, you would have chosen to leave your body (i.e., die). If this happened, we would not have had the needed group force (combustive energy) to cause an awakening in all of our brothers and sisters. This is not meant to imply that the whole of the planet will awaken at this time.

The ones who will awaken are the ones who are members of the soul family that is preparing to graduate.

Some of these family members are the ones who are causing the most problems here on the planet. There are other soul families who live quite happily and peacefully, until they come in contact with the sleeping, power-hungry, greedy members of our soul family.

Fortunately, these other soul families have a great tolerance for us, because they are new to the Earth and as such, they have a direct contact to God. In this direct contact, they have the means for great forgiveness and understanding and love. (Think of the South American original inhabitants, the one who are mistakenly called Indians. Many have been enslaved by the gold miners, who overworked them, subjected them to poisonous chemicals, and leave a polluted wasteland when they leave.)

Ages begin and ages end.

Your class is not the first class to graduate…

and it will not be the last.

Many here upon the earth warn that if precautions are not taken at this time, those in control of certain weapons might destroy the planet so that it can never again be used as a school. This simply isn't true. If humans get too out of control, Mother Earth... your "nanny" can protect Herself (hurricanes, floods, earthquakes, violent polar shifts, plagues, and pestilence... She knows what she needs and when she needs it.)

Mother Earth is not at the mercy of humans; don't ever think She is.

And so ... the awakening lesson for today begins.

Remember to have your journal close at hand because you will want to record your thoughts and reveries. If you prefer a tape recorder, that will work also. If you prefer to read the poem out loud, please do so.

The Awakening Prose: Second Poem

Wednesday, February 13, 1985

Once again you climb the heights
And meld your mind with ours.
Not long ago there was a site
Where time would flow for hours.

Swirling in a dervish way
That brought some to their knees
Time would circle round you
And bring our world to thee.

High upon a mountain
Where few humans ever tread,
The secret of the swirling time
Is hidden....
It is said...
 That in the time before time
Which was no longer than a day
You wove your love all round us
Before you went away.
All round and over and through us
This love of yours did weave
And now tis on these lovely threads
We pull... so you can leave.

The threads of love stretch from you
And fill our world with song.
Our little angel has been away
From our hearts for far too long.

So now has come the appointed time
When all that came before
Be caught up and purified
And taint the earth no more.

As though a mighty genie
With a vacuum in his hand

Roams the earth from top to side
And clears the dirt of Man.
And so it is,
Our darling child
That you appeared on earth
To hold the sweeping energy
And free Christ from Its berth.
 "How can one mortal have such power?"
 Shhh.... Your thoughts can limit now

Release your thoughts,
Allow ours through...
Your answer shall be found.

An individual who works with
God has only to demand,
And unto that person
Shall be given
ALL at our command.

Be careful of what you wish for now,
For your thoughts are powerful tools
Shaping a beautiful landscape
On which to place a brave new world.

So unto you is passed this day
The keys to a kingdom new.
So that in harmony with all mankind,
New worlds will shine in you.

Surrounded you are on earth and heaven
By a powerful few
Who have the fate of all mankind
Locked in their hearts so true.

Know now that as you read this
Our words find true their mark
In each and every colleague
With whom you shall embark.

The way is simple

Yet manifest
And in you all shall rise
Like flour into bread dough
In thine, thy Father's eyes.

The power of exaltation
Is floating through the air.
The will toward divine creation
Will allow all men to share
The earth and all her assets,
So that none on earth shall need
And with love for God upon their lips,
All men will lose their creed.

Gone nations, churches, titles too,
All things that separate.
Come love and joy and wisdom,
Through heaven's open gate.

Go now in peace and joy and love....
Our time's about run out.
Remember that you...
Of all the world
Now bear the secret gift,
Your words carry the power
To heal the chasm and the rift.

For you ahead lies the road
The Masters have been shone.
Walk upon it gently,
With your brother by your side...
The love from whom you parted
Before the morning tide.

Cleave tightly to his council
For his words ring loud and true,
His only task upon the earth
Is to see the great Work through.

Remember now just how he came,
In times of ancient past.

Recognize him by his love
And know your bond will last.

Receive him in your heart of hearts
Rejoice that he is come
The Work shall start
And none shall part
The living, loving One.

From roof top to roof top
Rises the cheer
That God and Man are One.

From the union blessed here
Shall come the Fabled Son.
Out of these loins
Shall be brought forth
The Brotherhood of Man.

Know in your hearts that you are nobly
 prepared to receive the final Plan.

With your hosts on high
And your brother on the earth,
You shall carry forth the message
And take Christ from His berth.

Now to all who hear these words
Whether soon, or late, or never...
The truths herein ...
The message too ...
Are hidden from foolish view.

Only they who walk in purity
Shall find the hidden clue.

Go now in peace and love and rapture,
Great things are on the way.
We guide and guard and bless you
While we make ready the great day.

Lesson 8
The Time of Armageddon has Finally Come

As you know, the times are changing. Many have stated that we are in the end times; some have even said that the time of Armageddon is upon us.

This is true.

The time of Armageddon has finally come.

The closing chapter is finally being read.

The final act is being played out.

All things on earth have beginnings and endings. This is true whether it is a human being, a nation, a continent or an epoch.

This epoch of humanity is closing. The lessons that were being studied have been learned and there is no more reason to keep teaching the same old lessons. Therefore, a closing must come.

Ancient ways and ancient days

Will only hold you back.

Prophecy has it that Armageddon must come before the world is delivered into peace and happiness.

A thousand years of peace and prosperity will fall upon the earth after Armageddon comes.

But what is Armageddon?

What are the trials and tribulations that will accompany it all about? Do you have anything to fear, or will you be able to walk through all of it unscathed?

What will you be asked to do?

Who will provide the hidden clue?

Who will help you

See this through?

The world you know is ending. Is this so bad? Are you really going to miss the old order? Can you honestly say that you like the world the way it is?

No, of course you can't say that? Maybe a few years ago you would have been content with the way things were. But now it has gotten so out of balance that only a very few are content with the way things are. And none of these few are enlightened peoples. Only the greedy dark masters wish to cling to the old ways.

Maybe you should start rethinking the Biblical prophecy of Armageddon.

If it is frightening to you, maybe you should ask yourself whom you have been serving. Maybe you should even begin questioning who wrote the Bible and for what purpose.

If Armageddon sounds the death knell for a selfish way of life that benefited only a few greedy and power-hungry individuals, then doesn't it make sense that only those greedy individuals should be experiencing fear? If you aren't one of these people, why should you live in fear?

Armageddon is the time to clean up our acts. If you have been living out of balance with God's law, then you will be asked to change your way of life. Some people call this sacrifice. Some have said that when Armageddon comes we will all have to sacrifice. We will have to give up things. But remember that by sacrificing you will get in return a thousand years of peace and prosperity.

Sacrifice has been made into a cruel word. When you hear it, your mind conjures up images of ancient priests carving out the hearts of innocent young virgins. Remember that sacrifice comes from the word sacred which comes from a Latin word which means to make holy or to return to God.

Yes... you are being asked to sacrifice. But if you understand that the sacrifice you are being asked to make is simply to return the planet to God, then the sacrifice will be much easier to make.

Returning this planet to its pristine state is the sacrifice you will be asked to make. Returning everything upon the planet to the same state of innocence and purity that existed before you arrived... that is your mission.

Armageddon is about destroying all that is out of balance. Armageddon can be compared to the cleanup crew that is sent in to put a house back in order after a raucous party.

Those of you who are on this planet legitimately have nothing to fear from Armageddon. Those of you who came to this planet to learn or to teach have nothing to fear.

There are others upon this planet who did not come to learn, they came to plunder. While they have been here, they have enslaved many of those who came to learn. We, in the angelic kingdom, did not rush in to interfere; we simply manipulated the invaders so that they could be used as teachers. They were savage instructors at times, but please remember that the earth plane teaches lessons of the material plane. Some of these lessons are so horrible that one student would never be able to help another friend and student learn it.

It was in cases like these that we were able to utilize the presence and skills of the invaders. They have served as useful tools. But if we allowed them to continue to run amok, they will destroy the planet. It is time for their games to end. They have used and enslaved the race of students who came to earth legitimately. We in turn used them to help us make the students strong, cunning, fearless, and intelligent. They have served their purpose, now it is time for them to leave.

Those souls who came to the earth school to learn their lessons have learned them. Those souls who came to the earth to rape, pillage and plunder will no longer be allowed to do so. We are shutting down the earth school and all those who have not completed their lessons will be asked to do so immediately. Even the invaders will be asked to wake up and ship out.

Salvation and Wholeness

Do you not like the way we have put things? Do you believe that you will not be asked to sacrifice? Do you believe that sacrifice is for someone else? Or do you believe that no sacrifice should be asked of anyone? Do you believe that you should simply turn your faces to God and say loudly and resolutely,

"We are here and we know you are our God. Come save us and take us into a thousand years of peace and prosperity."

After you have said this, then you stand back and wait for the heavens to open up and the great hand of God to reach down and lift you up to heaven where you will be saved.

Is this what you want to believe?

Or are you one of the ones who wants to believe that the planet earth will just keep turning and turning until all of you have died and a whole other group of believers and skeptics occupies the planet. Do you believe that every generation has its prophets and false prophets who proclaim the end times and howl and cajole their spineless and stupid followers into paying a very good price for the salvation that only the prophets can bestow upon them?

When will humans realize that no one can save them?

They can't buy their salvation with worthless earth money. Salvation has its origin in the word "safe." Safe comes from a Latin word meaning whole. People who are seeking salvation simply want to be saved, to be made safe, to be made whole once again.

To be made whole, you must join with that part of yourself that never became caught up in the earth experience of material illusion. You must become one again with the higher and greater part of yourself. You must come home to the God who created you and from whom you have been separated. This is salvation, this is wholeness. Wholeness can't be bought. It can't be begged.

Wholeness is a condition that will exist when certain conditions are met. Wholeness is a state no different than baking bread or fixing a car. You do certain things, and certain results will be achieved. There's nothing magic about wholeness. You want it, you ask for it. You ask to be shown the way to wholeness and then you do what God tells you to do. Every human has a path to wholeness. There's no one path for everyone. That's why religions only enslave.

Religion comes from the French word "religiere," which means to bind back. Religions hold you back. God and only God can move you forward. That's why if you are seeking salvation, don't try to buy it, because preachers don't have it to sell. Ask God for wholeness...and then listen and let your inner spirit move you in the right direction.

The end times are here.

How do you prepare yourself? What have you been told to do by your priests and preachers?

Pray and pay. Pay and pray.

Take out the "r," and you have pay and pay. Give the "r" to father and repeat once again the few sacred words that haven't been perverted. "R" Father...

Let's B Sirius now...
Seriously now!
 "Our Father who art in Heaven...
Hallowed be Thy name...
Thy Kingdom come...
Thy Will be done...
On Earth as it is in Heaven."

The Path of Wholeness

In the previous writings we have given you many clues as to what you can do to awaken.

We have shared with you the secrets of awakening prose and explained how you could use the channeled poems to help you awaken more rapidly. We have explained how the times are changing and just how you will be affected. We have told you what you can do to accelerate your shift into this new state of consciousness.

Those of you who receive these writings are a very select and advanced group. Do not think that I am flattering you. I do not believe that flattery serves any purpose except to make one feel temporarily superior to others. I am only stating truth. Those who receive these messages are souls who have spent many lifetimes upon the earth school studying and preparing for the work that would be required of them in the last days upon the earth.

Those last days have arrived.

And now I say to you...

"It is time!"

You must awaken now and accept your duty as it was given to you in the beginning. We have given you many different techniques for discovering and accepting your duty. But we cannot accept it nor find it for you. Each and every one of you upon the earth was given freewill. You can choose to awaken or you can choose to stay asleep. We would be violating our prime directive if we interfered at this point. We can encourage you, but we are not allowed to do it for you. The choice to awaken or to stay asleep is up to you. But you must realize that the consequences will also be borne by you...and be borne for the rest of eternity.

You are in a critical time upon the earth. The planet was invaded eons ago by the dark brotherhood. These dark workers have worked throughout the ages to enslave mankind and keep him attached to the planet in a state of slavery and servitude. As these dark lords grew more savvy in the ways of the earth, and as their intelligence grew sharper they were able to devise more effective methods of enslaving and controlling the innocent humans. Humans are too trusting of everyone and everything. Simply look at the sweet innocent lovelies of the New Age movement and see how easily they fall dupes to any wise guru who sits cross-legged and chants Oms of peace and love.

You have no idea how many lovely young men and women have become the helpless mind-controlled slaves of cult leaders around the world. You all remember Jim Jones and Jonestown. This was only one experiment in mind control. It was an experiment that went sour and was just about to be exposed. If those people had lived to tell their stories, the world would have been made aware of the horror that was just about to descend. The mind controlling techniques, of the great dark brotherhood, are so horrible and devious that they truly defy description. But these methods are fact and they are here upon the earth today.

The mind-controlled become helpless tools of the strong. They become the meek who shall inherit the earth. But what will be left of the Mother earth when they finally inherit her? The strong will mine and use everything that earth has to give including her human slaves, and then the invaders from other worlds, the dark brotherhood who have enslaved mankind will move on to other more fertile worlds. Worlds that have not yet been raped by their dark kind.

The invaders are just about to make that jump to other worlds. They realize that they have depleted the earth of her resources, and since they don't want to take the time to restore and replenish the planet, they will simply make one last push to create the tools and machines that will transport them to other worlds that haven't yet been despoiled by their kind. Virgin worlds where innocent young souls can be exploited and enslaved just as the humans were so many lifetimes ago.

But before they make their exit to other worlds they have to make sure that they take with them everything that is of value upon the earth. All the precious metals. All the precious stones. All chemicals and atoms that will help them in the creation of their new kingdom.

And how are they going to gather up these things in record time?

Why my dears, they already have a pack of willing slaves ready for the working. Whether it is mining the gold or building the rockets. The slave masters have their humans working at breakneck speed to create the ships of plunder that will leave in the night with all that is valuable from the planet. Possibly even the water and the air.

When these dark lords leave, they will leave behind a planet that is unfit for human habitation. At least that is their plan. Of course, they also plan to enslave several group souls and take them also. Certain prime body types will be chosen for their DNA and these human bodies will be used to breed the new slave race on other worlds.

Do not think that we are writing in parables as we write this. For too long now we have been gentle in the way we have delivered our messages. But you have now finished your coddling period and it is time for you to know the truth. It is time for you to accept that you are being called upon to do something. You must make your own voice heard. You must rise up and do something before it is too late for you, your family and your world.

ONE WORLD GOVERNMENT

Is it the curse or the cure?

In a few short years there will be a united world. This has to be. Only a world that works as one can protect itself from being raped and destroyed by plundering invaders from other worlds.

But realize this and realize it fast...

At the moment, those who are clamoring the hardest and the loudest for a one world government are the very ones who have invaded and plundered your world.

Read the last sentence again. Make sure you understand it. Your very existence depends on you understanding what we are saying and realizing the urgency. Read it once more:

"At the moment those who are clamoring the hardest and the loudest for the one world government are the very ones who have invaded and plundered your world."

Right at this moment both the legitimate dwellers on these planet and the invaders are vying for control of the planet.

If the invaders win,

You will all become their slaves.

This enslavement will not just last for one life.

It will last for all eternity.

If your present body is too old or too frail, then you will be enslaved at a physical level just long enough to be enslaved at a soul level and then you will be killed and forced to incarnate in a stronger and sturdier body so that your slave masters can work you until you drop, and then force you back in another body.

This pattern will continue to repeat itself until your masters have no further use for you and then you will be discarded like the trash you will have become.

Will it be possible to salvage you at this stage? Maybe yes, maybe no. Some may be salvageable, others will simply have their soul essence dispersed to the far ends of the universe, and they will become one with all that is.

Are you beginning to understand the seriousness of our words? This is not a game you are playing. You cannot go to church and ask forgiveness and hope God will reach down and pat you on the head.

God sent those of us who dictate these messages to our scribes on earth to tell you that it is time to wake up and begin to shake off the lies you have been fed. It is time to remember who you are and get on with the task of reclaiming the earth from the false lords who invaded with their advanced technology and enslaved and fooled you.

Wake up!

You must take control of your world

Before the illegal aliens invaders do...

And the invaders are very close to winning right now.

To Win The World,

They must first capture the USA.

Look at what they have done to your country in the past few decades. Do you really think that good honest Americans could have destroyed your country the way it has been destroyed? The invaders have taken control of the minds and bodies of your politicians. Those that they have not been able to blackmail or buy, they have brainwashed or controlled with other powerful techniques of mind control.

Drugs and hypnosis are being used

On the Congressmen, Senators, Governors and Presidents

Who claim to be acting in your best interests.

Oh, do not roll your eyes and wonder what type of inflammatory messages we are dictating tonight. You know in your heart that what we are saying is the only thing that makes any sense in these times.

You have been purifying your heart and your soul. You have been doing this so that you can better serve your God. And now your God is telling you that if you don't serve Him and serve Him now, then you may never get another chance.

The Invaders are about to seize the planet and take complete control of Her. To do this, they must stay in power in the United States of America. To prevent them from gaining control of the world and establishing their version of the one world government...one that is based on a slave state...then you must take back control of your country. Take back the United States of America and return it to its original purpose which was to be a beacon of truth and light for the whole world.

You have purified yourself and you have become strong. And if you doubt me when I say you have become strong just realize that you will be tested now or later, but there will never be a point in your string of lives when you are stronger than you are now. You are at the pinnacle of your lifetimes.

This is the mission for which you have prepared for eons.

Look back into your past lives and see the old teachers who gave you the tools and strength to play your part. Do not let the torture and programming at the hands of the dark lords throw you off your path. See through their illusion. Accept your place in the world. Look into your heart and see where and how you can help.

You must take back your country, because it is only in reclaiming your country that you can stop the onslaught of the invaders who will continue to dupe and control naïve souls... until they control all the souls upon the earth. Do not forget, their mind control techniques have been perfected to such a high degree that they can also control the disincarnate soul.

In other words,

You don't have to have a body

To become their slave.

But they are not invincible.

They are already preparing to leave. They can read the signs of the times better than you can.

Armageddon is coming.

It's time for the rats to be thrown out.

Wake up...

Throw them out now!!

So that they don't enslave you and take you with them.

In Search of a New Form of Government

Look at your legislators. Do you want any of them as your representatives? There must be another way. Go find it! Start talking to your friends and to your neighbors. What can you do to restore this country to the principles on which it was founded? Or were those principles also part of the illusion set forth by the invaders? Can any law ever be written that binds humans together into a country? How can the world be governed for the highest good of all?

Has it ever been done upon the planet?

A one world government must be implemented to save the earth from destruction and depletion. But it must be a government based upon the Will of God, not upon the wills of the invaders who only came to mine the riches of the earth, and enslave the little people to do the dirty work for them. As they overstayed their welcome, they grew to like the power that enslaving the simple humans gave them. They strutted and basked in the play and pretense of power that enslaving the little people gave them. These invaders have their own world and their own life plans. They are not of our worlds. They do not honor our God. They do not fear His wrath. And they have turned many of you from the path of your God. Many of the slaves became so much like the slave masters that over the lifetimes it has become almost impossible to tell them apart.

The wake up call has been sounded.

It is time to rise…

And make yourself and your message known.

If not now, when and if not you, who?

Each soul on earth has a part to play at this crucial time in the evolution of the earth souls. If you don't play your part, then who will? And if your part isn't played, will the play be lost?

For want of a nail the shoe was lost.

For want of a shoe, the horse was lost.

For want of a horse, the battle was lost.

For want of your piece of the puzzle,

The whole future may be lost.

Can you afford to take this risk?

What can you do right now?

You have been given the tools to awaken to your higher wisdom. Use them and all others that come your way. Be careful at this time not to become enslaved by the dark brothers who are using subtle techniques of mind control, hypnosis and energy work. Be very careful about the people you allow to touch your body or work with your mind. Be careful of the groups you attend. The best advice right now is to be your own council, teacher and healer.

Spiritually you have come as far as you need to come to be able to do what you need to do. Now you need to take the tools you have learned from your years of inner work and go out into the community and apply them.

Become active politically right now. Register to vote and join a political party. It doesn't matter which party. All parties need to be cleansed of the dark brotherhood. Become active. Take your light out into the community and shine it.

Speak your truth.
 Speak it loud and strong for all to hear.
Reclaim your country, reclaim your school.
Become the masters of your destiny once again.

Cast off your shackles.
Rise up and take your place next to your God.
He is returning.

Throw out the dark lords!
Return your Father's planet to the beauty
In which He left it.

You will have help in doing this. As we have said in previous updates, the feminine creative force is returning to the planet. This force always returns as the ages close. This is your true spiritual Mother. Do not confuse Her with the Mother Earth. Mother Earth is the nanny who raised you. In these End Times you will have the help of both your Father and your Mother. Call on them often.

Things to Remember

The dark lords use you to enslave yourself. You have been programmed in other lifetimes to believe you are not good enough, not spiritual enough, not bright enough. They did this to keep you in your garden meditating while they stole your world.

You are pure enough to be a receiver. But do not receive blindly and deafly. Remember that there are dark lords who have been trained in the art of mind-control through telepathy. The moment a human opens up to receive; the dark lords can begin dictating their misinformation and disinformation.

Misinformation is easy to see through because it is all lies. But disinformation is harder to detect because the lies are woven in between truth. You have developed your heart mind in the last few years. Now is the time that you must put this heart mind to use in detecting the lie. Not just the lie in your own transcribed information, but in all information. Information that comes in the form of scribed work, as well as in newspapers, magazines, television and radio. Your heart mind now holds the key to truth.

Now is the time to begin in earnest your inner work
As well as your outer work.
It is only with the combination of the two
That the lies will be exposed.

First you must inform yourself with truthful information.
Then you must act.
An informed society is a free society.
The truth will set you free.

Part III

Rayelan's Story

Rayelan Allan and the Obergon Chronicles

One morning, in the late seventies, Rayelan Allan was walking through her living room on her way to feed a very demanding cat and a hungry dog. Just as she turned to walk into the kitchen she heard someone tell her, "Get a pen and paper. We're going to teach you how to how to take dictation." She stopped and looked around; thinking the television or radio was on. The demanding cat was yowling like a wild lion. The dog was whining and dancing around. The animals didn't care if she had heard a voice, they wanted to be fed, and fed right this minute!

Rayelan was sure she had heard something, but the yowling and the whining were so loud, she could hear nothing but her bossy animals demanding their breakfast. She continued into the kitchen and fed the animals. She then made her morning cup of tea, picked up her newspaper and sat down at the table. Then she heard it again.

"Get a pen and paper. We're going to teach you how to take dictation." This time she knew for sure she had heard a voice. But there was no one in the house. A hundred different thoughts ran through her head. "My god, I'm hearing voices." Rayelan had a BA in psychology and was about to begin her masters. She was married to the Chairman of the Physics Department at the Naval Postgraduate School. How would she explain this to her husband? What if their friends found out? Did she need to see a psychiatrist?

The voice spoke again. This time it had a tinge of irritation. Not wanting to make the voice angry, Rayelan quickly looked for something to write with. The first thing she found was a pencil. She picked it up and grabbed a piece of white typing paper. The voice seemed to sigh,

"We told you to get a pen. If you are going to learn to take dictation, you must also learn to follow orders."

Rayelan was flustered, nervous and a little frightened. She didn't know if there was a pen in the kitchen. She looked for the pencil holder, hoping to find a pen. But there was none. She remembered her husband had worked on his notes at the dining room table the night before. Maybe he had left one of his pens. She hurried to the dining room. There on the table was a ballpoint pen and an ink pen. Before she had a chance to choose between the two, she heard the voice again.

"Use the ball point pen. And use the yellow legal pad."

Rayelan was bewildered. Not only was she hearing voices, but the voice could see what was lying on her table. The voice continued,

"When you are learning to hear our voice and transcribe our words, you must devote all your attention to the words we are saying. If you use a pencil, you will be distracted by the scratching sound it makes. If you use white paper, you will be distracted by the glare. In the future, we want you here at 8:30 each morning, ready to take dictation. Arrange your schedule accordingly and make sure you have enough pens and yellow legal pads."

The voice continued,

"Now write down everything we say."

The voice paused as Rayelan picked up the pen, sat down and pulled the legal pad toward her.

"My name is Isham, and I am here with Candor. We are not dead. We are talking to you telepathically. We have been asked to teach you how to get your own thoughts out of the way so you can take our dictation without injecting your own feelings and opinions."

Rayelan couldn't believe how easy it was to hear the voice. She also marveled that the words did not come faster than she could write. Isham explained to her that she was being prepared to take dictation from the "higher planes." He said that the work she was going to be doing was very important to the evolution of the souls on the planet. He stressed again how important it was for her to learn to get out of the way and not interfere with the messages she was receiving.

Rayelan studied with Isham for many months. Then one day, Isham said, "You have completed your training, it is time for you to meet your first teacher." Isham then introduced her to Nystr, pronounced "Nis ter."

Nystr had a very proper English accent. His style was very different from Isham's. Isham was like a strict teacher, Nystr was kind, funny and loving. Rayelan now looked forward to her morning meetings. Nystr worked with her as if he were a psychologist. He helped her understand her pain and let go of her anger.

On the surface, Rayelan's life seemed ideal. She was 29. In perfect physical condition. Her body was toned through yoga, running and hours of exercise. Her husband was a respected nuclear physicist. They had a lovely home in the middle of a forest on the Monterey Peninsula, one of the most beautiful places in the world.

Her life was filled with afternoon teas, cocktail parties and dinners with visiting Admirals, Congressmen, Ambassadors and an occasional Secretary of Defense or visiting head of state. Before she married, she didn't own a cocktail dress or an evening dinner dress. Now she had a closet full of them.

From the outside looking in, her life seemed enchanted, like a romance novel. She and her husband seemed to be a perfect couple.

But inside, her feelings were much different than they appeared. Her marriage was not happy. When they were not entertaining or being entertained, her husband came home and drank himself to sleep every night. The closeness she had enjoyed when they first met had quickly vanished.

As she glided through the parties at the Navy School, she watched the naval officers with their wives and girlfriends. She saw their love, their happiness and wished she could trade places with them. When Nystr began working with her, he had to scrap away layers of facade and armor.

Her daily meetings with Nystr sometimes lasted two to three hours. He taught her about nutrition, and the necessity of balance in her life. He helped her pick books from the bookstore, and he miraculously brought people into her life at exactly the right time. After several years of working with Nystr, one day Rayelan was told that she had graduated from his lessons and she would soon be meeting her new teacher.

Rayelan was devastated. She had come to love Nystr. He was everything she had always wanted in a partner. He was interesting, compassionate, caring and very wise. If only he had a body to match that beautiful voice. For about a week Nystr prepared her for his departure. Then one day, Nystr introduced her to her new teacher.

Shamus was as different from Nystr as night was from day. He spoke with an Irish accent and said he was really a Starship Captain. He said he had been picked to be her teacher because they had a very close connection during the lifetime when he reached enlightenment and subsequently freed himself from the earth cycle.

Shamus had a wicked sense of humor and absolutely no sympathy or compassion for her hurt feelings or unfulfilled dreams. When Nystr would join with her in the mornings, his entry was gentle and his first words were always, "Welcome my child, thank you for joining with me on this day."

Shamus would come storming in with a yell, "Get out of the way, it's my turn at the helm!" Shamus told her that she had been badly damaged in her early life and in previous lives. He told her that Nystr was a healer and while he was teaching her to receive from the higher planes, he was also healing her. Shamus told her that it was his job to teach her.

For several years Shamus taught Rayelan about many different things from ancient history to secret societies. After the two had worked together and become comfortable with each other, Shamus began to invite "guest lecturers" in to deliver the "lesson of the day."

In 1981, one of the "guest lecturers" dictated two stories. These were the first stories of the Obergon Chronicles. It took ten full years for all the stories and lessons to be dictated. The last few came in 1992.

At the time Rayelan was receiving these writings, she believed she was in contact with ascended masters, angelic beings, or some other cosmic representative of our Lord and Creator.

After Rayelan married Gunther Russbacher, CIA, ONI and a Navy SEAL, she was confronted with a reality that she had not yet explored. Conversations with her husband, Gunther and with his boss, a four star Admiral, made her realize that a lot of channeled information was not coming from representatives of God.

She was told that through various techniques of mind control, human based organizations, such as the CIA and NSA, were trying to shape the thought of the world by tapping into a human longing to know the Truth.

She was told that certain groups had long understood how powerful religions of the past had successfully controlled human thought for ages. These groups realized that modern day religions could no longer be used by them to introduce new ideas. Religions of today have their holy books written down and preserved, therefore, it would be difficult to introduce new dogma.

Not only this, most followers of modern day religions can read the Holy Books and interpret the scriptures for themselves. It is not easy to distort or grossly misinterpret the Holy Books in today's world.

Because of this, the groups who wished to use religion to control the masses realized that they needed to introduce *new* religious texts to the world through modern day prophets. The prophets would receive the new religious texts through various machines and techniques created by government and private agencies.

The information that would be transmitted would be created in their think tanks. It would then be transmitted to their chosen receivers, i.e. "Prophets," through various techniques that fall under the heading of "mind control." In most cases, the receivers of the information believe with all their heart, that they are hearing the voice of God or God's representatives.

Rayelan was told about several New Age channels who are receiving their information from New World Order think tanks, and who are shaping the people of the world for the coming New World Religion. She was also told that the group of individuals, who oppose the New World Order, is employing similar techniques to get their information to the public. The opposition to the New World Order, a group of men who refer to themselves as Faction Two, appears to be in possession of historical texts that record earth's history almost from the beginning.

Rayelan was never directly told that the Obergon Chronicles were transmitted to her through government mind control techniques. However, knowing that she has been married to two high level government employees who were involved with Electronic Warfare and mind control, it is now her belief that The Obergon Chronicles were transmitted to her through a form of voice to skull electronic transmission.

When she confronted her husband, Gunther with her feelings, he responded that it didn't matter where the information came from if it was true. Gunther's boss had told her that her information was true. She asked Gunther how he knew it was true. Gunther replied that there were "vast libraries" of information regarding the history of the earth and the universe that had not been released to humanity because the time wasn't right to do so. He went on to say that the group with whom he worked, used various New Age Channels to release the part of this work that they felt would not damage the psyche of the world. Rayelan tried to press him for more information. She was unable to do so. He fell asleep. She later was told that Gunther had built-in programs to control how much information he could release. If he came too close to releasing something that was still highly classified, he would begin to ramble nonsense and then fall asleep. While Rayelan was convinced that Gunther believed the Obergon Stories were real, she was never able to learn the original source for the Obergon Chronicles, until she traveled to Austria in 1994.

In 1994, while Gunther and Rayelan were in Austria, they stayed at a Templar Lodge, which had been in Gunther's family for over six hundred years. While she was there, she had dinner each evening with members of the Austro-Hungarian royal families. She was told the lodge was a secret meeting place for the modern day descendants of the Knights Templars and other people who are working to stop the New World Order from imposing a One World Government.

One Evening, during the dinner conversation, she was told, by a member of the Habsburg family, who was also a Templar, that the Templars have huge underground libraries full of information that is slowly being released to the public.... as they are ready for it. She was told that much of the information in these libraries came from hermetically sealed chambers deep below King Solomon's Temple.

During the Crusades, the Knights Templars built their stable over the Temple ruins. They did this so they could excavate the Temple without anyone realizing what they were doing. The library they brought back and eventually stored in the salt mines near Salzburg, Austria, is believed to be a duplicate copy of everything that was in the Alexandria library when the Romans burned it. Legends say that the information in this library dates from Atlantis, Lemuria and from other civilizations throughout the Universes.

These Templars believe they come from the royal blood of the House of David. According to their beliefs, the House of David, via a son of Noah, is descended from the star Sirius. Gunther is also a member of the Hungarian royal family. He believes the royal house of Esterházy is also descended from the star Sirius. "Ester" means star, "haszy" means descended from or "house of." The "star" that the Esterházy's believe they are "descended from" is Sirius.

Gunther Russbacher is a highly intelligent, well-trained intelligence operative. If he believes the Obergon Chronicles are true, then he must know the truth behind the stories. He must also know the reason that Rayelan was chosen to be the vehicle who received and released the stories to the world. One of the questions that people continue to ask is, "What part did the Obergon Chronicles play in the meeting and marriage of Gunther and Rayelan?

Note from Rayelan - 2006

The last time I saw Gunther was in 1994. He met Jane in 1996 while he was in prison in Austria. When he was released from the Austrian prison in December of 1996, he was supposed to catch a plane to California to pick me up so we could fly to Florida where we had scheduled a lecture on the Obergon Chronicles and mind control.

Instead, he disappeared for a month. When he surfaced he was in jail in allanLos Alamos, New Mexico. He called me. He thought I was Jane Ryder, a woman he would eventually marry. His mind was so messed up that he thought he had only had one wife. He thought Jane was the wife who had fought the Bush Administration with him. He thought Jane was the wife who had helped him complete the transfer of Austrian and Templar gold from the Philippines to back to Austria. He had NO memory of a wife named Rayelan.

After Gunther married Jane, I met a retired Marine officer named David Lee. When we finally decided to get married, I first had to convince Gunther that he and I HAD been married and he had to sign divorce papers.

I stopped publishing allanRumor Mill News in 1997 and was working as a dispatcher while I finished studying for the California test to be a teacher again. David not only encouraged me to finish the classes I needed to become a teacher, he encouraged me to write the book, *Diana, Queen of Heaven*, AND start Rumor Mill News once again... but this time as a webpage.

✝ Gunther died August 8th, 2005.

✝ My beloved husband, David died October 5th, 2005.

Several weeks after David died, I was moved to write the following for Rumor Mill News.

THIS IS THE MOST IMPORTANT ARTICLE YOU WILL READ TODAY

From http://www.rumormillnews.com
Posted By: Rayelan
Date: Wednesday, 19 October 2005, 1:57 p.m.

In spite of the grief I am feeling because of my husband David's unexpected passing, I am feeling OTHER feelings too.

Many of my closest friends are also feeling these "inexplicable feelings." And now, after reading other things here on Rumor Mill, I realize that others, all over the world, are feeling this also.

I have especially seen the following, (taken from the article below) in close friends and family:

"I have watched the egos of some cling desperately to beliefs and conclusions which no longer serve them.

"Rather than release old patterns, forgive and move forward, the majority of the time and energy is used defending these old patterns."

The only thing I can add to the above is this:

Not only have I seen people defend their old and worn out beliefs, I have seen them blame OTHERS instead of looking into their own hearts.

This is a time of rapid spiritual growth. Those who cling to the past and the way they USED to think and to do things in the past... will rapidly be given lessons that will either FREE them from the past or will cause them to spiral down into behavior patterns that will cause them to be stuck in concrete, with no hope of forward movement on the spiritual level.

For each and every one of you...

It is time to look deep within your own hearts and let go of all hate, anger, judgement, blame and all other negative thought forms.

Take a good look at your family members. If you are holding on to some kind of anger or hurt that was caused by them, it's time to let go of it.

If you can't bring yourself to call the person and say you are sorry. Or if you KNOW that the person is so stuck in their own mental, emotional or physical problems that a call from you would ONLY add MORE gasoline to the flames of anger that already exist between you, then you MUST ask God, the Angels or Jesus to intercede on your behalf.

YOU... not them... YOU are the one I am concerned about here. YOU are the one that I want to see transcend. It would be nice if your estranged friends and family could transcend too... but unless they are reading this... they can't be helped except by YOUR prayers.

We are rapidly coming to an end of a cycle. Some people, me included, have been feeling my/their body/ies vibrate. I have felt this in the past when the earth was going through an "uplifting" a "raising" of vibrations.

Said in other words, the paradigm is changing. That which came before will vanish before our eyes.

The writers who write for RMN have been using the word "seachange." The world is experiencing a "seachange." The outer manifestations of this "seachange" may be seen in changes of governments. Countries that have been savagely ruled by dictators may see the people empowered to rise up and depose the dictators. Countries that have been ruled by corruption may see that corruption exposed.

Years ago I wrote about the "Truth and Reconciliation" courts. While we may NOT see these courts, I KNOW they exist and are doing their work. We may suddenly see many wealthy men form non-profit organizations that really DO help the disadvantaged. We may suddenly see men and women who have been possessed by power and wealth suddenly realize that power and money mean NOTHING if you have sold your soul for it.

Some of these people may genuinely have realized this on their own. Others will have been ordered to do this by the "Truth and Reconciliation" courts. Their choices will have been "give your ill-gotten gains" to those you stole it from, or face prison and death.

If you have recently experienced situations with friends and family that seem completely inexplicable, then YOU need to clear your mind of all anger, hurt, remorse, guilt, or other feelings. You must immediately send unconditional love to the person that you wronged or you FEEL wronged you! It doesn't matter if this person is living or has passed into that other dimension that we mistakenly call death!

U... you are living in this 3-dimensional world... are the one who needs healing. YOU can ONLY heal yourself with forgiveness. It doesn't matter how serious or how PETTY the problem is/was. It is TIME! It IS time! YOU must take the reigns now. NO ONE ELSE can do it for YOU! YOU must initiate the "truth and reconciliation." YOU must realize that the person was doing the best they knew how to do. YOU must realize that some people are damaged from birth. Some people carry DNA patterns that affect their brain chemistry giving them mental and emotional problems. YOU must realize that some people have been SO damaged in childhood that they only KNOW this kind of damage. YOU are the one reading this. YOU are the one that has to reach out!

If there is NO way you can bring yourself to reach out and physically talk to the person, then you will have to talk to God, Jesus, the Angels, or your OWN higher SELF! You are the ONE who is still suffering from the pain. YOU are the one who is being given the opportunity to FREE yourself from this kind of pain.

ONLY BY FREEING YOURSELF from the chains of pain that keep you stuck in you old reality will YOU be able to join the rest of us who are moving up to the next level.

I don't know what the next level will bring, but I do know that many of the people who have been around me will no longer be around me. Why? Because they will refuse to admit that there is anything wrong with the way they are leading their lives and making decisions.

Please do NOT think that by merely releasing all of this to Jesus or God that you will be rid of it. No... you must take the time to really FEEL... maybe for the FIRST time in your life! You are the ONLY one who can be honest with yourself. HONESTY and TRUTH are the ONLY things that can free you from the bags of garbage you have been carrying for years.

Don't think that by throwing out those people who cause you pain or problems that YOU will solve anything. You will only attract MORE people of the SAME vibration who will cause you MORE pain and problems.

This is NOT a time to hide from yourself. It is a time for you to look in the timeless mirror of SELF REFLECTION. It is the mirror of your SOUL. It is the mirror that ALL of us are terrified to view. But ONLY by standing naked before this soul mirror will YOU be able to release ALL of your old baggage and MOVE forward into this new world that is being created.

As I said, it doesn't matter if the person you are angry with is dead or alive. The so-called dead are just millimeters away from us. The walls that used to separate those who are in material form from those who are in spirit form are rapidly thinning. Don't be surprised if your loved ones show themselves to you. However, they can ONLY touch you with love if YOU exist in total and complete love.

If you are holding on to blame, guilt, anger, hate, envy, and any of the other 7 deadly sins, it means that YOUR vibration is too LOW, too DENSE to be aware of the love that is surrounding you.

ONLY YOU can do something about this.

The train is coming... and it is coming fast. ONLY YOU have the power to step up and on to this "train." The ONLY way that you can step onto this train is in love.... complete and total unconditional love!

The earth is changing. Many are choosing to leave rather than face what is coming. Many do NOT have the skills or the ability to face what is coming. Some of too ill mentally or physically to withstand the vibrational change. These people will make the transition to the other dimension through the doorway we call death. But they will NOT be dead. They will quickly be healed of all their earthly problems and they will be asked to help those of us who are still in body. If you have lost a loved one, wait for an appropriate time period, and then reach out to that loved one for help. They are right next to you! Their loving arms are embracing you, guiding you and protecting you. They will help you understand what is taking place.

If you TRULY want to be part of the change. If you TRULY want to be part of the new world that is coming, then YOU must examine ALL of your emotions. YOU must be brave enough to truly LOOK at yourself... (I am including myself in all that I write.) ONLY by looking at ourselves and our actions can we free ourselves from all the negative emotions that are attached to our past actions.

YOU have the time to make the needed atonements with loved ones living or "dead."

Please believe me when I say that the MOST important task YOU can take on today is sending pure unconditional love to ALL people who have wronged you, to all people that YOU have wronged, and all people who have who have hurt you and BEEN hurt by you!

It's time to forgive everyone... family, friends, strangers, politicians, dictators, and human monsters who have done and still do unspeakable things to others. We MUST forgive them.... this does NOT mean that we must allow them to continue the unspeakable acts that they are still doing or that they have done. It is time that Justice comes swiftly to these people. Those who lived and stayed in power by the sword will perish by the sword.

Those who lived and stayed in power by graft and corruption shall be given a choice. They can go to prison, or they can spend the resting of their lives making restitution to their victims.

The change I am talking about is NOT one that people can escape. It is NOT one that is being brought about by humans. The bread is rising. It is a process that is simple. You add flour, water and yeast...

and you wait... if all the ingredients are pure and active, then the dough will rise. It's a simple rule of the universe. The same rule applies to what is happening now. The souls are rising. The ones who are still in body must cast out all the impurities they are still carrying or their "dough" will fail to rise. If it fails to rise, then you will NOT have the needed strength to move into the next dimension.

Do not be afraid that you will be condemned to hell for all eternity. It will only mean that you may not arrive at the same destination as those who release all their impurities and allow themselves to rise....

"Allow YOURSELF to rise....

Like flour into bread dough...

In THINE, thy CREATOR's eyes!"

I will repeat ONE more time. This is the MOST important message you will read today!

In love,

Rayelan

The Amazing Life of Rayelan Allan

It was 2AM. Rayelan pulled out of the radio station parking lot and eased her car onto Highway 280. Her mind was not on driving. She had just publicly charged the President of the United States with treason. She was scared and nervous and afraid of reprisals. She would never have gone public on her own. She did it to keep her husband from being murdered in prison. He was a Navy SEAL team commander with sensitive knowledge of government crimes. Someone had just tried to kill him. Publicity was the only way to keep him safe. The radio show was her first. The callers were brutal and their attacks made her forget important details. Her self confidence was in the sewer. She didn't want to face another audience but tomorrow was already booked solid. She felt her attempt to bring attention to her husband's story was a fiasco and that she had made them both look like idiots. She hadn't. Her story had been well received. Her mind should have been on her driving. But it wasn't. It was back at the studio, reliving her humiliation. She never saw the car that slammed into her rear bumper. Her car crashed into the guard rail and careened out of control. Out of the corner of her eye, she saw a dark van headed straight at her. It was obvious he intended to push her off the overpass. She floored the Cadillac. The van continued to bear down. Suddenly another car clipped her rear bumper as it forced itself between her and the van. What was he going to do? Shoot her? Were they going to stage an accident and say she was dead when they found her? She accepted her imminent death, but in a split second, reality changed. The small grey car was not ramming her, it was ramming the van. She remembered what her husband said earlier, "Don't be afraid. My SEALs will be with you."

A burst of automatic weapons fire interrupted her concentration. In the rearview mirror, she saw the van stopped in the middle of the empty freeway. Before she had time to think, an explosion rocked her car. She looked again. The van was in flames.

In the next two years, six more attempts were made to kill her. On Christmas Eve, 1992, she sat in her darkened room, with a Glock 9 millimeter in her lap. The Director of the CIA had put a contract out on her. If she survived the night, and the flight, she would be under the protection of her husband's Godfather, the President of Austria...Up until 1989, Rayelan lived what appeared to be an idyllic life on the Monterey Peninsula. How did this idyllic life turn from a fairytale into a nightmare? She had been the wife of the Dean of Science and Engineering at the Naval Postgraduate School. Her life was filled with cocktail parties and dinners. Senators, Congressmen, Admirals, Generals, Cabinet Secretaries and Presidents had dined at her table. Her private time was spent studying metaphysics, yoga and developing her natural psychic abilities. When she began to hear voices, she believed she was receiving messages from master teachers. She would not learn the whole truth for many years. As the inner masters taught her, they also arranged "accidental" meetings with living masters, such as the Dalai Lama, Krishnamurti, Wayne Dyer, Indian shamans, yoga masters and others.

Her love of history gained her a reputation as an esoteric scholar, researcher of ancient mysteries, and an expert on secret societies, in particular the Knights Templars.

A near fatal bout with viral meningitis produced an out of body experience that changed her life forever. In a classroom on another plane, she was taught about the holographic universe, the atomic akashic memory, genetic memory and the settlement of the planet earth. She was taught a method for removing pain and trauma from the physical body and the DNA. The method was called Activated Cellular Memory (ACM), and she was told it would change the world. When she recovered, she began teaching the ACM Method.

After her husband's death in 1988, Rayelan moved to New York City. She lectured and gave workshops at the United Nations. She saw clients for private ACM sessions. She soon relocated to Washington DC. Within a few short months, she had a large clientele stretching from the United Nations to Capitol Hill.

One of her clients, the Chairman of the Senate Foreign Relations Committee, asked her to become his administrative assistant to oversee a psi-warfare program he funded through his Committee. This program is now known as Remote Viewing. As she was deciding whether to give up her clients and take a government job, she married a Naval officer she had known for years.

It turned out that her new husband was more than a Naval officer. He was the number three man in the CIA, a member of the Austrian royal family, the Godson of Kurt Waldheim, and a Knight Templar.

After surviving a four-year nightmare as the most famous political prisoner of the Bush Administration, her husband was freed and they fled to Austria. They stayed at a Templar Lodge in Salzburg where she was tutored by members of the Habsburg royal family who were Templars. She learned the truth about her lineage. She was told why the Knights Templars went to the Holy Lands, what they found, and why they have remained hidden for 800 years.

In the December 1996 edition of RMNews, the magazine she and her husband, Gunther, started they published "Operation Open Eyes." It was his explosive account of a secret government mind control project that created Manchurian Candidates. In January

1997, they were scheduled to blow the lid off government mind control cults and new age channels.

Then in late December of 1996, her husband disappeared. Rayelan went forward with the exposé of cults and new age channels. Two months later, her husband surfaced, but he had no memory of her or their marriage... AND he had a new wife, an English film producer.

Rayelan continues to publish RMNews. Because she has access to the intelligence community, RMNews is rapidly becoming the leading online Alternative News Site. For more information of RMNews go to: http://www.rumormillnews.com.

Rayelan is the author of *Diana, Queen of Heaven, The New World Religion*. For more information about this extradinary book, go to: http://www.dianaqueenofheaven.com

David Lee Feb.1999 for The P³ Times

The Rayelan Allan Interview

By Theresa de Veto, Publisher of
http://www.surfingtheapocalypse.com

> *The following is an exclusive interview conducted with Rayelan Allan, Founder and Publisher of The allan-Rumor Mill News Agency, a web-based news magazine that was started by and for government whistle-blowers. (http://www.rumormillnews.com)*

> *At one point in her life, Rayelan was part of the New Age community and believed she had been chosen to receive channeled messages from the star system Sirius. After a strange set of circumstances, she found herself married to a Naval Officer who, at the time, was also the number 3 man in the CIA. From him, she learned that her channeled voices were originating from a more earthly source. . . namely the Office of Naval Intelligence.*

> *Through a bizarre journey that included a trip to Austria where her husband revealed that not only was he a Knight Templar but that the messages that had been transmitted to her in these "channeling" sessions came from ancient manuscripts the Templars had retrieved from King Solomon's Temple during the middle ages. Rayelan discovered that many New Age channels are receiving messages in the same way she received them, via modern technology. She also learned that there are several competing factions involved in these transmissions.*

> *Rayelan's amazing story will take you beyond the world of channeling, into the covert side of the U.S. Intelligence world, the New World Order, alien technology and more!*

> *This interview was conducted via email over a period of months by Theresa de Veto Founder/Editor of the web magazine Surfing The Apocalypse — http://www.surfingtheapocalypse.com.*

> *The views expressed here are not necessarily the views of Surfing The Apocalypse or the interviewer.*

Q: Rayelan, most people who know you know you as the publisher of Rumor Mill News, one of the most respected of the Internet alternative e-magazines. You were the wife of the CIA operative who was dubbed "The October Surprise Pilot," and you are the author of a book on the death of Princess Diana.

Your public image is that of a researcher and writer who is trying to alert people to the danger they face from a group of powerful people who believe in a One World Government. You are also the one who has introduced the concept of Two Factions that are vying for control of the world.

But there is much more to Rayelan Allan than the side you present in Rumor Mill News. You were successful and well known long before you married CIA operative, Gunther Russbacher. You traveled the United States giving workshops and private sessions. You lectured at the United Nations. You were active in politics and were considering going to work for a Senator on Capitol Hill.

I would like to explore some of the other aspects of your life. One of the most fascinating to me is your book, The Obergon Chronicles. I would like to begin with it.

Q: What are The Obergon Chronicles?

A: The Obergon Chronicles are a series of biographical stories about beings from the star system Sirius who came to earth.

Q: Where did the Chronicles come from?

A: I "channeled" them, in the same way New Age Channels bring through their information.

Q: Who were these "beings" from Sirius, and why did they come to earth?

A: It is my belief that many humans carry the souls from Obergon. They came to earth because their home planets were destroyed when a neighboring sun became a red giant. The beings were not finished with their lessons on the material plane when their worlds were destroyed.

The elder brothers and sisters were sent out to prepare a new planet which would become a "school" for the younger souls. This new planet was Terra.... Earth. The Obergon Chronicles are the stories of the misadventures these older brothers and sisters had while trying to fulfill their missions and create a planet that was suitable for the continuation of lessons by the Children of Obergon.

The stories that make up the Obergon Chronicles not only deal with the difficulties involved in preparing a new planet to receive a new class of students, but they deal with personality traits such as vanity and lack of compassion. The stories are focused on certain main characters who appear to represent the archetypes found in all sentient life. The seven deadly sins and the seven virtues are presented, but the stories don't use a sledgehammer approach to pound home their point. If anything, the stories are told in the same way an onion is peeled.

Each story makes the reader's mind expand to the point that the reader is able to take on new concepts. In the dedication, it says that the Obergon Chronicles are dedicated to the Children of Obergon.

The stories that are included in "The Obergon Chronicles" mainly deal with four characters. Atalon and Raelon are two souls that were created as an experiment. Their father, Odon, was trying to create a Super soul. At some time in the future, Atalon and Raelon will join together for a mission that only a Super soul can perform. The other two characters are Shalma and Xanos. They are one soul that has split into two souls so it could very quickly complete its lessons in the material world and gain the knowledge it needed to perform its primary mission on the planet Terra.

There are many other minor characters in these first stories. Bits and pieces of their stories were "dictated" to me, but I have never taken the time to piece them together. These minor characters each have stories of their own that will make additional books.

Q: How did you come to write the Obergon Chronicles?

A: I had no choice. I know this sounds funny, but it is the truth! I was racing to get to an appointment in Los Angeles. I had just sold a short fantasy book to Disney and I was on my way to sign the contract. I was rushing to get out the door and into my car. The drive from my house to Los Angeles was about six hours, and I had a 5PM appointment.

I had been "receiving" messages from "outside" my own consciousness for about three years. "Channeling" is what the New Age movement calls the phenomena. The messages I was hearing were dictated to me by a man's voice. At the time I was receiving these messages I genuinely thought I was a New Age Channel who was receiving messages from an assortment of ascended masters.

That day, as I was racing to get out of the house and into my car, the voice of my regular "teacher" i.e. spirit guide, said, "Sit down, we need you to take some dictation."

I protested saying that I would miss my appointment. The voice became so loud and persistent that there was really nothing I could do but sit down and "take dictation." Two stories were "dictated" at this time. The first story in the Obergon Chronicles, "Atalon and Shalma" was dictated, and "The Story of White Eagle" was dictated. At the time, I did not realize the two were related. They are completely different, but they illustrate lessons the Children of Obergon need to understand.

Q: How did you feel about it when you first began to hear this voice? Did you think it was time to see a psychiatrist?

A: In the late 70's, when I began to hear voices, I had just graduated with a BA in psychology. When I first heard the voices, I believed I was manifesting all the symptoms of schizophrenia or multiple personalities. I didn't want to tell anyone about it, and yet I knew I needed to talk to someone. I called a psychiatrist and told him I was "depressed," and made an appointment. After several appointments, the psychiatrist told me that nothing was wrong with me and I was simply "opening up" spiritually.

At the time, I did not question this, I just thought that I had been lucky enough to find the "one" enlightened psychiatrist in the area. Now I wonder if the "psychiatrist" I called was working for the government!

He told me about a healing circle that met in Carmel, California, a few miles from my home. Dorie D'Angelo, the Angel Healer of Carmel was the leader of the group. I began attending Dorie's healing circle on a weekly basis. Through the people I met at the group, I realized there was a whole world I never knew existed. The people who attended these circles did things and talked about things that I had never even imagined.

Q: What made you think you were a "new-age channel?"

A: I met a woman at the healing circle who channeled a being who gave people advice, sort of a cosmic Ann Landers. She volunteered to help me understand what was happening to me. After working with her and her spirit guide for a few weeks, I came to believe that the voices in my head were part of burgeoning phenomena that was soon to be called "channeling."

On the advice of the friends I met through the healing circle, I started taking a Yoga class. I also studied nutrition, meditation, healing, spiritual awakening and a whole array of things that are now labeled "New Age." I mention the "New Age" label only because at the time I got into all of this, the term had not been created. The term "New Age" arrived at about the same time Shirley Maclaine came along. At the time I stumbled into this world, it was called simply, "Walking the Spiritual Path." Most of us who had been "walking the path" felt that Shirley Maclaine's approach to spiritual truths was like instant oatmeal; it filled you up, but lacked the real nutrition.

You asked if I felt I was going crazy. The answer is yes. Even through a psychiatrist had certified me "sane" and assured me I was only "opening up" spiritually, at home and in my social life, I was surrounded by physicists and their wives who would have thought I was insane if I had told them what was happening to me. Because I was married to a physicist and understood his mindset, I knew there was no way that any of his colleagues could understand what I was going through. I knew if I opened up and said anything about my spiritual path; it would cause problems for me... and my husband.

The world we lived in was so different from the way things are today; that I can barely believe it was only 25 years ago. I would like to take a moment to try to paint a picture of the world I was living in when I began hearing the voices.

In 1975, when I became the wife of the Chairman of the Physics Department at the Naval Postgraduate School, the military tradition and formalities were still grounded in the 1950's. The Postgraduate School is where members of the military go to get Master's degrees and PhDs. It is the graduate division for all the military academies.

The culture of the School was anchored to the formal military way of life. The formality had been fading ever since the Viet Nam war, but when I got there in the mid 70's, it was far from gone. I was told by the other wives that I *had* to join the Faculty Wives Club and eventually I had to head it. The woman who led me through the paces, and taught me what I needed to do to fulfill my duties as a Chairman's wife, was the wife of a retired chairman. She invited me to a "wives luncheon." She told me that the women "dressed" for these luncheons. I had no idea what she meant by the term, "dressed." As I walked into the luncheon, I felt I had stepped back into a world of southern elegance and gentility.

Having been a Haight Ashbury hippie seven years earlier, the change was like night and day. I quickly learned that my wardrobe did not fit in. My platform shoes and mini-skirts had to go. I replaced them with afternoon "tea suits," sensible pumps and gloves. I was part of a world I didn't understand, and I was sure they wouldn't understand the "Spiritual Path."

I made the decision not to discuss the things I was learning in my classes and through books with any of the faculty members or their wives... this included my husband. Because of this decision, I began living a double life. During the day, while my husband was at work, I read, attended classes and had friends over for tea and talk.

In the evening, we had social commitments, and I became the perfect hostess and wife. When my husband was promoted to Dean of Science and Engineering, our social engagements increased. As the wife of a Dean, I was expected to do a lot of entertaining. I often had a house filled with heads of the military academies, scientists from Los Alamos, high level Washington bureaucrats, Admirals, Captains, Congressmen, and Ambassadors. Talking about my life on the spiritual path was something I wouldn't even have considered doing at these parties.

At the time, I was not interested in politics, the military, government, or any of the things that fascinate me now. I learned to be a good cocktail conversationalist. It is surprising the things you can learn at cocktail parties. Can you imagine what I could have learned if I had asked the right questions, rather than just listened?

Q: You state that "the messages were dictated to me by a man's voice." Was this voice "inside your head," or was it as if someone was in the room speaking to you?

A: The first time it happened, I really thought someone was in the room with me. I began hearing the voices during one of the only times in my life that I was not working outside the house or going to school. The only thing I had to do each morning was feed my white cat and our three-legged German shepherd. One morning, as I walked past the dining room table on the way to feed the animals, I thought I heard something. I looked to see if the radio was on, or if my husband had come home. There was no one around and the radio and TV were not on, so I figured it was something outside. I fed the cat and dog and started to walk back to the bedroom.

The dining room table was in front of a wall of windows. The picture windows looked out over a forest. There were no curtains or blinds on the windows. The view of the forest was completely unobstructed. As I passed the dining room table, on my way back to the bedroom, I heard the voice again, this time more clearly.

"Get a pen and paper," it said. "We're going to teach you how to take dictation."

I looked around because the voice was so loud and clear I really thought someone was in the room with me. In other words, the voice was *not* in my head. It appeared as if it was coming from somewhere in the house. I didn't know what to do, so I followed orders and picked up a pencil.

The voice spoke again, "I said, get a pen." I could hear annoyance in his voice as he explained further. "A pencil makes too much noise, it will distract you. Get a pen."

"Oh my God," I thought, "Not only am I hearing voices, but the voices can *see* me." I put down the pencil and picked up a pen. I sat down at the table and pulled a white note pad to me.

The voice explained further, "A white pad will reflect too much light. While you are learning to take dictation, the fewer distractions you have, the better. Use a yellow legal pad."

There was a yellow legal pad on the table. I picked it up and positioned my pen to begin taking dictation.

The voice began, "My name is Isham, I am here with Candor. We are not dead. We are communicating with you using a form of enhanced telepathy. Our job is to teach you how to get out of the way so your own thoughts don't interfere with the dictation and distort the meaning. Once we are sure you can do this, we will introduce you to your first teacher."

Isham told me that I was to meet with him for a half hour every morning between 8 and 8:30am. Isham taught me how to get my own thoughts out of the way so I did not add my own thoughts to the information that was coming through. He then passed me onto my first teacher whose name was Nystr (pronounced like "mister"). Nystr had an English accent and was charming. He acted in the capacity of teacher, counselor and healer.

I soon loved Nystr as much as I could love anyone. He was my best friend, as well as my teacher. I studied with him for about two years... maybe longer. Nystr helped me emotionally, intellectually, and spiritually. When he told me that he had done everything he could for me and he was going to pass me over to my new teacher, I was heartbroken. I felt I had lost my best friend.

I thought nothing could be worse than losing Nystr, but for a while it did get worse. The new teacher was nothing at all like Nystr. He was an arrogant and brash Irishman named Shamus, who was neither gentle *nor* kind. He did not teach through gentleness and love. He taught using jokes, personal attacks and ridicule. He went against everything that I had learned about the spiritual path. He wasn't a saint, he was a rogue, and he was proud of it!!

It took a while, but I eventually got used to him and realized that he was preparing me for work in a world that behaved just like he did. He was trying to "toughen" me up, so I wouldn't collapse in a "sea of tears" the first time I was attacked. Once I discovered that he wanted me to take my messages to a world of men and women who behaved just like he did, I understood what he was doing. I eventually came to love him as much as I loved Nystr. Unlike Nystr, Shamus was able to bring in "guest teachers" from "higher planes." It was some of these "guest teachers" who "transmitted" the Obergon Chronicles to me.

Q: How long were you able to live this "double life," and what happened to change things?

A: I lived the "double life" from the time I started receiving the messages until 1985—about six years. The reason things changed is that I had a near death experience that changed my life forever.

In January of 1984, I came down with viral meningitis. I lay in bed for two days with a headache that was so bad I could not even move. My husband finally took me to the emergency room. The ER doctor examined me and called in a neurologist who did a spinal tap.

I can remember lying by myself in a dark room listening to the doctor and my husband, who were in the hall, talk about me. The doctor told my husband I had viral meningitis. At that time there was nothing that could be done. The doctor was very matter of fact. He told my husband, "Take her home. She'll either die or get well."

I was given pain pills, which allowed me to sleep. One night, during my long recovery period, I was awakened by a voice

It is time. It is time!" The voice said. Thinking it was the television, I ignored it. Then with more emphasis, the voice said again, "IT IS TIME!"

I looked in the direction of my closet, because the voice seemed to be coming from there. Instead of seeing my closet doors, I saw a scientific laboratory filled with students and a teacher. Everyone was staring at me, waiting for me to join them, so the class could begin.

As I took my seat on a stool at one of the experiment tables, the instructor announced that today we were going to be studying the holographic nature of the universe. He explained that everything in the universe carries with it the memory of everything that it has ever been or done... from the beginning of time. Each atom carries the part of universal history that it has experienced. From the interaction with all other atoms, due to close proximity and transference, all atoms can become a hologram of the entire universe.

He said that the very atoms that make up a person's body are chosen by the soul to help the soul successfully accomplish what it came to earth to do.

The instructor moved on from atoms and talked about how DNA is formed and how DNA carries the history of every ancestor and everything the ancestor had experienced up until the moment the DNA was passed on to the fetus.

The instructor quickly changed subjects again and said, "The cells of your body carry with them the memory of everything, good or bad, that YOU have lived through in this life. Past trauma is re-lived over and over again because the cells are still holding on to the "energetic emotional charge" that created the memory of the incident. The past trauma becomes a millstone which keeps you bound down and incapable of reaching your potential. As a result, you are incapable of fulfilling the life plan you chose to fulfill, prior to incarnating. The traumatic memories will trigger over and over, and will continue to do so until the cellular memory is cleared.

The instructor approached me, closed his eyes, and bowed his head. He inhaled a long slow deep breath, held it for a moment and then forcefully exhaled in my direction. I felt a bolt of energy enter my body. In the moment of exhalation, the instructor imparted to me the knowledge that I now "knew" the secret of activating cellular memories and clearing them out of the body.

I also received information that my "class on earth" was nearing its graduation, but before they could graduate and leave the material plane, they needed to get rid of their excess baggage, the traumatic and painful memories that are stored at a cellular level. After the teacher imparted my lessons, I knew the process was inside me and it would rise to the conscious mind as I cleared my own cellular memories and got rid of my own emotional baggage.

The transfer of information from the instructor to me took only a moment. The instructor went from student to student, passing on to each of them their new gift. Then the instructor said that he was going to show the class what each level of the clearing process felt like. He started with the cells of the body.

I felt a hand on my head. I assumed it was the instructor. I had always hated to have the top of my head touched. Whenever anyone touched me in this way, even the ministers who blessed me, I would panic and fight to get the hand off my head. Suddenly all the old feelings of panic and fear returned.

I was suffocating in terror. I heard the instructor's voice, "Breathe! Breathe in a long, slow deep breath. Don't hold it. Exhale immediately. See your breath as a circular, continuous connected breath. Breathe!"

As I breathed in this manner, I relived a childhood incident when my brother put me into the box where my family kept firewood. I knew it was filled with spiders and other bugs. My brother put his hand on my head and pushed me down so he could close the lid on me. Then he sat on the box to keep me from getting out. It was dark, it was cramped. I felt things crawling on me. Suddenly I couldn't breathe. I felt I was dying. I began to scream. My grandmother heard my terrified screams and rescued me.

The terror of this event was still stored in the cellular memory of my body. The hand on my head was causing me to relive the original event. I felt claustrophobic. I felt panic. I was unable to breathe. I felt I was dying.

"Breathe through it." I heard the instructor say. "You are fine, you are safe, you are protected. Breathe, and let it go." I did as I was told. With each breath, I faced the fear. Finally I knew I had released the trauma, not just from the moment, but from the past as well.

For an instant I became a child again. But this time I was not "trapped" in the wood box. I was in the wood box because I was playing a game with my brother. As I released the painful memories, which were trapped in the physical cells of my body, I was also able to rewrite my personal history and undo the damage.

Opening my eyes, I saw the other students were breathing in the same long slow continuous manner. It appeared each one of them had just relived a traumatic experience, as I had done.

The instructor then said, "Now I am going to show you what it is like to remember something from your DNA." Once more he closed his eyes and inhaled. As he exhaled, suddenly I was standing in the woods watching my father split a log with a wedge and a sledge hammer. I was holding a baby boy in my arms. My father was in his early twenties. Suddenly something flew up from the log and struck me in the lip. I began bleeding all over myself and the baby.

My father looked up and saw what had happened. He had tears in his eyes. "Honey, I am so sorry. I am so sorry." He pulled a piece of steel from my upper lip and pressed a cloth to my lip to stop the bleeding. Part of the wedge had broken off, flew up, and struck me in my upper lip. Then my father put his arm around me, took the baby and walked me back to the cabin. I had never seen the cabin before, but it looked familiar, like a picture in the family album.

My father called me by my mother's name. I realized that I was reliving one of my mother's memories. Then I remembered the scar on my mother's upper lip. I had just experienced a DNA memory of something that happened before I was born. The baby boy was my older brother. The cabin was one my parents had lived in when they were first married. The incident had happened 10 years before I was conceived. I later asked my mother how she got the scar on her lip. It had happened exactly as I had experienced it.

I could tell by the expressions on the faces of the other students that they had also relived a similar DNA memory.

The instructor then stood in front of the class and said, "Now I am going to show you how it feels to access the memories of the stars." He instructed the class to place their index finger over their heart. He told them to press down with their fingernail until they could feel the pressure in one small spot.

"Draw all of your consciousness into this area," he said, "Begin to breathe the long, slow connected breath. This is your heart chakra; it is the center of your body. It is the place where Father-God and Mother-Earth meet in love. Father-God is spirit, Mother-Earth is his opposite, she is material. He is without form, She is with form. Humans were created in the image of their Father and their Mother. A human carries the spirit of their Father and they wear the material body of their Mother. When a human comes into a perfect state of balance the energies of the Father and the Mother can meet in the heart chakra. Remember to breathe, breathe slowly and continuously.

"The Mother's energy is red. She enters into the balanced physical body through the base chakra. The Father's energy is white. He enters the body through the crown chakra. There are seven chakras. Mother and Father each travel through three chakras and meet in the center on the human body... the heart chakra. When this happens to a human, mystics and psychics see the heart chakra radiating a beautiful pink aura. Mother and Father are communing in love.

"Continue drawing all of your energy into the space beneath your fingernail. Choose one cell and go deep inside of it. Remember to breathe. Focus all your attention on that one cell. See yourself going into the cell. Breathe.... Now pick an atom and place your consciousness inside the atom."

The instructor had barely finished his sentence when I felt a loud roaring sound. It sounded like a jet engine. I literally felt my entire body being sucked backwards through the area where my fingernail was pressing. Everything went black. I felt like I was traveling at the speed of light inside a black tunnel. Suddenly I broke free of the darkness and found myself sailing through space. The stars were beautiful. I was joyously happy. I sailed through space as if I were a small plane.

I was in my child body. I was seven or eight. I did flips and dives and barrel rolls. I swooped down on a planet and saw beautiful deer like creatures bounding over tall grass which resembled wheat. I sailed in closer for a better look. Suddenly I found myself in the body of one of the deer creatures. I felt its joy and happiness as it ran side by side with its mate, leaping and bounding over the tall grass like two dancers performing an intricate ballet. I felt the intelligence and the love of these creatures. They were not dumb animals, they had souls and feelings and thoughts very much like mine. They were on the planet developing their ability to think and reason. The male deer was a mathematician; the female was a philosopher who told me she was going to be a famous Greek playwright when she got to Earth.

Something else happened while I was in the body of the female deer person. It's taken me a long time to piece together the strange sensations I felt while on the Deer Planet. I am just now beginning to comprehend what had really taken place. It's not time to talk about it now because I still don't fully understand it.

The stars called me again and I left the body of the deer people. I again sailed through the universe. I was headed for my home which I knew was near Sirius. I was racing home because I longed with all my heart to be back with my Father and my family. But the joy of being out of body and free to wander the universe was overwhelming. I was exhilarated with my newly found gift of flight. Instead of making a Beeline for home, I played in the universe. I circled and swooped down on several more planets.

On the last planet I visited, I sat at the top of a high canyon looking at the beautiful turquoise river that flowed below. There was dark green grass growing on the banks. The rock walls of the canyon were a beautiful blue, the color of lapis lazuli. Every now and then there was an orange streak in the blue. The colors were bright and exhilarating. I couldn't stop looking at them. While I was sitting, in a semi-trance, staring at the beauty, I heard sounds. The sounds had the ring of language, as if I were listening to two people talk.

I watched the river below. Soon two creatures appeared. Their bodies were human like. They had two legs and two arms with five fingered hands. Their heads were large and reptilian looking. They were greenish brown and covered with scales. They pulled themselves out of the water and lay down on the green grass near the water. I heard their laughter and felt the love that these two creatures had for each other. The longer I looked at them, the sadder I got. On an alien planet, light years from Earth, I saw and felt true love and devotion, things I had never known.

I sat there for a while, feeling sorry for myself. But then, the thought of going home and seeing my Father and my brothers and sisters, once again filled me with joy. I decided to stop visiting other planets and head straight for home as fast as I could. Once again I started sailing through space doing flips and rolls and thoroughly enjoying the freedom that being out of body gave me. Suddenly a huge white wall appeared in front of me, blocking my path. I skidded to a stop to keep from crashing into the white wall. I sailed to the right, but the wall was still there. I sailed to the left, but I could not get past the wall. I stopped and stared at it.

The white wall wasn't a wall. It was an off white roughly woven robe which was like a cross between burlap and light weight canvas. At the bottom of the robe were two very large feet wearing dark brown sandals. I suddenly realized that the being in the robe had his hand on my head keeping me from going anywhere. I heard his words inside my head,

"Where are you going in such a hurry?"

"I'm going home," I replied.

"You haven't even started your work on earth. Turn around and look at your home world. You have the secret of preparing your fellow students for their next evolutionary leap. Without your presence, your piece of the puzzle will be lost and the entire evolutionary experiment could fail."

I looked back at earth. I saw the planet ringed in a brown haze. The haze was the anger, hatred, rage, perversions, wars, and man's inhumanity to his fellow man. I shuddered and said silently, "Thank God I am out of there." Then, like a petulant child I crossed my little arms and told the man, "I won't go back. I don't want to go back. I'm going home, get out of my way. Don't you KNOW who I am?"

I could sense that the man in the white robe was very amused. Instead of answering my question, he asked:

"How is your husband going to feel when he wakes up in the morning and finds your dead body in bed next to him?"

Suddenly I could see into my bedroom. I saw my husband and in the next instant I was back in bed next to him. I hit with a jolt. I was wide-awake and filled with more energy than I had had in months. I got out of bed and made notes about what had just happened.

As the weeks went by, I began to regain my strength, but I was still very weak. I still had to spend many hours in bed. I used the time to practice the breathing technique the teacher taught us. As I breathed I felt different sensations arising in different parts of my body. Sometimes the sensation was very slow to leave. In these cases I channeled energy into the area. I noted that when I did this, the sensation quickly went away.

Sometimes I went into the memory that was attached to the sensation. Other times I simply experienced the sensation without looking deeper to find out what was behind it. I soon discovered that the sensations were like little cans of garbage. I could toss out the can without going through the garbage and re-experiencing it, or I could choose to go through the garbage and feel all the pain once again. I quickly decided that it was easier and faster just to dump the can without going through the garbage.

By April, I had recovered. When I got out of bed, I knew something had changed. I went from my deathbed to a hectic schedule. I had never been interested in politics or city government. Now I found myself on an adjunct planning committee for the city of Monterey. In addition to this, I accepted a job as fund raiser for a non profit heritage organization. I became the assistant editor for the newsletter of the local woman's Democratic club. Then I became the media coordinator for Senator Gary Hart's 1984 presidential campaign. I had never been interested in politics before my near death experience.

At this same time, I began experimenting with the new clearing process I had learned in the near death experience. I was experimenting with music, to balance the chakras; and breath, to clear the stored memories. I invited a group of friends to join me and learn the method as a group. I also was doing private sessions on an experimental basis with a group of volunteers.

By 1985, a friend and I were conducting Activated Cellular Memory (ACM) workshops... that is what I named the clearing process I was given during my out of body experience.

In 1987 I began to travel throughout the United States giving private and group sessions. The feedback from people who attended the workshops was incredible. Almost 98% of my students were able to release themselves from their bodies and travel through the universe as I had done. Each of them brought back valuable lessons from their journeys. They were also able to let go of much of the emotional garbage that had been trapped in their cells. Several women who had been in therapy for years told me that one session with me cut straight to the root of their problems and they were able to let go of the trauma.

Q: It is clear that you continued on your spiritual path, did you also continue on the political path?

A: Yes, I did. For a while I worked within the normal political organizations. Then I met a woman named Barbara Honegger. Barbara had worked in the 1980 Reagan campaign. When Reagan was elected she moved to Washington and took a job in the West Wing of the White House. She was the woman who was doing the research for implementing Reagan's alternative to the Equal Rights Amendment.

In 1983, Barbara realized that Ronald Reagan had no intention of ever implementing his ERA Alternative. She was extremely disillusioned because she genuinely believed in what she was doing. It took a great deal of courage for Barbara to resign her position in the Reagan White House and to publish her letter of resignation in the Washington Post. She was in the headlines for weeks. The National Organization of Women (NOW) picked her up and made her into a celebrity. The only thing that took her out of the headlines was KAL 007 being shot down by the Soviet Union.

Unknown to me, Barbara was from my area. When I saw a letter from her, to the editor of our local newspaper, I picked up the phone and called the only Honegger in the phone book. It turned out to be her mother's house, but Barbara was there and answered the phone. I was producing a radio show at the time and asked her to be a guest.

We became friends immediately and worked on a number of projects together. In 1984, Barbara had been the women's coordinator for the Jesse Jackson campaign. I had worked for Gary Hart. Both our candidates lost to Walter Mondale. Neither of us could support Mondale, so we batted around ideas of what we could do during this election year.

Barbara had evidence that the Reagan Campaign had stolen Jimmy Carter's debate briefing books and had used them to get an advantage over Carter during the debates. She even had photographs of the Carter Debate Briefing books lying on a table in the garage where the Reagan campaign team was preparing for the debate. She spent a few weeks putting together this research and writing an article. In those days, there was no place to publish articles like this. I don't know if it was ever published.

After she finished with this project, she and I discussed Reagan's Armageddon beliefs. It was 1984, and we both believed that Ronald Reagan was thoroughly in the grip of Christian Armageddonists who believed that the Biblical prophecy of Armageddon had to be fulfilled during Reagan's presidency.

The man Reagan appointed to be his Secretary of the Interior, James Watt, believed that it was fine to mine and log all of the earth, because our generation was going to be the last generation of people on earth. His famous quote "We don't have to protect the environment, The Second Coming is at hand," echoed the way many of the people who surrounded Reagan felt.

Barbara and I decided to put together a paper on Reagan's Armageddon beliefs. We turned the paper into an 8-page flyer that could be folded, addressed and mailed. We then addressed and mailed them to every radio and television station and every newspaper and magazine in the world.

About that time, I suffered a relapse. I don't know if I came down with meningitis again, or if I had never really recovered from the original illness. I ended up in bed for a few more months. It was during this time that I really practiced the lessons I had learned during my "Near Death Experience." I also used that time to listen to tapes and do a little reading. Reading was hard, because I couldn't sit up or bend my head. Most of the time, I just lay there and stared at the ceiling.

I was very angry with God and blamed Him for my illness. One day, after mentally screaming at God for hours, I was very exhausted and felt that I could finally sleep. I don't know if I actually went to sleep, or if I was awake when this happened. But I heard a voice. It said,

"Do you know what your problem is?" I didn't know what the voice meant, so I didn't answer. "Your problem is you think and act like a soldier, and a soldier never surrenders. You hate that Christian expression of, 'surrender to God'. You won't surrender to anyone, not even God."

The voice continued, "Instead of surrendering, why not just give up the fight? Stop fighting God! God doesn't fight back, therefore it isn't a war; therefore you *can't* surrender."

"You have to have two groups fighting each other, before you can consider it a war. Two armies have to fight each other before one can surrender. In *your* "battle" with God, the only one fighting is you. Stop fighting God. Just give up the fight!"

"You spend so much time being angry at God for putting you in bed that you don't even realize that He has given you a wonderful opportunity to be alone, in the solitude of your "cave," so you can spend some time working on yourself."

At this moment, I remembered my near death experience, and I knew that God had given me this "free time" so I could use it to work on all the garbage that was stored inside of me.

I spent about two and a half months in bed that time. The only reason I got out of bed was because a friend told me about an Archbishop in Santa Barbara named Warren Watters. I don't know why, but I KNEW that this was the man who had to baptize me.

I made an appointment to go see him. When I met him, we made the arrangements and I was baptized the following weekend. I stayed in his home with Warren and his wife, Ellen. Warren was 93 and Ellen was in her 80's. They were the most wonderful and loving people I had ever met. They both had a radiance surrounding them that everyone could see or feel.

Near the end of the weekend stay, Warren asked me if I wanted to be ordained in his Church, the Church of Antioch. I knew nothing about it, but I was certain that God would not have sent me there if I was not supposed to be ordained.

Warren and Ellen had a small chapel attached to their beautiful red-tiled adobe home. There were about four rows of pews with an altar at the front. It looked like any Christian church, just smaller.

During the ordination, Warren suddenly became very quiet. Ellen asked if something was wrong. The day was very hot and I think she was worried he was ill. He replied that Master Melchizedek had just joined us. I saw Ellen look up. Warren had his eyes closed. I looked up and saw the most incredible vision.

The ceiling had vanished. In its place was a multi-tiered cone that went up until it completely disappeared. Around each circular tier there were hundreds if not thousands of people watching me be ordained. Warren later said that this was the Ashram of Melchizedek and I had just been ordained into it also.

After the ceremony, I asked him about the other people who had been ordained into the Ashram of Melchizedek. He told me that this was the first time in his life that anything like this had happened to him. I asked him who Melchizedek was. He told me the few things he knew about Melchizedek, who was the original High Priest of Jerusalem. None of what he told me made any sense to me. It still doesn't. I may have been ordained into the Ashram of Melchizedek, but until I understand what this means, I have chosen to do nothing. This was one of the major lessons my teacher, Shamus taught me, "When you don't know what to do, do nothing."

After I came home from Santa Barbara, I spent most of my time working on the Activated Cellular Memory process. I put together classes and flyers and began teaching it. All the while, I was also working with Barbara Honegger on her various quasi-political projects.

In 1986, a crisis developed in the Middle East. Ronald Reagan had just ordered the bombing of Libya and he was threatening to bomb Syria. The Biblical Armageddon scenario looked like it was about to play out. Barbara and I went into action again. We needed to rewrite, update and reprint the information we had gathered in 1984.

One of Barbara's friends was the pianist, Byron Janis. He just happened to be visiting in our area at the time we were working on this. Barbara and I had been trying to figure out how we could get a copy of our work hand delivered to Pope John Paul II. Byron told us his wife was a friend of a woman who went to high school with Pope John Paul II. Byron also told us that he was a close friend of Nancy Reagan. We gave Byron our information. Within 48 hours of handing this information to Byron, Reagan stopped his threats to bomb Syria and the Armageddon scenario never raised its head again during the Reagan years.

Did the Pope and Nancy Reagan avert Armageddon in 1986?

I don't know. Someone should ask them.

Q: I know from prior conversations with you that during this time you had some experiences that are even stranger than the ones you have just described. You said some radio personalities and other well-known people have told you to keep quiet on these experiences because they feel you will lose your credibility. Do you feel you can share these experiences now?

A. I have been cautioned about talking about certain things. I have often wondered if the people who cautioned me to stay silent on these things were really worried about my credibility, or if they were trying to keep the lid on things. All right, for the first time ever in print, here's the story!

In 1986 I was taken to Mars by the Admiral who I later discovered was Gunther's direct boss and his uncle. This trip to Mars was three years *before* I married Gunther and *four* years before I officially met the Admiral.

This story is a hard one for me to tell. I am not sure how to begin. I still wonder if it actually happened, or if it was just a realistic dream. The experience was far too real to have been a dream. It is possible that I only traveled in my astral body. My psychic grandmother took me on out of body journeys when I was a child. The trip to Mars could have been a dream, or an out of body journey. But a very big part of me believes that it really happened.

In 1986 there were a series of events that happened within the span of a day, maybe two. This was right in the middle of the work Barbara and I were doing to get out the Armageddon information. The first event happened when my spirit guide, Shamus, told me that the Golden Armada was coming to earth tonight. He told me to go outside and look up in the sky.

A friend was with me. We went out. It was cold and damp. We stayed out for a very long time, but saw nothing. Finally I told Shamus that he had better give us a sign or we were going back inside. Before I even got the words out of my mouth, the biggest and bluest "falling star" I had ever seen, streaked across the sky. We had our sign, so we knew we had to stay out in the cold!

My friend went back inside and brought out blankets. We stayed outside looking up in the sky. Finally she pointed in a certain direction and told me to look past all the stars to what would be the edge of the universe. I followed her suggestion and sure enough, I saw the same thing she was seeing. What we saw was something that looked like giant fireworks. This occurred in 1986. I have now seen this phenomena in a few science fiction movies. They call it a star gate. I believe a fleet from another part of the Universe entered Earth's space that night.

Shamus said leaders of the Galactic Federation were coming to the Earth to attend a meeting of all the world leaders, which was being held in the Grand Tetons. Shamus said representatives from all inhabited planets would be in attendance.

Just at that moment, we heard the doorbell ring and went back inside. It was another friend. We sat there talking about what we had just seen. Finally one of us pointed to the plush rug. There were marks forming on it that looked like footprints. We all looked at the rug, and sure enough, it looked like an invisible person was walking toward us.

At that time in my spiritual development, I knew no fear. I asked who it was and what he wanted. Suddenly I could see the person. He was dressed in a silver flight suit. He introduced himself as Commander Shubreadth and said that he was there to ask my permission for the C-Cubed unit to be installed.

I knew that a C-Cubed unit was for Command, Control and Communication. He said it was to guide the Golden Armada in their journeys to and from earth. I asked him why he wanted to put it in my house. He answered that I had divine protection around me and if it were in my house, it would be safe. I asked a few more questions, all of which he answered to my satisfaction, so I gave him permission to set the C-Cubed unit up.

Suddenly, a group of similarly dressed beings began carrying all sorts of things into my condominium. Instead of building it in the condo, they built it in the stairwell. About halfway through their installation, the doorbell rang. Needless to say, it scared all of us out of our skin. It was about 1AM. We all wondered who would be ringing the doorbell at that time. I think we must have unconsciously feared it was "the men in black."

It turned out to be one of my nieces. She said that she was driving by, saw our lights on and knew something was going on. One of the reasons we jumped when the doorbell rang was because it was the back door and not the front door. When I asked my niece why she came to the back door, she said that she did not feel comfortable going up the stairs inside the stair well. The back door did not have a stairwell. The stairwell was where the C-Cubed module was being built.

When she got inside the condo, she looked over in the far corner, where the installation of the C-Cubed module was going on. No one had yet said anything to her about what had been happening. "What is going on over there?" she exclaimed. She could also see the men in silver uniforms carrying in the boxes from which they constructed the C-Cube module.

After the installation was complete, commander Shubreadth came back and said that they were finished. He said that it was a self-running installation. He said that when it was no longer needed, it would fade away.

About two or three in the morning, my niece and friends left. I put on a white night gown and went to bed.

The next thing I knew, I was standing in a dry creek bed. The dirt was red, and somehow I knew I was in Arizona. It was night. Everything was illuminated by the moon. I looked around and saw ten or eleven other women. They were all in their nightclothes as I was. No one spoke. We walked around slowly, looking at each other and our surroundings.

Suddenly, without sound, a golden ball began to materialize. It was about fifteen to twenty feet high. A door opened, and a man with white hair and blue eyes walked down the steps. "It is time to go." he said as he motioned us to get on board.

I was one of the first inside. I was almost directly across from the door. There was a bench that ran along the edge of the round room. Each woman sat down in front of her own window. There were twelve windows and the door. The man sat on a seat in front of the door. He said that we were going for a short ride. He told us to look out the windows because the view was going to be beautiful. I followed his advice.

I don't remember him telling us we were going to Mars, yet I knew that was where we were headed. I could see Mars in the distance. The red planet grew larger and larger, until it filled the entire window. I could see that all the women were now looking out the windows on my side of the Golden Globe.

Without sound or warning, the man with the white hair stood up and opened the door. We had come to rest on the red planet. Our trip took about half an hour or less. One by one, the women silently filed out the door of the Globe. Not one of us had spoken to the others.

Each woman was met by a man in a gray uniform with yellow piping and patches. I watched the other women as they were led to different areas. The place where we landed looked like a freeway underpass system. There were several large entryways which led down into the red planet. The Golden globe had landed on a flat piece of ground which seemed to set on top the underground passages. There was a fence or guardrail around the landing area. The section where we disembarked was the only place we could exit.

I was the last to leave the golden globe. As I stood at the doorway I saw two of the women who had been in the globe with me. They were walking with their arms around the men who had met them. It appeared as if they knew and loved the men.

There was no one there to meet me. I looked at the man with the white hair. He read my mind and sent back the answer. I am your guide. He walked away from the landing area and the underground passages. He headed toward the red rocks that were in front of us. I can remember thinking; "There is an atmosphere on Mars. Why haven't our scientists told us about it?"

I heard the man answer me, "If they told you, there would be an overwhelming rush to colonize Mars. We don't want that."

As we walked closer to the red rocks, I could see that there were caves carved in the rocks. The man corrected my thinking. "They aren't caves, and they aren't rocks. These are living structures. On earth we would call them apartments, but these apartments are made from living crystals. The crystals create an energy field that keeps the people who live in these structures in perfect health. When the Martians lived here, there was no sickness, there was no death."

I climbed the rocks and walked inside one of the structures. I could feel something touching me. It gave me a shiver. I heard the man tell me, "Don't worry. It will not harm you. It is sensing your energy system. If you spent the night here, you would go home in perfect health."

My mind was already thinking, "How can we bring these crystal beings to earth?"

The man silently answered, "We already have. We are trying to duplicate the process that the Martians used to make these structures." I quickly discovered that not only could the man communicate with me telepathically, but he could put pictures in my mind. The man showed me the dome-like structures that they had created using the crystal beings in a mixture of concrete like substance.

The man said he had more to show me and started back down the hill. He stopped at a wall that came up to his waist. The wall had hidden a passageway that led down into an underground structure. The man went ahead of me. The light was filtered. It took a moment for my eyes to adjust. When I got to the bottom of the stairs I saw a long hall with picture windows on each side.

When I first saw it, I thought that it must be some kind of indoor zoo. The windows appeared to hold different scenes. I don't know why I thought it was a zoo, but that was the first thought that popped into my mind. I could almost hear the man laugh as I thought 'zoo'.

He told me to take a look and tell him what I was seeing. As I approached each picture window I saw that there was no glass. I could look through the picture windows at scenes I couldn't understand. I didn't know what I was looking at. Some of the scenes appeared to be swirling clouds and fog. Other scenes were of meadows and grass. "Could it be a picture album left by the people who used to live here?" I asked.

The man didn't laugh at my question. "That is a very good thought, but no. This was not what Mars looked like."

The man read my mind and realized I had no idea what I was seeing. He said, "This is a space-time portal. When the Martians knew they were going to lose their atmosphere, they knew they had to find a new planet on which to live. Earth was their first choice. It was nearby and easily accessible with their spacecraft. But earth was in a creation process thirteen million years ago."

The man told me that the Martians did not have the technology to travel in spaceships outside of this solar system and none of the planets in this solar system were ready to support life. He said the Martian scientists turned their attention to creating space/time machines.

About half way down the long hall, the man stopped me and pointed to a window. This is the portal to earth.

I thought you said that earth was not habitable 13 million years ago. It wasn't, he replied. This portal leads to earth, approximately 50,000 years ago, earth time. From a Martian point of view, it is 13 million . . . minus 50, 000 . . . earth years in the future. Come with me and have a look.

The man stepped through the window or portal. He stood there waiting for me to join him. I looked in and tried to figure out what kind of room he was in. It was dark and glowed with a green light. I really couldn't see anything but the man.

Once I stepped through the portal, it closed behind me. We were in some kind of underground cave. We stood on a rock platform that was surrounded on all sides by water. It was very dim; I could not see anything very well. From the water I heard a voice. It was irreverent and humorous, "Are the two of you going to stand there all day, or are you going to come with me?"

I looked down and saw a creature that looked like a dolphin with the head of a catfish... a really cute catfish! The man led me to the stairs and we walked down into the water. There were two dolphin-like creatures waiting for us. He grabbed the fin of one and gestured for me to do the same thing.

I heard the dolphin creature tell me that the Martians designed the entrance to earth to make sure no one could get through the portals unless they were invited and wanted. The dolphin-like creatures were the guardians of the portals. Without them, no one could ever find their way out of the portal and onto the earth.

The two dolphin creatures swam for a very long time. Finally they skidded to a stop up a golden brick ramp. The talking dolphin creature said, "This is where the two of you get off. We will see you on the other side."

The man with the white hair was the first to climb to his feet. He offered me his hand and helped me up out of the water. I felt strangely refreshed and alive. Almost like there was something in the water that nurtured me and healed me.

As I was thinking the thought I heard the man reply, "When earth was younger and non-polluted, ordinary water was healing water."

I walked by his side to the doors at the top of the ramp. He pushed the two doors open. The first things I saw were beautiful columns and temples. The colors were vibrant turquoises and orange and yellow. The land was lush with trees and grass. I saw the two dolphin creatures swim out from under the temple.

There was a canal that surrounded the area. The water was crystal clear. There were many other types of fish swimming in the canal. When the people saw the dolphin creatures, they fell to their knees and seemed to pray before them.

I looked at the man, he answered, "The dolphins are sacred to these people. The dolphins take care of them. They don't appear very often. The people haven't noticed us yet. The dolphins are telling them about us. Wait a moment; you are going to be surprised."

After a few moments, a young man came over to us. He kneeled before us. I tried to pull him up but the man with me stopped me. When the young man stood up, he said, in perfect English, "Welcome to Egypt. I am your guide."

We followed the young boy down the steps of the temple. The man told me that the dolphins had read our thoughts and instantly taught the boy to speak our language.

The young boy led us through their city. There were no cars; none were needed because the area was not large enough for cars to be needed. There appeared to be thousands of people living there. Their skin was medium brown and their facial features were similar to the people of Italy. They were very beautiful.

We were taken to the edge of the city where the fields that grew the crops were. I could see fields of green with people working. There were also trees and bushes. Everything was so beautiful it looked like a park.

The young boy handed me an orange fruit that looked like an apricot. I looked at the man, "Eat it," he said, "You will never in your life taste anything as sweet."

The last thing I remember is the wonderful sweet taste of the fruit. The next thing I remember is floating through space. I was lying horizontally. I could faintly remember being told to keep my eyes closed. I fought to open them. Above me I saw a space ship. I was in some kind of beam that was moving me through the roof of my apartment and putting me back in my bed. I was dressed in a long white night gown, and I could feel the silk fabric flutter against my arms.

I fought to stay awake long enough to write myself enough notes so I would remember my trip

When I woke up the next morning, there was red dirt in my bed. I wondered where I could have gotten red dirt on my feet. Then I saw my notebook wide open on the bed stand. The first word I saw was MARS followed by Golden Globe . . . and other key words. By the time I had finished reading the code words, I had remembered the entire experience.

I called one of my friends into my bedroom. I told her what had happened to me and showed her the notes I had written. Then I showed her the red dirt in my bed. Four years later, I met the man with the white hair on Offutt Air Force Base. He was my husband's BIG boss. He was also my husband, Gunther's uncle. He was also the one who took me to meet the King of the World.

I have wanted to tell the story of my trip to Mars for a long time. Friends who know the story have advised to keep it to myself. They fear it will cause me to lose all credibility.

I don't know if I went to Mars. I know there was red dirt in my bed when I woke up. Did I go to Mars or just to Arizona? I can't give you an answer. What I do know is the man in the dream turned out to be my husband Gunther's boss, a four star Admiral in Navy Intelligence, and at the time I met him in 1989, on Offutt Air Force Base, he was the Director of Covert Operations for the CIA.

If the Admiral did not take me to Mars, then someone went to a lot of trouble to make me think that he did. About a week after I met the Admiral on Offutt, he took me on another journey. He took me to meet the King of the World. The only two times I have gone on unusual journeys in my physical body, it has been with the Admiral.

Q: What did you do after you realized what had happened? Did you lecture about your trip? Did you make it part of your work? How did it affect you, and do you think it had any impact on what you were doing at the time?

A: I don't think it had any impact on what I was doing. In fact, I can only remember telling one friend about it. She was staying with at the time. I brought her into my bedroom to show her the stains left by the red dirt. For some reason, it was very upsetting to me, and I wanted to put it out of my mind. I continued doing workshops, seeing clients and when Barbara needed my help, I helped her.

Q: In 1988 your husband, John died. You moved to New York City and began teaching and giving workshops in the ACM method. You also were traveling to Washington DC to see clients and give workshops. You met Senator Claiborne Pell at this time, How did that happen?

A: A friend introduced us. She knew about his interest in Near Death Experience, and she knew that a Near Death Experience (NDE) changed my life dramatically.

While I was talking to the Senator, I told him about the Activated Cellular Memory process. He wanted to experience it, so I gave him a private ACM treatment. Senator Pell had just hosted a large conference on the Near Dear Experiences. There is a book written about the conference. It is called "Proceeding of the Symposium on Consciousness and Survival. An Interdisciplinary Inquiry into the Possibility of Life Beyond Biological Death" The book was published by the Noetics Institute in Sausalito.

Senator Pell was impressed with my experience and the depth of my information and abilities. Each time I was in Washington, I called him. We usually met for lunch or dinner. On one visit, he told me that his committee was funding a top-secret project that dealt with a number of the things the Soviets had pioneered in the psychic world. I was familiar with the psychic work the Soviets were doing. I was very interested in his project and we discussed it several times.

At this same time, in California, Barbara Honegger was working on a book exposing the main scandal of the Reagan/Bush years, The October Surprise. She was helping one of the men who had just been charged with lying to a judge. The man, Richard Brenneke, had told a judge that a career CIA operative named Donald Gregg, (who had just been nominated by President Bush to become the Ambassador to South Korea), was involved in the October Surprise.

All nominees for Ambassador have to be confirmed by the Senate Foreign Relations Committee. Senator Pell was the Chairman of that Committee. Because Barbara knew Senator Pell was a friend of mine, she asked me to hand deliver a packet of information regarding Donald Gregg's involvement in the October Surprise.

I agreed to do this. On my next trip to Washington, I made an appointment and delivered the packet. The Senator said he would look it over and we would talk about it over dinner that evening.

We went to a Thai restaurant in Georgetown. As we walked in, Senator Pell said hello to many different people. One man, at the far end of the room, stood up, waved and said, "Hi, Senator." In other words, it was obvious that everyone there knew who he was.

We sat down, looked at the menus and ordered. After the waitress left, Senator Pell, pulled out the packet I gave him, dropped it in the middle of the table and began to talk very loudly and sternly. Many people would say he was yelling at me. I have rarely been talked to like this by anyone, especially a United States Senator. He was angry that I had used our friendship to try to influence his vote on Donald Gregg. His voice was so loud that everyone in the restaurant stopped eating and was staring at us. I was not about to let him ruffle my feathers or upset me.

When he stopped yelling at me, I said, very politely, "Are you finished?" He nodded. In a firm voice I said, "Just because we are friends, you are saying that you do not want to know about crimes and treason being committed by high ranking government officials?"

I could see that the other people in the room were riveted on our conversation. I can't remember how he responded to my question, because what he did next completely knocked me off center. In the same loud voice he had used to berate me, he said, "Do you remember that project I was telling you about? I want you to come to work for me and oversee it."

I was stunned into silence. He lowered his voice and asked me if I would become his assistant in the Foreign Relations Committee. He had earlier told me that the project was being carried in the Foreign Relations Committee budget. Knowing we were still being watched by almost everyone in the restaurant, I told him I would think about it and give him an answer in a few days.

We finished dinner with no more unusual happenings. The Senator took me home. I talked with my hostess for an hour or two and then went to bed.

That evening, at about 2 am, the feel of someone brushing up against my neck awakened me. When I opened my eyes, I saw a man in a black cape. He was wearing a large black hat that flopped down over his face. I felt he was trying to suck blood from my neck. I was terrified and petrified. I could *not* move a muscle. I was frozen either in fear or by other means.

I knew that if I allowed this man to suck my blood that I would die. Instantly I knew what I had to do. I had been taught sacred words to ward off evil. I could not speak or move, but I could think. I began thinking the words as strongly as I could.

Kadoish, Kadoish, Kadoish, Adonai Sabeyoth
Kadoish, Kadoish, Kadoish, Adonai Sabeyoth
Kadoish, Kadoish, Kadoish, Adonai Sabeyoth

After the first syllable, of the word Kadoish was thought, the man in the cape quickly raised his arm to shield his face. It was as if I had hit him. With the second set of words, the man backed away from the bed. He was still looking at me, ready to strike again if he could.

By the time I had finished the third set of words, my voice came back. I repeated the words out loud.

Kadoish, Kadoish, Kadoish, Adonai Sabeyoth

Kadoish, Kadoish, Kadoish, Adonai Sabeyoth

Kadoish, Kadoish, Kadoish, Adonai Sabeyoth

Each time I said them, I grew stronger. Each time I said them, the vampire grew weaker. The man, or astral body, that had touched me felt physical, I felt the touch of his hands on my neck and shoulders. But as my voice grew stronger and I was able to forcefully speak the sacred words, I saw him begin to dissipate. As he dissipated he retreated further and further from me, as if he felt being close to me would cause him harm. He finally backed up into my closet and vanished.

I stayed awake most of the night thinking about what had just happened. I knew Senator Pell had friends who were advanced enough in their psychic abilities to be able to manifest out of body and do things in their astral bodies. I believed that whoever had visited me was probably associated with the Senator in some way. The next day I called and read him the riot act. I have often wondered what the spies who tap all the phones in Washington must have thought when I accused him of visiting me in his astral body.

Of course he denied that it was him, but some of the things he said made me believe he knew about it, and had possibly ordered it. During my tirade, he asked again if I was going to take the job. I told him I would give him an answer once I got back from Virginia Beach.

My husband John's ashes had been scattered on Virginia Beach. I wanted to say goodbye to him before I closed that chapter of my life and moved on. I rented a red Mustang convertible and drove from Washington DC to Virginia Beach. It was a beautiful sunny day. I put the top down and let my hair blow in the wind. It was a beautiful day, and I wanted to put the vampire completely out of my mind.

When I got to Virginia Beach, I chose to stay at the Cavalier hotel, across the street from the beach. I put on my two piece suit, grabbed my towels and walked down to sunbathe. I had not been there long when I saw two men in trench coats on a catwalk to the left of me. It was hot and sunny, why were these men wearing overcoats? When I looked at them again, they were taking pictures of me with a camera that had a long lens. I remembered that Senator Pell told me I had to undergo a background check. I figured these men were part of that background check.

I decided that I looked great in my two-piece and wondered if I could ask them for copies. I lay back down and relaxed as the sun warmed and relaxed me. I was thinking about the "vampire" attack the night before, wondering if I had dreamed the whole thing, or if it had really happened.

Suddenly I felt a stabbing pain in my stomach. It was so intense it felt like someone had hit me with a hot knife. It took a while for me to recover from the pain. When I did, I noticed that I had started bleeding. I figured it was my menstrual cycle and chalked up the excessive pain to stress. I wrapped the towel around me and used it to mop up the blood as it flowed down my leg. I hurriedly ran back to the Cavalier Hotel, trying to keep from leaving a trail of blood behind me.

Once I got back to my room, I realized that the amount of blood I was losing was definitely *not* normal. I waited for a few hours to see if the bleeding would subside. It didn't. I was afraid to go to a hospital. I had been working with Barbara on the October Surprise project and I was afraid I might be killed if I went to a hospital. I wondered what to do.

I realized that I needed a friend in Virginia Beach to help me, and yet I didn't know a soul. My late husband had grown up in Virginia Beach. He had dated Edgar Cayce's granddaughter. I decided to call the Cayce Institute and tell them the whole story, including the reason I couldn't go to a regular hospital. It turned out that the grandson of Edgar Cayce's doctor had just moved back to town. He was a friend of the woman I was talking to. She arranged an appointment with him.

He was able to stop the bleeding long enough for me to catch a plane and fly back to California where I could be treated by my family doctor. By the time I got off the plane, I was bleeding heavily again. The pain was unbearable. My mother drove me directly to my family doctor. He examined me and said that he felt I was suffering from an ailment called metropathia hemorrhagica. It is excessive uterine bleeding brought on by stress or grief. It mimics childbirth. The uterus goes into contractions. Because there is no baby to push out, the uterus pushes itself out.

I had lost a great deal of blood. He advised me to get a blood transfusion. I declined the transfusion due to the fact that our blood supply was not pure in those days. He said I would have to spend about six weeks in bed.

During my illness, Senator Pell called almost daily. He told me he was planning a trip to Pakistan and he wanted to take me with him as his assistant. I told him that I was too weak to go.

Q: What kept you from accepting the job with Senator Pell? Was it the so-called "vampire" attack?

A.: No. At that time, I didn't associate the vampire attack with the loss of blood that happened the next day. I didn't even associate the men on the cat walk with the loss of blood. I was planning on accepting his job offer just as soon as I was well enough.

Q: You just said you didn't associate the loss of blood with the men on the cat walk. What did you mean by that?

A: At the time I thought they were taking pictures for my background check. But since that time I have discovered that there are "beam weapons" that look like a camera with a long lens. Men who work for intelligence agencies believe I was hit with some kind of microwave beam.

Q: So what was it that kept you from taking the job?

A: I met Gunther Russbacher, fell in love and married him.

After six weeks of bed rest, I was feeling almost back to normal. I was still very weak and could only stay out of bed for about six hours at a time. My mother asked if I felt well enough to drive her and my niece to Tacoma, Washington. I said if we could stop whenever I got tired, I could do it.

As we were entering Medford, Oregon, I suddenly become so weak that I believed I was passing out. I knew I had to pull off the road and find a motel. I took the first exit. Only one motel had vacancies. There was no place else to go, and since I was so weak I was about to pass out. We stayed at that motel.

We checked in about 4pm. I lay down and took a nap. At six, I woke up. My mother and I wanted to go to dinner. My niece didn't want to go, so I ordered room service for her. While we were waiting for it, I turned on the television. There had just been a horrific automobile accident a few miles north of Medford. Many people were killed in the fiery crash.

My niece's dinner came and my mother and I walked down to the restaurant, to have dinner. The restaurant was roped off. It looked closed. As we started to walk away, a woman came running after us. "Do you want to eat dinner?" she asked. I said yes. She opened up the rope and she showed us into an empty dining room. I can't swear to it, but I believe she actually put the rope back up, to block off the entrance.

We ordered and as we were waiting for our dinner to come, a tall, thin man approached the entrance. He stood at the entrance for a while, looking over the dining room as if he was looking for someone. The room was empty except for my mother and me. When he saw us, he came in and sat down one table away from us, in the non-smoking section.

As he stood, at the entrance, I said to my mother, "I know that man. He's a navy officer. I know him from the Navy School."

I thought about the first time I had ever saw him. It was at an afternoon cocktail party for visiting dignitaries. He was dressed in a dark suit, standing at parade rest, on the perimeter of the room. I said to a friend, "He looks just like Sean Connery. Do you know who he is?" My girl friend was the wife of one of the other Deans. We walked over to talk to him. He fidgeted and squirmed and barely answered any of our questions. A few moments later, our husbands came over and led us away. I later found out that he was there as bodyguard for one of the dignitaries

After he seated himself in the restaurant, the first thing he did was light a cigarette. I quickly reminded him he was in the non-smoking section. Instead of getting up and walking away, he put out his cigarette. By that time, the waitress had brought him a glass of California house wine. He tasted it and complained bitterly to me and to the waitress.

I sarcastically said, "It's obvious you don't know anything about wine."

He puffed himself up and declared, "My family has been in the wine business for six hundred years. I know *everything* about wine."

I replied in a condescending voice, "It's obvious they weren't making wine in California or you would know better that to order house wine!"

He was silent for a moment. It looked like he was thinking about wringing my neck. He then turned to my mother and said, "Is she always like this?"

My mother nodded her head and said, "Yes."

Then he looked at me again. "Don't I know you?"

"Yes," I answered, copying the shy way in which my mother had answered.

Then, with much agitation he started shaking his finger at me saying, "You. . . you're . . . you're that *dean's* wife. What's his name . . . Dyer! You're Dean Dyer's wife!"

I shook my head yes. I knew he couldn't have forgotten me. I first met him in the mid to late 70s. Each time he came to the Navy School after that, I loved to tease him. He was so solemn and all business. I loved saying things I knew would get a reaction from him, such as, "I don't see why the Navy won't let women fly planes or be on submarines." I could literally see steam coming out of him as he stifled his response so he wouldn't offend the Dean's wife.... Meaning me!

There were many of those kinds of moments, but the moment I remember him best was in the early 80's. The Naval Postgraduate School was getting a new Superintendent. The new man was Commodore Robert Shoemaker. Commodore Shoemaker had been a POW in Viet Nam. He was one of the men who had been held the longest by the North Viet Namese. The post at the Navy School was his first command position since being released from the Hanoi Hilton.

His installation was one of the most formal ones that I had attended. It was held on the lawn in front of the main building of the Navy School. The Navy School had been the Old Del Monte Hotel, where kings and queens, movie stars and famous people from all over the world used to vacation. The architecture is a Spanish four story white building with a red tile roof.

The installation was being held on the outside bandstand. Around the perimeter there was a sea of naval officers in their dress blue uniforms. Each had a sword at his side. There were more officers than normal at this installation. Many former POWs had come to pay their respects to Commodore Shoemaker. I found out later that Gunther was at the installation because he had been a POW in the undeclared war in Laos.

After the ceremony was over, my husband, John had to get his briefcase from his office. We walked into the main building and up the stairs to the mezzanine where the Deans' and Superintendent's offices were. While my husband went into his office to get his briefcase and make a few phone calls, I went into the ladies room. I caught a glimpse of myself in the mirror. I was wearing a black and white sleeveless polka dot summer dress. I had on a black patent belt with matching high heeled black patent sandals. After fixing my hair and putting on more lipstick, I started to step out the door into the long hall that led to my husband's office.

As I opened the door I saw two Navy officers. They were in their dress blues and having a sword fight. One of them was a much better sword fighter than the other one. He quickly knocked the sword out of his opponent's hand. Another officer came running up with two glasses of cognac. He gave them to the swordsmen. The winner raised his glass, as if he meant to toast the loser, but instead he turned to me.

I was still frozen in the doorway. He came over, put one hand on the wall near the door, and raised his glass. He was so close to me I could see the hairline scar above his lip. I was uncomfortable, almost frightened. He was so forward. I was not used to this kind of treatment from Navy officers.

At that moment, my husband, John came out the door of his office. He saw what was going on and said to the man, "That's my wife sailor, touch her and you're a dead man." John then grabbed me by the arm and pushed me down the hall ahead of him. As we quickly walked away, I asked John who the man was. "He's a spook from DC. Don't have anything to do with him." John had never said that about anyone before. Needless to say, it made me even more curious as to who this Naval officer really was.

Now, here he was, in Medford, Oregon; sitting next to me in a restaurant. He admitted that he never knew my first name and I admitted I never knew his last name. He introduced himself to me as "Gunther Russbacher."

"Gunther?" I said, "I remember you as "Bob." He looked uncomfortable for a moment and replied.

"My mother was Austrian. When we came to this country after the war she would introduce me as her "bobby." She couldn't say "baby." The Americans thought my name was "Bobby," and it stuck. As I got older I became "Bob." It sounded like a reasonable explanation. I didn't question it at the time. I later found out that Bob was the nickname of his Navy Intelligence alias, Captain Robert Andrew Walker.

As we talked, I realized that the spark of joy I always felt when I saw him was still there. There was fascinating chemistry between us that had never been explored. After we finished dinner, he asked if we would join him for a nightcap. My mother said she needed to get back to the room to be with her granddaughter. I agreed to meet him in the cocktail lounge after I walked my mother back to her room.

I returned to the bar and stood in front, about to open the door. There was a small window next to the door. Through the window I saw Gunther. I heard his voice as he laughed and joked with the men who were with him. Then, out of no where, I was stopped in my tracks. I heard a voice, as clearly as I could hear the voices in the bar. It said, "If you go through that door, your life will change forever. Are you strong enough?"

I thought about everything I had just been through. Losing a husband, moving from a small town to New York City, being attacked by a vampire and almost bleeding to death. I figured if I could go through all of this and survive, I could go through anything. I pulled open the door and entered.

Gunther saw me and motioned me to a table, away from the men in the corner. A waitress came to take our orders. She was awfully curious about who I was and why I was there. I answered all of her questions and she left. She returned with my beer and his cognac. It took me a year to figure out that she was not a waitress. Her name was Marilyn. She was an Air Force Colonel and part of Gunther's team.

After she left, Gunther lifted his glass and said, "Once a Templar . . ." I quickly raised my glass, smashed it into his, in the traditional Templar toast, and finished the toast for him ". . . always a Templar!"

He looked startled, "How did you know that?"

"I am a student of esoteric history and the Templars are my main interest. I have researched them for years. I have even lectured on the Templars at the United Nations." I boasted.

He looked at me and said, "You may think you know about the Templars, but no one knows the truth about the Templars. No one."

I was just about to argue with him, when suddenly, he began to physically change. This was long before the term "shape shifter" came into use. I could not believe what was happening to him. There in front of me, a slim, balding man with dark brown hair began to bulk up with muscles. His brown eyes became blue, his dark, thinning hair became blonde, thick and wavy. I could not believe what I was seeing.

He looked at me with a look that seemed to be a million light years away. He lowered his voice and whispered, "I am Atalon, and you are my other half. I have searched the combined universes for millions of years. Now that I have found you, *no one* will *ever* be able to separate us."

I was floored. There was no way he could have known about The Obergon Chronicles and Atalon. At that time, only about a thousand people had read the story. Those were the people on my once a month mailing list.

He quickly came back to normal and asked, "What the hell happened?" I didn't know how to answer him. I was so upset and knocked off center by what had just happened, that I decided to change the subject and ignore what had just happened. Gunther had just become Atalon, the soul that was created to join with my soul. Atalon was the soul who was my other half. I had been searching for him for years. Now that I found a man who said he was Atalon, I was so overwhelmed I couldn't even talk about it. I quickly changed the subject, and tried to pretend that the "Atalon" part of him had never appeared.

I searched for something to ask him in order to change the subject. When we were in the restaurant, Gunther said he was an assistant U.S. Attorney out of Denver. My friend Richard Brenneke, who was part of the October Surprise, had just been charged with perjury, by the U.S. attorney in Denver. I wanted to ask Gunther some questions about the case. What I did not know was if I was jumping out of the frying pan and into the fire… or line of fire! I knew I had to phrase my question carefully.

I said, "If you're a U.S. attorney out of Denver, you must know Richard Brenneke."

I was not prepared for his response. The strong and confident man, who sat across from me, collapsed into a shaking puddle of tears. I couldn't believe what I was seeing. One moment he 'shape shifts' into a handsome young man who says he is my other half, and now he crumbles into a fetal position and tears literally spurted from his eyes. I could hardly believe this was the same Naval officer who always seemed to "in control" at the Naval Postgraduate School.

Gunther tried to gain control himself by grabbing the edge of the small cocktail table. He grabbed it so hard he made the table shake just as he was shaking. He said haltingly, through his tears, "I know Richard. I love Richard. They're framing Richard."

I could not believe it. The emotion in his voice told me that not only did he *know* Richard, but he cared about Richard, like a friend or brother. All I could say, was, "You really *do* know Richard."

"Richard's my cousin. We were raised together in Winnemucca." I knew Richard was from Winnemucca, so I figured Gunther was telling me the truth. How could anyone fake this kind of emotion?

"Richard's being sacrificed." he said.

"What do you mean?" I asked.

"Lower your voice." Gunther cautioned me. "Those assholes in the corner are FBI."

Gunther and I spent the rest of the night talking. At about 5 am he said, "Let's get married." I could hardly believe I said yes. I didn't even know him. Yes, we had friends in common, and yes, we were both used to the navy life. But he was a stranger to me. I couldn't believe that I had agreed to marry a stranger. But even as I thought this, the thought vanished. I remembered the way he 'shape shifted' into Atalon, and I realized that I had finally found my other half. What did it matter if I didn't know him? We were brother and sister, the children of the Great Lord Odon. Here before me, in a hotel in Oregon, was the soul mate I had dreamed about my whole life. After finally finding him, was there any doubt we would marry???

Several days later, we were in Tacoma Washington. He said he had called his boss earlier and requested permission to marry me. He said the answer would be coming, via the phone, any minute. The telephone rang. It was a friend of his, from the CIA, who had done the background check on me. The friend told Gunther there was no way we would be cleared to marry.

His friend read off the list of reasons. After Gunther was told that my best friend was Barbara Honegger, he looked at me and said, "You're Barbara Honegger's best friend?"

I nodded yes and watched as he slapped himself on the forehead.

He turned back to the phone. He listened for a few more minutes, then turned to me again.

"Did you try to rob a jewelry store in New York City?"

"Of course I didn't," I protested.

"Well the FBI has that in your record."

"What jewelry store?" I asked

"The one in the Plaza Hotel," he replied.

I had only been to the Plaza once. I knew the day that I had been there. A girl friend had taken me there to see the necklace she was going to talk her boyfriend into buying for her. I later found out that her boyfriend was an old friend of Gunther's. Their fathers had known each other in Germany during the war.

"How did the FBI know that I was there at that time?" I asked.

He repeated the question over the telephone. A few minutes later Gunther turned to me and asked, "Were you just about to go to work for Senator Pell?" I shook my head yes. "He was having you checked out for a security clearance."

"What do you mean?" I wanted to know.

"You were being followed by the guys who do background checks." Gunther replied. "You passed your background clearance for working for a Senator, but *not* for being my wife. Your friendship with Barbara Honegger is going to cause us problems."

"What do you mean, my friendship with Barbara is going to cause us problems?" I asked him.

Gunther replied, "They told me we have to wait two years before they will even give us an answer. This is the policy after someone like me gets divorced and wants to marry again." I didn't think about it at the time, but he never answered my question about Barbara.

He quickly added, "Or we can get married in the morning and face the consequences later."

The next morning we flew to Reno in his private Learjet and were married. We returned to the plane and headed back to Washington.

The pilots had bought us a bottle of wine. Gunther opened it and poured us each a glass. We were sitting together on the back seat of the Learjet buzzing with happiness and excitement. The pilot's voice interrupted us. "Chief," I heard him say, "Our air space has been violated, we've been ordered to arm." I couldn't have heard him right. Did he say "ordered to arm?"

The telephone in the back of the plane was not working. Gunther got up and went forward to talk to the pilot. I followed Gunther to the cabin and listened as the pilot told him our air space had been invaded by a small prop job. They had been ordered to arm. Gunther looked out the windows.

The Lear jet had fuel tanks on the wings. Gunther said earlier that they were there so the jet could make it to Europe without refueling. There was no reason for me to think any differently . . . until now.

I saw the front of the fuel tank slowly open. I saw missiles moving out of the pod. A thousand questions filled my mind. What kind of a plane was I flying in? Who had I just ?

The next few seconds moved in slow motion. The copilot said to the pilot, "Nose cannon fully armed . . . missiles locked in position." It was true… I had seen missiles.

The pilot told Gunther that a small plane had entered our airspace. He said that Nellis had scrambled a fighter escort to force the plane down and take us home to Boeing field. Gunther and I returned to the rear of the plane. Gunther asked me if I had heard what had been said. I nodded. He looked distressed. He should have been. We hadn't even been an hour, and already he was beginning to face the problems that his boss, "the Admiral" had known would arise.

I sat in silence for a moment, trying to figure out what was more important; wondering about what kind of plane was out there and if it was going to shoot us down, or wondering what kind of plane I was in and who these people were?

Gunther was sitting by my side looking troubled. It was as if he had suddenly realized what he had done and the danger he had put me in.

"What kind of a plane is this?" I whispered weakly. So many thoughts were running through my head. I couldn't believe that a Navy Captain would have a plane like this—even a Navy Captain that was attached to a U.S. Attorney's office wouldn't have a plane like this!

Who was this man? I had heard stories about our government being involved in drug trafficking. Had I just a government drug trafficker? Drug dealers had planes like this. International crime figures had planes like this. I remembered seeing the international bank accounts in his briefcase. I remembered how he talked about his "family." What kind of "family" had I married into?

I was preparing to hear the worst. I figured I had married the "Mob." Gunther gently took my hands and said; "Honey, this is the Blackbird." he was talking about the Learjet. "It was William Casey's private jet. After he died I got it."

Barbara Honegger had just read me an article about William Casey, the former Director of the CIA. Casey died just as he was about to tell the whole story to the Iran/Contra committee. I had read other stories about Casey's clandestine trips to Central America in a Learjet. Was this that Lear jet?

Gunther continued, "Up until 1986 I was the number three man in the CIA."

I had prepared myself for the worst . . . Colombian drug dealers. . .Sicilian mob family. . . but nothing could have prepared me for this . . . this WAS the worst. I had married the number three man in the CIA!

"No," I said as if trying to make him take it back. My mind was reeling with everything I had seen and heard. "I don't understand. You can't be CIA. You're in the Navy."

"I am a deep black cover operative. I have been for almost twenty-eight years."

"You mean you're not a Naval officer?" My voice was trembling. I was angry and upset. I hated the CIA, but if he was really a Navy officer, maybe it wasn't as bad as I thought!

He laughed, "Don't worry, you married a Naval officer. That's my cover. I received a Congressional Commission in 1968 as a Naval officer. Over the years my rank is advanced, on a regular basis, just as though I was in the Navy. That's the way it works with all of us. "

I wasn't satisfied with his answer, "Are you CIA or are you a Naval officer?"

"I am both . . . or I was both." This answer gave me even less comfort. "Now I don't know what I am." He continued, "I fell out of favor in 1986 and I still haven't landed."

"What happened in 1986?" I questioned.

"One of my planes crashed in Central America."

Could he possibly be talking about the plane crash that started the whole Iran/Contra investigations?

"You don't mean Eugene Hasenfus's plane, do you?" I was familiar with the crash. It was October 5, 1986. Anyone who was familiar with the beginnings of the Iran/Contra mess knew about Eugene Hasenfus and the Southern Air Transport cargo plane that went

down in Nicaragua. It was the papers found on board his plane that
started the investigation into the illegal arming of the Contras.

He nodded his head. "It was one of my planes." I used to run a stock
brokerage company called National Brokerage Companies. It was set
up to launder black budget CIA funds so they could be used for covert
operations. I bought the plane with NBC money."

I took a deep breath and tried to absorb everything that he was
saying. Too much was coming too fast. I didn't have the necessary
information base for me to understand it all. Maybe Barbara could
have made sense of what he was telling me. But the details and the
covert intrigue were incomprehensible to me. It was almost as if he
were speaking another language.

I heard the pilot speak, "Mrs. Russbacher," he said. It was the first
time anyone had called me Mrs. Russbacher. "Look out the windows
below the wings. You will see our fighter escort."

I looked out the window, and sure enough, two military jets were
off our wings. The pilot spoke again. "They're here to escort us home.
We can't let anything happen to the Chief." The pilot said this as he
walked to the back of the plane. Gunther offered him a glass of wine.

The pilot continued, "Did he tell you that he's the best pilot in the
Navy? He's the real "top gun."

Gunther hadn't told me anything about flying except that he had
lost a plane in Viet Nam. Gunther and the pilot talked and laughed
about a trip they had just made to Oklahoma. Then they started
talking about a house in Baja California where they spent time
relaxing. It was clear they had known each other for years. As I
listened to them talk over old times and old friends, some of whom I
knew, like Richard Brenneke and Harry Rupp, the reality of what was
happening began to sink in.

The Naval officer I had just married was a deep black covert CIA
operative. I had married a CIA agent! I couldn't believe it. I had
married one of the very men I had vowed to throw in jail. I couldn't
believe it. Now I was slapping myself on the forehead in disbelief!

He had married Barbara Honegger's best friend. Barbara was the
author of the first book on the October Surprise. I had married a CIA
operative!

What I really couldn't believe was I loved him, in spite of the fact
he was CIA. For years I had thought about nothing but breaking up
the CIA and stopping their illegal drug and arms running. But now, as
I stared into his eyes, love ruled the day, and nothing else mattered! I
remembered how he turned into Atalon, and I knew that it didn't
matter what or who he was. He was my other half, and for better or

for worse, now that we had found each other, we would be together for all eternity.

Two days later, the FBI arrested him at a family dinner—in front of my entire family. They told me that he wasn't a Naval officer, he wasn't CIA, he was a low-level conman who had been marrying and defrauding wealthy widows. I objected and told them they were mistaken. I described the Learjet, and the missiles. I told them about the fighter escort from Nellis. I told them to call the pilot; he would tell them who Gunther was.

The FBI placed the call for me, and handed me the phone. I told the pilot what had just happened. I asked him to tell the FBI who Gunther was. What he said almost knocked my feet from under me. "I'm sorry Mrs. Russbacher," the pilot said, "but I don't know your husband. I just met him the day before yesterday."

I couldn't believe what he just said. I remembered the stories he and Gunther told about their trip to Oklahoma and Mexico. I remembered the way they punched each other and played like brothers or best friends. I remember the pilot telling me he knew Richard Brenneke from Saudi Arabia. Now the pilot, who told me, less than two days earlier, "We can't let anything happen to the Chief," told the FBI he didn't know Gunther.

That evening began an eight-year nightmare that was filled with a horror and terror. In September of 1989 I began doing battle with the largest and most evil empire in the world, the United States Intelligence community. I walked through the valley of the shadow of death and I knew fear, but I also knew God would not have placed me so strategically if there had not been a very good reason.

At that time it never occurred to me that my husband and I were going to be used to bring down a president and expose the worst pattern of related scandals in the history of the United States. Some Presidents leave office through losing an election, some resign, others are assassinated. George Bush was forced to lose an election.

As I watched Gunther being led away in handcuffs, I could not even imagine that two years later, Gunther and I would be used to keep George Bush from winning the 1992 election.

I have always heard that God uses people in mysterious ways, but it was not God who was using us. It was my husband's boss. It was the same high ranking Admiral who had caused my late husband John to walk on egg shells whenever he visited the Naval Postgraduate School. It was the same high-ranking Admiral who had taken me to Mars in 1986.

During the first year of my marriage to Gunther, the Admiral manipulated events and watched our reactions. He studied us until he was certain of our love for each other and of my strength. He played with our emotions and watched our pain as if we were laboratory animals. And then when he decided that we were strong enough to endure more, he proceeded with the rest of his plan and began using us to tell the story he wanted exposed . . . The October Surprise, and George Bush's role in it.

This Admiral could have stepped in at anytime and put an end to our suffering. But he didn't. He watched us, he listened to our conversations, he read our mail. He needed to be sure that we would fight to stay together no matter what they threw at us. He needed to know that I believed Gunther *was* Atalon . . . my other half. He needed to be sure that if we were backed into a corner, I would be strong enough to hold up my end as we fought our way out, even if it meant taking on the President of the United States.

This Admiral had a plan for us. A plan that I couldn't even begin to understand, because in the beginning, I did not know the man I had just married was involved in the October Surprise. I didn't know that my husband was the one man who could connect all the scandals and bring down the Bush administration.

Almost eleven months from the day we married, Gunther was released from the county jail in Missouri where he had been held. We paid a price for his release. He pled guilty to four counts of fraud and was placed on five years probation. If he violated his probation during those five years, he would go to state prison for twenty-eight years. The price was high, but we had been apart for eleven months. Gunther had a heart attack while in custody. I was afraid he might die before we had a chance to live together.

At the time, I didn't know Gunther was released for a reason. He was needed to fly a top-secret mission. I didn't know there were people behind the scenes who were working just as hard as I was to get him out. I thought it was my actions that were responsible for the prosecutor's change of heart.

Once Gunther was out, he told me that he had to report to Offutt Air Force Base in Omaha. He said there was a meeting going on and he had to be there. At Offutt I met his boss, the Admiral, the man who had pulled our strings. Had I known what the Admiral had in mind for us, I might have chosen to leave Gunther at Offutt and go into hiding.

Gunther and I lived through three and a half years of hour by hour terror. We were 'slimed' by the media; Gunther was poisoned and beaten. He was set up and put in the 'hole' repeatedly. I had people shooting at me, ramming my car and trying to push me off cliffs and overpasses. At one point I was sent out of the country and put in protective custody in Austria.

After over four years as the most visible political prisoner of the Bush Administration, Gunther's sentence was vacated, and the Missouri State appeals court ordered the state to release him. However, the order was not carried out. Gunther was transferred back to the St. Charles County jail and held illegally while the prosecutors decided what to do.

Gunther had been used to expose the treason committed by the CIA and George Bush. While in prison Gunther had been cruelly punished. Numerous attempts were made to kill him. To save his life, I organized a letter writing campaign that involved all 50 states and many foreign countries. I wrote articles and went on radio and television describing the beatings and punishments he had been subjected to. My letters brought help from all sides, conservative, liberal and middle of the road.

As Gunther waited to be released from the county jail, his tormentors were planning their final attack. One day, without warning, Gunther was taken from his cell and forced to undergo open-heart surgery. His sentence had been vacated. He should have been free! Instead, he was told to take his chances with the doctors. He had no choice. It was the surgery or a prison knife. His heart condition had been worsened by the many years of incarceration, but he didn't need a quintuple heart bypass. It was done to kill him or disable him permanently.

The first I heard about this came in a fax from Gunther's attorney. The jailers would give me no additional information. Neither would the hospital. For five days I lived a nightmare not knowing if my husband was dead or alive. At the time, I had pneumonia and not enough money to see a doctor, let alone fly back to Missouri to try to help.

Five days later, the phone rang. It was Gunther. His voice was weak. He told me the doctors had left him for dead after the surgery. He said no doctor checked on him for four days.

On the fifth day he was taken back to the jail and thrown into a cell that was covered with urine and feces. The stench of human excrement and waste caused him to gag. When he gagged, he broke the stitches in his chest. He asked to be moved. It was denied. He asked that the cell be hosed down. It was denied. The jailers brought him a bucket and rags. They stood outside his cell and laughed as he struggled to clean the cell himself. This act of unspeakable human cruelty was what galvanized the informed American public.

Hundreds of thousands of letters began pouring into Missouri and to the White House. Help came from every direction. Amnesty International assigned their London office to investigate the charges. The

ACLU sent two attorneys. The conservative CAUSE Foundation stepped forward. Newspapers and magazines and radio talk shows spread the word and Americans came forward with letters faxes and phone calls. Veterans threatened to march on Missouri and worse!

Seeing they had a tiger by the tail, the Missouri officials cut a plea bargain with him. They allowed him to plead guilty to the charge of defrauding TWA, out of the price of a one way ticket, from Pittsburgh to St. Louis. If he didn't, he was told all the charges that had been vacated would be re-filed and he would spend forever in the same jail that had just tried to kill him. Gunther pled guilty to defrauding TWA out of a ticket. Four years in jail, and the destruction of his health, and the only thing they could get him on was the price of a $50.00 airline ticket.

Gunther is the only person to ever claim that George Bush was flown back from the Paris October Surprise meeting in an SR-71. Gunther became known as "The October Surprise Pilot." The October Surprise is the hub of the wheel that connects all the scandals of the Reagan-Bush years. George Bush knew that if it were investigated in depth, all his illegal deals would be exposed. He had more than a political career at risk; he had his family empire and fortunes at risk. If he had been exposed, not only would he have been indicted, but most of his family and friends would have gone with him.

While Gunther was in prison, he wrote essays on the Federal Reserve Banking system and on the non profit foundations that were created with Federal Reserve money. The essays showed that the men, who own the Federal Reserve, use non-profit think tanks, like the Ford and Carnegie Foundations, to influence every aspect of life in the United States.

Gunther knew that all presidents since 1913 were owned and controlled by the International bankers who own the Federal Reserve Bank. The same money and people, who were involved in the overthrow of the Austro-Hungarian Empire, went on to overthrow the government of the United States of America. This banking cartel grabbed control of the money system of the United States in a midnight session of Congress on December 23, 1913. Gunther taught me that the Federal Reserve is neither federal, nor does it have a reserve. He used to laugh and say, "Federal Express is more Federal that the Federal Reserve. At least it was started with CIA money!"

Bush's family had been deeply involved in this treasonous takeover of America's banking. George H.W. Bush's father Prescott worked for John D. Rockefeller. Rockefeller was one of the people who owned part of the Federal Reserve Banking System. Gunther's essays on the Federal Reserve were released in early 1992. They were among the first in recent history to tell the whole truth.

There was another reason George Bush feared Gunther Russbacher enough to try to kill him. Bush knew Gunther had the power to place the world on a gold standard once again and thereby put an end to the looting of nations by the international bankers! Gunther and several men from his team knew about the gold in the Philippines *and* he had the connections to transfer it out of the Philippines.

There is a war taking place in the monetary system. This war started hundreds of years ago. The players that vied for power five hundred years ago, are the same players, i.e. their physical and ideological descendants who are fighting today. These players are divided into two camps. One camp consists of the royal families, which at one time or another, (with the exception of the British monarchy), were all under the banner of Austrian Empire. The other side is made up of international bankers and the British monarchy.

Gunther is a Habsburg Baron on his father's side, and a member of the Hungarian Esterházy family on his mother's side.

The international bankers destroyed the Austro-Hungarian Empire in the late 1890's. Since this didn't destroy the Habsburgs completely, WWI and WWII were started to finish the job and drive Austria and Germany into the ground.

During WWII, there was a group of men, in Austria and Germany, who understood the full picture. They had tried to work with Britain and the United States to bring the war to a quick conclusion. But their overtures were rebuffed. These men were all part of the royal family. The men who headed the group were all Knights Templars. These men were Abwehr (military intelligence) officers. The Abwehr was headed by, Admiral Wilhelm Canaris.

Canaris used his position as the head of military intelligence, not only to plan the assassination of Adolph Hitler, but he used his power to smuggle gold. The gold he smuggled had been stolen by Hitler from the Austrian treasury. The gold was not just ANY gold. It was Templar gold and Canaris was the head of the Templars.

For fifty years the gold lay hidden. If it had been brought back into Austria before the 50 year hidden agreement had expired, the gold would have been claimed by Israel as war reparations... and it would have gone directly into the banks of the International banking cartel.

After WWII, members of the royal families were ordered to sign contracts stating that they would never try to restore the monarchy. Gunther never signed this agreement. This is the reason he and his mother were sent into exile. Gunther is one of the last pure-blooded royals of the old Austro-Hungarian Empire.

When Gunther and his mother were exiled in 1954, it was done to keep any legitimate heir to the Austrian throne from establishing a power base within Austria that could eventually help him regain the throne. Because Gunther had not signed the contract with the global slave masters, he became the highest-ranking true Habsburg. Because of this, it was his job to bring home the gold.

George Bush feared Gunther because he was the only person who could bring the hidden gold back into Europe. Once it is back in Europe, it will be used to create a gold standard, not just for Europe. . . but for the world. Once that happens, the Federal Reserve Banking cartel is over! When this happens, not only will George Bush the First be finished, but his entire way of life will be finished. (Please don't think I lump George W. Bush into the same category with his father. They are as different as night and day. George H.W. Bush is *far* more similar to his business partner and successor, William Jefferson Clinton.)

Almost immediately upon his release from jail in December of 1993, Gunther became the central figure in the transfer of a huge amount of gold from the Philippines to Austria. I was told that the gold would be used to destroy the Federal Reserve and the New World Order.

The gold returned to Europe in December of 1994. It first went to a smelter in Greece where the bars were melted down and the Swastikas removed. The gold was then distributed to the countries whose treasuries had been looted first by Hitler and then by the Russians. There is enough gold to put every country in Europe on a gold standard, with some left over for other countries. When the gold based currencies go into effect, this will mean the end of the age-old enemy of the Habsburg bloodline... the "illegal aliens" who own and control the Federal Reserve Banks and use the sweat of the American people to finance their New World Order!

Gunther's health had suffered under the stress of the recent open-heart surgery as well as his confinement for the last four years. His liver was swollen, his pancreas was failing, and his kidneys were shutting down. He was afraid to go into an American hospital. He felt he would be killed. Several men, who were also involved in the gold transfer, took him to Austria.

He was arrested for entering on illegal documents. During the arrest, he suffered a heart attack. He was taken, via helicopter, to a hospital. The charges were eventually dropped, I joined him in Austria and we tried to complete the gold transfer, get our commission and retire somewhere to recuperate.

What appeared to be a done deal soon became a nightmare of tangled threads that stretched from the gold mines of King Solomon, to the gold teeth of Hitler's holocaust victims. Gunther and I were impeded at every turn. Representatives of the Austrian government told us that the Jews felt the gold we were trying to bring back into Europe came from the teeth of their grandfathers.

Gunther and I had been told that the gold was from the Austrian treasury and had been stolen by Hitler in 1938. We had been told that the symbol for Austrian gold, a fox, was still stamped on all the bars. However, we weren't told that the bars also had HH and the swastika stamped on them. The HH stands for Hitler Helvetia. Helvetia is a Latin name for Switzerland. The Swiss were Hitler's bankers.

While waiting for the gold transfer to go through, Gunther and I stayed in a lodge outside of Salzburg. Gunther told me that the lodge had been in his family for over 600 years. He said it belonged to the Esterházy family of Hungary. His mother was an Esterházy.

While we were at the lodge, we had dinner each night with members of the allanHabsburg family. Most of the people we had dinner with were the members of the family who had refused to sign the Allies agreement regarding the restoration of the Monarchy. As a result of this, they were stripped of their lands and wealth. The ones who signed the agreement and said they would never try to restore the monarchy were given their titles, lands and wealth.

I discovered that the Lodge where we stayed was not an ordinary lodge. It served as a meeting place for some of the highest-ranking members of the opposition to the New World Order. It was at this Lodge that I learned that the opposition to the New World Order is not just made up of Habsburgs, but of Knights Templars.

I learned that the Habsburgs who are part of the Opposition to the NWO are all Knights Templars. I was told some of the history of the Templars. The story is too long to tell here.

In 1994, Gunther and other members of Faction Two, who are Knights Templars, arranged for the Philippine gold to be returned to Austria.

One of the men who arranged this transfer and knew Gunther was the one who had to do it, was the very same Admiral who had caused us so much grief. Admiral William Johann was the illegitimate son of Admiral Wilhelm Canaris. But he was only illegitimate in the Habsburg line; in the Templars, he was considered the legitimate head of the order.

After several months in Austria, trying to close the gold transfer, we had run into betrayal, intrigue, lies and disinformation. Gunther was growing weaker and sicker. His heart pain was unbearable. He had suffered two or three heart attacks and had been taken to emergency rooms. The doctors in Austria put him on the heart transplant list. They told us the doctors in Missouri had butchered him and the only thing that would save his life would be a heart transplant. Gunther was in tremendous pain from his heart. To stop the pain, he started drinking. We did not know that his pancreas had shut down which caused the alcohol to go directly into his blood stream. I thought he had become an alcoholic overnight, and I was furious with him.

He was in no condition to complete the gold transfer. After weeks of put-offs from the Austrian National Bank, he finally realized that if he were to ever accomplish what his ancestors have been trying to accomplish for hundreds of years, he would have to let go of everything. The commission on the gold deal would have made us two of the richest people in the world. Because of the way we had been treated at the hands of our "out of control" government, we had plans for publishing and film companies that would begin to educate the people about the conspiracy to make them eco-slaves of a One World government.

It was hard to let go of the dream of awakening the world, but there was no other way for the gold to get back into Europe. On a train from Salzburg to Vienna, Gunther finally decided that the only way to save the gold deal, was to give it away . . . all of it.

He called Kurt Waldheim, the man who had been instrumental in keeping both of us alive during his years in prison. Kurt Waldheim was the president of Austria while Gunther was incarcerated in the United States. Now he was the head of a non-governmental organization called, The League of the United Nations.

Gunther and I went to Dr. Waldheim's office in Vienna. Waldheim was with the King of Denmark as we entered the outer office. (I have since discovered that there *is* no King of Denmark. However, I still believe the man I met WAS the legitimate King of Denmark. I have researched the Danish royal line and can NOT find his picture. But he resembles many of them.)

Gunther and I were told to wait until Dr. Waldheim and the King had finished their business. The King soon left and we were ushered in. In a few sentences Gunther explained what was happening. Waldheim gave him the name of a man within the Foreign Ministry and arranged a meeting. Waldheim then showed us out, stopping to introduce us to Helmut Kohl, Chancellor of Germany, as we left his office.

Gunther turned the gold deal completely over to Waldheim, including all the commission. When his American partners, who had financed the deal, for a *large* share of the commission, discovered what he had done, they stopped funding us. This left us penniless on the streets of Vienna. Gunther called the American Embassy in Vienna, where he had been CIA station chief in the 70's. He asked for help. They told him, due to the Haiti crisis, he had just been reactivated into the Navy. He was told an airplane would come to take us back to the United States.

I felt another set-up coming on. Gunther had been on probation when he left the United States, and he would be arrested if he returned. No matter how hard I tried; I could not make him see what was going to happen. In anger I told him I was not going to stand by and watch him end up in an American prison again. I left him in the hotel where the U.S. Embassy had put us up. I caught a midnight train, from Vienna to Frankfurt. From Germany, I took a plane home to California.

When I arrived home, I learned Gunther had been arrested for not paying his hotel bill. A hotel bill that I *knew* had already been prepaid by the United States Embassy! He was sentenced to two years in an Austrian prison.

In a letter that Russbacher wrote me from prison on November 26, 1994, he gave the partial history of the gold transfer which was code named Operation White Robe. This is what he wrote:

'Let me give you a bit of background for Operation White Robe. It begins with the U.S. government imposing an embargo against the Swiss in WWII. They (the Swiss) had been making deals with the Nazis. They allowed them to use their rail systems to bring war materials to the German troops of Italy. In return, the Swiss were the true bankers of the Third Reich.

To further the true meaning of hypocrisy, the Swiss received coal from Germany. (the Swiss have none of their own). The U.S. government went straight for the jugular and imposed an all out food embargo. Almost 60% of Swiss food was imported from other European markets. The Swiss told the U.S., in 1944, to go to hell and they began importing foodstuffs from South America. The vessels flew Liberian and Swiss flags. The U.S. put a halt to that in December of 1944.

The Swiss had almost all of Hitler's gold, which he had seized from Jews, the National Bank of Austria, Belgium, France and numerous other countries. The gold was a real sore point for the U.S. They wanted it in their hands. The Swiss, operating on orders from Hitler's men, began the long and worrisome transport of the metal to Argentina and Paraguay. After March of 1954, the gold bars and chunks of used gold were shipped to a remote area of the Philippines.

There it has remained until we (*Ed. Note*: meaning Gunther, Rayelan and the group they worked with) entered the picture. Only a hundred or so people knew about this horde of precious metals. The White Robes (The Knights Templar) became involved because great gold monstrances (crucifixes) as well as solid gold chalices and coins were robbed from many churches (Catholic of course). It became a brand new quest for about 30 of us. Most of these men were my seniors and have long since died without fulfilling their cause. With the deaths of my two best friends in Laos this February, (1994) I was the only one left who was empowered to move the gold.

Even though it looked to you that I was a recent player in the gold transfer, the truth is, I have known about it my entire life, and I knew that eventually the gold would return to Austria. It will return to Austria in 1995, 50 years after the end of the war.'

While Gunther was in prison in Austria, I worked in an answering service. While I worked there, Gunther and I started allanRumor Mill News. On December 23, 1996 Gunther was released from prison in Austria. On the 26th, he would have had access to the money in a small bank account he set up years before. There was enough money in the account to bring me to Europe, and take care of us until he got the rest of his affairs in order. We were joyously planning the rest of our lives together.

On December 23rd, a film producer from England, named Jane Ryder met Gunther outside the Austrian prison. Jane had made several trips to California to visit me. She told me she was doing a film and needed information. I gave her everything she requested, including a copy of The Obergon Chronicles.

After she read The Obergon Chronicles, she said something that should have alerted me as to what was going to happen. She told me she believed she was Shalma. Shalma was the earth woman that Atalon, my other half, i.e. Gunther, kidnapped and removed from Earth. To make Shalma fall in love with him, Atalon used mind control to erase the memory of her soul mate and true love. Then Atalon used mind control to make Shalma believe she was in love with him.

After several phone calls to me, Gunther and Jane vanished for one month. During that month, I went through with the lecture Gunther and I set up to expose government mind control and government created "new age channels." This was January of 1997, and this was the first time that I had ever talked about The Obergon Chronicles.

When Gunther finally surfaced, he was in jail in Los Alamos, New Mexico. He had no memory of me. He thought Jane was his wife. For a short time, he regained his memory and told me that he had been subjected to mind control. Did Jane subject him to mind control? Or were both of them victims of our government?

In the Obergon Chronicles, Atalon/Gunther subjects Shalma/Jane to mind control so she will not remember her soul mate. In real life, Gunther was subjected to mind control and forgot he was married to me, the soul that was destined to join with his, Rayelan/Raelon.

Gunther was transferred from New Mexico to Missouri to face charges there. After a short time in Missouri, Gunther lost his memory again. He no longer remembered he had ever loved me, been married to me, or what we had gone through together. I called to tell Gunther that Allan Frankovich, a documentary film maker who was Jane's partner, died of a heart attack in Houston. In a voice that sounded like evil incarnate, Gunther told me, "He didn't die of a heart attack, it was a blood clot, and if you don't leave me alone, YOU'RE NEXT!"

Gunther pled guilty to charges in April of 1997. He agreed to leave the country and never return. He and Jane moved to England. They were married a few months later. Gunther had not bothered to divorce me. I have not talked with Gunther since that time.

Q: Gunther Russbacher "shape-shifted" into a totally different person in front of your eyes and said that he was Atalon, the main character from your book "The Obergon Chronicles." Many years later, this still must seem totally surreal to you. What do you make of this now?

A: I still find it hard to believe. After knowing what I know now, about mind control and holographic projections, I wonder if this was done to him through some kind of outside technology. What happened to him that first night was different from the other times I saw him "shape shift."

Q: You mean there were other times?

A: The second time it happened was later on the first night we met. We were in Gunther's hotel room when he suddenly changed into a Roman soldier. He began quoting from Marcus Aurelius' Meditations. These are famous writings which were written by a Roman Emperor and soldier. For years, I had known that I had been the co-Emperor with Aurelius. I was his cousin, a man of few redeeming virtues, named Lucien Veras. Because of this connection to Aurelius, I had read a great deal about him. When Gunther 'shape shifted' into Aurelius and began quoting verses from his Meditations, I became even more certain that Gunther and I were the two halves of a soul.

Another time he "shape shifted" in front of me occurred in July of 1990, right before we got to Offutt Air force Base. We had stopped at a restaurant in Iowa. While we were there, we were joined by Garret Henderson, one of Gunther's friends; the one he thinks was killed in 1994. Since Garrett was one of my "sources" for Rumor Mill News, I know that he wasn't physically killed; only the alias, i.e., the name Garret was killed. While I was in the restaurant bathroom, Garret put LSD in my coffee. I did not drink my coffee when I came out. It was cold. Just as we were getting up to leave, Gunther grabbed for it and finished it off with one gulp. I remember seeing Garrett try to grab it, but I did not understand the significance at the time.

Gunther and I checked into a motel. We were exhausted and I fell asleep immediately. When I awoke, I saw the most incredible thing I have ever seen. Gunther was pacing the floor of the motel room talking to himself. Each time he would speak, he became a different person. His voice would change, his face would change, even his height appeared to change.

I still barely knew Gunther. We had only been married two days when he was arrested and transported to Missouri. I had not seen him in almost 11 months. For all I knew he could have been a multiple personality type.

After he recovered enough to make a phone call, he told me that Garrett had put LSD in my coffee. Gunther explained that what I had seen were all of his aliases.

To show me that he was not "crazy," he "shape shifted" into each alias in front of me. He told me that there was nothing abnormal or alien about this. It didn't take any special magic skills; it took a CIA laboratory, drugs, electrodes and hypnosis. He said it took two full years to create a full alias.

When Gunther shaped shifted into "Bob," the naval officer, I could see the Sean Connery look-alike I fell in love with so many years ago. Then he shifted into Emery Peden, the stockbroker. He looked old, fatter and ordinary. Then he became a man he called Jerome, another stockbroker. Jerome was in his late 60's or early 70's. Gunther went from being a 30-year-old Navy pilot, to a 70-year-old arthritic stock- broker in just seconds.

There were a few more aliases. James was the U.S. Attorney. David was the State Department officer. Gerhard was the German intelli- gence officer. There was also a Russian KGB agent, a Middle Eastern terrorist, a German terrorist, and even a few women. He did not change physically when he became the women. He said he only imitated them on the phone.

While we were in Winnemucca, Nevada, the place where he and Richard Brenneke were raised, he became an American Indian and told me the story of how the White men took his land and killed his people.

Another time occurred in front of a large number of people. When we were in Austria, Gunther stood in front of a picture of one of his ancestors. We were in a museum and were surrounded by dozens of people. In front of everyone, he assumed the same pose as his ancestor, and suddenly, he *was* his ancestor! For a moment, Gunther and the picture looked identical. Then he stepped away and became Gunther again. I could hear the people who were taking the tour with us gasp. Some of them took pictures.

Q: You state: "He (Gunther) said he had called his boss and requested permission to marry me." Being someone who has not had much exposure to military life, it seems odd to me that someone would have to ask permission to marry. Is this standard protocol, or was there something special about Gunther's situation?

A: Gunther told me this was standard operating procedure for a covert operative. I have never asked about it, I just accepted his explanation.

Q: At critical junctures in your life, there always appeared a "voice" of guidance. Who/what do you feel this voice is/was? Do you still hear this voice?

A: No, I no longer hear voices; I now have inner "knowings." Sometimes I am awakened in the night, or sometimes I will be driving and suddenly I will "know" something. Many of the puzzle pieces that have been unconnected will suddenly fit into place. When I do my homework and check things out, I discover that the inner "knowings" are always right.

Q: What do I think the voices were?

A: As hard as it is for me to admit it, I believe I was used in some kind of mind control project by Navy Intelligence.

Q: What made you think you were *not* a "new age channel?"

A: It was another Admiral who first spilled the beans and let me know what had happened to me, and why I now think of myself as a Navy intelligence project, rather than a New Age Channel.

This happened while Gunther was in prison in Austria for entering the country without a passport. This must have been April or May of 1994. Admiral Raeder and several of Gunther's friends and relatives would drop in and visit me. During one of these visits, Admiral Raeder talked about the New Age Channel JZ Knight.

"She was one of our early models," he said. I asked him what he meant and he told me that her first husband was a dentist who did special jobs for Navy Intelligence. One of the jobs they asked him to do was put receivers in her teeth.

The Admiral told me that this was an early version of the technology they use now. I asked him why they were doing this. He told me that their enemy, i.e., the New World Order, was using New Age channels to subtly change the world we live in.

Admiral Raeder told me that his group was using New Age channels to release the real history of the planet earth. He talked about the new technology that was later used on JZ. He said it was a form of enhanced telepathy that had been developed for NASA. I remembered the first time I heard the voices. The man, who called himself Isham, told me that he was communicating with me using a form of telepathy. I slowly began to realize that the Obergon Chronicles and the rest of my "channeling" had not come from ascended masters, it had come from Navy Intelligence operatives. The Admiral at the Naval Postgraduate School, at the time I began "channeling," was Admiral Sam Linder. I found out many years later, and Admiral Linder's first name was Isham.

Admiral Raeder began talking about a few channels that were in his group. The way he spoke about them, it sounded like he was talking about me and the Obergon Chronicles. I don't think I actually put two and two together until after he left. I later asked Gunther about it. Gunther was non-committal. He said it was possible that someone did this to me, but he did not confirm it. . . at the time.

In a strange coincidence, that I still wonder about, one of the men at the lodge in Austria started talking about the Obergon Chronicles. He said the stories had been discovered in King Solomon's Temple. Did someone tell him to say this to make me believe that even though these stories were channeled to me via Navy Intelligence, that they were true? I don't have an answer to this. As you can see, I still have many unanswered questions.

What the man at the lodge said, fits in with what Admiral Raeder said when he told me that his group was using New Age channels to release the real history of the world.

One of the last things Raeder told me was that JZ Knight's ego got in the way and she began distorting the information they were transmitting to her. He said she taught them a lot, and by the time they got to the other people, (I am now sure he meant me,) they knew enough to put the new people through some kind of spiritual training first. He said they did this to make sure the channels wouldn't dissolve into lower emotions once they realized how powerful they were. When he said this, I realized that the years I had spent with Nystr were for this reason.

Q: It often appears as if you were placed in situations deliberately by someone or something. As if there was a greater plan that you were being groomed for and manipulated into becoming a part of. Do you have any idea who it was that was placing you in these situations and what it was that they hoped to achieve?

A: I know the man who first manipulated us was Gunther's Boss. Admiral William Johann. I also knew him as Admiral Tom West, Admiral Meyer, and a few others whose names I can't remember right now. Admiral Johann is the man who took me to Mars back in 1986 - three years before I married Gunther, and four years before I officially met Admiral Johann. Shortly after I met Johann on Offutt Air Force Base, he took me to meet the King of the World.

Admiral Johann was poisoned in 1993 and left the scene. I know he is still alive, I saw him briefly in 1999. I don't know what he is doing or where he is. After Johann left, Admiral Raeder seemed to replace him. I think that Gunther and I were being set up to start some kind of new religion. But I don't know for sure.

At the time Gunther disappeared with Jane, Gunther and I were scheduled to give a lecture in Florida on mind control. He was going to blow the lid off the Manchurian Candidate program and the religious cults who were programmed using mind control. The Moonies are the most famous example of this, but there was Waco, the Order of the Solar Temple, and Heaven's Gate. And these are just the one that we know about!

Gunther was also going to expose a type of mind control called "overlays." This is where an agenda, such as "saving the environment" or being adamantly 'anti-abortion,' is overlaid on your own personality. Sometimes I think that removing Gunther from me and erasing his memory of me was punishment for me for talking him into exposing the things about mind control that he did expose. He wrote an article called Operation Open Eyes. This article goes into many of the things I listed above. (Ed. Note: This article is included in Gunther's section of this book.)

I also think I started thinking for myself, and was no longer "controllable" by Gunther or his bosses. Maybe Gunther and Jane are now being used for the project that Gunther and I were supposed to carry out.

I wish I could say for sure what it was all about, but I don't know. I wonder if I ever will.

Q: In Obergon Chronicles, the character Atalon has the power to "alter the most private thoughts of Terrans," in fact much of Obergon reads as a primer on Mind Control. Did you realize this at the time it was dictated to you?

A: When the Obergon Chronicles were first channeled to me in 1981, I had never heard of mind control. I don't think anyone outside of the intelligence community had heard of mind control in those days. Frank Sinatra starred in the film Manchurian Candidate. It had just been released when President Kennedy was assassinated. The film was pulled off the market for almost 20 years. That film and a few other low budget films about Korean brain washing were all I knew about mind control, and I really thought it was all "Hollywood hype." When I wrote the Obergon Chronicles, it never occurred to me that the type of mind control Atalon used on Shalma was possible. Now I am sure it is.

Q: Jane Ryder stated to you that she believed she was Shalma from The Obergon Chronicles. In Obergon Chronicles, Atalon used mind control techniques on Shalma to make her forget her soul mate and to make her love him (Atalon.) Now it seems, in this context that Jane (Shalma) is taking revenge on Atalon (Gunther) by making him forget his soul mate in this lifetime, (you, Rayelan.) How do you work this out in your mind? Was Obergon used as a script to also control you and Gunther and Jane? Or is there something else going on here?

A: I think you hit the nail on the head. It appears that Atalon, in the body of Gunther, is being taught what it feels like to have your soul mate stolen from you through mind control.

While Shalma was under Atalon's control, she had no memory of the soul mate she loved with all her heart. Now that Gunther (Atalon) is with Jane (Shalma), he has no memory of his soul mate, Rayelan (Raelon).

The only thing that gives me any solace is a part of the Obergon Chronicles which talk about Raelon's betrothed, Fanra. Fanra is Raelon's twin soul. They matured on a soul level together and they were betrothed by their fathers. They also have some kind of mission to carry out here on earth.

Over a year after Gunther left me, I met a man who many people say is like my twin. Our backgrounds are almost identical. We even have pictures of us at age 18 that look identical. If the Obergon Chronicles are true, and if I am Raelon, I have wondered if my new husband is Fanra.

And then there is that other part of me who thinks all of it was created to pull me into some kind of covert operation. Sometimes, I believe that Atalon and Raelon were created to make me believe that

Gunther was my other half, and that no matter what the consequences were, I had to stay with him until we had finished our operation.

I am certain that defeating George Bush was one part of the operation. Maybe that was all of it. However, there were things that happened in Austria, including a remarriage in a Templar Ceremony, that make me think there might be more to come one of these days. After this re-marriage, Gunther said to me, "No one will *ever* be able to separate us now!" At the time, I believed him. Sometimes I wonder about that sacred ceremony. Sometimes I wonder if I am *still* married to Gunther.

Q: What would you do if you heard a "voice" now?

A: I would tell it to shut up, leave me alone and get out of my life. In this day and age of electronic mind control devices, I really can't imagine how anyone can take "new age channels" seriously. The sophistication of the mind control operations that are being conducted by our government and the New World Order should scare everyone.

Not only do they have machines that can put voices in our heads, they have devices that alter brain waves in an entire area. If they want to turn an entire town into psychopathic killers, they can do it. If they want an entire country to see and hear a new Messiah, they have the tools to do that. If they want to project an image of Jesus or Mohammed in the sky, they have the technology to create holographic images that not only can be seen, but can be heard. And these are just what the machines can do.

When you add hypnotism and drugs, you can add a whole new and even more frightening aspect to mind control. Most of this is covered in an article called "Operation Open Eyes" which was written by Gunther. He described the process of creating a Manchurian Candidate, someone who is programmed to carrying out a mission, usually an assassination. Gunther's boss in Austrian Intelligence came to California—shortly before the 1999 Columbine High School shootings in Colorado, to explain to me how the New World Order is using mind control in a modified Hegelian Dialectic to change society.

Hegel's famous Dialectic changes society by using an "antithesis" to change the "thesis" creating a "synthesis." Using this method, a powerful group can introduce an "antithesis," such as gun violence and mass murders to bring about legislation that will disarm America. In this century, each time a nation was disarmed, such as in Nazi Germany, Russia, and Cambodia, genocide has taken place. The only reason the United States has not already fallen victim to a

One World Government, is because we have guns. The Second Amendment is not about protecting ourselves from lions, tigers and bears; it is about protecting our Constitution, our country and ourselves from our government.

Q: It sounds like what you have experienced is a combination of mind control, spiritual encounters and actual physical journeys, what advice would you give to someone on how to discern between the three?

A: I wish I had a simple and easy way for people to know how to do this. Sadly, I have not discovered the way. When someone is having a voice "channeled" to them by an intelligence agency or other nefarious earth based group, it is impossible for them to tell the difference between this and a true spiritual channel. I do believe real "channels" have existed. I have known some of them.

One group of women who I truly believe were receiving information from spirit guides, "channeled" a book called, "Growth of a Soul." Each person received different parts of the book. They wrote them on any kind of paper they could find. When they presented the book to the publisher, they gave it to him in a grocery bag full of pieces of paper. He and his wife, my teacher, Dorie D'Angelo, pieced together the book like a jigsaw puzzle.

Phylos, the Tibetan, channeled a book called "Dweller on Two Planets." It was published in the 30's or 40's. Phylos is the spirit guide who channeled the book, "Growth of a Soul" in the early 50's. It was not published until the 70's. I knew Josephine Taylor, one of the women who was part of the channeling project. I believe she was a true channel. She started channeling as a child in the late 1800's. I met her when she was close to 100 years old.

Q: After your conversation with the Admiral about the enhanced telepathy, you came to believe that the "voices" were actually being transmitted to you by Naval intelligence. Then later, you were told by the man in Austria that the Obergon Chronicles stories had been discovered in King Solomon's Temple. Do I understand you correctly when you say that it appears as if there are different "factions" behind the mind control/transmissions as well? And that one of these "factions" might actually be transmitting the truth?

A. When I was in Austria, I was told by the men I met at the Templar Lodge that their group is using mind control technology, i.e. "space based telepathy" to tell the real history of the planet earth. They told me they are doing this to bring up the awareness of the population. I was told that soon they are going to release absolute proof that the history of the planet we have been taught through religions and history books is wrong.

The men at the lodge told me that if they released this information to a society like we had in the 50's, the people could not accept it. That is why society is being changed through the introduction of new concepts through new age channels. This group appears to be giving their "channels" the real stuff. The process they use to channel this information is telepathy. It is "enhanced" telepathy which uses some kind of radio or microwave to put someone else's thoughts in your mind.

I have been told that one or two of the "channels" who were developed by Faction Two–the anti NWO faction, have actually developed the ability to communicate telepathically. This is all that real channeling is . . . telepathic communication with other sentient beings, no matter where or in what form they reside.

I also know that the other side, the World Order, also use new age channels. They use them in various ways, but usually they are used to create a spiritual community in which mind control and programming can be easily used with no questions asked. The Moonies, Jonestown and the Temple of the Solar Order are the best examples of this kind of programming through channels. They have also been used to "put" songs in the heads of some of the most famous 60s musicians and song writers.

Q: So, what I understand that you are saying is that there are two factions that are transmitting information through so-called "channelers" One of these factions is doing this for control and to promote a New World Order Agenda, while the other one is actually transmitting the true history of the planet earth? When you read channeled information are *you* able to distinguish between the two?

A: This is a very good question. It would be nice if I could give two or three good ways for people to distinguish the lies from the truth. Sadly, if there is an easy way, I haven't found it yet. I used to think that I could tell who belongs to which group by looking at the messages they produced. If they talked about a One World, then I usually put them into the New World Order group. Then I realized that that both groups talk about a One World. The difference in their approach is one group believes in human sovereignty, and the other group wants to take most of humanity back to the days of serfs and peasants.

However, even knowing this, you can't always count on being able to use this tool to decide if the "channeler" is promoting a New World Order, or if they are simply being realistic and understand that humans are going to have to learn how to live together and cooperate so they don't use their advanced technology to destroy civilization. The long and the short of it is, there is no hard and fast rule for being able to tell who is good and who is bad.

One of the lessons all of us are learning right now is discernment. Using your own discernment is the key to understanding most things. Discernment can also be used to draw into your life the books and teachers you need. Once you have mastered "the art of discernment," and are sure you can trust it, then you don't have to use outside 'tools' or 'tricks' to be able to tell is something is good or bad for you. You will simply "know" at an inner level.

Q: You know that there will be people who read this and think that you are delusional or worse. What do you have to say regarding this?

A: I have been under attack ever since I started sharing my information. Over the years, the attacks have ranged from name calling, to attacks on my animals, to assassination attempts on me. When you compare being called a name versus having speeding cars and bullets aimed at you, it tends to put things in perspective. Name-calling doesn't bother me.

I still get called names due to the articles I write for Rumor Mill News. Most of these names are unprintable. Back in 1998, when I said that Hillary Clinton, was going to run for the Senate from New York, I received hundreds of angry emails telling me I was insane. Many people demanded that they be removed from my mailing list. Last year, when I published an article about the Aztlan Liberation Army, and their plan to take back the South Western United States for Mexico, I was also subjected to hundreds of angry and insulting emails. Just this week, a major newspaper published the same information.

There will always be people who are afraid of the truth. When they don't like the message, they attack the messenger. This is just the way it is and always has been. Everyone who pushes the fabric gets treated like this. Galileo was censored, tried by the Inquisitors, tortured and imprisoned. Until human consciousness changes, there will always be people who attack things they don't like, don't understand, fear, or don't want exposed.

When you choose to do what I do, you have to face all the possible consequences, no matter how bad they may be. If you feel that what you are doing is more important than the consequences, then you continue your work. As the years go on, you eventually get used to the name-calling. You learn how to deal with it, or you stop doing the work.

I have learned to use my own discernment to decide which attacks need to be countered, and which ones need to be ignored. This is the key! Ignore the things that won't hurt you, and deal with the attacks that will.

One of the last pieces of advice Gunther gave me before he disappeared was, "If something happens and I am not around to protect you, make yourself so incredible that you become un-credible."

He explained that people who might want to silence my message would rather discredit me than kill me. Dead people become martyrs, discredited people remain nuts, kooks, conmen, and charlatans.

If I have a choice between being dead or discredited, I am going to choose to be discredited. George W. Bush is President. I am working on a book that charges his father with treason. When it is published, I hope that President George. W. Bush will choose to discredit me rather than make me a martyr. With this article, I have given him all the ammunition he needs!

About The Interviewer

Theresa de Veto is the Founder and Editor of http://www.surfingtheapocalypse.com, a comprehensive website that deals with controversial, hidden and late-breaking news addressing a myriad of topics.

Coming from a background of broadcast radio and the music industry, she conducts interviews with interesting, innovative and mysterious people; those persons the "controlled" media would never dare approach for an impartial discussion. Her many interviews may be found on her website located at:

http://www.surfingtheapocalypse.com

Copyright © 2001

2006 Note from Rayelan:

> *In the interview I did with Theresa de Veto, I talked about my out of body experience and my trip to the planet of the Deer People. I said that there was more that I couldn't go into at the time because I didn't fully understand everything.*
>
> *I didn't fully understand what had happened until I watched President Ronald Reagan's funeral. The funeral was one the most dramatic funerals in history. It even surpassed Princess Diana's. I don't know how watching*

his funeral filled in the missing pieces of my puzzle... but that's what happened. I now KNOW the rest of the story!

The Quarantine of the Planet is Over!

Saturday, 12 June 2004

Today I saw something that can only be called a superhighway home. It is force field that stretches between the earth we know and another body. The other body may be a planet, or a ship. I don't know what it is. I just know that all of you who are reading this came from there. We came to earth together and we have not been able to leave. Once here, we are here until we finish our lessons... all of us are here until all of us finish our lessons.

For a long time now, I have known that our planet is quarantined. I was told that beings on earth have a virus and because of it, no soul is allowed to leave the solar system. What is the virus? It's not physical. It's one that affects the spirit. It's a virus that changes pure souls of light into dark beings who know evil... the knowledge of good and evil... While I am certain evil exists elsewhere in the universes, the kind of evil that exists on earth is so rare that those souls who are infected with it are forced to stay here until they cure themselves.

What I saw today tells me that we have finished our lessons and it is time for us to start going home. Today I knew that souls from our family will be traveling this super highway home for the next 100+ years. Some of us will go early, some of us will stay until all the family members have left earth. We can leave no one behind! I have argued with agents about this quarantine theory of mine. I now realize that I cannot change anyone's belief system. If you don't believe what I am about to say... that's fine. I will not try to change your beliefs, so don't bother trying to make me prove it to you. If what I am about to say doesn't feel right to you... then stop reading. There are a lot of other things on RMN to read... go read them... don't make me waste my time trying to convince you of something that you simply cannot be convinced of until the time is right for you!

With that being said... Here goes:

I come from a group of souls whose planet was destroyed before we finished our development in the material world. Most people who are part of Rumor Mill News (RMN) are also part of my family. After today's revelations, I know that the reason I created RMN was to unite our family.... especially the more advanced ones who have chosen to help the less advanced. It's possible we have some on RMN who are not family members... who are spies from the other side... some who even actively work for the government while pretending to be high, wise and spiritual teachers. RMN also has readers who are soul-friends, but from other worlds... not ours.

Needless to say... there are NO aliens on earth... because we are ALL alien to earth! Earth has always been a school. It is a wonderful school. It has taught many different kinds of lessons using many different kinds of physical forms. At one point on earth a school for philosophers and mathematicians existed. The bodies that these souls wore were very similar to deer. These souls needed no hands. They were not builders. All they needed were brains that could think... and plentiful food. Once they had learned the lessons of philosophy and mathematics, they began to apply it to all forms of sentient communal life. The philosophy they developed could be compared to the enlightened spiritual teachings of the great masters. Once the phase of communal living in an enlightened state was achieved, these same philosophers and mathematicians had to learn about love. The bodies changed slightly... they still had the body of a deer, four feet... but they also had arms... to hold, and embrace, and gently touch the face of their beloved. They did not look like the centaur of old with its large and clumsy horse like body. They were loving gentle creatures who lived in a world that spanned earth and the spirit realm from which we all come.

As a benefit of living so close to our Origin, these beings had powers above and beyond anything we can even imagine these days. Their powers were never used for evil because the lesson they were learning was LOVE... All they knew was love... innocent, gentle, sweet, pure LOVE. Love for no other reason than LOVE. However... if you only know love... how can you ever be sure that you will not fall into evil... hate... anger... lust... the seven deadly sins??? How can a soul that has never known anything but love survive in a world where evil, deception, cruelty and pain exist? Can they be certain they will not follow a clever talking evil pied piper, who leads them down a slippery slope of deception into realm of evil that can do permanent damage to their soul, and turn them into a being that can infect others with the same soul aberration that now keeps them quarantined on planet earth. If the story I am telling plucks a chord in you, then please read the links below so you will have more of a foundation on which to build the next chapter.

Is This a Picture of a Soul Catcher?

What is This Strange Dark Cone?
Is It A Soul Catcher At Work?

By Rayelan Allan

The launch of the space shuttle Atlantis on February 8th was one of the most spectacularly beautiful ever. But something strange happened that has NOT been widely reported. A long, dark cone, extending from the shuttle's bright exhaust plume to the full moon near the horizon appeared. Some described it as rainbow-like, and some observers wondered how a dark shadow could possibly extend from one very bright object (the shuttle plume) to another (the full moon).

Mystifying shuttle shadow

By Boston Globe Staff, 2/27/2001

The launch of the space shuttle Atlantis on Feb. 8, on a mission to the International Space Station, was one of the most spectacularly beautiful ever. Lifting off at 20 minutes after sunset and eight hours before a full moon created spectacular visual effects, best captured in this photo by Pat McCracken of NASA headquarters. But many people were mystified by the long, dark cone extending from the shuttle's bright exhaust plume to the full moon near the horizon. Some news accounts described it as rainbow-like, and some observers wondered how a dark shadow could possibly extend from one very bright object (the shuttle plume) to another (the full moon).

Several years ago, I had an Instant Message conversation with John Lear. During the conversation he asked me if Gunther had ever told me anything about the buildings and structures on the moon. I answered yes and proceeded to tell him that Gunther had told me about a Moon Base.

He quickly sent back an instant message that asked, "Did he ever tell you about the structure that is a soul catcher?" I was stunned.

Gunther had described, in great detail, an ancient structure which was built by extraterrestrials that "shot" souls to earth and "caught" them after their trip to earth was finished. I was amazed that John knew about it.

Gunther told me that his mother was descended from the Hungarian Esterházy family. The Esterházys are best known as the benefactors of Hayden. The Hayden conservatorium is in the old Esterházy castle east of Vienna, Austria near the Hungarian border.

The Esterházys believed they were descended from people who came to earth from the star Sirius. "Ester" means "star," and "haszy" means either "descended from" or "House of." In other words, the word "Esterházy" means "House of the Star" or "Descended from the Star." The Star was the star Sirius.

Gunther told me that the Esterházys believe that their ancestors had to come to earth because their home world was destroyed. He said that original settlers built ships that took volunteers to earth to physically settle and begin to prepare the earth for the later arrivals.

He said the main body of souls traveled as a soul group from their home world to the star Sol, the Sun around which the Earth orbited. The soul group resided in the Sun until preparations had been made for the souls to travel to earth. When a soul was ready to individuate in preparation for going to earth, the soul was shot out of the Sun and went to the Moon.

Gunther said that at the time this was going on, the Planetary Federation had a quarantine on the Planet Earth. No one was allowed to interfere in the "breeding experiment" that was going on. When one of the souls from the Sirius Group was ready to travel to earth to reside in a body, the Federation would "shoot" the soul to earth with their "soul shooter" which was on the moon.

When the soul had finished its lessons, there was a "reverse soul-shooter" in the Great Pyramid. The body would be placed in a sarcophagus in a mineral brine. Low levels of electricity were sent through the mineral brine. When enough water had evaporated, there was a sudden flash; the body was instantly transmuted into atoms. This string of atoms, to which the soul was still attached, was shot out the "reverse soul-shooter," through the slanted opening in the pyramid. This was done only when the opening and the moon were aligned. On the way to the moon, everything physical fell away from the soul and it was "caught" by the device on the moon that was set up by the Federation to "shoot" and "catch" the souls that were assigned to earth.

I don't remember much about what John Lear told me about the "soul catcher" that he knew about. What I do remember is that it was being used for a negative purpose rather than the purpose it had been created for. It was catching souls, but it was catching them to enslave them, not as part of the two way transportation method that had been built to gain entry to a quarantined planet.

Take a look at the above picture which was taken at the launch of a Space Shuttle. If I had been asked to draw a picture of the "Soul Shooter" on the moon, shooting a soul to the moon, it would have looked just like this! The more I look at the photo, the more I wonder.

If there really is a soul shooter and/or soul catcher, could an exchange of souls have just been made? Could one of the people who was on the shuttle now have a different soul?

See Also: John Lear's Disclosure Briefing from the 11.2.03 Art Bell Show.

- ❥ http://www.rumormillnews.com/cgi-bin/ archive.cgi?read=39442IN SEARCH OF THE SOUL CATCHER

- ❥ http://rumormillnews.com/ SOUL%20CATCHER%20ADDENDUM.htm

The Deer People

Monday, 14 June 2004

I don't know why the Deer People had to be eliminated from Earth. What is very interesting to me is this: For the first time since I have known about this story, I am questioning why... why did they have to be eliminated? Why couldn't Deer People and humans co-exist?

Now that I have asked myself this question, I now wonder if maybe the Deer People and humans did co-exist for a short time. When the Earth School graduates a class, there is always an "overlap" of old students and new students. When the bodies changed, there was also an overlap. We can see this with Cro-Magnon man and Neanderthals. I am certain there have been many other "overlaps," but I do not think those in charge of the official version of history will share them just yet.

When I was made aware of the Deer People, the story, as I know it, involved a Special Operations Group (SOG) from our present time. The SOG went back in time to round up and kill all the Deer People.

What is *very* important to understand right now is: I do not know if we have reached the point in *this* time, where the Special Operations Group (SOG) was dispatched to go back in time, and kill the Deer People. In other words, whoever dispatched the SOG to go back in time and kill the Deer People had access to time travel.

I don't know if the SOG team came from the future or another dimension. I also don't know if the mission took place in the past, or if it will take place in the future. Something went wrong with the original plan. I don't really know what it was, but it appears as if when the Deer People were transported to earth, they loved it so much they chose NOT to give up their Deer bodies.

The Deer People had a very important role to play in the future of Earth. If they did NOT give up their Deer bodies and incarnate as humans, Earth civilization would not have occurred in the way it did. Not only did something go wrong with the original plan, but something went wrong with the plan to FIX the original plan.

As a result of this glitch, there is the possibility that we are running on two time lines right now, and at some point in the future... the very near future... these two timelines are going to merge.... and to do this, the Deer People who are alive in one of the time lines, have to die! But why? Why was the Special Operations Group dispatched from this time? Because a person was alive in this time period... the latter part of the 20th century...who had known the Deer People... she was a soul who had lived with the Deer People and shared a body with one of them. This person was trusted and loved by the Deer People.

Those who believed (or knew) the Deer People had to die, also knew that if this person went with them and allowed them to read her mind, the Deer People would lay down their Earth bodies with no fear, hatred or anxiety, and go back to their home planet. Many of their soul family still live in their Deer bodies on that planet.

That person was me. The SOG mission took place at the exact time in 1984 that I was having my out of body experience due to spinal meningitis. If you remember from the interview conducted with me by Theresa de Veto from Surfing The Apocalypse; during my out of body experience, I visited many different planets. One of these planets was the home of the Deer People. I entered the body of a female Deer Person who was studying to be a philosopher and writer for a life on earth in ancient Greece. Her husband was studying mathematics and advanced physics. While I was in the body of the female deer he and I discussed what his race was being prepared to do. They were the ones who would be bringing mathematics, science and philosophy to earth. They would be the ones who gave Terrans the foundation for the world we now live in.

There were many things involved in getting the Deer People to leave their earth bodies. The Deer People had gone off course in their evolutionary plan. Their purpose on Earth was to develop their minds... *only* their minds. Somewhere along the line, a glitch crept in. I can't tell you where, when, or what this glitch was. I can only speculate. I suspect that one of the Deer People interbred with a human because the Deer People developed hands and arms. In the Bible it says, "The Sons of God mated with the Sons of Man." I have always believed this passage to mean that extra-terrestrial beings came to earth and mated with earth women. I suspect the same thing must have happened to the Deer People.

It's possible that the same extra-terrestrials who changed things on earth for the humans, also changed things for the Deer People. I don't know when this happened. Possibly on their own planet, possibly after they came to earth. Because of this, they entered an entirely new evolutionary path that was not their intended path.

The path the Deer People was intended to follow on earth was one that developed their mental side. The Deer People were preparing for lives as some of the greatest philosophers, writers and mathematicians of all time. Instead, they were seduced by love in its highest form.

How could this be a bad thing? It could only be a bad thing if it prevented the original mission from being accomplished. And it did.

There was one other thing that complicated things. The bodies the Deer People lived in could not die. They lived on an island in the middle of the Pacific Ocean. There were no other beings on that island.

I do not know this for sure, but I suspect that the Island on which they lived is one of the Islands that is part of the Philippines. The Deer People were alone on that Island. For all they knew, they were the only beings on the planet.

The Deer People developed the ability to love. However, one other thing complicated things. One of the Deer People had also developed the ability to hate. This is the reason I think there were outside genes in the Deer People by the time they got to earth. The Deer People were preparing to become philosophers and mathematicians. They did not have emotions.

It appears that whoever created the Deer People wanted them to be like computers. They didn't want to have anything to interfere in the mission the Deer People needed to accomplish. The deer people were meant to bring the foundations of civilization to earth. They were expected to bring language, mathematics, social orders, and more.

All of this was to have been created in their minds before they set foot on earth. But something happened. They did not appear in a place where humans lived. They chose to live by themselves and experience all of the feelings of joy and pleasure that love could give.

However, there was one who was different. Not only did he choose to experience the emotion of love. But he chose to experience all emotions…. Not just the seven virtues, but the seven deadly sins as well.

This was the Deer Person who used his mind to develop science… perverted science. Science can be used for both good and evil. This Deer Person used his mind to create evil. He had done little damage until the SOG went down with the intent to kill the bodies of the Deer People, thereby freeing their souls.

When I first was told about the Deer People, I was only told about the mission to kill them. I was told about the person who had lived on the Deer Planet and I was told that this person agreed to accompany the Special Operations Group back in time in order to talk to the leader of the Deer People, who was a close friend of the One who agreed to help kill the bodies of the Deer People.

I was told that the Leader of the Deer People would use the mind of this person as a way to leap from Earth back to his home world. The person who went back in time had the ability to act as a "mental" time and space transporter for the Deer Leader… a bridge from Earth to his home world.

When I was first told this story, I didn't connect the dots. I didn't realize the person I was being told about was me. The Deer Leader was transported back to his home world over a bridge I made. Evidently while I was out of body and in the body of the female Deer Person, my own physical body was being transported back in time.

In other words, "I had a foot in each world and the leader of the Deer People could use the 'highway' I created to return to his home planet. Once he did this, he remembered his original mission. The mission he and his people had spent eons preparing for. He understood why the Deer People had to give up their earth bodies and go home. It only took him an instant to remember, and once he remembered, he was able to telepathically share his 'awakening' with all his Deer People.

The one Deer Person who had developed the ability to hate was not in the group when the Deer People laid down their bodies and left Earth.

One of the men in the Special Operations Group had a rifle. He was the only one with a weapon. It was brought because the Deer People were extremely strong, and it was feared that one or more might resist. When the leader of the Deer People realized that all Deer People had to leave Earth and return home, ALL the Deer People knew it instantly. Their souls traveled home on the same intergalactic highway that my body and soul had created for the Leader. The moment the souls departed, the bodies fell and died.

The Special Operations Group vaporized the bodies. The man with the gun and several others in the SOG went in search of the other Deer People. Before he departed, the leader of the Deer People said that several of his family were missing. I do not remember how many. What I do remember is something happened. Something went wrong. The other Deer People were not killed nor did they return home.

The Deer Man who had developed both sides of his emotional body was one of the Deer People that was missing. As the SOG was getting ready to depart, the leader of the Special Operations Group asked the man with the gun to account for all the bullets and shell casings. Nothing from the future could be left in the past.

The leader of the SOG asked for the rifle. The sniper gave it to him. The leader checked the bullets and asked for the casings. There were not enough casings. The sniper had fired one shot. Had he killed or wounded one of the Deer People? I was never told.

The SOG began to search for the missing shell case. But then another screw up happened... the man who had carried the rifle

and may or may not have killed some of the renegade Deer People…
vanished. I suspect he joined the Deer People.

The SOG searched for him and for any sign of the missing Deer
People or their bodies. No trace of them could be found. The SOG
could not stay past a certain time or not only would they not be able
to return to their own time, if this happened, it would alter the time
line for all of Earth.

The SOG returned back to this time… aware that their mission was
not completely accomplished and as a result of this, there could be a
"wrinkle" in time. The man who told me this story believes that the
SOG did create a "wrinkle in time." He says that this "wrinkle" could
have created two time lines. Two parallel worlds. He believes we are
now entering the time frame where the two worlds come together.
We are entering the "Wrinkle in Time."

The time window I am talking about is from now to 100 years in
Earth's future. In other words, the orders to carry out this SOG
mission came from somewhere in this time frame. However, the
people who made up the SOG were chosen was from the 1980s
because that was when their bodies and their minds were the
strongest. The SOG was chosen because of the souls who were
involved. The 1980s were chosen as the date because the SOG
members were at their prime AND …a time window opened in the
1980s.

The memory of the trip back in time was erased from the minds of
the men who were part of the SOG. Only one person remembered the
trip. But not really. The memory was there, but it was hidden under
layers of denial that such a thing could really have taken place. That
person was me. At the time, I was an ordinary human living an
ordinary life.

The out of body experience that was caused by the meningitis was
overwhelming enough. Knowing that my body was also taken that
night, without my permission, was something that was just too much
for me to remember.

I changed after the mission that involved the Deer People. I
attributed this change to the information I learned while out of body.
I now believe the enormity of my change had little to do with being
taught the Activated Cellular Memory Method and flying around in
space. My entire focus in life changed. I went from being 100% on a
spiritual path, to being 100% consumed with politics.

Two months after I recovered from meningitis I became Gary Hart's
media coordinator for his 1984 run for President. He lost to Fritz
Mondale, and I came down with meningitis again. This time I stayed

in bed from July until November. I was too weak to even lift my head off the pillow.

The SOG consisted of less than 20 people. I believe most of these men are still alive. I also believe they have had memory blocks put in their minds. Or maybe, since we haven't approached the time in our future when the mission actually takes place, maybe they have no memory because it hasn't been formed for them yet.

Maybe I am different.

As we move closer to the time when the decision will be made to activate the SOG from the 1980s, we will have the opportunity to redo the glitch that created two timelines. When this happens, the timeline of earth will shift.... again.

While I was watching President Reagan's funeral something very strange happened to me. For a moment I was somewhere else watching souls who were building a super highway for the rest of us. I realized that the super highway I saw being created was very similar to the one that had been made for the leader of the Deer People. I knew that the souls who were building this new "super highway" were sacrificing themselves and the lives they had lived on Earth in order to keep one foot on Earth and the other out in space... each person/soul was building on top the shoulders of the others... each reaching out a little farther in space... until finally the super highway will connect all of us to the home from which our soul family came.

The people who are building this "super highway" are the ones who are manifesting symptoms we currently call Alzheimer's. At some point in the future, we will recognize what a tremendous sacrifice and gift they gave us.

Not all people are of our soul family... Not all people will resonate with what I am writing here. Our class... our soul family is approaching graduation time... We will soon be returning home and the planet Earth will be home to a new group of souls. This new group of souls will need bodies that are slightly different from the ones we are using.

Some people believe that the chemtrails are terra-forming earth in order to create the proper environment and the proper bodies for these new beings. We will see the new souls arrive soon. They will not arrive en masse until we have reached the point... somewhere between now and 100 years in our future... when someone realizes that the problem in the past with the Deer People has to be cleaned up... and cleaned up properly.

So... there may be a time-loop for a while... until the problem with the Deer People is fixed properly... for all we know, we are caught in this time loop right now... going round and round... repeating and repeating....

Earth has been quarantined since our class arrived 10 to 50,000 years ago. The first of our class arrived 50,000 years ago. Most buzzed on in about 10,000 years ago. But some of the "newbies" were so busy elsewhere in the universe that they only got here about 3,000 years ago. I am not sure how long ago the Deer People came to earth... It could have been millions of years ago for all I know.

We have all learned what we came to Earth to learn and it is now time for all of us to clean up our garbage and leave. We are needed elsewhere. Our time for study is over... we must prepare to leave... and that is what some of our soul family are doing for us right now.... they are preparing our path home!

Approximately 4 and a half million people are creating a soul bridge... a super highway home for the rest of us. The ones, who are building the Super Highway for us to escape Earth's quarantine and return home.... have Alzheimer's.

Next time you are with an Alzheimer's patient, make sure to thank him or her for creating your pathway home. I still don't understand why the Deer People had to be eliminated. I do know that the reason I was chosen to go with the SOG was so the Deer People would suffer no trauma to their souls. If I had not accompanied the SOG, the Deer People would have had to be killed. Because I was there they immediately understood what had to be done and simply left their bodies. They did not suffer any soul damage at the moment of death.

Alzheimer's patients suffer no soul damage at their deaths. When they die, they step from one body into the next with no need for rehabilitation on the other side.

There are 4 1/2 millions souls who will greet the rest of us and act as nurses, counselors and old friends. The leader of this group is Ronald Wilson Reagan. His presence on Earth had to be so Great that all the members of his Soul Family would know him and trust him.

When it is time for our Graduation we will go like the Deer People, with no pain or trauma. The Super Highway will beckon our souls and we will be pulled on board for the ride home. When it's time for us to make the transition, there will be no fear, no pain... only peace and then jubilation!

I put all of these pieces together while I was watching President Reagan's Funeral. I believe the reason that the funeral was the longest, largest and most royal funeral the world has ever experienced, was because someone besides me knows the truth. Someone wanted to awaken this truth.

The Day I Met The King of The World

By Rayelan Allan, formerly, Rayelan Russbacher

I met the King of the World in July of 1990. I had been married to Gunther [Russbacher] about a year. Gunther had been in jail near St. Louis, the entire time. I was in California. I had not seen Gunther since he had been arrested two days after we were married.

I arranged for a film company, with whom I worked, to buy Gunther's life story for $40,000. The prosecutor agreed to take the money for bail, and released Gunther.

Gunther and I drove directly to Offutt Air Force base in Omaha. We stayed in VIP quarters on base. William Webster, the DCI (Director of Central Intelligence) was on one side of us, Brent Scowcroft, the NSA (National Security Advisor), was on the other side. George Bush was across the hall, and Dick Cheney was at the end of the hall. At the time, Cheney didn't rate being in the inner circle, he was only the Secretary of Defense.

William Webster wore red shorts and a red Hawaiian shirt when he was in the room. We were there so Gunther could upgrade his SR 71 flying. Gunther had been in jail almost a year. They needed him to fly a top secret mission to Moscow and they wanted to be sure he still knew how to fly! On the mission with Gunther would be Brent Scowcroft, William Webster, Gunther's boss, the DCO (Director of Covert Operations) an Admiral named Wilhelm Johann.

There was a fourth passenger, but Gunther would never tell me who he was. When they got to the Moscow airport, there was no translator, so Gunther had to do the translation. He said there was an old KGB spy who was a friend, so he and Gunther did the translating for the group. The old spy gave Gunther a pack of Russian cigarettes. Gunther had them in the pocket of his flight suit when he returned.

The Russian delegation included Mikhail Gorbachev. Gunther and his covert group of high ranking United States officials carried a treaty to Moscow for Gorbachev to sign. The day of this flight was July 26, 1990. This was one day after April Glaspie met with Saddam Hussein and gave him the green light to invade Kuwait.

The meeting on Offutt was from July 19 to July 22. Gunther and his group left from Reno Municipal airport in Reno, Nevada, the afternoon of July 26, 1990.

I watched at the edge of the runway while the four SR-71's circled and came in for a landing. Three of the planes were painted in desert camouflage. Only one was the standard black titanium. Following the four 71's came a white Learjet. This was the same Learjet that

Gunther and I had taken, a year before, when we fled his "handlers" and flew to Reno to get married. At the time we took it to Reno, it was black, with red pin stripes.

While we were staying on Offutt Air Force Base, William Webster called our room and told Gunther to look out the window. We were in a room that had full view of the flight line. We saw a white Learjet that looked just like our old "Blackbird."

I was listening on the phone when William Webster said to Gunther, "That's your plane. We painted it white and renamed it 'The Pigeon.'" Gunther shouted some colorful words and banged the telephone on the wall as if trying to hit Webster.

The sound of laughter came from the room where Webster was staying. It was so loud that it could be heard through the walls. Gunther stormed out the door of our room and went to pound on Webster's door. I stood in our doorway watching it all.

"Let me in," I heard Gunther roar.

"You think we're crazy?" a voice replied.

"I'll break this door down." Gunther threatened. "Let me in. I'm going to pound you into toast."

At that moment, two men dressed in dark suits approached Gunther. One said, "Captain, don't you think you should go back into your room before we have to get nasty?"

Gunther looked at them, calmed down and walked back into our room, slamming the door behind him. He went back to the wall that adjoined Webster's room, and pounded on it again.

"Just you wait, I'll get you guys. Your time is coming!" Gunther yelled this at the top of his voice.

I could hear laughter and voices, but I couldn't understand what they were saying.

On July 26, four SR 71's flew to Moscow, only three came back. One was left in Moscow, along with the pilot, a man I did not know. The other three planes, their pilots and passengers flew back in a close wing pattern that registered on radar as one plane.

We left Offutt on the 22nd of July. Gunther flew the flight out of the Reno airport on the 26th. We left Omaha and had driven non stop to Winnemucca, Nevada. We arrived at the Red Lion Hotel about 2pm on the afternoon of the 23rd.

Gunther requested a specific ground floor room near the front of the hotel. Gunther and I had taken turns sleeping as the other drove for a day and a half. We were tired, but not sleepy. All we wanted was a hot bath and something to eat.

As we walked into the room Gunther said, "This is A CIA room. Turn on the television. There is a CIA training channel." I followed his orders, and sure enough there was a very unusual black and white film playing.

"Watch that," Gunther ordered. "It's a training film. It will teach you how to search a house with the owners home and they won't have the slightest idea what you are doing."

I sat on the bed in front of the television. Gunther went into the bathroom and took a hot bath.

In the film, there was a group of men sitting in a circle in a small room. I could not believe what I was seeing. There was a young William Webster, along with a young Zbigniev Brezhinsky, Stansfield Turner, Vernon Walters, and some I didn't recognize. They were discussing how to enter homes while people were present and search the home or plant listening devices.

There was also a narrator for the film. Instead of standing nearby and telling us what was going on, the Narrator was in a 1961 Cadillac convertible and he was taking us for a tour of a CIA community that had just been built in Florida.

The camera showed us the names of all the street signs. They all had names that sounded like sea creatures from Greek legends. The community had curving and circular streets. The streets were set up in such a way, that no one could enter the community without being seen, and they couldn't drive fast enough to do any damage and get away without being caught.

The top was down on the convertible and the driver's face could be seen very well. Behind the wheel of the convertible was a very young George Bush. He was the narrator of the training film. Bush said that it was 1961, and a Catholic had just been elected as President. Because of this, it was time to start selling Catholic bibles door to door.

The next scene involved Jean Kirkpatrick as a leery housewife who does not want to open her door to two unknown salesmen selling Catholic Bibles.

"What are you?" One of the men asked Kirkpatrick, "An atheist? Or do you just hate Catholics?"

"No," Jean, the housewife protested.

"Then you won't mind letting us come in and show you this Bible." One man said.

The two men walked past her into the house. One of them sat down in the living room and pulled out the bible. He began the sales pitch. The other man asked for a glass of water. Jean, the housewife, started to get up and get him one.

The man who wanted the water told her, "No...no, you sit right there and look at the pretty pictures. I can find a glass by myself."

The man with the Bible, mesmerized the housewife, while the other man did whatever it was that he had come into the house to do.

Gunther later told me that part of this training film was the implied knowledge that a very powerful form of hypnosis was being taught to CIA operatives. This powerful form of hypnosis was imported from Nazi Germany after the war. A watered down version of it is called Neural Linguistic Programming. The man with the Bible, used this rapid form of hypnosis on the unsuspecting housewife while the other man did the dirty work. When he was finished, they thanked the housewife for her time and left with a $400.00 check for the Bible.

Gunther said he taught this Super form of NLP to CIA operatives at a school for Operatives in Waco, Texas in the early 60's. The school was called The Life Management Institute, LMI. William Sessions, the former Director of the FBI was a councilman in Waco at the time.

The film was longer. After the Bible session, George Bush came back on and drove around in the Cadillac convertible and talked a little more about something. Suddenly I was so tired I could not stay awake. I wanted to watch this film, but there was nothing I could do but close my eyes and lay back on the bed.

This was about 2:30 PM. I awakened at midnight. I had slept almost 10 hours.

This was not usual for me. I am lucky to sleep continuously for four hours at a time, no matter HOW tired I am. Gunther wakes up every hour on the hour to do a perimeter check. He says it is a "leftover" from Viet Nam. But on this afternoon, both of us slept for almost ten hours.

When we awoke, we were both groggy. Gunther said we had been drugged. I looked at my arm, and sure enough, there was a tell tale needle mark. I did not remember anything about where I had been or what I had done. We were both so upset and wary about what had happened to us that we stayed awake until early morning, constantly on our guard wondering what else was going to happen. As soon as it was light, we checked out and drove to Reno where Gunther needed to pick up an SR-71 flight suit.

A day later, Gunther flew his mission to Moscow. After he came back, we drove to Castle Air Force Base in Merced, California. We were told that Gunther was going to be promoted to Admiral and we were going to be given a post at Whidby Island in Washington State. Instead of this, he was arrested and our year long nightmare began again.

Many months later that I ran into an old friend I trusted. She was a hypnotherapist. I told her about the missing time and she suggested that we do a session. Once she had gotten me into a relaxed state, she asked me to talk about everything that had happened from the time Gunther was released from jail in St. Charles, Missouri to the time he was arrested on Castle Air Force Base by the FBI.

From the relaxed state I was able to remember two men coming into the room in Winnemucca and taking me out the sliding glass doors that led into the parking lot. I was dressed in white short shorts and a sleeveless pink blouse. One of the men grabbed a pair of sandals for me. They were not the kind of sandals that you would wear with shorts. They were 2 and a half inch wedge ankle straps. I saw that the men had backed a van up to our sliding glass doors. They put me and Gunther in the van.

When I got out of the van we were on a runway. I saw Gunther being led, as if in a trance, into a waiting plane. I was taken to a helicopter and we immediately took off.

The helicopter landed on a deserted World War Two base somewhere in the Nevada desert. The buildings looked like they hadn't been touched since the end of the war. I was taken into one of the buildings and put into a chair that looked like a dentist's chair.

The man who was with me was the CIA station chief from St. Louis. A man I knew as Roger. He looked at the arm where they were going to put the needle. On that arm I had a rash that is called "Hoalie Crud." It is similar to athlete's foot. I don't know how or where I had picked it up. I have recurrent flare-ups. Each time I have one, I have to see doctor for a prescription.

I hadn't had the time to see a doctor, so I still had the rash on my arm. Roger put a piece of scotch tape on the rash. He pulled it off and gave it to a man. The man left the room. When he came back, he had a swab that he handed to Roger. Roger swabbed my arm and that is the last I remember of that episode.

The next thing I remember is climbing out of the top of a vessel that looked like a submarine. The vessel was in a concrete tunnel or canal which could have held water. Or there could have been track under the vessel.

I was dressed in a pair of khaki pants, and wearing a white polo shirt. I had on the wedge sandals that the man had picked up for me. I was with Gunther's boss, the Admiral named Wilhelm or William Johann. The clothes I was wearing were his. He had worn them the night Gunther and I had dinner with him and his wife in the Officers Club on Offutt.

The pants were way too long for me. Someone had taken the cuffs and pulled them to one side and tied them up with rubber bands. The cuffs were tight around the ankle and puffed out like harem pants. From a fashion point, it looked good. I felt a woman had to have dressed me!

We were inside an underground base. The men who were there were wearing gray uniforms with yellow trim. There were two huge metal doors. One was directly in front of the submarine. The other was to the left of the sub. There was a long tunnel to the right of the Submarine that was filled with small cars, like golf cars, that were going to and fro very quickly.

The Admiral pointed to the huge door to the left of us. We walked over to it. There was a smaller door cut into the huge door. There was a button to be pressed. The Admiral pressed it.

"Why are we here?" I asked

"The King of the World wants to meet you," The Admiral replied sarcastically.

I wanted to ask who that was, but there was no time, a buzzer sounded and we entered a room that was a museum. The glass cases where the treasures were kept were incredibly low. I am only 5 feet tall, but the cases were so low that I had to stoop over to see what was in them. Most of what was there had the Templar cross on it somewhere. At the time, I can remember thinking, "so this is where all the missing treasures are."

The only thing I can really remember seeing is the Crown of St. Stephen. I do remember that I was looking as fast as I could for the Spear of Longinus. The Spear of Destiny that pieced Jesus side when he was on the cross. For some reason, I knew it was here in this underground installation.

A door at the end of the room opened, and a man, about 5 feet 6 inches tall entered. He had white hair and was wearing glasses with thick black rims. He was wearing a light blue shirt with an emblem on it. It was the compass from the center of the CIA logo. It was stitched in dark blue. The man who entered the room dismissed the Admiral as if the Admiral were a busboy. I realized that this must be, "The King of the World."

He put his arm around me and led me out the door from which he had come. To the right of me I saw a mess hall filled with hundreds of people. They were talking and laughing and acting as normal as any other group of military men and women I have observed.

To the left, I saw a long hall. The King of the World had his arm around my shoulders as we walked down the long hall. He was talking to me the entire time. I cannot remember what he said. And I do not remember anything more than the walk down the long hall, with many doors. The floor was gray linoleum tile.

At the end of the long hall was a door. The King opened it. The first thing I saw was a fountain in the center of the room. It was a round stone fountain. In the center there was a tree that grew about ten feet above the fountain. There was water flowing into the fountain down waterfall type walls that were near the trunk of the tree. I had never seen a tree like the one in the room. It looked like a very old bonsai tree. In other words, it appeared to be a tree that was supposed to be a huge tree, but it had been pruned and kept as a small tree.

The King said to me, "This is where we keep the spare parts from our cloning lab. Come, let me show you what we have here."

He steered me to the left side of the room. There were long, low metal tanks. They were about four feet in width and each one was about 20 feet long. There were three of them lined up next to each other. They were filled with a liquid that contained very fine minerals. It resembled sea water, but with a huge amount of salt and minerals.

In the tanks were small sea creatures of several different sizes. The sea creatures moved around, slept, searched for food, bumped into each other and floated in the mineral brine.

The King pointed at one of the sea creatures that was shaped like a triangle. "This one has a liver in it."

He pointed to one that was rounder and bigger than the others. "This one has a heart in it." He pointed to a small round one. "That one has an eye." Pointing to another one, "That one has a kidney."

He put his hands on my shoulders and turned me around, "Over here we have the arms and legs, hands, and fingers." I saw that the other side of the room was filled with the same kind of long and low tanks which were filled with legs and arms and other things, including the strange looking sea creatures.

The King pushed me quickly through the cloning storage room and into a wonderful room filled with roses and orchids. At some point the King told me that when an organ was needed, they activated the tracker and found the one that had been grown for the person who was requesting it. All the sea creatures had implanted chips in them that were coded so the organs could be tracked and found when needed.

The sea creature was put in an organ transplant container... similar to the Coleman ice chests we take on picnics, and transported to where the transplant was going to be performed. The King told me that the creatures were not killed. They were "re-planted" with a seed from the original donor, and the creature was sent back to the lab where the organ would grow and be kept safe until it was needed again... if ever.

I remember walking through the roses and the orchids thinking how beautiful they were and how wonderful it was there.

And that is the last thing I remember from my meeting with the King of the World.

One thing I did recall very clearly, and it was my only real proof that something had happened to me. The rash I have does not tan. If you have a tan, and then get the proper treatment to cure the rash, there will be a white spot in the middle of you tan, where the rash used to be.

When I awakened from my missing time, there was a white spot where the rash used to be. I guess Roger treated the rash with the appropriate medicine before he injected me with whatever he gave me.

Gunther later told me that I was privileged to too many top secret conversations on Offutt, and all Roger was doing was putting in a block so I wouldn't remember anything.

I remember a lot of the conversations that happened at Offutt. While I was there, I had the feeling of being in a spy movie. For some reason, I remembered an old film I had seen as a child. I believe John Wayne was the star. It was about a soldier who was captured by the North Koreans during the Korean War and was subjected to brainwashing. He had a book of matches with him, and he wrote key things inside the book so they would jog his memory and keep him focused on what was really going on.

I decided to do the same thing. I figured the only time when I was safe enough to write myself notes, was when I was in the stall in the ladies room. I remember telling Gunther that I had a urinary tract infection. This gave me cover to explain why I was going to the bathroom all the time. I heard him tell this to someone who became suspicious as to why I kept excusing myself and going to the ladies room.

Even in the ladies room I wasn't really sure I would be unobserved. So I would sit on the john and bend over my purse, as if hunting for something. While my hand was in my purse, and I would write short keyword notes to myself, on scraps of chewing gum wrappers, receipts, or anything else that was at the bottom of my purse.

I have a habit of going through my purse every six months or so and throwing all the junk away. I know myself well enough to know that I write telephone numbers on scraps of paper, therefore, I have to go through everything that is in the purse and look at it before I throw it away.

It was several months after I had been on Offutt Air Force Base with Gunther that I went through my purse and discovered the cryptic notes I had written to myself in the ladies bathroom. Each one jogged my memory.

I am sure there are still things I have forgotten, but I am also sure that I remember a lot more than I am supposed to remember.

One of my vignettes will be about the UFO's that landed in the Persian gulf shortly before Kuwait was invaded. Another will be about the 12 million aliens that are coming to earth. These are conversations that I overheard from Gunther's cousin Larry Pauley, A.K.A. Robert Steigler, and another cousin Garret Henderson, a man I later found out was Richard Brenneke's half brother.

Gunther told me that these two men were killed in Cambodia in 1994 on a mission to rescue the last of the POW's that came out of SE Asia before Ron Brown normalized relations with Viet Nam. All the rest of our boys who were left behind, were killed. However, I know that Larry and Garrett aren't dead. Their aliases are dead. But the men who played the part of Larry and Garrett are very much alive, or at least they were in November of 1999 when I met with them in San Antonio, Texas.

Beware of Phone Men, Cable Installers, and Diapers

Posted on http://www.rumormillnews.com
By: Rayelan
Date: Thursday, 11 October 2001, 3:34 a.m.

After I married Gunther Russbacher, ONI, CIA, in 1989, I began to realize that things were not at all what they appeared to be.

Before I continue this, for readers who don't know the story of my marriage to Gunther, let me quickly say that he was arrested two days after we married and he stayed in prison almost the entire 10 years of our marriage. We spent about 9 months together, and most of that was in Austria.

One day, as I was having a phone installed in my new house, the phone man motioned me over, handed me a telephone and said, "Your husband wants to talk to you."

Gunther was in prison at the time. He was in Terminal Island, near Long Beach, California. Prisoners are only allowed to make collect phone calls. Had the phone man accepted a collect call? I never knew.

Gunther told me that the telephone man was installing a special scrambler that would make it impossible for the FBI to listen in on my conversations.

The next day, while I was making lunch for the man who was installing the TV cable, the phone rang. It was Gunther, "Let me talk to the turkey." he said.

"What turkey are you talking about?" I asked.

The cable man held out his hand for the phone and said, "He means me!"

They talked for a while and then the cable man handed the phone back to me. (The cable man re-appeared in our lives four years later to help us work on the Philippine gold transfer!)

Gunther told me not to worry if the cable man stayed in the house all day. It never occurred to me to ask Gunther why. In hindsight, I wonder if a hit order had been put out on me and the cable man was there to make sure I stayed alive!

One of the funniest things that ever happened was at the same house. One day I noticed a very strange panel truck parked across the street. It was light pink and blue and had the name and address of the company written on the side.

The name was something like: "The Dipsy Doo Diaper Service." The address and telephone number were in San Francisco. I thought this was very strange, because I lived in the Santa Cruz mountains, about an hour and a half from San Francisco. Why would anyone use a San Francisco diaper service if they lived in the Santa Cruz mountains?

One day when Gunther called, I told about the panel truck. He told me to go outside and look at the license plate. He told me what the letters would be before I got there! And he was absolutely right! Gunther told me that it was a "pool vehicle" that had been checked out of San Francisco. He said he had been informed of it by a friend who ran the CIA office in San Francisco. He also told me that anyone in government could recognize these vehicles because of the license plate number.

Then he told me to stand in front of the truck and continue talking to him. I did as he told me. He said a few things that I did NOT understand. Suddenly the panel truck started its engine. Backed up... away from me... spun a u-turn and sped away!

I knew Gunther had told them something that made them do that, but he never told me what it was.

Another funny thing happened as I was waiting in the San Francisco Airport to catch a Southwest Airlines plane back to Missouri. The gate attendant walked up to me and asked, "Are you Mrs. Russbacher?" I answered yes and wondered what had happened. She responded, "Our President wants to speak with you." When I got to the counter, she handed me a telephone. I said hello. The man on the other end said, "Your husband wants to talk to you." with that he put Gunther on the line.

Gunther told me to always fly Southwest Air because it was the "Company Airline" and I would always be safe on SWA.

One of the strangest and most puzzling things that happened involving government agents disguised as cable men, phone men, diaper service men, etc... happened after Gunther left me and married Jane! (He married Jane before he divorced me.)

One day the doorbell rang. Before I answered it I looked out the window and saw a phone truck parked in the driveway. I opened the door and a phone man asked if this was 2525 Howard Way, I said yes. He then handed me an envelope and said that he had a work order. I told him there was nothing wrong with the phone.

"I know," he said, "But here is the work order."

It didn't dawn on me until later that he knew there was nothing wrong with the phone... If he had a work order to fix my phone, how did he know the phone worked???

I pulled out the work order. There was a small piece of paper inside a larger yellow paper. On the small piece of paper was a poem. Even after all these years, I can still remember it:

The Gunther Russbacher
Who Lives With Jane
And the One you Married
Are Not the Same.

To find the One
Who has the real Face
You must Look in the Darkest Place!

Try Langley VA
And have a nice Day!

The moment I looked up, the telephone man grabbed the envelope out of my hand. He left without saying a thing. I was too stunned to do anything.

I ran back in the house and wrote down the poem before I forgot it. I looked out the window in time to see the phone man drive away. It was then that I recognized him as one of Gunther's friends.

Needless to say, I could continue telling these stories... but I think you get the idea.

In May of 1991, after Gunther went public with what he knew about the October Surprise and George Bush's involvement in it, things began to get even stranger for me.

Gunther was not able to get a 'secure line' for our conversations anymore, so I had to learn a secret code language to talk to him. He called it "slingo."

I also realized that the government could tap any communication I had... including mail, phone, fax, or with a friend at a restaurant.

One day Gunther sent a man to deliver a message. The man, whom I knew and trusted, stopped by, unannounced, with a picnic basket. He said, "Let's go to the beach!"

I grabbed some towels and we went to a beach that had a high cliff next to it.

After we sat and ate our lunch the man said, "Let's go for a walk."

We walked to the edge of the water, where the sand is packed down. He bent over, picked up a stick, and began writing in the sand.

He told me, through the messages he wrote in the sand, that there was an FBI van parked on the cliff listening to everything we said. He also told me that he was probably being tracked by satellite from NRO. The man was an Admiral in Navy Intelligence.

After he wrote that, I understood why he bent over the words that he wrote, he knew the satellites could read what he was writing, so he hid the words with his body.

He wrote, "Package will be delivered to Congress tomorrow! Don't worry if you don't hear from Gunther. He needs to go get the package."

He then told me NOT to discuss any of this with anyone because everyone was listening to everything I said. He said that Gunther sent him because Gunther was afraid that I might do something that would alert the Feds if I didn't hear from him for 24 hours. This was happening during the election of 1992. George H. W. Bush monitored everything we did.

Gunther was right, I probably would have created a crisis on the fax networks we used at the time to get out the word! And if the government knew that Gunther was out of contact with me, they would probably think that he was 'out of pocket' and start looking.

What was the package that Gunther had to go get??

It was the cockpit video from the SR-71 he flew President Bush back from the Paris meeting which finalized the October Surprise.

Twelve men from Congress viewed the tape. They were flown in Navy jets to an aircraft carrier. They were then put over the side of the carrier onto a craft that was lashed to the side of the carrier under the part of the runway that sticks out. The craft had a center part where a submarine could surface without breaking the surface. The men were worried about being tracked by satellite.

On the submarine, the Congressmen were shown the video tape, which had a timestamp and a location, i.e. latitude and longitude, stamp on the bottom.

The congressmen were also briefed on a number of other things.

When Gunther returned, he called me and told me that he had been to the dentist. That was our codeword meaning he had been checked out by his men. In our code language I was able to discover that he had flown from Missouri to Maryland and finally to the aircraft carrier out in the Pacific. He also told me that they almost shot a kangaroo. The next day I discovered what he meant when a pilot from a Quantas Airliner said he was contacted by a Navy ship and told to get out of the airspace or he would be shot down.

At the time, I was living in California and Gunther was in prison in Missouri... (John Ashcroft was Governor at the time. Ashcroft was *not* very happy with George Bush. Ashcroft felt that Gunther was going to be murdered in prison and Ashcroft would be blamed for it.)

I did not find out the whole story of what went down that day until I went to Missouri to visit Gunther. Even in prison, our conversations were monitored. The only way he could really communicate was with a tic tac toe pencil we used to play games.

I smuggled a lot of information out of prisons while I was married to him. I often wondered what would have happened if any of these messages had been confiscated.

One of the after affects of all the government eavesdropping that I went through while I was married to Gunther, is the knowledge that *nothing* I say or write is private. I simply assume the "boys" listen in on *all* my conversations!

Since 1989 I have known that most of my conversations were listened in on. That's why my sources *never* (or almost never) give me any information over the phone.

One of the recent ways they had been passing "bits" of information to me is by leaving trash in my front yard! I live on a street where kids walk to and from school. There is *always* a candy wrapper or popsicle wrapper in my yard.

One day, I mentioned, over the telephone, that one of my sources had left me a message in the trash on the front yard. I come home for lunch around noon, and pick up any trash that is there. As I picked up the one piece, I saw that it had the symbol we use as a sign the message is from a trusted source.

Several days later, after I had put the message out on the internet, I told a friend, over the telephone, where the message came from.

Guess what?? It is *now* three to four weeks later... and there has not been one piece of trash on my front yard!

Have the kids stopped throwing their garbage on my front yard... or is the government cleaning up my trash hoping to find another note from my source!

Don't you just love it! Your taxes are keeping the trash picked up out of my yard!

The Day after the Gathering of the Children of the Light

I have chosen to enclose this piece because it occurred after Sister Thedra's Gathering for the Children of light on Mt Shasta and it is very typical of the way information was given to me in those days. —Rayelan

September 2, 1986

It is good that you have chosen to work with us on this day. The recent gathering has left you full of new information and the ability to tune into even higher frequencies. It has also given you the personal knowledge that what we have been dictating to you is valid and timely in the world right now. So it is with great joy in our hearts that we welcome you up to an even higher level of transcriptions and transcribers. In other words the messages you receive from now on will originate at even higher levels than the ones you have previously received.

Because of your very special relationship with Shamus he will still act as the connector. In coming years he will no longer be needed in this capacity, but he will remain near you because you have requested that he do so.

What we want to talk to you about today is the new quality of love that is emerging on the planet at the moment.

Many people have reached a stage in their own development at which they feel unable to carry on any longer in the old way of relating to people. The love vibration has changed, and many people upon the planet have misinterpreted its signal.

In the sixties, when this vibration was first introduced to the planet in a very small dose, people tried unsuccessfully to love everyone in the old way which had previously been reserved for just one person. Communes were organized which were based on community loving which usually had a sexual side to it.

Because many of the people who were members of these communes still had not ascended from their lower chakras, the energy that arose from the "loving" was not the energy of love. It was a combination of the energy of sex and power.

Conquest was the practice of the time, not love. Conquest disguised as a communion and sharing. The message of love for all upon the planet was received and heard, but it was not understood and therefore was not properly put in practice.

The love which descended to earth in the sixties is a love that will connect the entire world. It is not a sexual love. Indeed, if sex is seen as a part of it, then the new love is not being practiced. This is not to say that sex is not a valid tool in the transformation process of a couple devoted to each other and the Work upon the planet. The Sexual union can be a major source of the transformational energies, but it cannot be used between strangers; it must be used between two souls who are dedicated to achieving higher consciousness through the union of two opposite forces, the yin and the yang.

It is most easily practiced between a man and a woman, but sometimes the partnering is same sexed because one person carries the yin and the other the yang. Yin energy is not exclusively the domain of females and yang is not exclusively the property of males. The perfect combination of energies is when one female who carries the yang energy joins with one male who carries the yin energy. Then all poles are balanced and the transformation to higher levels can be easily reached. But this is not to say that all combinations of energies cannot be used successfully to enable two dedicated people to reach the spiritual heights. It simply takes a longer time for them to refine the energy in their own bodies.

In other words, if a female carries the yin and her partner is a male who carries the yang, then it is first necessary for each of them to bring into balance within their own bodies the yin yang energies. (Remember the lesson from the Atalon and Shalma Story. Atalon had to find the other half of his own soul before he could find and unite with he true mate.)

If the female of the couple has no masculine energy running, then she must first learn how to run masculine energy before she can enter into a union with a man and hope to achieve perfect balance as a couple.

Let's take this one step further and try to understand the attraction of a man for a man and a woman for a woman. Many women these days have been running a double dose of masculine energy. Therefore they need a very female woman to balance out their energy. This is why they are attracted to another woman for companionship rather than a man. However, once they get beyond the social stigma attached to making sexual love to a woman, they forget, even at the unconscious level, what the purpose of the search has been, and they enter into sexual unions merely for the sex of it.

In reverse the same thing is true for men. Men who have a double dose of feminine energy seek a masculine man to satisfy their balance requirements. They do not realize that a union with a woman who is running yang energy could satisfy their needs for balance. This desire for balance is what leads these people to seek sexual partners of the same sex. What is needed to learn right now is that the same balance that is sought can be found by partnering with a partner of the opposite sex who is running the opposite energy.

As was stated earlier, all combinations of partners who have come to each other with a true dedication to seek the higher paths together and combine their energies in a devoted way to enable each of them to attain awakening in this life, will have success, but it is the combination of the male running yin and the female running yang which will achieve the results in the quickest amount of time.

Since the sixties there has been a whole group of men who have been learning to soften their masculine energy. These men have been bringing in the yin energy to balance out their own yang energy. This was first evidenced by the fact that these men chose to wear their hair long and take part in practices previously reserved for women, such as raising children or cleaning the house. There has also, more recently, in the seventies been a rise in the masculin- ization of women. As you have noticed there have been more women becoming the heads of households. This has been an exclusive domain of the man. Women have entered the work force, they have adopted men's clothing, and they have cut their hair in very masculine styles. They have accepted into their lives the yang energy.

> (2006 Note: Remember in Raelon's Mission, Odon lamented about how nice it would have been if his children had followed the path he set down for them rather than complicating things by following their own paths. Because of this, Atalon and Raelon did not join together and undertake the job of raising the younger souls who were just beginning to individuate. The male souls who individuated under Raelon were more feminine. The female souls who individuated while Atalon and Anteb were in charge of the Obergonian Mystery Schools were very masculine.)

But now we need to discuss the fact that many of these yin men and yang woman have chosen to overdo their opposite energy. In other words, women have chosen to run 100% yang energy which totally overshadows their own basic yin energy, and vice versa for men.

Men who fall into this category are usually unable to function in the real world.

Many of them end up living in the woods or on the streets of the major cities. Women who choose to run 100% yang energy usually choose not to have children. They choose fields which have primarily been totally masculine. They dress and act like men. Fortu- nately there are very few of either extreme. But you have all seen one or two examples of these types of people. If you happen to fall into this category yourself, you first must recognize that you are out of balance and then you must take steps to put yourself into balance.

Putting yourself into balance is the subject of another talk, but right now we can say that the new body workers that are emerging onto the planet can help you put yourself back into balance. It is simply easier to heal the person physically through energy rather than to heal the person mentally through the old way of psychoanalysis. Through healing with energy the old patterns simply slip away and we don't have to understand them. If they are no longer there what is the point of trying to understand them?

This is the future of the psychoanalytic movement: Healing the psyche through bringing the two energies into balance and eliminating all that is of a lower nature, or outworn patterns.

There is much garbage that clutters the bodies of humans on the earth right now. We feel that by bringing the bodies into balance energetically, the garbage will be disposed of painlessly and permanently.

That is all that we will say on the subject of healing. Later we will add more to this.

It is now time to return to our original thoughts on the new emerging love that is now being focused upon the planet.

As we said, many people were made aware of this ray of love back in the 1960ws. Only it was interpreted in light of the old information they had in their bodies and their akashic records, i.e.; the records of all their lives upon the planet.

What was not understood is that the earth is entering a new phase which has never been known to the souls now upon the planet. This is not to say that the earth has never known such a phase. Remember, the earth is a school and has been used as a classroom for many millions of years. The latest classroom went into construction approximately 18 million years ago and it is just now graduating its first class of PhDs.

Remember, the earth has graduated people from the physical, but now we are going into a graduation that involves all of us. Those of you who are still in body, and those of us who have graduated from the earth plane and are now helping to serve humanity by working with you through various channels. This phase is the graduation of all our family from the earth school. We are all preparing to go home.

This is a difficult concept but we know you can grasp it. Imagine a soul coming to earth to learn a lesson, then that soul divides into a million parts and each part enters into a human body to learn a particular lesson. This is what happened, only it wasn't just one soul, it was a family of souls who had divided from the one soul state in their previous training. They came to earth as twelve souls and then they divided into twenty-four, except this really wasn't the way either. It is difficult to explain the full concept to one who is still in body and that is why we simplify it. Later we will continue on this vein until we have sufficiently explained it to you.

What happened when the first original souls made their journey to earth is they divided themselves into many different pieces and began to populate the entire planet. Remember the original tribes of Israel. There is some truth to what is told there.

But you also must know that there were certain uninvited guests on the planet, travelers who were told to leave the earth school but who violated this command and stayed. What you do not know about these travelers is that they, too, were part of the plan, and they have been playing a role. It is now time for these actors and actresses to awaken to the fact that they were sent by higher beings to help in the education of the beings on the planet. And so, since it has been proved to those guardians of the planet earth that the souls who were sent to school on the planet have finally learned their lessons and can now leave with their entire family, it is time for the forces of opposition who have been helping to educate the souls to awaken to who they are and stop the negative way of learning that they were charged with bringing to the planet.

In other words, it is time for the planet to stop learning through pain and begin learning through love.

This is the force that is now descending to the planet: a new ray of learning, a ray that is based on love not pain. Many are having difficulty accepting this new ray. They are used to the old way of grinding down the rough edges through painful process, and so they try very hard to keep the painful processes in their lives.

Many couples will even try to invent problems in their relationships where none existed before. The love vibration can frighten people who have not yet reached a sufficient spiritual level of development in which most of the lower vibrations have been removed. The love vibration will quickly pull up and out every piece of incompatible energy. It will be like shaking a huge dirty rug. All the dirt will be brought to the surface and removed.

This is what has been occurring in many relationships. People who are in relationships at the moment must realize that they are there for a specific reason. In other words, there was something left undone that had to be finished very quickly. Those who are not in relationships at the moment can thank yourselves for studying very hard so that you do not have to go through this painful way of learning as the love vibration makes itself known upon the planet. But please know that soon you will have the opportunity to join with someone and work together for your higher states of consciousness. That is, if you are a soul who needs to join with someone. There are many souls upon the planet who are a perfect blend of yin and yang and therefore do not need the outside help of another soul to achieve higher enlightenment.

Realize that you might be one of these souls and do not mourn for your aloneness.

If you are a soul who has been having trouble with your mate, just step back from the situation and know that God will resolve it in the best possible way for the highest good of both of you, if you will get out of the way and let the God Force do its work.

The vibration which is now descending to earth will bring about a sense of cooperation between all the peoples of the world. It is a recognition of the fact that we are all children of the same parents and when the family moves, it must move together, or at least make provisions for those who choose to stay behind or go to other schools. But the main part of the family is getting ready to move forward and we ask that those of you who understand this message work forcefully to see that the message is carried forward.

There are new energies also being released upon the planet which will insure the eventual success of the love and cooperation ray.

These new energies will be discussed later.

What needs to be recognized right now is that the love is a nonpersonal love. Any trying to personalize it will result in personal setbacks. It is a love of cooperation and family, not of individuals. Individual relationships will of course exist, but they will be for balance and healing, not for education as they had once been. It also will be impossible to maintain more than one personal relationship. Multiple involvements simply will not be able to withstand the new energies on the planet.

Sexual involvements with more than one person will cease. One to one commitments to the Work will replace all relationships.

The individual becomes the unit of the day, but the individual who chooses to work in harmony with one or more, will have the added group energy to help with ascension.

It still must be remembered that group energy is not group sexual energy. It is group cooperation and love for a goal. It is dedication to a purpose higher than any of the group members.

A goal of sex or money or power will not bring happiness in this day. It never did, but that is another topic. People who work together must first decide what their larger goal is. It is never making money. It is never surviving on the planet. If you are indeed working for God, God will provide. So do not set your goals on raising money or bringing in cash. If you only concentrate on cash it will not come. Ask yourself what you plan to do with the cash. If it is desired merely to make you comfortable and serene, if you only want money so you don't have to be in the rat race, then you will continue in the rat race until you have raised your expectations of yourself and the money you want in your life.

If you want money to bring you serenity, then you will not get either. If you seek first serenity and then from it ask that all your needs be met, then you will find serenity.

If you seek money to make you dreams come true, seek first your dreams and the money to see them through will appear.

Too many higher consciousness people seek the money first and lose themselves in the making of the money. Be careful that this does not happen to you.

Chart out your plans for your Work upon the earth and then go forth and do it.

Remember the manna from heaven is given to you new each day to see you through.

In many ways money becomes the way that the higher aspects of yourself keeps the lower aspects of yourself on track. Remember that when the money dries up you may be needing to change directions.

Use money as your compass. If you are making it, then you are doing something right. If you are making it and you are not happy, then stop what you are doing and start seeking. If you are not making money and are unhappy with no joy in your life, then use this as a lesson from the universe that your path needs to be looked at more carefully.

People who are given great ability to generate money must realize the great responsibility that comes with the generating of money.

Think carefully about how you are using it. If you are using it merely to have the best possible life on the planet, then ask yourself if you would allow your mother or sister or brother to starve and be in pain while you enjoy the pleasures your money will buy. If you are using your money merely for yourself, this is what you are doing.

All money must be shared. You/we are a family. If one suffers, we all suffer.

This is the message of the new energy of love. We are a family. We are not separate units. Each individual unit must become strong in itself. But all units must cooperate to the mutual benefit of all.

This Is The Message Of The New Day

It has been good working with you on this day. I am the Master Morya and you have heard my voice many different times without knowing it was I who was speaking. Now that you know it is my vibrations and energy that you sense, we will be working together more.

There are many others who await their turn. You will be bringing through great messages to share with many, and you will be bringing through messages to share with just a few. You will be told the differences.

You have also accepted the job Of the Scribe for the Mother. We ask that you remain true to your commitments. We have invested much time and energy in your training. Do not allow your personal interpretations of personal events in your life to keep you from your promised duties.

All is working out in your highest good, remember that now and always.

You will be provided for just as we provide for all our beloved younger brothers and sisters. Do the work that you have agreed to do and you will be given all that is needed.

We love you and guard you and protect you. Be with us now and always.

MASTER MORYA AND THE BROTHERHOOD OF LIGHT WORKERS FOR THE NEW AGE OF ENLIGHTENMENT UPON THE PLANET

bye bye bye bye bye bye bye bye

remember us? we're the same old gang, we just now share with you who we are.. bye bye bye bye

Voices From the Pits of Hell

Political Prisoners in the United States of America
How it feels to be the wife of a prisoner

"There but for the Grace of God, Go I"

By Rayelan Allan

May 28, 2000

"Vicarious" is such a wonderful word. It describes the act of learning or experiencing through the imagined participation of another's experience. Imagine how easy it would be to learn life's difficult lessons, if all we had to do was live life 'vicariously' We could avoid all the pitfalls that cause pain and suffering..

While I am not sure if vicarious learning works for subjects like physics and mathematics, it does work for other kinds of learning. How many of you know a younger brother, who has vowed he will never do drugs, because he has seen what they did to his older brother? How many little girls, who saw their older sisters get pregnant and end up on welfare, chose other paths for their own lives? These are examples of vicarious learning.

People learn from good examples, and bad examples. For a vicarious lesson to be really effective, the teacher needs to be someone you can empathize with. It doesn't necessarily have to be a relative or a friend. You can learn vicariously from the lives that have been lived by people you read about or see in documentaries. The person doesn't even need to be real. Good fiction, with a good message, can teach people vicarious lessons about bravery, honesty, loyalty, and service to others.

Stories of personal suffering can also teach vicarious lessons. When I made the decision to share every aspect of the life I lived as Gunther Russbacher's wife, I did so because I hoped that other people could vicariously learn all the lessons I had learned, and thereby escape the horror, tragedy, misery, and agony that I went through.

At the time I married Gunther, I was teaching several different processes for self healing and self improvement. With a background in psychology, a thesis in bio-feedback, and years of workshops in stress reduction, meditation, and self improvement classes; I had developed a process that was quickly learned and produced noticeable results in a short time.

When I married Gunther, my life changed overnight. The first thing I realized was, after all the years of 'clearing' and other exercises, I had not conquered my own dragons. I was not the pure, pious and centered person I thought I had become. I still had fear. I still had grief, anger, hate, sorrow, despair, and a thousand different kinds of mental anguish I had never felt before.

But I still had students who had been with me a very long time. They walked a dedicated path of inner growth and devotion to a higher creative power. At that time, I put out a short monthly newsletter called, 'The Light Age Journal'. It was my own personal journal of my travels into 'The Light Age'. 'Light Age' in this sense had many levels of meaning. The bronze and iron ages were named after the tools; therefore, I felt the age of computers, lasers, and fiber optics should be called, 'The Light Age.' I also saw that we were at a time in history that humanity has the opportunity to transform on all levels, and step into a world of light, not darkness.

Two days after I married Gunther, my calm and serene life changed. I went from a world of truth and light, through the Looking Glass, into a world of shadows and lies. My new husband, a man I 'thought' I had known since the mid seventies, was arrested in front of my entire family. The FBI agents told me he was a conman on a crime spree marrying and defrauding wealthy widows. His arrest made the front page of our local paper. The humiliation was unbearable and extremely humbling.

I was the local girl who left our little town and became a buyer for Nordstrom's and an Editor for Publishing Company. I was the one who married a nuclear physicist who was the Dean of Science and Engineering at the Naval Postgraduate School which is located on the beautiful and wealthy Monterey Peninsula. I traveled to Washington D.C. to do interviews with people like Treasury Secretary, Angela 'Bay' Buchanan. I had just been asked to move to Washington D.C. and become the Administrative Assistant for the powerful Senator who was the Chairman of the Senate Foreign Relations Committee. I was too smart to marry a conman.

But the front page of our small town paper said that is exactly what I had done.

The only other time I made the front page of our local newspaper was when I started a company that taught women how to enter the business world. The headlines that once read 'local girl makes good', suddenly became, 'Local girl falls for conman'.

Shame and humiliation were not emotions I had experienced a lot before then. After I married Gunther, I became intimately acquainted with these two emotions.

After the FBI left with Gunther in handcuffs, I went to bed for two days and begged God to let me die. Somewhere in the black pit of despair, a light went off. I began to remember 'little things' that made me question the story the FBI had told me.

The Learjet we took to Reno to get married had stinger missiles on the wings and a nose cannon. I remembered the pilot and co-pilot talking with Gunther about their trips to Mexico, Central America, Oklahoma and about things that had happened years ago. I also remembered hearing the pilot lying, as he told the FBI agent who arrested Gunther, that he had just met Gunther the day he flew us to Reno. I remembered that Gunther told the pilot that he would re-pay the cost of the flight. They even joked about all the government officials that have gotten in trouble for misusing government jets. Then I remembered the FBI telling me that the Learjet was NOT a government jet, it was a private jet.

How many private jets have stinger missiles on their wingtips? It was obvious that the FBI was lying, the pilot was lying, and Gunther wasn't saying anything. Once it sunk in that I had been lied to, the shame and humiliation were transformed into righteous rage and I vowed that I would find out the truth about who I had married.

The fact that Gunther had transformed himself into Atalon on the night we met, and told me he was my other half was probably the main reason I stayed married to him and fought to prove who he was. I wasn't fighting to prove to the world who Gunther was, I was fighting to prove to myself that I had not married a 'con man'.

Before I married Gunther, I had been helping researchers and writers investigate various scandals involving the CIA. Because of this, I had contacts within the intelligence community. Once I realized the FBI was lying, I got out of bed and started making phone calls. Within days of requesting information about who I had married, I received calls from three men who identified themselves to me as the Station Chiefs from Frankfurt, Tel Aviv and St. Louis. Each man told me they had known Gunther for over thirty years and he was a Naval officer attached to the CIA. They confirmed that Gunther WAS the man I thought he was. He was the Naval officer I had met, many years earlier, at the Naval Postgraduate School.

Because I had been lied to, and the world around me had suddenly turned upside down, I didn't really trust anonymous voices over the telephone. To further verify who Gunther was, I flew to Washington D.C. and asked the Senator for whom I had almost gone to work, to tell me the truth. The Senator grabbed my hand, and led me into a dark foyer that separated his office from the outside door to the main hall of the Capitol Basement. With both doors closed, in almost complete darkness, the Senator said, "Raye, you have married a very good man. Just hang on for a few months and this will all be over." I tried to ask more questions, but he had already opened the outside door and walked me down the hall to the ramp at the back of the Capitol Building. I later found out that the dark foyer was the only place in his office that he was sure was not bugged. Even though the Senator did not tell me much, he told me enough to put an end to my shame and humiliation.

Now that I knew Gunther was not the professional conman the FBI told me he was, I figured I was finished with shame and humiliation. But this was before I experienced the master emotion manipulators of the American prison system. Each time I visited Gunther in jail or in prison I was subjected to prison guards who had perfected the art of making prisoners' families feel like the dregs of society.

Sometimes, after traveling for days to visit Gunther, I was turned away because I had arrived too late. Sometimes I was told that I could not see Gunther because I had not been cleared. Sometimes guards, who towered a foot above me, got up in my face and screamed as loud as they could.

At one prison, visitors had to be searched. I had to remove my under wire bra and pass it out to a guard who examined it. When I still did not pass the metal detector test, I was led back to the room where the guard examined everything I was wearing. This meant I was stripped down to my underpants in front of a female guard. No matter how much I took off, the metal detector kept going off. I could tell that the guards suspected I was smuggling in contraband. Just before I was about to be taken away for a body cavity search, the guard asked me to take off my shoes. Without the shoes on, the metal detector didn't go off. The range of emotions I went through started with irritation, advanced to anger, transformed into embarrassment, heightened into fear and settled over me like a black cloud of dread.

At other prisons, I was turned away and not allowed to visit because I was wearing open toed shoes, sleeveless blouses; pants they said were too tight, boots or some other dress infraction. One time, after driving from California, where I live, to Missouri where he was in prison, I was turned away because I did not have a slip under my denim skirt. At that prison, women visitors are required to pull up their skirts and show their slips to the guards before they are allowed in the visiting room.

When you have a loved one in prison, the visits and the phone calls deplete your checking account instantly. All calls from prisons and jails have to be collect and they cost a dollar or more a minute. If a wife is on welfare or working at a low wage job, she usually has her phone disconnected after the first month. Then there is no contact except through letters and visits. Many times the prisoner is held in another state and the family is too poor to visit more than once a year, if at all. All of this happened to me. When Gunther was in Prison in

Missouri, I could only afford to visit him about three times a year. We had to conduct out marriage via telephone and letters.

For the first year and a half of our marriage, Gunther and I kept our mouths shut and did not go public with what had happened to us. We tried to handle our problem through the legal system. All of this changed in an instant when an attempt was made to kill Gunther. In a recorded telephone call to Rodney Stich, Gunther told him the truth about why people in the Bush Administration wanted him dead.

Gunther was married to the best friend of the woman whose book, 'October Surprise' charged President Bush with treason. In a half hour telephone call, Gunther revealed to Rodney that he was the pilot who had flown George Bush back from the Paris meeting which concluded the October Surprise deal. Gunther told Rodney that if he was killed, Rodney should give me the tape so I would understand why he had been killed.

Instead of remaining silent, Rodney played the tape for Harry Martin, the publisher of the Napa Sentinel. Harry published the story on the front page of his Thursday newspaper. On Monday, the article was front page in the nationally distributed Spotlight newspaper. Before I had even heard the truth from Gunther or Rodney, I received a telephone call from a radio talk show host asking me what it felt like to be married to the October Surprise Pilot. I had no idea what he was talking about.

Shortly after the attempt on Gunther's life, the publication of the articles, and my first appearance on world wide short wave radio, two important things happened. William Webster, the Director of the CIA resigned suddenly, and the Senate and the House both convened long over due Task Forces to investigate the October Surprise.

The October Surprise is the Granddaddy of all the scandals of the Reagan and Bush years. All the other scandals can be traced back to the deal the Reagan Campaign made with Iran to delay the release of the 52 hostages from the Beirut Embassy. Because President Carter could not free the hostages, he looked weak and ineffective; therefore, Ronald Reagan won the election. The moment I told my story on the radio, Gunther and I became overnight celebrities in the world of government whistleblowers.

The positive thing about being infamous as the wife of the October Surprise Pilot was I no longer felt shame and humiliation because my husband was in prison. These two emotions were replaced by fear and an overwhelming sense of helplessness. After the first radio show where I had to be in the studio, there was an attempt to run me off a freeway overpass. Gunther's Team members were following me that night. I saw them smash into the van that had just tried to run me off the overpass. I saw the van explode in flames. I later learned Gunther's team had fired a shoulder held rocket launcher into the van. Many months later Gunther told me his boss had ordered the 'Team' to 'immediately terminate' any assassin who tried to kill me.

The more Gunther and I went public, the harder life became. Gunther was poisoned, beaten, and denied his heart medication which caused him to suffer numerous heart attacks. He was placed on work assignments that were torture for someone in his condition. Everyday a new crisis arose that had to be handled immediately. The worst crises always happened over long weekends, like the three day Memorial Day holiday when all the courts were closed and there was no one I could appeal to.

I was married to Gunther for 9 years. During that time, he was free about 9 months. The rest of the time he was in county jails in three states; federal prisons in more states that I can remember; and finally in an ancient prison in Austria. I have been the wife of a prisoner. I have been bankrupted. I have had times when there was no food in the house. I have stood in lines at food banks. I learned to buy my clothes at Goodwill instead of Nordstrom's.

I waited in line at prisons with people that I wouldn't have crossed the street to help, years before. I met the wives, the mothers, the grandmothers and children of men that we refer to as the 'dregs of society'. And I learned that they were just like me. Most were middle class. Some were teachers, chiropractors, doctors. Others were on welfare or holding down menial jobs. Others were farmers struggling to save the family farm while still trying to help their son or husband who was in prison.

Most of the prisoners I met were incarcerated for drug use. All prisoners, no matter where they are incarcerated or what they are in for, live lives of stress, medical neglect, beatings, rapes, poor health, bad food, depression, loneliness, and alienation from family and friends. Imprisoned fathers mourn over the problems their children encounter and grieve when their wives leave them for another man.

An American prisoner's life is not that much different from prisoners in third world countries. Torture, deprivation, inedible food, little or no medical care and NO dental care, are the same in the United States, as they are in the third world. In the United States, torture can't be blatant. Prisoners can't be strapped down and tortured with electric prods. Instead, they are isolated in freezing solitary confinement cells, or cells that are so hot the prisoner can barely breathe. They are beaten by guards or other inmates. Sometimes they are even murdered.

One of the things I learned from my life, in and out of prisons, is that we never know when we or someone we love could become a prisoner. Dr. Hulda Clark, a 76 year old microbiologist who is challenging the American Medical establishment knows what it like to be a prisoner. Ed McCabe, the author of a book on oxygen therapy spent years in a federal prison. Congressman George Hansen, the author of a book on the IRS called 'To Harass our People' spent four long and torturous years in the AmeriKan Gulag. Rodney Stich, author of 'Defrauding America' and three other books exposing the connected pattern of government corruption, also knows what it is like to be a prisoner in America.

The names of government whistleblowers who became government dissidents and then government prisoners are too long to cover completely. Chip Tatum, Ron Rewald, Trenton Parker, Bob Hunt, Al Martin, and Les Coleman are prisoners and former prisoners I know personally.

None of the people named above ever thought they would end up as prisoners. None of their wives, children and families ever thought they would have a husband, son or father who was a prisoner. In our country, in this day and age, any of us can be free today and in jail tomorrow.

I wrote this article, because I wanted you to 'vicariously' learn what it was like to be married to a prisoner. I wanted you to feel what I went through every day, not knowing if Gunther was dead or alive, was being beaten, was in solitary confinement – freezing in the winter and suffocating in the summer. I wanted you to understand that no matter how rich you are, the lawyers and phone calls quickly deplete your funds and you are reduced to poverty.

Most families are destroyed when a loved one goes to prison. If they had been middle class upstanding citizens, they are embarrassed to admit they have a family member in prison. They usually drop out of their church or clubs. Sometimes they even move away from their hometowns and go where no one knows them. They lose their support system. Most develop severe depression which gets manifested in different ways. Children are affected the most. Many become antisocial and sometimes end up in prison. Some turn their pain on their father and hate him. Others turn their pain on themselves and commit suicide.

The American system of corrections is broken. Prisoners and their families cannot fix it because they have been broken by a broken system. I took you on this vicarious journey because I wanted you to become a prisoner's wife, father or son, for just a few moments. I wanted you to know how it feels to have your loved one locked up in place where neither of you knows if he will live to see the next morning.

Some of these prisoners are innocent. Others have committed crimes that should never have been labeled crimes, such as smoking marijuana, innocently driving a car that had drugs in it, stealing food, exposing government corruption, being in the wrong place at the wrong time, or being the fall guy. Prisoners cannot help themselves because they must focus their attention on staying alive. Most family members are in too much pain to try to fix a broken system. The only hope the broken prison system has of being fixed is you.

Before you or a loved one becomes a guest in the AmeriKan Gulag, don't you think you should try to fix it? If you still don't believe our prison system in broken, then ask Congressman George Hansen how it felt to spend days chained and shackled on a transport bus, with your feet and legs swelling and the shackles cutting into your skin. Ask him was it was like to pull his own teeth. Ask him about his health problems that were caused by medical neglect.

If you want to see the photos of the scars left on Congressman Hansen from his 4 years in the Amerikan Gulag, you can read his entire story at:

http://www.rumormillnews.com/cgi-bin/archive.cgi?read=22130

I did not write this part to teach anyone how to fix the broken system. I wrote this because one of you will be touched by it and YOU are the one who will figure out how to fix this broken system. You are the one who can change the system so that no man or woman will ever have to know the agony of a prison system that destroy souls, create monsters, perpetuates lives of crime, and offers no hope of reform or rehabilitation.

Part IV

Gunther's Story

Gunther Karl Russbacher
July 1, 1942 — August 8, 2005
R.I.P.

Who was Gunther Russbacher?

March 2006

As you read the following articles, some written by Gunther, others written about Gunther, please keep in mind that this is the same man who said:

*"I am Atalon and you are my other half.
I have searched the combined universes for millions of years.
Now that I have found you,
No one will ever separate us."*

Gunther Russbacher was a CIA operative. He had many different cover aliases. His two main covers were Robert Andrew Walker, Captain, USN; and Emory Peden, the owner and operator of National Brokerage Companies. Under the alias of Emory Peden, Gunther was the CIA banker. Under the alias Robert A. Walker, Gunther headed a Special Operations Group that was made up of Navy SEALS and Delta Force.

As the head of this Special Operations Group, Gunther was called on to do many different things. One of those things was flying Vice-Presidential Candidate, George Herbert Walker Bush to a suburb of Paris. Mr. Bush, (who was CIA director in 1976), arranged with representatives of Iran to hold the 444 American hostages until after the American election for President.

In 1980 the presidential race was so close that the only thing that could tip it either way was for the American hostages to be released or for the release to be delayed.

President Carter was dealing with Iran behind the scenes. So was Vice President George Bush and many in the group who made up the inner workings of the Reagan Campaign. The Reagan campaign offered the better deal. They gave Iran forty million in cash plus the promise of giving Iran all the weapons they needed to fight their enemy, Iraq. The hostages were released the day Ronald Reagan was sworn in as President. The arms started flowing to Iran from Israel in January of 1981.

When I married Gunther in 1989 he told me he was a CIA operative. I told him that I was helping a friend investigate the "October Surprise." Gunther neglected to tell me that HE was the pilot who flew Bush to the meeting in Paris that concluded the deal to delay the release of the hostages

2006 note from Rayelan

The October Surprise Articles by Harry Martin

I have often wondered why Iran hasn't blackmailed both Presidents Bush. But then again, maybe they have black-mailed them both. Maybe the real reason for the Iraq war was to put an end to the threat of another war with Iraq... or to give the Shiite part of Iraq to Iran.

The following series of articles was written shortly after an attempt to kill Gunther was narrowly averted. Gunther's life was saved because someone drugged him and he was NOT able to go on the mission that had been planned. The helicopter he was supposed to have been on, crashed. One of the people who was killed was the blonde woman I met in Medford, OR. She was a Colonel in the Air Force. I have often wondered what her family was told to explain her death. — Rayelan, 2006

Bush Made Deal With Iranians, Pilot Says

Navy flier testifies he flew Bush to Paris for deal to block release of hostages

By Harry V. Martin

Copyright © FreeAmerica and Harry V. Martin, 1995

Exclusive to the Napa Sentinel

A BAC 111 aircraft, which had been reconfigured to carry a sufficient amount of fuel to travel 3,600 miles, left Andrews Air Force Base in the late afternoon of October 19, 1980. The aircraft's destination: Paris, France. The Passengers aboard the aircraft included the command pilot U.S. Navy Captain Gunther Russbacher, Richard Brenneke and Heinrich Rupp, on the flight deck; and in the cabin was William Casey, soon to be the Director of the Central Intelligence Agency; Donald Gregg, soon to be the ambassador to South Korea; and George Bush, the future Vice President and President of the United States and former director of the Central Intelligence Agency. There were also Secret Service agents aboard the aircraft.

This is the weekend—three weeks before the November 1980 Presidential Election, that Bush has claimed he spent at Andrews Air Force Base.

Testifying to this flight is Russbacher, the pilot. The Navy pilot is currently at Terminal Island, a federal prison, awaiting an appeal on a charge of misuse and misappropriation of government properties, misuse of government jets, and misuse of government purchase orders for purchase of fuel. He was also a member of the Office of Naval Intelligence and worked with the Central Intelligence Agency. Russbacher's alias is Robert A. Walker. Russbacher now becomes the second crew member of that flight to testify to this clandestine episode that may have changed the politics of this nation and which has been labeled the "October Surprise." Brenneke was upheld by a Federal jury when he testified about the flight. After his testimony he was charged by the Federal Government with perjury, but a Federal jury acquitted him upholding his testimony that the flight actually took place. The trial was held in Portland, Oregon last year.

Russbacher, in an exclusive interview, states that Bush stayed at the Hotel Crillion in Paris. Russbacher has stated that more than one flight was involved, but that this was the initial flight at which time an agreement was made between Bush and Casey and the Government of Iran to delay the release of American hostages in Iran until after the November 1980 election. Former President Jimmy Carter and several Congressmen are now asking for an investigation into the "October Surprise."

According to Russbacher statements, Bush stayed only a couple of hours. He attended a meeting at the Hotel Crillion and at the Hotel George V. Russbacher, Brenneke, and Rupp stayed at the Hotel Florida. Bush did not return on the same BAC 111 aircraft or return with some of the people he had flown with to Paris, but instead Russbacher flew him back in the SR-71. The aircraft was refueled about 1800 to 1900 nautical miles into the Atlantic by a KCl35.

The returning flight with Bush landed at McGuire Air Force base at approximately 2 a.m. on October 20. Russbacher states that Bush, while in Paris, met with Hashemi Rafsanjani, the second in command to the Ayatollah and now the president of Iran, and Adnan Khashoggi, a Saudi Arabian businessman who was extremely powerful. Arrangements were apparently made to pay Iran $40 million to delay the release of hostages in order to thwart President Jimmy Carter's re-election bid. The $40 million was the beginning of terms that created the Iran-Contra scandal that is now being reopened by Congress.

Russbacher is concerned for his life, but feels that the other pilots will now come forward in a new Congressional investigation. He indicates that there is a growing division within the Central Intelligence Agency. There is no one higher than the CIA, but there are groups within the company (term used by insiders for the CIA) that are very, very strong. And the group or clique that I belonged to, in my opinion, was probably the strongest but there are other factions that are at war with themselves, Russbacher states." You have these groups that are answerable to no one. Well, they are answerable to one man, on top, and he doesn't seem to care how the problems are resolved, just as long as they are taken care of." The man Russbacher is referring to is President Bush.

On the eve of an announcement of a Congressional investigation into the October Surprise, Russbacher was to have taken a helicopter trip with Navy Intelligence officers, but he did not take the trip. The helicopter carrying several Naval Intelligence officers was reported to have crashed near or on Fort Ord in California. Russbacher, who was willing to tape this interview, states that had he been on the helicopter he would be dead right now. In fact, because of that crash, Russbacher wanted this interview taped for safety reasons.

He believes that the other aircrew members are in danger, as well, but feels that they are ready to come forward and testify, as did Brenneke last year.

Israelis are Blowing Whistle on Bush Administration

By Harry V. Martin

First of a Series

The thread is unwinding and the deeds and misdeeds of high U.S. Government officials are beginning to surface. But why has so much information concerning George Bush's trip to Paris, the Iran-Contra scandal, the growing INSLAW scandal all suddenly surfaced?

There have been too many double crosses involving the Central Intelligence Agency and Bush—international double crosses. At the heart of the problem are three nations, Iran, Iraq and Israel. The Bush Administration has been pushing a pro-Arab stance at the cost of Israel. In fact, according to court documents, the United States supported the manufacturing of chemical weapons by Iraq as a counterforce against Israel in the Middle East. The Bush Administration links to oil favored a more pro-Arab stand.

It began in early 1980, when pollsters for presidential candidate Ronald Reagan reported that if President Jimmy Carter was able to obtain freedom for 52 American hostages held in Iran, he would win the election. The Carter Administration was in negotiations with Iran at the time and a release looked promising. The Reagan-Bush campaign was wary of a possible "October Surprise" by the Carter Administration that would result in the early release of the American hostages. Actually, the Iranian government was tired of the hostage issue and wanted to have an early release. They were bickering over release of frozen assets or military replacement parts to support their squadrons of American fighters. At the same time, Iraq was threatening war against Iran. Carter also considered the possibility of a second rescue attempt, but American officials leaked that information to the Iranian government and they dispersed the hostages to many different locations.

Concerned with the possible election turnaround, officials of the Reagan-Bush campaign, notably John McFarland and William Casey, held meetings in Washington, D.C. at the Mayflower Hotel and in Madrid, Spain with representatives of the Iranian government. The concept of an arms-for-hostages deal was consummated. According to Israeli testimony, the Iranians were ready in September 1980 to release the hostages, but the Republican contingent did not want release until after the November 1980 elections. The meeting in Spain were sufficiently productive to warrant a final meeting in Paris between October 18 and October 22. It was at this meeting that agreement was reached on the hostage question and a payment of $40 million was made to the Iranian government through a Luxembourg bank.

Two pilots have now stated that Casey, Donald Gregg, who worked for the CIA under Bush, and Bush attended the meeting. They were flown out of Andrews Air Force Base late in the afternoon of October 19, 1980 Bush was returned, according to Navy pilot Captain Gunther Russbacher, after a few hours in Paris. Russbacher states he flew the SR71, the Blackbird, from Paris to McGuire Air Force Base in New Jersey, arriving on October 20. Refueling was done 1800 to 1900 nautical miles over the Atlantic by a KC135.

Strangely enough, Bush made no public appearances during that time, three week's before the election, and has yet to prove where he was during the "missing" 21 hours. According to the pilot, Bush only stayed a few hours in Paris and was flown back to the United States. On October 21, the Iranians changed their entire negotiating position with the Carter Administration, the results of a completed deal with the Republicans.

The Israelis were the go-betweens, helping to establish the links between the Reagan-Bush people and the Iranians. The Israelis were used to ferry equipment to Iran, and in one case, an Argentine aircraft was shot down by the Soviet Union in Russian airspace. The aircraft, flown by Israelis, was carrying U.S. military equipment to Iran. Much of the equipment shipped to Iran, began weeks after Reagan took office, was stripped from NATO units in Europe and not from U.S. bases within the United States. The U.S. did not have a sufficient stockpile of arms in the country and resorted to taking weapons from the Reforger stockpile. Reforger was a massive military exercise (war game) staged in Europe with all NATO participating.

But once the Reagan-Bush team came to power, Bush began to push a pro-Arab position within the government, or, in essence, a pro-oil position. This irritated the Israelis and they felt the United States was beginning to betray them. Israel made a deal with the Soviet Union for closer relationships and also sought more Soviet Jews for immigration, thus keeping the Likud Party in power. Israeli agents are the ones who broke the story of the Iran-Contra scandal in a Lebanese newspaper, as a retaliation against Bush. It is also the Israelis who witnessed arms deals, including the transfer of Inslaw's PROMIS software, in a Chilean meeting. The same names, Dr. Earl Brian and Donald Gregg come up in those testimonies.

The U.S. had also selected Iraq as the stabilizing or balancing Arab force in the Middle East. Israel and Iraq had a good working relationship, as did Iran and Israel. The U.S. also assisted in building up Iraq's chemical warfare base as a counter to Israeli military might. But Saddam Hussein began to show that he was not going to "follow orders" and thus the scenario of the recent Iraqi war unwound. But the U.S. does not want Hussein out of power.

Iran, in the meantime, is anti-Arab and anti-Jew, but has made accommodations with both segments of the Middle East.

More Damaging Testimony Given

Hostage deal, Inslaw cases connected in Congressional probe
    By Harry V. Martin
    Second in a Series
    Copyright © Napa Sentinel 1991

The code word for George Bush in Iran is Bosch Batteries—a name used often when the United States was clandestinely engaged in illegal arms shipments to Iran. It was also used to herald his brief presence in Paris on October 19, 1980. Though the President denies that he ever went to Paris to make arrangements for the detention of 52 American hostages until after the U.S. elections in November 1980, more testimony is coming forth from people who claim to have been there and were part of the sophisticated plot.

Navy Captain Gunther Russbacher broke "radio silence" last week in an exclusive Sentinel article which has been picked up by some newspapers and news services, and national radio. Russbacher, who is in Terminal Island awaiting an appeal on charges of misuse and misappropriation of government properties, misuse of government jets, and misuse of government purchase orders to purchase fuel. These charges stem from his position with the U.S. Navy Intelligence and a CIA mission involving a government Lear Jet. Despite his imprisonment, he has continual contact with Naval Intelligence. Russbacher's intelligence background coincides with his story. He says he piloted the BAC-111 that flew Bush, William Casey and Donald Gregg to Paris to meet with Iranian officials to arrange a $40 million transaction and arms shipments to Iran in exchange for delay of any hostage release prior to the election. Russbacher also stated that he flew Bush back to McGuire Air Force Base hours later in the SR-71, the Blackbird.

But Russbacher is not the only one to come out of the woodwork to claim Bush went to Paris. From a jail cell in Tacoma, Washington, former CIA operative Michael Riconosciuto, told Congressional investigators that he was the man who transferred the $40 million to a Luxembourg Bank. Why is Riconoscuito in jail? Early this year he signed an affidavit testifying that the U.S. Justice Department did reconfigure INSLAW's PROMIS software to be used by the CIA and Dr. Earl Brian, a very close associate of former Attorney General Edwin Meese, and also a former cabinet member of Ronald Reagan's California cabinet. He claims in the affidavit that members of the U.S. Department of Justice warned him that if he testified before the House Judiciary Committee investigating the theft of the sensitive PROMIS software, that he would be arrested. Within a week of his affidavit, and after it was published in the St. Louis Post Dispatch and The Napa Sentinel, he was arrested by Drug Enforcement agents in the state of Washington and held without bail. Most of his records have been seized. According to Riconosciuto, the theft of the PROMIS software grew out of a need to obtain funds to reward Dr. Brian for his work in arranging the hostage agreement. Among other things, Dr. Brian also owns United Press International.

Richard Brenneke, an international arms dealer and former CIA operative and pilot for Air America, testified before a Federal Court that he took part in the Paris flight. The Federal Government tried Brenneke for perjury, attempting to disprove his claims. A jury acquitted Brenneke of the charges. At the trial, former CIA agent and now South Korean Ambassador Donald Gregg who both Brenneke and Russbacher claim to have participated in the 1980 Paris meeting, said he was never in Paris for the alleged meeting. However, he presented testimony to the court that he and his wife were at Rahoboth Beach in Delaware on the date of the Paris meeting. He produced photographs of his family on the sunny beach. But an expert technical witness said the cloud formations in the photograph could not have been recorded over that beach at the time, the weather was far from sunny that day. Gregg was brought into the CIA while George Bush was its director under the Richard Nixon administration. Gregg is believed to have been one of several moles within the CIA under President Jimmy Carter that staged the "October Surprise" in an effort to defeat Carter's re-election bid.

Also, Gary Sick, an Iranian expert of Carter's National Security council, has outlined the history, actions and interactions, of the "October Surprise." Barbara Honegger, a former Reagan White House aide, has written a book called "October Surprise" in which she details the meetings prior to and in Paris, the names of people who attended and the results of those meeting that Bush said he never attended. Abolhassan Bani-Sadr, who was president of Iran when the hostages were being held, is coming to the United States to promote his book, "My Turn to Speak." It also contains the same general allegations that the Reagan-Bush team paid to block the release of 52 American hostages in order to assure victory at the polls.

Bush has released copies of his 1980 campaign schedule, but there is about a 21 hour gap (Nixon's Watergate tape had an 18 minute gap) in his whereabouts. The trip to and from Paris involved about that amount of time.

Media Almost Broke Bush-Iran Story Several Years Earlier

By Harry V. Martin

Third in a Series

Copyright Napa Sentinel, 1991

Before the revelations about the October Surprise, in which George Bush is alleged to have flown to Paris in 1980 to delay release of 52 American hostages from Iran, the American public almost learned the truth. In the first years of the Ronald Reagan Administration a small tempest was created over the Reagan campaign camp allegedly obtaining President Jimmy Carter's briefing book to be used as debate notes. The national news media was unsuccessful in arousing public attention to the situation. Even John Stockwell, a former CIA operative, boasted on the air that Reagan would win the election because of "filched material."

But that episode, as small as it appeared, was only the surface of an iceberg. Actually, the media had focused on the wrong problem. The Reagan-Bush campaign drew a lot of information from the Carter White House during the 1980 election campaign. The Reagan-Bush campaign was so worried that President Carter might do something to obtain the release of the hostages before the election, that William Casey, with the involvement of people active in the Former Intelligence Officer's Association, systematically set up spy networks in the White House, itself. Key members of the CIA from Bush's tenure as director, were left in place-though President Carter had been warned to purge the CIA of Bush and Nixon men. Several moles within the

White House and the National Security Council reported directly to Casey, who in turn reported to Reagan and Bush, but mainly Bush. Reagan was not totally informed of all the details.

One of the pieces of information that the moles inside the White House learned was that Carter had planned a rescue mission, a mission that ended in a desert disaster. According to several books and the San Jose Mercury News, among others, three retired Air Force officers, who were overseers to the Contras, also planned the desert rescue operation. The same people involved in the Iran-Contra scandal, which grew out of the alleged October 1980 deal in Paris made between the Reagan-Bush team and the Iranians, were tied into the rescue mission. Reports that have surfaced from the intelligence community indicate that the rescue attempt may have been sabotaged. Eight American servicemen died in the fiasco. The Iranians were also informed of the rescue attempt through the moles at the White House. The Director of the Center for Strategic and International Studies and Association of Former Intelligence Officers, Stephen Halper, had "far reaching access to the most sensitive materials." Richard Allen, to become Reagan's National Security Advisor and later disgraced, was circulating the day-to-day memos of President Carter. The CIA had virtually vetoed Carter's first choice for CIA chief and successfully pushed for the appointment of Stansfield Turner. Turner is believed to have played a key role in the October Surprise. He believed he would be reappointed.

CIA head under the new Reagan Administration.

The future of American politics, the Iran-Contra deals, arms for drugs shipments, and even the war in Iraq, all had their embryo in the 1980 election campaign. Close to the election, Reagan's own pollsters showed the election was too close to call. Richard Wirthlin, the pollster for the Reagan-Bush campaign, said that if the hostages were released before the election Carter would gain a boost of 5 or 6 percentage points in the polls, or even as much as 10 percent, giving him a sure victory for that election.

Pilot's Full Account of Bush's Paris Flight

By Harry V. Martin
Copyright, Napa Sentinel, 1991
EXCLUSIVE REPORT
(Fourth in a series)

Navy Captain Gunther Russbacher, who worked with Naval Intelligence and the Central intelligence Agency, received a phone call at his home in St. Louis, in mid-October 1980. He was told to meet a TWA flight and take it to Washington, D.C. From there he was met by a car and brought to the Base Hospital at Andrews Air Force Base. At 1900 hours (7 p.m.) he was greeted by two military personnel in flight suits, handed flight papers and boarded a BAC-111 aircraft. Destination? Paris. Purpose of the mission? Unknown at the time.

Richard Brenneke was doing a preflight check when Russbacher closed the cockpit door. He had no knowledge of who else was aboard the aircraft. Brenneke has already testified that he was on the aircraft and his testimony was held up by a federal jury. Russbacher testifies that he did not look into the passenger cabin until he was over the Atlantic. The aircraft refueled at Newfoundland. There was also an Air Force officer aboard, according to Russbacher. It landed at Le Bourget Airport near Paris.

Who did Russbacher see in the cabin?

- George Bush,
- Donald Gregg,
- William Casey,
- two security people, and
- a woman, believed to be Jennifer Fitzgerald, Bush's Chief of Protocol for the White House.

Heinrich Rupp was not on the BAC-111, but did fly a Gulfstream aircraft to Paris. He met Brenneke and Russbacher in Paris. Vehicles were waiting for the passengers, some of these vehicles were from the U.S. Embassy.

The pilots and crew checked into the Hotel Florida and within three hours Russbacher was called back to duty. He was to fly Bush back in the SR-71, the CIA's Blackbird, from a French Air Force Base to Dover Air Force Base. But because of security leaks in Paris, the aircraft was diverted to McGuire Air Force Base in New Jersey. The flight of the Blackbird took one hour and 14-1/2 minutes, being refueled 1800 nautical miles over the Atlantic.

The SR-17 model was the YF12 A, a two-seater. According to Russbacher, Bush had few words to say on the return flight. The pilot stated, "Hold on, we're going out." Bush is reported to have replied, "It's a fast ride." Bush is a former Navy pilot. Bush was met at McGuire by an Air Force colonel who later became a four-star general.

Brenneke was the first crew member to reveal the trip to Paris and much has been done to discredit him. At his perjury trial, Brenneke's defense shot holes through Donald Gregg's testimony that he was not on the flight or in Paris. Gregg showed photographs of him and his wife on a sunny beach in Maryland, stating he was there and not in Paris. Weather experts testified that the weather conditions that day did not match the photograph. Gregg, who has been named by former National Security Advisor Gary Sick and former President Jimmy Carter, as a mole for Bush in the CIA, was a long-time CIA operative who has recently been appointed ambassador to South Korea.

A French intelligence memo does exist claiming that Bush did come to Paris in October 1980 and received French assistance. The meeting in Paris was to delay the release of 52 American hostages held by Iranian radicals. The Republicans sought to delay the release until after the elections in order to prevent President Jimmy Carter from winning the election should the hostages be released early. A total of $40 million was transferred from a Mexican account and Bush presented a draft of the transfer to the Iranians. Within six weeks after Ronald Reagan was inaugurated, covert shipments of arms were sent to Iran. When the shipments were discovered around 1985, it became known as the Iran-Contra scandal. But the origins of that scandal began in the flight to Paris. George Bush has never been able to account for this time and Secret Service memos about his whereabouts are also conflicting. Casey was never able to prove his whereabouts either. And Gregg's' excuse was shot down in a court of law.

How do we know Russbacher is telling the truth? Obviously, his credibility is critical to the story. Russbacher is currently in a federal prison on Terminal Island near Long Beach. A nationwide search for records relating to Russbacher was undertaken by Tom Valentine of Radio Free America, The Napa Sentinel and other cooperative news media. The search included public records, classified information and information from highly reliable sources within the intelligence community.

Russbacher has been directly linked to both Rupp and Brenneke through the Habsburg Trust, the Ottokar Trust and the Augsberg Trust. These trusts control billions of dollars and some of the funds were funneled by Rupp to Aurora Bank, a failed Institution. Russbacher will not discuss the trust. Independent research has also discovered that Russbacher may be the "banker" for the CIA, its number three man. This means that he would have knowledge of various secret accounts the CIA is operating. The search also revealed that F.B.I. has a great interest in Russbacher because he could possibly lead them to monies siphoned off Savings and Loans institutions and funneled into secret CIA accounts, and also used to finance gun and drug running.

CIA and intelligence figures made Russbacher sign a contract that he would not get married for two years, especially after a divorce from his wife, Peggy, an F.B.I. informant. Russbacher violated that contract and was married. Russbacher's wife, Raye, was told by an Army Intelligence Officer in San Francisco that she and Russbacher would have to separate. Within a few days after their marriage, Russbacher was arrested on several charges, held in jails for months at a time. Each of the charges was dropped and in every single case the criminal investigation files and court records were sealed, which is highly unusual. A fellow prisoner in Terminal Island, Ron Rewald, had the same problem. He was tried in a state court but the prosecutor came from the U.S. Justice Department. Rewald was not allowed to introduce evidence showing his CIA involvement and his records and court case are sealed. Michael Riconosciuto, another CIA operative, is currently sitting in a Pierce County, Washington jail. All his records have been seized and he is being held without bail, after testifying to CIA and Justice Department involvement in the INSLAW case.

Through a special arrangement, Rewald has met with Russbacher and was skeptical at first of Russbacher's background. But after future exchanges and the matching of names, dates and places, Rewald is certain Russbacher is who he claims to be. Rewald was involved in a covert CIA financial institution in Hawaii and had prominent Air Force generals and high ranking intelligence officers working in the firm.

The most damaging evidence against Russbacher's claim comes from Barbara Honegger, who wrote *October Surprise* several years ago. Honegger has been a long-time friend and associate of Raye Russbacher, who married Gunther about two years ago. Honegger has called several media people, including Valentine and the Sentinel to say that Russbacher is a "pathological liar." Honegger's work has been challenged by such people as Phillip Agee, a former CIA officer, and John Stockwell, a CIA agent. Honegger states that Russbacher is not who he appears to be, that he isn't in the Navy and that he has a criminal past. After further questioning, Honegger admits her entire information has come from a Modesto, CA. attorney named Mark Coleman, Russbacher's appointed public defender when the pilot was charged with misuse of a government aircraft and misuse of a government purchase order. The case was declared a mistrial and under threats of sending Raye Russbacher to prison for unauthorized access to a military base, Russbacher pleaded guilty to a lesser charge and is serving a short term in Terminal Island, with tremendous freedom within the institution. Honegger says that Brenneke denied knowing Russbacher.

Mark Coleman admits that Brenneke has admitted knowing Russbacher, but will not confirm times, places and dates. Coleman also admits, under heavy questioning, that he couldn't find anything to verify or deny Russbacher's background, including no employment records. An F.B.I. officer did testify at Russbacher's trial that Russbacher was doing work for them. Coleman finally admits that the basis of his knowledge of Russbacher comes from Peggy Neil, Russbacher's ex-wife and F.B.I. informant.

A court record in Missouri shows that Russbacher pleaded guilty to four counts of investment fraud and was sentenced to 28 years in prison. The judge, reviewing a secret file at the trial, gave Russbacher full probation and allowed him to go to Hollywood to negotiate a movie call The Last Flight of the Blackbird. The prosecutor in the case, Mr. Zimmerman, was fired. The F.B.I. had also arrested Russbacher for kidnapping his niece and dropped the charges. He was arrested for impersonating a U.S. Attorney.

There has been a very swift campaign to immediately discredit Russbacher, a familiar pattern associated with Riconosciuto, Rewald, Brenneke, and Anthony Motolese, another CIA operative who blew the whistle. The swiftness of the discrediting campaign has been witnessed by both the Sentinel and Valentine. Moments after the two separately interviewed Coleman, the U.S. Attorney in Central California called to inquire about the interview. Honegger also called immediately, stating Coleman had told her about the calls. Why? The Russbacher case is closed, why the calls?

Honegger writes in her book, "I grew not only to like, but to love Ronald Reagan as an individual." She indicates that she did not publish her book until after Reagan left office because of her "love" for him. Yet in 1984, Honegger left the Reagan camp and campaigned for Jesse Jackson for President. Some specific references in Honegger's book to a former associate of the publisher if the Napa Sentinel are known to be seriously incorrect, because of first hand knowledge of that person's direct interrelationship to the incident cited.

Honegger's work, however, is excellent in some areas and she was the first to publicly expose the October Surprise. Her book, unfortunately did not sell well.

The fact there is no history for Russbacher in a nation that tracks every detail of a person's movements through Social Security cards, and employment records, is not surprising. A high ranking CIA agent in St. Louis has verified certain aspects of Russbacher's story, and a senior U.S. Senator has also verified Russbacher as being "a very good man" and knows of the Habsburg connection.

Russbacher had several code names, one being Gerhardt Mueller, another Robert A. Walker and sometimes just Raven. He traveled on a Swiss passport and spent a lot of time in Europe on assignments.

He logged 750 flight hours as the command pilot of the SR-71. He had some association with the USIS and MI6 intelligence units.

No one has verified Russbacher on the actual aircraft that allegedly flew George Bush to Paris, but the man and his history are recorded in the more secret annals of American records. Raye Russbacher had serious doubts about her husband, but she has close ties to the Naval Postgraduate School in Monterey, California. Her late husband was the dean of science there, and it was there in 1981 that she met Russbacher in a hallway, in full uniform, having a sword fight with a fellow Naval officer. The Intelligence Community opposed Russbacher's marriage to Raye because of her association with Honegger and her liberal political background, from the early Haight-Ashbury days in San Francisco, to her campaigns. Raye Russbacher was Gary Hart's Central California coordinator. Russbacher was to be "free" for two years. And in looking at the various times he was held in jail or on Terminal Island, it almost amounts to two years.

It is also reported, but not confirmed, that Russbacher has no difficulty leaving Terminal Island on Naval Intelligence business. Prison officials would not comment on that aspect, neither a denial or a confirmation.

Secret French Memo on 'October Surprise'

By Harry V. Martin
Copyright, Napa Sentinel 1991
Fifth in a Series

The SDECE, the French equivalent to the American CIA or Russian KGB, apparently monitored George Bush's trip to Paris in October 1980. The monitoring was done because French officials were also involved in the meetings with the Iranians, as were the Israelis. The trip is alleged to have been to delay the release of 52 American hostages held in Iran until after the November 1980 Presidential election.

The man who had the memo was Col. Alexandre de Marenches, head of French Intelligence or the SDECE. There were other foreign powers involved with the Paris meeting, directly and indirectly. According to Navy Captain Gunther Russbacher, who claims to have been the command pilot that flew Bush to and from Paris, the BAC-111 used in the Andrews Air Force Base to Paris flight was retrofitted for the journey and owned by the government of Saudi Arabia. Russbacher reported that information on KING radio in Seattle on Friday night. A French Air Force Base outside of Paris was used for the return flight of Bush to the United States on the SR-71 Blackbird, according to Russbacher's testimony.

Ironically, the Reagan-Bush team gave the Iranians an advanced check for $40 million, drawn off of a Mexican bank. Allegedly Maurice Stans was responsible for getting the money to Mexico and Michael Riconosciuto has told investigators from the House Judiciary Committee that he made the arrangements for the $40 million payment. Riconosciuto is currently in a Pierce County Jail in the state of Washington, being held without bail, after blowing the whistle on the Justice Department's illegal use of INSLAW's PROMIS software.

Former White House National Security Advisor Gary Sick and former Iranian President Bani-Sadr also claim the meeting in Paris did take place. Neither George Bush, George Casey or Donald Gregg have been able to concisely provide information on their where-abouts during this period of time, and even Secret Service memos on the whereabouts of Bush are conflicting. Bush remained off the campaign trail at the time, two and one-half weeks before the election.

Information received by the Sentinel yesterday from the U.S. Department of Justice, indicates that Russbacher does have legit-imate CIA ties. The Justice Department commented about the Russbacher articles, "You're pointed in the right direction." Richard Brenneke has testified that he was on the flight to Paris with Bush, William Casey, and Donald Gregg. The government tried him for perjury because of those statements, and a federal jury in Portland upheld Brenneke's testimony. The government later tried to indicate that Brenneke did not know Russbacher, and therefore, he could not have been the pilot of the Paris-bound aircraft. But documents that have recently surfaced show that Brenneke, Russbacher and Henrich Rupp, another pilot who claims to have been involved, are all closely related to the Habsburg Trust or the Farnham-Ottokar Trust, a vast fund of billions of dollars, some of which were used in a Savings and Loan Scandal involving Rupp. Not only do these documents support Russbacher's ties with Brenneke, but tapes in the possession of Russbacher's wife, verify the close relationship between Russbacher and Brenneke. In fact, evidence points to the fact they are cousins and basically grew up together. Brenneke was raised in Winnamucca, Nevada, the same town that Russbacher's father is buried.

The record of what is happening to known CIA operatives who claim they were involved in the October 1980 Paris meetings?

♦ Richard Brenneke tried on five counts of false statements to a federal judge.

- Heinrich Rupp tried on fraud counts involving the Savings and Loan scandal.

- Gunther Russbacher arrested for kidnapping, investment fraud, desertion, impersonating a U.S. Attorney and a U.S. Marshal. All court records are sealed and he is in Terminal Island for six months.

- Michael Riconosciuto for manufacturing methamphetamines and held without bail.

All enjoyed top security clearances and were involved in multiple CIA-Intelligence operations from gun running to the sale of Exocet missiles to the Argentine government for use against the British Navy.

The General Accounting Office has launched an inquiry into the alleged Paris meeting. Congress is considering conducting an investigation, as well. The GAO is an investigative arm for Congress.

French Connection, the Smoking Gun

If Bush went to Paris, the French and U.S. have documents to prove it

By Harry V. Martin

Copyright, Napa Sentinel, 1991

Sixth in a Series

If there is a smoking gun in the allegations that George Bush flew to Paris in October 1980 to arrange for the delay of the release of 52 American hostages, it will be found in a file cabinet in the French SDECE office, or in secure U.S. government computers.

While Bush was allegedly in Paris, the French intelligence service (SDECE) was asked to make certain the Vice Presidential candidate was not seen. French security succeeded in that task and wrote a routine memo on the incident. A man who spent 18-years in the U.S. intelligence service has testified that he actually saw that memo in December 1980 in the files of the CIA. The file of the Paris meeting was given to the CIA on November 18, 1980. The agent testifies that Bush had to meet with three different factions of the Iranian revolution. The meeting took place at the Rafael Hotel. The agent not only names Bush, but also William Casey, Donald Gregg, and Richard Allen as participants. Bush did not attend the first meeting, only the second.

Afraid that Bush would be recognized by the French press, his aircraft landed at the military part of Orlee. He was whisked away in a closed car and brought directly to the Rafael Hotel. He was there for about two hours, the agent states. This agent has the highest CIA clearance and worked the entire time in the Directorate of Operations in the CIA and was with the Agency since 1965. The agent also testified that the $40 million the Iranians received as a "down payment" in the deal was actually funds left over from a $60 million illegal contribution to the Committee to Reelect the President (Richard Nixon's 1972 reelection campaign) from the Shah of Iran.

In a taped interview, to be released by the Napa Sentinel to KING Radio in Seattle, the agent states that Bush was "out of the loop" from midnight, October 18, 1980 to 5 p.m., October 19. He states that Bush was in a meeting with Hashemi Rafsanjani, representatives of the Ayatollah Behisti, and Javad Bahonar. A key figure was also there for the French SDECE, Robert Benes, the son of Czech President Edward Benes who died in 1948 when the Communists took over his country.

The agent further testifies that Maurice Stans obtained the funds from Mexico. After November 20, 1980. Col. Alexandre de Marenches, head of the SDECE met with President-elect Ronald Reagan in California and presented the Paris meeting report to him. He did not visit President Jimmy Carter. The French intelligence chief warned Reagan not to trust the CIA.

The U.S. agent said Bush and the CIA go back to 1959 and 1960. A memo from FBI Director J. Edgar Hoover was sent in 1963 to CIA agent George Bush addressing the assassination of John F. Kennedy and the possible reaction of Cubans in Miami who might have believed Fidel Castro was responsible for the plot.

But that is not the only smoking gun that could prove the Bush trip to Paris, a trip that he denies. The computers in Washington have codes buried in them, codes that would identify the Bush-Paris activity. In fact, using the right code name and code number, a complete history of the trip, the manifest of the aircraft and other details, including briefing notes, would emerge. According to three separate CIA sources, the operation was conducted in three stages and had three codes:

- ❥ Part one was Magdelen.
- ❥ Part two was Maggellan.
- ❥ Part three was Michaelangelo.

Each has a separate code access. The Maggellan access code is reported to be 0221-001-666. Some of the records can be found at Quantico and others at Andrews Air Force Base. The source of this later information could not be double checked.

Navy Captain Gunther Russbacher, who has been verified by several separate agency members and intelligence sources, claims he flew Bush to Paris in an aircraft owned by the Saudi Royal Family, the aircraft was a reconfigured BAC-111, which refueled in Newfoundland. Russbacher's credibility has been a see-saw for awhile because much of his files are missing, and like many agents has a strange and sometimes silent past. Russbacher, is currently serving a short sentence in Terminal Island for allegedly impersonating a U.S. Attorney. The U.S. Defender's Office indicates that the information published about Russbacher is "on the right track." Others have confirmed the same thing.

But the Sentinel has not been totally satisfied with the complete testimony of Russbacher and has pressed other sources and Russbacher, himself, for more detail. Records will now prove that Russbacher is the cousin of Richard Brenneke, who was acquitted of perjury by a federal jury. He was charged with perjury when he testified that Bush went to Paris. Brenneke originally denied knowing Russbacher, but now admits he knows him. They virtually grew up in Nevada together after their families secretly left Austria after World War II and were recruited by U.S. intelligence. Russbacher identified Brenneke as a member of the flight crew.

One of the difficulties in tracing the steps of CIA agents is the smoke screen, disinformation and attacks on their credibility. The Sentinel has learned that Russbacher escaped from a U.S. Federal Prison in Seagoville, Texas in 1975. On national radio, Russbacher openly admitted the escape and said he was placed on the escape list and spent 10 years in Europe and the United States, working with the CIA. The fact that he has been in the United States and the focus of public attention, he has never been rearrested for the escape. But sources very high up in the intelligence community verify his authenticity.

After receiving information from other sources and pressing Russbacher, he has confirmed the reports of other intelligence officials that Robert Gates was also on the aircraft that flew Bush to Paris. "Gates had a strong hand in it," Russbacher finally admitted. Russbacher, who did not originally seek publicity on this case, was very reluctant to bring in Gates' name. Gates has just been appointed by President Bush to head the CIA and is facing Senate confirmation. Intelligence sources indicate that Russbacher is a key figure in CIA financial matters.

The smoking guns are out there, it is a question of whether they will be found or destroyed. The French have a bitter hatred for the CIA and it is plausible they might use the French report to blackmail the President, especially on matters related to the new European Community and Common Market.

EDITOR'S NOTE: Because some of this information has been verbal or on tape, the Sentinel cannot attest to the complete accuracy in the spelling of some names.

Secret Service Can't Account for Bush

Under sworn testimony, guards don't know where Bush was for 23 hours

By Harry V. Martin

Copyright, Napa Sentinel, 1991

Seventh in a Series

Presidential Press Secretary Marlin Fitzwater stated at a press conference, "The President was on the campaign every day that period. He was on the campaign and he never went to Paris. And anybody who wants to give me a date I can prove it." Thus, the defense of George Bush was made. The then Vice Presidential candidate did not go to Paris to make a deal with the Iranians to delay release of 52 American hostages until after the November 1980 election.

In May 1990, in a Federal Court in Portland, Oregon, a jury found Richard Brenneke not guilty of making false statements alleging Bush went to Paris in 1980. At this trial, two secret service agents in charge of Bush's security in October 1980, swore under oath they could not state definitively or even with a high degree of confidence, where Bush was at all times during the campaign. They could not state where Bush was from 9:25 p.m. Saturday, October 18 until Sunday evening at 7:57. This is direct testimony in the federal court.

Bush claims that he had gone to Chevy Chase Country Club at 10:30 a.m. on Sunday, October 19. But the Federal Bureau of Investigation investigated this possibility and reported that no one at the country club could be found to substantiate this. Bush claims he had lunch with Supreme Court Justice Potter Stewart and his wife. The Justice is dead and his wife has no recollection of that luncheon.

At the time of Brenneke's trial for perjury, the Secret Service could not say where Bush was for the missing 23 hours. Assistant U.S. Attorney O'Rourke, who was prosecuting Brenneke, could not find any information on Bush's whereabouts, either. Brenneke, in a recent letter to Fitzwater, stated, "If the government could not prove in court where Mr. Bush was for one 23 hour period discussed in the trial, how are you going to do it for this and, perhaps, other periods?"

Brenneke has asked a direct question to Fitzwater and to 26 other individuals. The other individuals include former President Jimmy Carter; Congressman Tom Foley, Speaker of the House; Congresswoman Pat Schroeder; Senator Mark Hatfield; Senator Robert Packwood; Congressman Ron Wyden; Iran-Contra Special Prosecutor Walsh; Michael Scott, Brenneke's attorney; Richard H. Muller; Gary Sick; Robert Parry; John King of Associated Press; Martin Killian of *Der Spiegel*; Frank Snepp of ABC; Peter Jennings of ABC; Ralph Blumenthal of *The New York Times*; Phil Insolata of *The St. Louis Post Dispatch*; Larry King; Abe Rabinovitz of *The Jerusalem Post*; Shigeo Masui of *The Yomiuri Shimbun*; James Long of *The Oregonian*; Philip Stanford of *The Oregonian*; Jodi Solomon of JFS Speakers; Jacques de Spoelberch of J de S, Inc.; Rev. William Davis of the Christic Institute; and Dr. Robert Hieronimus. The question: "Did Mr. Bush, Mr. Allen, Mr. Casey, Mr. Gregg or anyone from, involved with or in any way associated or affiliated with the Reagan campaign, the Bush campaign, or the Reagan-Bush campaign visit any foreign country at any time during the summer or fall of 1980 and meet or negotiate with any Iranians, any Iranian representatives, or agents of any Iranians regarding anything? If so, was this done with the prior or subsequent knowledge or consent of either candidate? Again, if so, were any discussions, overtures or contacts reported at once to then President Carter?"

Brenneke became embroiled in this controversy when he attempted to defend his close friend, former Nazi pilot Henrich Rupp, who has been a CIA operative for many years. Rupp was charged with fraud in a Savings and Loan scandal and sentenced to 42 years in prison. The sentence was reduced to two years. Rupp claims to have piloted an aircraft that brought several high Republican campaign people to Paris in October 1980 to make a deal with the Iranians not to release the hostages. Brenneke testified on behalf of Rupp concerning his CIA connections and the October 1980 flight. After the testimony, Brenneke was tried on five counts of perjury in connection with his testimony, primarily that Bush and his close associates flew to Paris in 1980.

At one point in Brenneke's trial, Donald Gregg, now ambassador to South Korea, and also reported subject of a Federal Grand Jury indictment for perjury, told a federal jury he could not have been in Paris in October 1980 and produced a picture of he and his wife on a sunny Maryland beach. Weather experts shot down his testimony, saying the weather conditions were adverse the day Gregg claims to have been at the sunny beach.

Both Rupp and Brenneke indicate that the people in Paris to make a deal with the Iranians included George Bush, William Casey, Robert Gates, and Richard Allen.

U.S. Navy Captain Gunther Russbacher came forward in early May and claims that he was the command pilot of the aircraft flown to Paris. Russbacher's background in the intelligence community has been independently verified by many intelligence sources throughout the United States. Brenneke is elusive as to his full knowledge of Russbacher, but he readily admits knowing Russbacher's wife, Raye Allan. But this week Brenneke confirmed with Tom Valentine, of the Sun Radio Network, that he knew Robert Walker. In the first articles concerning Russbacher's claims, he stated that one of his aliases was Robert Walker.

Brenneke also confirmed information that was never published prior to the Russbacher interviews in the Napa Sentinel, that the BAC-111 was a reconfigured Saudi aircraft. Brenneke indicated that there were only about three BAC-111s available in October 1980, but no one knew about the aircraft being reconfigured. Brenneke indicates that the aircraft flew non-stop, but Russbacher indicates it was refueled in Newfoundland. Rupp has admitted the aircraft was refueled in Newfoundland, as well.

But what shocked Brenneke the most was the revelation made in last Friday's Sentinel of the code words of the mission:

- Part one was Magdelen.
- Part two was Maggellan.
- Part three was Michaelangelo.

The code number is 0221-001-666. This information has never been made public before the Sentinel article and Brenneke was genuinely shocked at their publication. Though the information had come from other intelligence sources, Russbacher was asked what the code names were without being supplied any clues or hints. The Sentinel had preknowledge of at least one of the codes in order to test Russbacher.

Brenneke provided some key information about the SR-71, information that is not classified, but also not of common knowledge. This information will be used to again test the validity of Russbacher's statements. The Sentinel has continually tested the man's validity time and time again. Even though the newspaper has verified his background in the intelligence community, it cannot absolutely guarantee he was one of the pilots. But then, nobody can guarantee the Brenneke or Rupp claims, either. In each case, the men have slightly contradicted each other and sometimes their own testimony, but there has been no major deviation from the main claim that Bush was in Paris in October 1980. Brenneke has confirmed his association with the Farnham-Ottokar Trust and the Sentinel has documents to prove that association.

A French intelligence memo and the codes could shed light on the entire controversy. The French memo, delivered to President-elect Ronald Reagan in California in December 1980, details Bush's presence in Paris and also the complete details of the various meetings held between the Republicans and the Iranians.

The Sentinel also published information linking Robert Gates, now facing Senate confirmation hearings as CIA Director, to the October 1980 flight.

In the meantime, Michael Riconosciuto, who claims he made the money transfer of $40 million as a "down payment" to the Iranians, is reported to have suddenly been moved from his Pierce County, Washington, jail cell and taken to an unknown location. The Sentinel has no direct confirmation of that move. Riconosciuto was a key witness in the Congressional investigation of the Justice Department and also a witness for a low-key Congressional investigation into the October Surprise. Seattle's KING Radio was set to interview Ricono-sciuto on the weekend, but his sudden transfer may have blocked the interview.

Though all parties agree that Bush was in Paris, there seems to be some sort of disinformation campaign going on to cover up all the principals involved in the flight, including the name of Gates. Three separate intelligence sources have indicated Gates was aboard the aircraft as either a pilot or a passenger. Several individuals who are pushing their respective books, are challenging each and every researchers, which only adds to the confusion and disinformation campaign. Each of the researchers have strong, valid reports, but they differ slightly from their prospective.

A U.S. attorney with knowledge of the background of each of the individuals involved, an investigative reporter in Florida who has talked with his intelligence sources, and a former CIA operative, all have stated, "You're on the right track."

Who is this man who claims he flew Bush to Paris?

By Harry V. Martin
Copyright, Napa Sentinel, 1991
Eighth in a Series

It was in the beginning of May, that U.S. Navy Captain Gunther Russbacher's name came into play in the Napa Sentinel and on the national news. He claims to be the pilot who flew George Bush to

Paris to participate in the negotiations with the Iranians to delay the release of 52 American hostages until after the November 1980 election.

There have been some challenges, naturally, to his statements. Through various intelligence and news sources, the Sentinel has been able to verify Russbacher's long intelligence background. To expound about the credibility of Russbacher's claim, it is important that his background be partially disclosed.

The man was born on July 1, 1942 in Salzberg, Austria. His birth certificate reads, Gunther Karl, Baron von Russbach, Count von Esterházy. On his father's side, he was descended from the Baron who had captured Richard the Lionhearted and held him for ransom. On his mother's side, he was descended from Hungarian royalty. The Esterházys had been advisors to the Emperors of Austria for generations. His Godfather, was Ernest Kaltenbrunner, the head of Austrian Intelligence during World War II. The records of Russbacher's family are kept in the family church in Salzberg. His family was part of the Gehlen group which was also called the Canaris group. (*Ed. Note:* After Kaltenbrunner died, Kurt Waldheim became Russbacher's godfather.)

After the war, several Austrian families, including his, had to leave Austria in order to avoid prosecution for working with the Nazis. Eighteen members of his family were forced into exile in the United States. His interests, as a youth, were in math, science, government and survival training, both in Oklahoma and in Nevada. He learned to fly at an early age.

In 1961, Russbacher entered the U.S. Army at Ft. Carson, CO. After basic training he was transferred to the North American Air Defense Command, where he obtained high levels of security clearances. He earned his cryptography credentials and had close meetings and ties with intelligence officers at Norad and Ft. Carson and at Ent Air Force Base.

That is basically the public life the government is quite willing to share. But in 1963, he was discharged from the military and "buried" as far as government records were concerned. At this point, Russbacher began to work with people from the Federal Building in Oklahoma City and was then transferred to the NASA school in Pasadena, TX. He moved around a lot from there, learning languages at military language schools, taught photo intelligence evaluation and aircraft thrust evaluation.

In 1965, Russbacher, who also goes by the name Robert A. Walker or Raven, was transferred to a facility at Langley Center. Most of the training at that time occurred at Air Force bases throughout the U.S., at the Center and in the Vienna, VA area. He was transferred to

advanced flight schools at Shepard Air Force Base, TX. From there he
went to Carswell Air Force Base, TX and then Nellis Air Force Base in
Las Vegas and then Cannon Air Force Base, NM. He operated in
Vietnam.

In 1968, he was assigned to the Office of Naval Intelligence with a
permanent commission. As a flier, he was sent to Nellis Air Force Base
and then to Beale for training on the SR program. He spent about
seven months in simulator training before having the first loner run in
the SR, Blackbird. He received his habu patch and logged a total of 750
hours front and stick time, and 150 hours as radar service officer. His
assignment with the SR was at Beale, Cadena, Mindenhall, Akrotiri and
in Turkey. The last runs of the Blackbird were out of Ramstein Air
Force Base, Kaiserslauten, Germany.

It is the Blackbird that Russbacher claims he flew Bush back in after
the Paris meeting. Originally, the SR-71 was called the RS 71 for Reconnaissance Strike aircraft. The aircraft is equipped with twin J-58 turbo-
ram jet engines, which equal 32,500 pounds of thrust per unit. The
speed is regulated by the nacelle spike, which are inlets which read
26.125 inches in length and can be changed from a fore to an aft
position, to change the positions of the spike, which will change the
power pack to turbo fans to ram jets. From 93 to 95 percent of the
frame of the aircraft is made of titanium. At operational speeds, not
top speeds, the center of the aircraft's skin gets anywhere from 510
to 515 degrees Fahrenheit while the temperatures along the engines
run anywhere from 1050 to 1110 degrees Fahrenheit. The exhaust
areas around the engines are a minimum of 1200 Fahrenheit. The
cockpit glass gets so hot that you cannot touch it even with a flame
retardant glove. The tires are 22 ply and contain aluminum pieces and
parts in order to dissipate the heat. The air in the tires is really
nitrogen. It travels at 32 miles a minute. The nose of the aircraft is
interchangeable to affix different kinds of sensors.

In 1972, Russbacher was still active Navy, but most of his 201 file
was closed due to frequent assignments with the CIA. The objective
of a 201 file is that you build a nice clean record that you can transfer
from military to civilian life. But because of Russbacher's intelligence
operations, much of his 201 file is spotty. Also in 1972, he was loaned
to the Department of State for Central and Eastern Europe and
attached to the black consular operations, a special operations group.
He was stationed at Badgodesberg, which was the U.S. Embassy in
Bonn, Germany. But he also operated out of Belgrade, Vienna, Rome
and Paris, plus a short term in Moscow. In Italy he worked with
counter revolutionaries and counter terrorists groups in liaison with
Italian intelligence staff and carbinieres. The object was to infiltrate

the Brigade Roso, Red Brigade. He was in Milan when the train station was bombed.

He also worked out of the consular general's office in Genoa, held Swiss and German passports under the name of Gerhard Mueller and Wagner. He worked with and against the Badermeinoff and Red Army faction. He helped get high level people out of Czechoslovakia.

In 1979, he was called back to Beale for updates and flew three tours on the newer version of the SR. He updated the global positioning system and firefly platforms at low darkness and red levels.

In February 1980, He returned to Langley, and then to St. Louis. He became an investment broker and financial planner with Prudential and Connecticut Mutual. After gaining the experience he opened up a CIA-proprietary company called National Brokerage Companies, National Financial Services, Crystal Shores Development Corporation and other companies. CIA money was laundered through these operations. He also attended Centerpoint, Phoenix which was a desert sabotage school. In October 1980, he was command pilot for the aircraft used allegedly to fly George Bush to Paris. The three code names for the operation were Magdalen, Maggellen and Michaelangelo. While he was in Paris, his cover was that he was attending the Connecticut Mutual School for advance planning in Hartford.

In January 1981, he was in Tegucigalpa, Honduras to meet with the resistance and continued the talks in Costa Rica and Cancun. Russbacher funded the group with low-level black funds channeled from European banks.

In February 1982, he returned to Frankfurt to discuss shipments to Israel after boats of Marseille harbor to Arab contacts. From March to July 1982, Russbacher was on Navy duty in and out of Monterey, and also loaned to the Looking Glass and Operation Michaelangelo. This involved details of using Reforger stored arms for shipment to Iran. Funds were transacted from Luxembourg City to Geneva and Zurich. His group met with Mossad (Israeli intelligence) people in Alicante for the final delivery of weapons to Iran. Aircraft was utilized from the Saudi, French, German, Austrian and Dutch government.

In October 1982, Russbacher was back at Langley (CIA headquarters), for briefing on the supply of arms to Afghani rebels. He met a special operations group at Islamabad and Ralapindi, Pakistan. Agreements were reached with the resistance people at Seven Rivers Junction in Afghanistan. Funds to finance the operation came out of financial sources in the state of Washington,

Oregon, Indiana, Florida and Georgia. Much of the heavy equipment was moved to Frankfurt.

Russbacher fell from grace with the CIA after his mission in Eastern Europe failed with the death of a U.S. Army major from Heidelberg.

In February 1983 he returned to Eastern Europe. The purpose of the trip was to acquire Czech plastique explosives and small arms.

In March to August 1983, he infiltrated the Pipefitters Union in St. Louis. A year later he was back in Afghanistan. Then back to St. Louis and then to Paris on hostage taking and counter terrorism assignments.

In March 1985, he was incarcerated at Seagoville, TX for an escape from federal conviction resulting from 1973 where he was caught with numerous bags of bearer bonds while dressed as a U.S. Air Force major.

From November 1985 to July 1986, he was attached to DOS consular operations service. he was active in Operation Clydesdale.

From July 1986 to August 1990 he was assigned to numerous internal U.S. operations for the CIA. In June 1989, he signed an agreement not to marry for two years, a common commitment for intelligence operatives after a divorce. But he did marry. He married a woman who was a political activist and who had lobbied against Donald Gregg's appointment for U.S. ambassador to South Korea. Gregg, at the time, was head of the CIA discipline committee. Russbacher was warned that his wife could be a KGB agent or possibly a mole for the State Department or FBI, entities that do not have a great love for the CIA.

Within days after his marriage, Russbacher was moved from California to Missouri. He pleaded guilty to an investment fraud and was sentenced to 28 years in jail. The judge, after reading a secret report, allowed Russbacher free on probation and the prosecutor was fired.

On his release he met with William Webster at Offutt Air Force Base. The trip was associated with the Lookinglass Command. He was ordered to fly to Castle Air Force Base in California. He was arrested by the FBI for trespassing and impersonating a Naval officer. These charges were dropped immediately.

He was then charged with impersonating a U.S. Attorney and misuse of government purchase orders, jet and fuel. The case was declared a mistrial. The prosecutor told him to plead guilty and therefore his wife would not be charged with trespassing on a military base. He was given 21 months in prison and is scheduled for release in December, though he has enjoyed considerable freedom.

In early May, Russbacher's boss in the Office of Naval Intelligence tried to have him transferred to Naval custody. A U.S. Senator from the Senate Judicial Committee has asked Russbacher to testify to the Senate and has personally assured him of his safety.

The Conclusion: Did Bush go to Paris?

By Harry V. Martin

Copyright, Napa Sentinel, 1991

Last in a Ten Part Series

Congressman Lee Hamilton has announced that there is not sufficient evidence to prove that George Bush went to Paris in October 1980 to negotiate a deal with the Iranians not to release 52 American hostages until after the November 1980 elections. The purpose of the meeting was to block any chance that President Jimmy Carter would create an "October Surprise" by gaining release of the hostages and thus assure his reelection to a second term. Hamilton has conducted a low level investigation into the October Surprise; the purpose of his investigation was to determine whether or not a large scale Congressional investigation into the allegations against Bush should be held.

Hamilton has apparently made no attempt to locate a French intelligence memo delivered to the CIA in December 1980 that reports on Bush's visit and the contents of the meeting between American civilian and Iranian government representatives. Hamilton, further, has not attempted to check Norad's computers for the code name Magellan and the code number 0221-001-666, nor have flight logs from any KC135 been obtained for the night of October 20, 1980, the night that an aircraft was allegedly refueled over the Atlantic, an aircraft that was reportedly carrying Bush.

Also, it is not known if Hamilton checked the sworn testimony of two Secret Service agents in a federal trial held in Portland, Oregon. The agents state under oath they cannot account for Bush's time for about 21 hours. Certainly, the wife of the late Supreme Court Justice Potter Stewart cannot confirm that she and her husband had lunch with Bush at a country club that Bush does not belong to, nor did anyone at the country club recall him being there.

Also, the transcript of the Richard Brenneke trial in Portland, Oregon, would show that Donald Gregg, now ambassador to South Korea and a person reported to be subject of a forthcoming perjury indictment by a U.S. Federal Grand Jury, lied on the stand. Gregg denied being in Paris on the dates in question, stating he was with his wife on a sunny Maryland beach that day, and even produced a photograph. Weather experts testified that the picture does not reflect the weather patterns that existed that day, which was not sunny.

Hamilton has not been able to account for the whereabouts of Bush, William Casey or Donald Gregg on those missing days in October 1980, in fact no one has, not even the men themselves.

Several witnesses have come forward, but how credible are the witnesses. Heinrich Rupp, a former Nazi pilot and long time covert operator for the CIA, says Bush, Casey and Gregg were in Paris. Rupp was sentenced to 40 years in a CIA-funded bank scam and his sentence was reduced to two years. Richard Brenneke, another long time CIA covert operator who flew drugs and guns, went to Rupp's defense and was charged with several counts of perjury. Brenneke was acquitted of perjury by a federal jury who believed he had flown Bush, Casey and Gregg to Paris. But Brenneke's health is broken. Gunther Russbacher, alias Robert A. Walker, alias the Raven, and several other aliases, has rushed to Brenneke's defense to claim he was in the command seat. He is now in Terminal Island Federal Prison for impersonating a U.S. Attorney. Russbacher's background provides solid proof of his CIA and Naval Intelligence background. The man who claims he made the money transfer of $40 million to the Iranians, Michael Riconosciuto, is a key witness against the U.S. Justice Department in the INSLAW case. He has provided testimony to the U.S. House Judiciary Committee investigation. Riconosciuto warned in his affidavit he would be arrested if he testified. He was arrested just one week after the affidavit and held without bail. He was to have been interviewed on KING Radio in Seattle but was whisked away to a midwestern federal prison for "psychiatric" evaluation.

All four of these individuals are known CIA operatives or contract personnel. All have taken a fall, save Brenneke, who was saved by a federal jury.

What is also known, is that the Carter Administration, according to Gary Sick, was on the verge of obtaining the release of the hostages in October 1980, which probably would have assured his reelection. After the date that Bush allegedly went to Paris, the negotiations with the Iranians collapsed. Moments after Ronald Reagan became President, the hostages were released. Within weeks, shipments of military equipment and spare parts were flown to Iran. Mossad agents have testified to the Iran weapons deal. The French have memos about the plan. The former President of Iran confirms the Republican-Iranian deal to delay the release of the hostages, and even former President Jimmy Carter, who had preferred to remain silent, has come forward to indicate that Gregg was a mole and was possibly responsible for the October Surprise. Gregg worked for Bush when Bush was head of the CIA.

Computers on flights in and out of Andrews Air Force Base, McGuire, French air fields, refueling planes, Brenneke's and Russbacher's flight logs, transportation systems, serial numbers of aircraft supplied by the Saudi Royal Family, the inventory of Reforger materials, French memos on file with the CIA and in Paris, and the diaries and campaign logs of Bush, Casey and Gregg, conflicting Secret Service memos, and transcripts of the Rupp, Brenneke and Russbacher trials are all smoking guns if Congress wants to check out documents.

Congress is wary of the impact another Watergate type scandal would have on the American people and with foreign nations. But perhaps, Congress is more worried about what **Gregg once told a Senate investigation committee probing the Iran-Contra scandal. "Back off or face martial law."**

EDITOR'S NOTE: Though we are concluding the series today, the Sentinel will continue to update its readers on further developments. All our material has been or will be sent to Congress.

Israelis Hold the Real Key to October Surprise
By Harry V. Martin
An Addendum in Two Parts
Copyright, Napa Sentinel 1991

EDITOR'S NOTE: O*n Friday morning, the publisher of the Napa Sentinel said on a Houston radio talk show that if anyone could break the Bush-Paris allegations, it would be the Israelis. The following article is an addendum to the eleven part series run in the Sentinel since May 3.*

If there is a smoking gun in the Bush-Paris affair, it will certainly have to come from the Israelis, they are the key to the entire October Surprise package. The Israelis initiated arms shipments to Iran as a counter to Iraq. When President Jimmy Carter ordered a halt to the Israeli weapons sales the Israelis may have set up the October Paris meeting that William Casey, Donald Gregg and George Bush allegedly attended in 1980.

The known facts leading up to this scenario are as follows:

1. In March 1980, a meeting took place at the Mayflower Hotel in Washington, attended by William Casey and Cyrus and Jamshid Hashemi. The two brothers were cooperating with the Carter administration, yet Casey told them he did not want President Carter to receive a political advantage by the release of 52 American hostages. Cyrus Hashemi reported the

meeting to the CIA. He died suddenly after revealing the information.

2. In July 1980, Casey, a U.S. intelligence officer and Mehdi Karrubi (now speaker of the Iranian parliament) met in Madrid. Karrubi is reported to have agreed to cooperate with the delay in the release of American hostages.

3. On October 2, 1980, a meeting took place at the L'Enfant Plaza Hotel in Washington, D.C. The participants of that meeting including Richard Allen (later named head of President Ronald Reagan's National Security Council), Marine Lt. Col. Robert McFarlane (then an aide to Texas Senator John Tower and later a national security advisor to President Reagan), Lawrence Silberman (an aide to Allen and now a Federal Court of Appeals judge in Washington, D.C.), Iranian Jewish arms dealer Hushang Lavie.

In the alleged Paris meeting, those in attendance are reported to be:

- ❱ George Bush, candidate for Vice President.
- ❱ William Casey, Reagan's campaign manager.
- ❱ Donald Gregg, a member of the CIA.
- ❱ Manucher Ghorbanifar, an Iranian born Mossad agent and arms dealer.
- ❱ Mohammad Ali Rajai, the future president of Iran.
- ❱ Ali Akbar Hashemi Rafsanjani, the speaker of the Iranian parliament.

The Israelis, because of their role of mediator between the United States and Iran and also as the deliverers of U.S. weapons to Iran after the conclusion of the meetings, are believed to have arranged the meetings in the first place.

Right after the alleged Paris meeting, the Israelis sent a shipment of spare parts to Iran for their American-built F-104 fighters, which was in contravention of U.S. regulations requiring U.S. approval of any shipments of U.S.–made arms to third parties.

Right after the alleged Paris meeting, the Iranians not only backed away from negotiations with the Carter administration for the release of hostages, but they also dispersed the hostages throughout Iran to prevent a second rescue attempt, a rescue attempt that was apparently leaked to them from the Reagan campaign headquarters and probably by Richard Allen.

After the hostages were released on January 20, 1981, Israel signed an agreement to ship arms to Iran. Former Iranian President Bani Sadr has verified the Israeli shipments to Iran. Israeli Defense Minister Ariel Sharon has consistently stated that all Israeli shipments of arms to Iran were sanctioned by the U.S. government. In 1982, Israel's ambassador to the United States is quoted in the Boston Globe as stating Israeli arms shipments to Iran were sanctioned and coordinated by the United States government "at almost the highest level."

Several Israeli Mossad agents have come forward to indicate full knowledge of the Paris meeting and subsequent shipment of arms to Iran. One of those agents is Ari Ben Menashe. (His testimony is in part two of this addendum to the October Surprise series.)

If the Paris meeting did take place, the Israeli government may have been able to blackmail the Reagan and Bush administrations. Richard Curtiss writes in the *Washington Report on Middle East Affairs*, "Whenever the Reagan administration and the hard-line Israeli governments of Menachem Begin and his successors went eyeball to eyeball, it was always the U.S. that blinked. The U.S. declined to press Begin on such topics as the Golan Heights, East Jerusalem, the invasion of Lebanon, the occupation of West Beirut, the Sabra-Shatila massacres, and even the Reagan Plan for Middle East peace. The Reagan administration apparently was vulnerable to highly damaging Israeli blackmail, and at least some top officials of both governments knew it." He adds, "It also explains how and why the Reagan administration so easily fell into the catastrophic series of arms-for-hostages blunders, clearly instigated as well as carried out by Israel, that became known as Irangate, or the Iran-Contra scandal. The renewed arms shipments in 1985 and 1986 were initiated by reopening exactly the same channels used in 1980 and 1981 by some of the same principals on both sides."

Curtiss, a retired U.S. foreign service officer, feels that the Israelis hold the upper hand and can blackmail Bush or, if Bush was not involved in Paris, could create disinformation about him being in Paris, anyway. "If Israel's disinformation squad has its way, the worst is yet to come." But at the same time Israel does not wish to be painted with the same political brush and would by leery of opening up such a scandal. It has also been noted that the Israeli lobby is making moves on Capitol Hill to prevent the opening of any investigation. Also, Israel is very dependent on U.S. military and economic aid and would not wish to jeopardize its close association with the United States.

However, Bush is putting a lot of pressure on Israel for an Israeli-Palestinian settlement and the possibility of yielding Israeli-captured lands. How hard Bush pushes will determine how much the Israelis will reveal about the alleged Paris meeting and arms shipments to Iran. Israel holds the key to the October Surprise.

Israeli Agent Names Names, Sources Reveal Bank Transactions

By Harry V. Martin

Second in an Addendum

Copyright © Napa Sentinel, 1991

Ari Ben Menashe, a 12-year agent of the Mossad, Israel's equivalent to the CIA, is doing a lot of talking these days. Menashe provided an affidavit to Congress which claims that Earl Brian, a close friend of Ronald Reagan and Edwin Meese brokered the illegal sale of INSLAW's copyrighted software in the Santiago, Chile office of Carlos Carduen in which Iraq was the principle buyer.

Menashe is now claiming that George Bush did go to Paris in October 1980 to make a deal with Iranians not to release 52 American hostages until after the election. Testimony of several agents on both sides of the Atlantic indicate that the Israelis were instrumental in establishing a meeting between the Reagan-Bush campaign organization and three factions of the Iran revolutionary government.

Menashe says that he definitely saw Bush in Paris in October 1980. Menashe states that Earl Brian and Robert McFarlane went to Iran to set up meetings with the Iranians on the hostage issue. The Israeli intelligence officer indicates that Prime Minister Menachem Begin wrote a secret memo instructing his inner circle to work quietly with the Reagan-Bush campaign and the Iranians. Menashe says that he actually saw the memo.

According to Menashe, a series of three meetings were held in Spain between the Reagan-Bush campaign, represented by William Casey, and Iranian officials. There was a fourth meeting in Barcelona, while the first three meetings were held in Madrid.

Menashe claims that William Casey personally invited him to Paris in October. The invitation was also extended to the military intelligence of Israel and to the acting director of the Mossad. Six Israeli representatives were sent to Paris for the meetings, with explicit instructions not to participate but to just observe. Menashe indicates the meetings took place at the Ritz Hotel in Paris on one of the highest floors of the hotel. He said that he saw Bush, William Casey and key Iranian officials. Menashe states that the head of the French intelligence (SDECE), Hamid Nagashian, deputy director of the Iranian Revolutionary Guard, aides to high ranking Iranians, William Casey, George Bush, Richard Allen, and Robert McFarlane were at the meeting.

The Sentinel received testimony late yesterday afternoon claiming that Bush was in Paris and presented a bank draft check for $40 million to the Iranians. The check was not left with the Iranians but was transferred to a Luxembourg bank. Here is the exact money route:

- Funds came from the Committee to Reelect the President (Nixon campaign funds).

- The funds, along with other CREEP money, came from Mexico.

- The funds were transferred to Gibraltar Savings in the United States.

- From there the funds were transferred to Atlantic Savings.

- Then they were transferred to Cloten Bank.

- The bank draft was sent with Bush to Paris and then placed in the Luxembourg bank.

The Atlantic account was under the name of Paul Hurt. William Jenson, who works with Bank of America, is alleged to have facilitated the transfer. Michael May of CREEP was the custodian of the funds and Roger Ailes allegedly played a key role in the transfer.

The source, already a key witness for Congress, indicates that Gunther Russbacher, the man who claims he flew Bush to and from Paris, is solidly legitimate and a key operative in the countermeasures field and ELITE, which is electronic surveillance and reconnaissance. The source also says that Richard Brenneke, another pilot who claims he flew the aircraft to Paris, is a very close associate and long time friend of Russbacher's. Russbacher, according to this entrenched intelligence source, indicates that he is only one of six pilots authorized to fly the two-seater SR-71, the CIA's Blackbird.

The source also indicates that there are flight records at Andrews Air Force Base showing that an SR-71 was flown into the base the night Russbacher claimed to have flown from Bush from Paris to McGuire Air Force Base in New Jersey in an SR-71. The flight log shows a SR-71 landed at Andrews from McGuire.

The source also indicates that there are three smoking guns to prove Bush went to Paris, each chiseled in marble, meaning nondestructible evidence. A special arrangement is being made to provide this information directly to Congress for a future investigation into the October Surprise.

The source also indicates that Menashe holds sufficient evidence on McFarlane to break the October Surprise case wide open.

According to Bob Woodward of the Washington Post, there was an Israeli-American agreement authorized which is still secret. It calls for counter-terrorist operations, which has been supervised by Lt. Col. Oliver North. This agreement, according to Woodward, was not known to Congress. The agreement was part of the Iran-Contra affair and has led to a series of covert actions.

Dead Men Tell No Tales

By Harry V. Martin

Senator Albert Gore has called for a formal investigation into the "October Surprise." A one-time Democratic presidential candidate, the Tennessee senator is considering a second race for the Democratic nomination in 1992.

But at the heart of the question of any investigation is: who would be the witnesses? The Sentinel has published a 13-part series on the allegation that George Bush and his Republican colleagues made a deal with Iran to delay the release of 52 American hostages in 1980.

As more and more attention is focused on the issue, little attention has focused on who would be the witnesses and what happened to many of them.

➤ CYRUS HASHEMI, an arms dealer, was approached by William Casey to set up the meetings with the Republicans and Iranians. He reported the contact to the CIA and died shortly after that.

➤ JOHN TOWER, a U.S. Senator who was deeply involved in the process through his then aide Robert McFarlane. Tower was the chief investigator in the Iran-Contra scandal. He died in a plane crash recently.

➤ ALAN MICHAEL MAY, who managed the funds for Richard Nixon's Committee to Re-elect the President. May allegedly transferred $40 million from a Mexican bank to various U.S. banks to Luxembourg as a "down payment" for the delay of the hostages. His name came up for the first time in the Napa Sentinel last week and he died of a heart attack this weekend at age 50. May had indicated a short time before he died that he feared for his life.

➤ U.S. SUPREME COURT JUSTICE POTTER STEWART, who Bush claims had lunch with him during the missing hours in October 1980, is now dead.

➤ WILLIAM CASEY, the former head of the CIA and principle negotiator in the alleged hostage delay, died on the eve of the Iran-Contra hearings.

➤ HEINRICH RUPP, the man who allegedly flew Casey back from Paris and a long-term CIA operative, was sentenced to jail for 40 years in a CIA bank scandal. His sentence was reduced to two years.

➤ RICHARD BRENNEKE, who also claims he was a pilot involved in the October Surprise and a long time arms dealer for the CIA, went to Rupp's defense and was charged with five counts of perjury. He was acquitted, but has recently changed his story saying he did not fly over in the BAC-111. He claims he flew Pan Am to Paris and flew part of the Paris party back to the United States.

🔾 GUNTHER RUSSBACHER, who claims he was the command pilot that flew George Bush to Paris in October 1980 and a long-time Naval Intelligence and CIA operative, is finishing a short term in federal prison on charges he impersonated a U.S. attorney.

🔾 MICHAEL RICONOSCIUTO, who was allegedly the man who finalized the money transfers for the deal in Paris and also a long time CIA operative, is being held without bail in a federal prison in Missouri pending a trial in the State of Washington for drug manufacturing. Riconoscuito had warned the media and Congress that he would be arrested if he testified in the INSLAW case. He provided testimony and was arrested within a week.

🔾 DONALD GREGG, who was a principle in the alleged meetings with the Iranians and former high official in the CIA, is now Ambassador to South Korea. Gregg's testimony in Brenneke's trial was rejected by a federal jury. Gregg is also supposed to be indicted by a U.S. Federal Grand Jury in Washington, D.C., soon on charges of perjury. Former President Jimmy Carter said that Gregg was the mole in the White House.

🔾 ROBERT GATES, implicated by Russbacher as having been involved in the deal, is seeking confirmation from the U.S. Senate as the new CIA director.

🔾 DR. EARL BRIAN, said to have been the liaison in setting up the preliminary meetings between the Republicans and the Iranians, has enjoyed extensive contracts with the U.S. government, including involvement in the INSLAW case in which he is alleged to have illegally sold INSLAW's PROMIS software to Israel, Libya, Iraq, Canada, Australia and South Korea. The INSLAW case is currently under investigation.

🔾 ARI BEN-MENASHE, an Israeli Mossad agent, has testified to the meetings in Paris and the Israeli role as an arms conduit. The Israeli Mossad is known for its disinformation, and thus Ben-Menashe may not be considered a reliable witness.

- ➤ RICHARD ALLEN, head of Ronald Reagan's National Security Council, was allegedly instrumental in the deal. Allen has already been nationally discredited.

- ➤ GEORGE BUSH, President of the United States and former head of the CIA, denies any involvement.

- ➤ RONALD REAGAN doesn't recall. He also couldn't recall being at any Iran-Contra discussions.

- ➤ MRS. JUSTICE STEWART POTTER, who was supposed to be having lunch with her husband and Bush at the time of the Paris meeting, does not recall the luncheon, but says she can't recall yesterday, either.

It isn't going to be easy for the Senate investigators. But there are a lot more permanent items on the paper trail that might break the case wide open.

Stay tuned.

FreeAmerica ©1995
Included with the permission of Harry V. Martin, publisher of The Napa Sentinel.
http://www.napasentinel.com

Articles by Gunther K. Russbacher

"I was born in Salzburg Austria on July 1, 1942 unto Elizabeth Maria Weissl/Esterbázy and Karl Gunther Russbacher. My mother was the heir to the Esterbázy estates. My father was of noble descent. He was known as the Lion of Salzburg."

And the Lion Cried

By Gunther K. Russbacher, Admiral, USN

Written June 11, 1992
Edited by Rayelan Allan Russbacher

The day was drawing to a close while the noise of the prison began to be unbearable. It seemed as if all the animals wanted to talk and yell at the very same time. The evening meal, consisting of burned pinto beans, dried out corn and spaghetti sauce with unknown meat was considered the fare of the day.

The noise of the young men housed in the maximum security (protective custody unit) section of the Missouri state penitentiary reached the usual levels as inmates taunted each other back and forth through-out the large housing structure, commonly referred to as the cell house of the Ozarks. The unit houses about 320 men - all of whom have either requested protective custody, were ordered into protective custody by and through order of the court or prison administration, or they were forced to 'check in' for their own protection due to incurrence of gambling debts, or that they failed to pay their prison pusher for drugs. Many of them cannot keep their mouths shut when it comes to the telling of tales about other inmates. Snitches, as they are called, are by far in the overall majority.

Lastly, there is another group of men who are forced to live under these deplorable living conditions. These men have committed no overt acts against other inmates, but rather and more so, pose a significant threat to the safety and security of the prison. They are the ones who have kept their honor, respect and dignity, even at the cost of incurring the severe wrath of the people running the institution. They are the ones who take freedom seriously—even to the point of attempting escape from custody. Many of them should not have been jailed or imprisoned at all. They represent the failings of a society with little or no social conscience. They dream of freedom; taste the freedom as they watch the numerous television programs avail-able to them. They, who are condemned to this place of higher learning feel not only lost, but also completely forgotten. It is a hell on earth. Hope, eternal hope, is the commodity panhandled by Bible toting fundamen-talist preachers, whose only goal is to 'rack up' another one for the Lord.

Yet there are these men who hold their heads high; find honor and dignity along with a little righteous pride, in all their little daily affairs. It is to these men that I tend to gravitate. These are the men, although few in numbers, who will stand by you when the going gets tough. Among all the scum which calls this place home, there is a man, who by virtue of his demeanor does not meet proper criteria, and does not fit in among the scum. I am proud to consider him friend. Maybe we are both so called misfits, and deserving the hell we live in. I can only hope not; hope that there is an end to all the shit and pain, and that we will be restored to our families, who even though suffering the same, or far worse pain, stand beside and behind us.

Although we come from somewhat different worlds - he from the east coast, and I from the west, we share the same low opinion of most of our fellow prisoners. Tony, as I shall call him, is a good man, and always there with a good word, or willing to help when profound trouble finds my cell door. We share the same dreams; dreams of wives, children, and better times. We, too, long for Mr. Bush's "kinder and gentler nation," knowing full well that such dreams can never be realized. I, as well as Tony, was in the wrong place, at the wrong time.

As the noise abates and everyone begins to settle down for another evening of doing nothing, all thoughts turn inward - to the family I left behind. They are the ones who really suffer.

I have ceased counting days according to the calendar. I count the days remaining until I am permitted the use of the telephone. I count the hours, days, weeks and months until I may see my wife again. All my waking hours are occupied by thinking about my friend, lover, wife and very best friend.

The days move with precision slowness, knowing that I wait for each and every sundown; the coming of night. Although I have received a twenty-one year sentence for alleged investment fraud, there is no release date in sight for me and for my wife and children.

Although they are not imprisoned, they too aren't free. The stigma attached to having a husband and father in prison has served to ostracize them from any form of normal life. For they are the family of a political prisoner. A man whom President Bush considers a most severe threat. A threat not merely to the national security of these United States, but also a serious threat to the re-election chances for the current president. I have the dubious honor of being a member of the national security establishment. Now, the very Agency which I have served for all my adult life, has not only turned against me, but has threatened to destroy my very family.

My troubles didn't begin a few months or even a few years ago. It doesn't take a great deal of intelligence to know when, where and how all these problems began. Born to Austrian parents during the middle of WW II was enough to bring my first years of life into conflict.

I was born in Salzburg Austria on July 1, 1942 unto Elizabeth Maria Weissl/Esterházy and Karl Gunther Russbacher. My mother was the heir to the Esterházy estates. My father was of noble descent. He was known as the Lion of Salzburg. It must also be noted that my father did serve in the SS Division Das Reich during WWII. At the end of the war rather than taking my father prisoner, he was permitted egress to England. There he was approached by the OSS and offered a position with the United States Intelligence Services. He accepted the posting and we began to prepare for immigration to this country. It was only later in life that I found out that we weren't the only family exiled from Austria. A number of relatives had also fallen to the hammer of WWII, and the phobia which ensued from Germany's loss of the war. I offer also that the position proffered to my father was basically the very same type of position he had occupied and executed during the years of WWII. In other words, the United States Government wanted my father to come to this country and assist in restructuring of the soon to be born Central Intelligence Agency.

We arrived in this country on December 10, 1954, at the port of Newark, New Jersey. My father had already been to the States a number of times, as early as 1948. As the CIA was formed and launched into life, we were already known as the Austrian family who was brought over to secure the freedoms of democracy against the global communist threat. No one made reference to my father having fought on the wrong side of the War. William (Wild Bill) Donovan made sure that his nucleus of operatives and case officers would not be held accountable for the many atrocities perpetrated, by the Germans, during the war.

The evening sun was slowly making its way across the dry hot dessert. Night time was only about four hours away. Soon another Nevada scorcher would be behind us. My parents laughingly turned to each other and my father said, "Don't worry Lisl, the boy can handle it much better than the adults. After all, didn't you notice him chasing the dog up and down the mountain, during the deep heat of the afternoon?"

My mother Lisl turned toward him almost whispering under her breath, "You know that I'll have to return to Dallas soon. Gunther will have to come back with me. I know that you would prefer to keep the boy with you, but remember, you and I can't be seen together anymore."

With tears in her eyes she rose and began to cross to the living room door.

"I want us to be together more than anything in the world. We managed to survive the terror of the war together only to be told, that we must come to the United States as total strangers. What right do they have to so torment us and continue to destroy our lives? At this rate Karl, it would have been better to remain in Austria and take our chances with the Allies."

Tears were trickling down her smooth and unmarred skin, causing rivulets of tears that turned into rivers of sorrow. She was my mother. The lady Esterházy/Russbacher; immigrant to this godforsaken hellhole of desert wasteland. She continued her virtual stream of tears as she began to pack her overnight bag.

This torment was not new to me. I all too well remember what transpired in Salzburg and Vienna. I might have been very young, but no one can ever say that I was very dumb. I remember that night. They brought word to mother that we had to leave the country. I remembered sneaking around on top of the stairs as the 5 men told my mother that we were being exiled from Austria because we not only cause a political embarrassment but also that Austria would no longer tolerate any member of the so called ruling family to remain in country.

Because I was a child I labored under many emotions. I would lose all my friends and relatives. There would be no one for me to turn to other than mother. I knew that father served in the SS Division Das Reich, and that he was considered a dead war criminal. Far too well the memory of the death notice of my father was burned into my mind. Although merely age three, it did remain imprinted in my mind. The Austrian officer, the American, the Englishman, Frenchman and Russian Colonel, calmly told mother that father had died in battle during the last big push of the war. Saddened by my loss, I began to withdraw from all activities my mother attempted to organize for me. The memory of father was all too recent.

That was the way it went for quite some time. Mother, was told she had a great deal of time before she would be required to pack up the house and leave. We left Vienna and returned to our comfortable estate in Salzburg. One day, after playing in the brook Glan, I arrived at the house as a staff car drove up. What great surprise... a person looking just like my father exited the olive drab staff car. I looked closer and screamed at the top of my little lungs...."Father ... You have come home to me." The stately gentleman reached down and took me into his large arms.

I was in seventh heaven. My father had come home. He had not died. Only later did I find out why such deceptive ploy was put into use. The Americans had offered my father a job and a new life in the United States of America. For me it was enough that my father was home. I was sworn to secrecy. From that moment on I was prohibited from writing or talking to any of our many relatives in Vienna. As far as all the others were concerned, my father was dead... fallen in battle.

I had become a conspirator. To what .... I surely had no idea! I did what I had been sworn to. I never again mentioned the name of my father for fear that I would compromise his life. I loved him, not only because he was the Lion of Salzburg, but because he was my honored father. True to Austria and Austrian tradition, I never referred to my father as dad, pop, or even daddy. For me he was Mr. (Herr) Father. It was a title I honored. All the other buergers called my father Herr Baron. I didn't know what that meant or dealt with. I was happy to have him home with me.

Thus Spake the Raven

By Gunther Karl Russbacher

(a.k.a. The Raven)

My mother's hand shook me awake. I opened my eyes. "Is it time?" I asked. My mother nodded. Behind her I could see my grandfather wiping tears from his eyes. We had known for weeks that the call would come. I didn't fully understand why I had to leave my home. I knew it had something to do with losing the war, but I was only twelve years old, and the war had been over for ten years. I didn't understand why I had to leave Austria.

Grandfather drove us to the airport and walked with us across the tarmac to the waiting plane. There were others gathered there that night. Eighteen of us altogether. We were all being sent into exile. It wasn't until years later that I understood that the Allies had ordered the highest ranking members of the Austrian royal family to be sent out of the country. In exchange for our exile, Austria would be allowed to become a sovereign country once again.

My Grandfather on my father's side joined us at the airport. He took from his coat a small gold lion that was the symbol of our family. My grandfather was the Lion of Salzburg, and I knew that someday I would become the Lion. As he pinned the small gold lion to my coat he said, "You come from an old and noble family. Don't ever forget who you are. You are the Baron von Russbach. Wear your name proudly."

My grandfather held me for a long time, and then my other grandfather hugged me. Finally my mother pulled me away and we boarded the plane. There were others on the plane that I had met at family gatherings. Young men and women who I recognized, but didn't know very well.

"Where are we going?" I asked my mother.

"We are going to a place called Oklahoma. There is a man there that I will marry. He is a good man."

"But what about my father?" I asked. "You are still married to my father."

"Your father is officially dead." Mother told me.

"No he isn't. You know he isn't dead." I was ready to fight.

"I know he isn't dead, and you know he isn't dead. But if we want him to stay alive, we have to pretend he is dead. How many times do you have to be told these things?" I could tell that mother was upset. At the time I didn't realize how much she loved my father. I knew their marriage had been arranged by their father's. I knew that the house of Russbach and the house of Esterházy needed to join and produce an heir. I was that heir. For the longest time I thought that my mother was indifferent to my father. Then I realized that she only acted that way because the pain of losing him while he was still alive was too much for her to handle.

First she lost her husband, then she lost her country, her property, her money, her title, her position, and finally the victors who had won the war and taken everything she had, would take the last thing she loved....her son...me.

I was born the first of July, 1942 in Salzburg, Austria. On my birth certificate, I am, Gunther Karl, Baron von Russbach, Count von Esterházy. On my father's side I am descended from the Baron who captured Richard the Lionhearted and held him for ransom. On my mother's side I am descended from Hungarian royalty. The Esterházys had been advisors to the Emperors of Austria for generations. The marriage between my mother and father had been arranged to cement family interests.

My Godfather was Ernst Kaltenbrunner, the head of Austrian Intelligence during WWII. Records of this are kept in the family church in Salzburg. My family was part of the Gehlen group which was also called the Canaris group.

I began learning the simple aspect of the craft when I was old enough to follow orders. After the war, several Austrian families had to leave Austria in order to avoid prosecution. Most of these families had belonged to the Gehlen/Canaris group.

Eighteen members of my family were forced into exile. Moving to the United States, not speaking any English, I had to learn to be one hundred per cent American within two years. A man I had known as a child in Austria appeared and took me under his wing. At that time I had a heavy German accent and the children in Oklahoma were very cruel. This man taught me how to lose the accent and speak just like an American. He had also lost his accent. This man became my new Godfather. He became responsible for my training.

I took great interest in math, science, government and survival training, both in Oklahoma and in Nevada. Instruction in school, at home, in the mountains, and in desert areas were a must. I learned to fly at an early age, as a matter of fact, at an age before I had a driver's license. Records of this endeavor can be found at Catlin Aviation, Will Rogers Airport in Oklahoma City, as well as the downtown air park in Oklahoma City.

I managed to put a business together at the age of fifteen. It was called the Triple A employment agency; the All American Agency.

In 1961 I entered the United States Army at Ft. Carson, Colorado. After successfully completing basic training, I was transferred to North American air defense command where I continued my schooling and was granted all types of security clearances. I earned cryptographic credentials. I was advised to go through an immediate OCS program. I met with intelligence officers frequently at Ft. Carson, at Norad and at Ent Air Force Base as well as in Denver, Colorado at their station headquarters.

In 1963 I took a discharge from the military and was buried as far as government records were concerned. In 1963 I began to work with people from the federal building in Oklahoma City, and was quickly granted the right to go to the NASA school in Pasadena, Texas. From there I was diverted, moved around, taught languages at the military language schools, taught photo intelligence evaluation, and aircraft thrust evaluation. I was also taught thrust dissipation and thrust design.

In 1965 I was transferred to a facility at Langley Center, and initially assigned an ensign rating with a provision that at a later date the commission would become a permanent position. Most of the training at that time occurred at Air Force bases throughout the United States, at the Center and in the Vienna area, that's Vienna, VA. I was transferred to advanced flight schools at Air Force locations at Shepard Air Force Base, Texas where I learned to aviate with jet aircraft. From there to Carswell Air Force Base, Ft. Worth, Texas. And then to Nellis Air Force Base, in Las Vegas, Nevada, from there to Cannon Air Force Base in New Mexico and numerous Naval installations and flight schools.

I arrived in Nam and had one hell of a lot of trouble. I came back through Techakawa, Japan, on medivac services and was transferred to Fitzsimmons in Denver, Colorado.

In 1968 I was assigned to ONI (Office of Naval Intelligence) with a permanent commission and began flying again. I was sent to Nellis Air Force Base for updates and from there to Beale for the SR program. I spent almost seven months in simulator training before having the first loner run. I received the habu patch. I logged a total time of about 750 hours, front and stick time, and 150 hours RSO time, (radar service officer). I was at Beale, Cadena, Mindenhall, Akrotiri, as well as in Turkey. The last runs were out of Ramstein Air Force Base, Kaiserslauten, Germany. All of the last runs were deep black.

For a resume on the unknowns of the SR, I will now tell you about them. This information has not been published. Originally the aircraft was to be called the RS 71 for Reconnaissance Strike aircraft. However through a fluke in the Johnson administration at the time it was unveiled, the person who introduced it to the public reversed the letters and that's how it became the SR program. The series was titled after the B 70 Valkyrye bomber.

The aircraft is equipped with twin J-58 turbo-ram jet engines which equal 32,500 pounds of thrust per unit. The speed is regulated by the nacelle spike which are inlets which read 26.125 inches in length and can be changed from a fore to an aft position, to change the positions of the spikes which will change the power pack to turbo fans to ram jets. What I am saying in essence, is that the faster the airplane flies, the faster it wants to go. Caution must be utilized, because if it's not held in check it will go so fast that the J58 engines would disintegrate through overheating and devour themselves in the process.

The aircraft is a flying time bomb. 93% to 95% of the frame of the aircraft is made out of titanium. At operational speeds, I'm not talking about top speed, the center of the craft's skin gets anywhere from 510 to 515 degrees Fahrenheit while the temperatures along the engines run anywhere from 1050 to 1100 degrees Fahrenheit. The exhaust areas around the engines are a minimum of 1200 Fahrenheit.

The cockpit glass gets so hot that we can't touch it even with the flame retardant gloves we wear. Tires are 22 ply and contain aluminum pieces and parts in order to Fahrenheit the heat. The air in the tires is not air, it is nitrogen. The tires retract back into explosion proof shields in the event that there's a blowout at takeoff or landing to avoid having the aircraft blown out from underneath you. The aircraft weighs approximately a hundred and forty thousand pounds, carries anywhere from 60 to 80 thousand pounds of fuel.

J-7 is the jet propellant that we use. Because it has a higher flash point than the J-4 which is commonly used in military aircraft. While you are operating the airplane you have to think of a minimum of four hundred miles ahead at all times because you're traveling at the speeds of thirty two miles per minute. The aircraft involves continual work, however it is not hand flown. In the transition to monitoring all systems engines, inlet spikes, and stability augmentation, careful watch has to be taken to manage and to watch your mock numbers and your altitude as well as the dynamic pressure keys.

Control problems are encountered in upstarts, that's when one inlet causes the aircraft to move faster on one side than on the other and causes an upstart which brings a lot of yaw. (Turning horizontally on its axis). At high speeds of any kind, side slips are deadly.

The following information about the airplane is not known. The nose of the airplane is interchangeable to affix different kinds of sensors. The main sensors that we can run are a pair of 48 inch focal length technical objective cameras which have a fifteen hundred foot strip of black and white or color film – it's a narrow field camera. The second part of the sensor would be a nose mounted optical bar camera which is also known as OBC. This is for long panoramic oblique shots, and can do a ten thousand five hundred foot film strip which is about sixteen to seventeen hundred frames, in color or in infrared, in mono or in stereo photography. Thirdly, we have a high resolution side looking airborne radar (SLAR).

The resolution is ten feet over four thousand miles in length. Lastly, the prior versions of the aircraft could carry a D-21 drone for a heightened effect. The drone is forty-three feet long and was attached piggybacked to the SR-71. But it was strictly used for "senior partner." This particular aspect of the aircraft was only used in Viet Nam. And it was a deadly game of chance because sometimes when you tried to fire off the drone the engines of the drone would misfire causing the aircraft to crash or disintegrate in the air.

The aircraft is fueled by a standard KC 135 Q. It takes anywhere from one to three KC 135's which are military equivalencies of 707's, to refuel the Blackbird. The main stations of the Blackbird are Beale AFB, near Marysville. That's where the ninth SAC strat recon wing is located. The second is Cadena AFB which is Air Force Navy, that's where the Habu comes from, the black snake with the side visual view, that's Okinawa. The third one is Mindenhall which is a Royal Air Force Base in England. The fourth one is Akrotiri which is in Cyprus. Your average run on the Blackbird was in stints of six weeks of duty and we rotated three to four times a year.

In 1972 I remained active Navy making the grade, but most of my 201 file was closed due to frequent TDY to the Company. The objective of a 201 file is that you build a nice good clean record that you can transfer from military to civilian life and have something to show for it, or within the military itself. But because of all my black cover operations, I ended up with a lot of gaps in my 201 file.

In 1972 I was loaned directly to the Department of State for Central and Eastern Europe, attached to black consular operations, a special operations group. Stationed while TDY at Badgodesberg which was the United States embassy in Bonn.

I was also in Belgrade, Vienna, Rome, Paris, and that was also when I did my first short term at the Moscow embassy. In Italy I worked with counter revolutionaries and counter terrorists groups in liaison with Italian intelligence staff and carbinieres. Our objective was lotocontinua. The Brigade Roso, I infiltrated the groups to review and construct funding for our own purposes so we could use them for our purposes. However, all that went sour. I was in Milan during the catastrophe, when they blew up the train station and all those people died. Also I was on the train going north to Trieste as they bombed the train out from underneath us.

I worked out of the consular general's office in Genoa, held Swiss and German passports under Gerhard Miller and Wagner. In BadGodesberg, I stayed at the Embassy guesthouse for three months while getting assigned to the consular general's office in Frankfurt, and from there to the United States information service in Frankfurt. I worked with and against the Badermeinhoff and the Red Army faction. I sanitized areas in Germany, Austria and East Berlin, during the pedophile crisis. There were no arrests.

I worked stations in Belgrade, setting up courier routes to Vienna. I utilized an American medical team, a husband and wife from our government to arrange extractions from Czechoslovakia.

In 1978 I took numerous trips to Budapest. This is where my ex-wife Peggy and my son Butch were along. Also to Bratislava and Pressburg, Czechoslovakia.

I was recalled to the United States on October 24, 1979. I went back to Beale for updates. Flew three tours on newer SRs, was command pilot or SRO. I updated the global positioning system and firefly platforms (This is important), at low darkness and red levels.

February 1980 I returned to SRs Center for instruction and school. I helped translate the first manual into Spanish. I was then SRs to St. Louis. I became and investment broker and financial SRs over a three year period. An insurance consultant for Prudential and Connecticut Mutual. As soon as I had enough experience I opened up a proprietary which was National Brokerage Companies, National SRs Services, Crystal Shores Development Corporation and so forth.

Through my assistants I funded numerous large projects for the Center. I met with the chief of station and developed liaison on a large scale to infiltrate labor unions, The Pipefitters, I got in as a broker and financial planner and continued my flight time logging hours in a diversity of military aircraft. I attended a convention of the company forces in Centerpoint, Phoenix, and attended Desert sabotage school in Gila Bend.

May, 1980 I went to DC to meet on flight scheduling for July and August. and Did numerous US and Foreign links for the Agency. I returned to Beale for five days of simulator on an improved SR and then flew back to St. Louis.

In October of 1980 I was command pilot for the flight in which George Bush went to Paris to finalize the deal to delay the release of the 52 Embassy hostages. The three code names for the operation were Magdalen, Magellen, and Michelangelo.

During the time in October when I was in Paris, I was allegedly attending the Connecticut Mutual School for advanced financial planning in Hartford, Connecticut. I spent Halloween with the family and drove them to Honor, Michigan where I began phase two of NBC growth. I talked to Denver groups, Red Hill Pennsylvania, and Michigan National Bank. We formed Crystal Shores secondary group to build on some fine lands. We had large credits at our disposal. We bought Crystal Shores resort and rebuilt it, there was no profit for me.

MDC Denver began looking for financial planner advice for future airport expansion, and we talked to investors in Miami.

In November of 1980 I buried my mother. In December of 1980 our house was flooded, we moved out and bought a new home. My wife, Peggy never asked where the money came from. She had never asked where any of the money came from.

January 1981 I went to Tegucigalpa, Honduras to meet with the resistance and continued the talks in Costa Rica and Cancun. I funded them with low level black funds channeled from European banks. At about this same time I attended a number of parties at the Naval Postgraduate School in Monterey, California. At several of these parties I met and talked with Rayelan Allan Dyer, the wife of John Dyer, Dean of Science and Engineering. In 1989 she became my wife.

In February of 1982 I returned to Frankfurt to discuss shipments to Israel after the boats of arms were priorily refused egress from Marseille harbor to Arab contacts. These were boats that we had already provided arms for. I provided logistical assets to C4 acquisitions for the Libyan crisis. You can check records for that with the East block aide.

From March to July 1982 I was on Navy duty, in and out of Monterey, TDY to Looking Glass and Operation Michelangelo. I completed the details of Operation Reforger in July, 1982; wherein we implemented depletion in the status of reforger arms agreement. I filed an assessment report to the Company on this. BND, which is the same as the west German intelligence service, the SDCE, which is the French security service, and the Benelux security services, also filed assessment reports. Transfers of such funds were transacted from Luxembourg City to Geneva and Zurich.

We met Mossad's people in Alicante for the final pass through deliveries of phase three of the Michelangelo plan to Iran. We utilized Saudi, French, German, Austrian and Dutch aircraft for further transport. Other transport was done by rail and truck through central and Eastern Europe, crossing by boat from Greece to the receiver nations.

In September of 1982 I returned to St. Louis where I stayed on and off, through Labor Day. On Labor Day, I spent time with the family, vacationed with the kids, and then took them back to school.

October 1982 I was called back to Langley for briefing on the Afghani arms supply.

I met a special operations group at Islamabad and Ralapindi, Pakistan. Agreements were reached with the resistance people at Seven Rivers Junction in the People's Republic of Afghanistan. We appropriated the funds through proprietaries and set up the so-called "frequent flyer" programs. The money came out of proprietary operations located in Washington state, Oregon, Indiana, Florida, and Georgia. Much of the heavy equipment was moved Frankfurt to receiver nations per reforger depletion agreements.

Intermediate offensive weapons were railed via containers to Cyprus for shipping to Afghani groups. We had a great deal of trouble in currency receipts. Other commodities were offered. This operative and case officer declined any such involvement.

January 1983 I was returned to consular operations for East European affairs. We liaison with the FBI in New York and the US Attorney's office to extract defectors from the Stasi _____(?) in East Berlin. The operation went sour; the target was terminated by East German border guards. One United States army Major from Heidelberg was left behind. I managed to cross the sector and make for a safe house in Spandau. A very close associate, a man who I called my friend, gave up his own life to save mine. I returned to Langley for debriefing and chastisement, after which I went home to St. Louis deeply troubled by the failure of the mission and the death of my friend. My wife interpreted my mood as trying to distance myself from her. She thought I was having an affair. I could not tell her the truth. Our marriage, which was based on a foundation of lies, was rapidly falling apart.

February of 1983 I returned to Eastern Europe, to Czechoslovakia to debrief a potential asset. It was determined that the asset was a liability and I beat a hasty retreat toward the Austrian frontier in lower Austria, in Nieder Oesterreich. The jaunt was for acquisition of Czech plastique explosive and small arms. The actual deal was later consummated by the West German security service and our Company people at the station's operations headquarters in Vienna, Austria. Many of the shipments passed directly through Austria. I organized shipments via rail to the receiver nations.

March to August 1983 I worked with the Pipefitters Union in St. Louis. That was infiltrational work. October 83 to 12-83 I financed packages and financial planning to corporations for major Internal Revenue Service deductions in the St. Louis area with all companies associated with us.

In March 84 I went back to Afghanistan to finish the last of the initial transactions and to collect cumulative data from the onset of the operation. From 4-84 to 7-84 I brought Barbara, my stepdaughter, to St. Louis and I also continued updating my flight training.

7-84 to 11-84 I worked in St. Louis as well as in Paris, back and forth on hostage taking and counter terrorism resolution. 12-84 I spent with the kids and family, brought Sandra, my other step-daughter, to St. Louis to be with Peggy. I was trying anything that I could think of to hold the family together. The situation was now deteriorating more rapidly than I was able to accept. I could not

explain any of my absences and my wife Peggy used her own imagination to explain them.

1-3-85 I proselyted (bought) a DOJ official to open and run the
National Business Corporation Dallas office in Mesquite, Texas. The
individual was under high level DOJ attack for money laundering,
which was part of the Nicaraguan business.

3-10-85 I was incarcerated at Seagoville, Texas for an escape from
federal conviction resulting from 1973 where I was caught with
numerous bags of bearer bonds while dressed as a United States Air
Force Major. We were unloading the duffle bags from a military
aircraft.

11-85 to 7-86 I was attached to DOS consular operations service
with an average assignment ratio biweekly. I did the Operation
Clydesdale in conjunction with St. Louis staff officers. The operation
was deemed a success after having sanitized the Phoenix, Los Angeles
and Miami areas. Also early in that year the divorce was filed.

7-86 to 9-86 I was in New York City with the family. Once again,
frequent absences did not make things very easy. The United States
Attorney in New York counts his great successes in RICO prosecu-
tions at the cost of several operatives' lives.

From 11-86 to 8-90 I was on numerous internal U.S. operations in
Deep Black cover.

In June of 1989 I signed an agreement not to marry for two years.
Such statements are common after divorces as many times men get
sloppy and talk out of school. In August of 1989 I ran into Rayelan
Allan Dyer. Her husband John had died in 1988. I fell in love with her.
It was the first time I had ever been in love. I think I had loved her
from the moment we had met back in 82. She told me about her
involvement in politics and her association with the group of
reporters who were trying to expose the October Surprise deal. I
knew I would never be granted permission to marry her. In July of
1989, just weeks prior to our meeting, she had flown to Washington,
D.C. to meet with the head of the Senate Foreign Relations Committee
to lobby him against Donald Gregg's appointment as Ambassador to
South Korea. **She had no idea that Donald Gregg was at that time
the head of the CIA discipline committee. And boy were we
disciplined!**

I don't really understand how I talked her into marrying me the day
after we met, but I did. We took a modified Lear jet to Reno and were
married. I had been told not to fly commercial jets because my car had
been firebombed by drug lords. Two days after we were married, I
was arrested. I was held for three months on kidnap charges. I was
charged with kidnapping my wife's niece. Those charges were

dropped and then I was charged with check forgery. The FBI told my wife I was on a crime spree from Missouri to California marrying and defrauding widows. They tried to convince her to annul the marriage.

The station chief from San Francisco told me that my wife was a KGB agent. Then I was told that she was a State Department mole and possibly FBI too. There was a lot of evidence that proved she was State Department. State uses people like her to "babysit" high level security risks, like her husband, John Dyer. At that time, he was one of the highest level nuclear and electronic warfare experts in the United States. She said she wasn't government. I believed her. Government papers are easy to forge and for that matter, easier to delete.

I was moved from California to Missouri where I was held on numerous charges until July of 1990. My wife and the ACLU put so much pressure on the prosecutor that he made a deal to let me go.

I had not seen my wife of two days in eleven months. When I was released I was ordered by my boss to report to Offutt Air Force Base in Nebraska. This is the Lookinglass Command. My wife objected, but finally agreed to go. We checked in at the gate where I was told that I was expected at temporary base housing. I was given the key to our suite and told where it was located. My wife and I were met by two of my men who took our bags and carried them up to our room.

During that time we met with my boss in ONI as well as with numerous of my people. We were invited to have lunch with William Webster. I was told that I would be asked to fly a mission to Moscow in an SR 71. My wife and I left Offutt and drove to Winne- mucca. We stayed at a Company hotel in a room that I have used frequently.

When we walked in the television was on. A CIA training film was showing.

The next morning we left for Reno. I had to get a flight suit to make the trip. There was only one such suit in the area. It belonged to a Navy Lt. Commander.

My wife took me to the Reno airport. The modified Lear jet that I had used since Casey died came in and picked me up. Four SRs also landed and the five of us took off. We stopped at Crow's Landing Naval Air Station in California to refuel and for me to give my mother-in-law some things I had bought for her.

I returned to Reno at two in the morning in great pain. The next day I was ordered to go to Fallon Naval Air Station in Nevada to pick up a set of whites. I was ordered to attend a meeting at Castle Air

Force Base in California. I was being promoted to Admiral. At Castle I was arrested by the FBI for trespassing and impersonating a Naval officer. These charges were dropped almost immediately.

I was then charged with impersonating a US Attorney and misuse of government purchase orders, jet and fuel. All these charges stemmed from the flight in which I had used my personal jet to fly Rayelan Allan to Reno to marry her. At the trial, which took place in November of 1990, the FBI liaisoned with the other agencies involved in the deep black operations, testified that I was working as an infiltrator in drug money laundering operations. This is the same man who advised me not to fly commercial airlines after my car had been firebombed in August of 1989.

After this agent's testimony the judge decided that the trial had been held in the wrong jurisdiction and he told the defense and the prosecution to meet him in his office the next morning. He was going to dismiss the case. The next morning the proceedings were declared a mistrial because my son had talked to the jurors. The prosecutor told me that if I pled guilty he would have me out of jail in March of 1991. If I decided to go ahead with another trial I wouldn't go to trial until June of 1991 and my wife would be charged with trespassing on military bases and go to jail for six months.

I pled guilty. The judge gave me 21 months in prison. I am scheduled for release in December of 1991.

In early May, my boss in ONI was trying to have me transferred to Naval custody. He told me that he needed my signature and my wife's signature on papers to this effect. I was told that he would be signing me out of Terminal Island so that he could meet with me and my wife at the same time. My wife had met him earlier at Offutt AFB.

The next thing I knew, a guard was shaking me awake. I was told there was an emergency with my family. I called my wife. I felt like I had been drugged. She was hysterical. A helicopter had crashed. She had called the CIA station chief in St. Louis. He had told her three navy men were killed. She thought it was the Admiral, myself and another ONI man that she knew. She told me quickly what had transpired. The last thing I remember was the Admiral handing me a glass of orange juice. I called around to find out what had happened.

My boss and the other man, who had just survived a plane crash where another one of our people had been killed, were in hiding. To protect myself I dictated information to a friend over the phone. This friend, Rodney Stich, decided on his own that the best way to protect me was to send this information to every member of Congress and every newspaper and radio station he knew personally. As a result, my involvement as the pilot in the October Surprise story came out. I am still incarcerated at Terminal Island.

I have met with a Senator from the Senate Judicial Committee. He has personally assured my safety if I cooperate with their investigation.

I have dictated this information to my wife who has transcribed it. Understand that I could not proof this copy for mistakes that resulted from her transcription.

...NEVERMORE

(This was dictated over the telephone. It was recorded. Some of the words were hard to understand, so if there is a mistake in spelling or in the actual word, it comes from not being able to understand the recording. —Rayelan)

Mind Control in America

Five easy steps to create a Manchurian Candidate

Gunther Russbacher sent the original pieces of this article to his wife, Rayelan in 1996. In December of 1996, Rayelan pieced together Gunther's many letters, and published the original article on "Mind Control in America" in the print edition of Rumor Mill News.

Several days before the Columbine shootings, a man from Austria came to California to meet with Rayelan and clear up some of the hard to understand passages in the original article. The man said he was Gunther's boss in Austrian Intelligence. Since Rayelan had never met Gunther's boss, the man provided information that only Rayelan, Gunther and Gunther's Austrian Intelligence superior would know.

The Austrian told her he had helped Gunther write the first part of the article on "Operation Open Eyes." The original article was hand written by Gunther and sent to Rayelan in several different letters. The man from Austria said that he had personal knowledge of the 5 Levels of programming, and that was the part of the article he had helped Gunther write. The second part of the original RMNews article was taken from other letters written by Gunther, alone. The man from Austria said he could only correct the part that he had helped write because he had no personal knowledge of Gunther's own mind control experiences, or how the United States used this method of mind control.

Shortly after the Austrian met with Rayelan, the tragedy at Columbine happened. Rayelan now believes that the Columbine killings were the beginning of the final push to take all guns out of the hands of the American people. One month, to the day, after

Columbine, another similar shooting occurred in Georgia. These killings are not random acts of teenage violence. These school killings are a planned, methodical attack on the American Constitution and the freedom which is enjoyed but taken for granted by citizens of the United States of America.

The method of the attack is designed to inflame anger and hysteria in the American public. The media whips up the anger and hysteria and keeps it fresh in America's mind, with continual graphic, around the clock, "overkill" coverage and commentary of the dead and wounded victims, the pain and suffering of the families, and the traumatic scars left on America's children. The President uses the hysteria of the moment to blame guns for the problems in America's schools and with America's children. In the heat of hysteria, Congress is pressured to pass more guns laws.

The hysteria and anger towards guns, propelled by the President and the media, continues to sweep across America. No one in media or being interviewed by the media, is allowed to speak rationally on the subject of guns. Rational people are shouted down by talk show hosts, as in the infamous Rosie O'Donnell interview with Tom Selleck. Members of Congress who try to point out the fact that existing gun laws don't work, because the Clinton Administration doesn't enforce them, are portrayed by the media as being "on the take" from the NRA.

No one is permitted to step back from the hysteria and consider, that no matter how many gun laws are enacted by governments, not even the total ban and destruction of guns could have stopped what happened at Columbine.

If there were no guns available to the two young men and their accomplices at Columbine, the killings would have happened anyway. A gun was not used to blow up the Murrah Building in Oklahoma City. Guns were not used to kill the 800,000 TsuTsis who were killed in Rwanda by the Hutus.

The children at Columbine and at the other schools across America were killed by other children. The "child killers" used guns, but they could just as easily used machetes or bombs. The man who drove his pick up truck through the window of Luby's restaurant in Killean, Texas used a high powered assault rifle to murder dozens of people. He could just as easily thrown a bomb through the restaurant window. The bomb would have killed more people than the gun, and the killer would have escaped alive. But a bomb would not have accomplished the first step in the planned take-over of America. That first step is the elimination of all guns in the hands of the American public!

Many of the mass murderers in the recent decade have committed suicide at the site of the killings, or they are killed by a law enforcement officer, once the various government agencies arrive. In several cases of school shootings, the "child killers" have been stopped by teachers or principles who had guns. If the adult school officials had not had guns, by the time the law enforcement officers arrive, more victims would have been killed. It is also possible that the "child killers" would have "self destructed" by committing suicide. Dead men and boys, tell no tales.

With the "child killers" dead, there is no way to trace back, to its origin in mind control programming, the true cause of the killing spree. If these children have been programmed using a Manchurian Candidate type of mind control, that has been around since the 1920's, and actively used since the Korean War, a trained psychiatrist can find the mind control tracks! For the psychiatrist to do his job, he needs a live "killer," and he needs the cooperation of the local law enforcement officials.

The only way to stop these shootings is to make the public realize that "Manchurian Candidates" do exist, and the kids who are committing these tragic crimes are victims of government mind control. The purpose of the shootings is to inflame the public against guns so that they force Congress to pass restrictive gun laws.

Once the guns are out of the hands of the American public, another twist in random mayhem will begin. More programmed "Manchurian Candidates" will begin anarchistic attacks on the public using bombs, knives, fires, Molotov cocktails, baseball bats and any other item that can be used as a weapon. Anarchy will sweep the streets of the United States.

The public will be disarmed and unable to protect themselves. Therefore, the government will step in and become everyone's protector and Big Brother! The government will do this by suspending the last threads of our barely surviving Constitution, declaring martial law, rounding up the dissidents, patrolling our streets with armed United Nations or NATO military, instituting curfew, and shooting anyone who disobeys any of the newly imposed laws. In other words, a totalitarian government will take control, and if you oppose them, you will be sent to the Gulags.

If the school killings escalate as a Rumor Mill News Source said they will, Congress will be bribed, blackmailed or threatened to pass the bills which will take away out guns. If this happens in 1999 or the year 2000, Bill and Hillary Clinton will be the permanent totalitarian rulers of the United States!

Programmed "Manchurian Candidates" as well as political and government leaders whose own personal agendas have been replaced with mind controlled New World Order "overlays," will work in tandem to bring the United States under the iron fisted rule of a One World Government.

There is enough research on mind control to convince any rational person that mind control and programmed assassins exist. Congress will not investigate this. Our Congress is either bribed with money or promises of high positions in the New World Government, or they are blackmailed and/or threatened with death or the death or their loved ones.

The only hope America has of exposing this and stopping it, is for a courageous community to demand that their district attorney look into the mind control aspect of the shootings. This courageous community must stand together as a united front. If only a handful of residents try to force their local government to investigate and expose the mind control behind the killing rampages, then that handful can be broken and defused using simple techniques of "divide and conquer," and "smear and attack" These courageous residents will be painted as mentally unstable, or as criminals and pedophiles. If these simple techniques of "breaking and diffusing the opposition" don't work, then the heavier guns of bribery, blackmail, threats and murder will be used. Only a well coordinated and informed public, with *no leader or spokesperson*, can expose the horror of what is really happening in America.

Why no leader or spokesperson? Because you can never be sure you are not putting a government infiltrator in charge of the attempt to expose the truth. In other words, the only person whose agenda you can trust is your own. This means, if you want the truth exposed, YOU have to do it.

One of the places where an investigator can begin research is with Satanic cults and children's mental institutions and in house drug rehabilitation programs. Almost all of the children involved in the school killings had attended a satanic cult or had been in a mental hospital. These are the two main ways of programming children without parental knowledge. The local authorities or researchers and investigators need to start there.

There have been many books written about CIA mind control programs, but no document or book has exposed the method used to create a programmed assassin. This article covers the basics of the program. Once you read this, you will understand how and why mass murders such as Columbine, take place. In the case of the mass murders using guns, these mind controlled assassins are being used to sow terrorism in order to force Congress to pass tougher, more draconian gun laws which do not stop terrorism, but take away freedoms Americans take for granted.

In the case of the children being murdered by children, this is a "CIA modified" "Hegelian Dialectic" technique. In other words, if you want society to become something different than it is, you must set up the conditions which will bring about the desired results. The German philosopher, Friedrich Hegel called it: Thesis, Antithesis, Synthesis. The CIA calls it: Crisis Creation, Crisis Solution, Crisis Control.

In the case of Columbine and other similar shootings the scenario is as follows:

THESIS: An armed America

ANTITHESIS: Horrific violence and mass murders committed by people with guns

SYNTHESIS: Draconian antigun laws that disarm America

The CIA's version of Hegel's Dialectic omits the Thesis, their version starts with the antithesis:

Crisis Creation replaces Antithesis:

Horrific violence and mass murders committed by people with guns, who were either programmed or in the employee of the CIA or other government agencies

Crisis Solution replaces Synthesis:

Draconian gun laws that take the guns away from everyone, including law abiding citizens.

Crisis Control Becomes the New Thesis

In the case of gun violence, the new thesis will resemble a police state, where only the government will have guns

To further illustrate the point. America is a nation full of guns and guaranteed the right to own and bear arms, by the Constitution of the United States.

America cannot be taken over by the New World Order and their socialist/communist agenda, if Americans are armed, (this is the Thesis, an armed citizenry), therefore conditions must be created that will cause the American public to demand that their Constitutional right to bear arms be rescinded.

These created conditions are called "The Antithesis" by Hegel; it is called Crisis Creation by the CIA. In the case of an armed citizenry, the antithesis, or anti-thesis, is random, senseless and horrific murders using guns as the weapon.

When these two conditions, i.e.; an armed citizenry and horrific gun violence, exist simultaneously, public hysteria can be whipped up making the public demand that their Congressional representatives outlaw all guns. This is called "The Synthesis" by Hegel; or Crisis Solution by the CIA.

The "synthesis" then becomes the new "Thesis" for a new triad in Hegel's Dialectic. In the CIA's version of Hegel's Dialectic, the synthesis i.e.; the Crisis Solution brings about the new Thesis which is called: Crisis Control.

When Hitler wanted to wipe Jewish DNA from all of Europe, he created similar "antithesis" conditions which allowed the passage of similar anti gun laws. If all Jews in Germany had been armed, how easy would it have been for Hitler to send them to concentration camps? An armed citizenry can protect itself from its government.

Hitler's plan to eliminate all gun from German citizens was so successful that Connecticut Senator Thomas J. Dodd, father of today's Connecticut Senator Chris Dodd, used Hitler's model to frame the Gun Control Act of 1968.

The Government's Diabolic Plan Must Be Exposed

If this horrendous, diabolic plan to disarm America is not exposed, we can expect to see many more killings like the ones at Columbine. Each subsequent episode will be 100 times worse than the others. In Columbine, the real people behind the killings were sending a subtle message to anyone who can decipher it: The bombs that were found were not intended to go off. They were merely there to let "key people" in Congress know what will happen the next time. In other words, instead of 15 people being killed, hundreds, maybe even thousands will be killed.

More than likely, there was a "Control Officer" handling these boys. If an honest police unit uncovers him, he will be sacrificed, just like Tim McVeigh. He will be portrayed in the exact way the Tim McVeigh has been portrayed. In other words, he will be part of "The Vast Right Wing Conspiracy," he will be a "gun nut," he will belong to an Aryan Christian group.

Once you read how "Manchurian Candidates" are created, you will fully understand what is behind the incidents like the school killings, the crash of Ron Brown's plane, The North Hollywood bank robbery, the massacre at Luby's, and the killings at the Capitol, (Tom DeLay was the intended target at the Capitol. Maybe he would be interested in how his would be assassin was created.)

Operation Open Eyes

An Overview of a Government Mind Control Program

Government insiders reveal how the United States Government finds, chooses, and creates "Sleepers" — mind-controlled, programmed zombies, also known as Manchurian Candidates.

How the Subjects are Chosen

By Gunther Karl Russbacher, Captain, USN

A preset group of our people (from the intelligence community) canvasses the county hospitals and immigration centers in order to find viable candidates. We locate and select people who have no close family or friends. Once they have been selected, they are put under heavy, Level One hypnosis. At this time a clear and definitive pattern of their usefulness is determined by our psychiatrists and field officers. If the candidate possesses a relatively high IQ, he will be filed in a category file, called "call file."

Levels One and Two

If the tested applicant has more than 120 IQ, a "recall" command and an accompanying "trigger" word will be written into his personality during the Level One hypnosis session. This "trigger" will activate his recall program when we are ready for him. We then systematically do a background search and create a file for future reference.

If there are no relatives, to speak of, the subject will be "recalled" and taken to a location of our choice. Further tests for vulnerability will be conducted at this location. If he passes these tests, he is then brought to Level 2 hypnosis where specific instructions are "written" (placed through hypnotic commands and suggestions) into his personality and he is given diverse small orders.

If the subject, upon release, shows that he has retained the instructions which were "written" into his personality, and if he carries out the small and unimportant work duties which were assigned under Level 2 hypnosis, he will receive a "recall service notice."

The timing of a "recall service notice" depends on how quickly we can determine that the programming which was "written" into the subject's personality has enabled him to complete his Level 2 work assignments properly. Once this determination has been made, a "recall service notice" will be given to him by a person, or "handler" to whom we have introduced him.

If the subject was not given a "trigger" word, the "handler" will use a quick and powerful form of hypnosis similar to Neuro-Linguistic Programming. The subject will be told when and where to report. The subject will have no memory of being given these instructions, he will just report on time to the proper location. If the subject was given a "trigger" word or symbol, he will report to the designated location upon activation of the "trigger."

Level 3

The next step is Level 3 hypnosis, where the subject will become an "overwrite" upon his own personality. An "overwrite" is a new identity or personality. It is similar to having multiple personalities, except the original personality is repressed or hidden under the "overwrite" and will not surface for a set period of time which is determined by the Programmer.

The "overwrite" is not a complete new identity. There is just enough information written into the subject's personality for us to determine his viability.

In the case of a Field Operative, Level 3 hypnosis is how the operative is prepared for a covert mission which requires a temporary new identity. Just enough information will be written in for the operative's alias and story to be believable by everyone, including law enforcement officials. In the case of a field operative who will be using this alias for only one occasion, his normal personality is not repressed, it is made recessive, but left alert.

For the field operative who is being prepared for a deadly covert mission, a Level 3 "overwrite" can eliminate all fear and nervousness, and allow him to function under the nose of his enemies without the added stress of being discovered. All operatives have to go to, and through these 3 Levels before they are fielded! Sometimes they go through Level 3 many times.

During Level 3 programming sessions, the new subject is told that anything his "friends," i.e. programmers, ask him to do, is okay, even though it may be against all laws of the land. At Level 3, the subject is also programmed to believe that he must and can do everything his "friends" i.e., programmers ask him to do.

Once Level 3 Programming has been "overlaid" upon the new subject's own personality, he/she is once again given a "recall service order" and is then discharged. The subject will be monitored to see how well he functions with his new personality. If everything goes well, he will be recalled for further programming.

The higher the IQ of a given subject, the further the programming goes! If the IQ is high enough we will study his abilities and our needs, and determine how the subject can be further used. Once this determination is made, the subject will be brought to "The Farm" or one of our numerous facilities throughout the U.S. and Canada for further and final programming. (Doctors Hospital in Dallas, TX is one of our main centers!)

Level 4

Once at the facility, we will put the subject into Level 4 hypnosis, a place where he no longer differentiates between right and wrong. The subject will be told he is a "Super Human" and all laws are written for other people. The subject's moral code, respect for the law, and fear of dying is replaced with new "Super Human" feelings.

This is the Level that turns a subject into a "Clear Eyes," i.e., a fully programmed "sleeper" assassin, who can commit crimes as serious as murder, and afterwards have no shame, guilt, or remorse.

The Level 3 Super Human "overwrite" replaces the subject's own morality and/or religious ethics with a program that makes him believe he is beyond all human laws. If the intent of the programming is to create a programmed assassin who will kill on cue, all morality, fear, and revulsion of bloody body parts must be eliminated. The Super Human "overwrite" eliminates both. The Super Human "overwrite" also gives the subject the feeling of immortality and invincibility.

If he has to perform a particularly suicidal or important assignment we do our job at Stoney Mountain facilities.

At Level 4, diverse programs can be written/or overwritten into the brain. Any command is accepted at this level. At Level 4 you can give the test subject a completely new personality and history. You are able to make him/her believe anything the program requires for the accomplishment of the desired project. In this case, a completely new person is being created, not just a partial personality as is Level 3.

Once the Level 4 programming is complete, the subject will be a different person with no memory of his former life. He will not be an amnesiac, he will have memories… ones which we gave him. He/she will be relocated to a new state and town and given a new life. Everything to complete the construction of the new person will be provided. Items such as driver's license, car, bank accounts, passport, credit cards, and birth certificate will be created or supplied by us and will be valid and legal.

The subject will also be provided with all the small things that ordinary people have in their lives, such as photos of his family. His family won't really exist, but he won't know this. He will have all the feelings of love, hurt or anger that normal family members feel for each other.

The photos of family and friends will be of deep cover agency personnel. If ever a mission goes "sour" and the news media starts looking for his family, the "agency created family" will be produced for a news conference or an interview. Agency personnel have been well coached and are trained actors and actresses. They will fill their roles perfectly, usually letting the public know that the "Clear Eyes" subject has always had a deeply troubled and violent past. The media will present the "Clear Eyes" as a nut case who went on a tragic and senseless rampage. Within a month, the public will have forgotten the incident.

Completing the new life and home, will be souvenirs from trips the subject has never taken, but yet remembers. There will also be small mementos of a life he has never lived, yet believes he has. Upon the completion of Level 4 Programming, the subject and patient (one and the same) now has an agenda that he believes is his own.

In other words, if the subject is going to be used to infiltrate a patriot group, religious commune, political campaign or environmental movement, the subject will be given all the knowledge and beliefs that are commonly held by people in his targeted group. The subject will believe that his fervently held opinions are his own. He will be believable to other members of the group.

Many politicians and government officials on a world wide level have been given "new agendas" through the use of Level 4 programming. Their own beliefs are replaced with the agenda of the programmers. They are given super human talents such as a photographic memory, and the ability to lie convincingly.

President Clinton is an example of a world leader who has been programmed with this technique. Senator John McCain and Secretary of State Madeline Albright are two other examples of an "agenda overlay" being "overwritten" onto the subjects own personality. In the cases of these people, their own personalities and memories are still present, to a large extant, although childhood and early adolescent memories are sometimes erased when this technique is used.

Once the future government leader is programmed, he will be recalled on a yearly basis and given hypnotic reinforcement of the original programming, or new programming will be "inserted" to modify the original programs. If no new programming is needed, the reinforcement programming can be done on a mass scale. In other words, "programmed sleepers" who are part of a lecture audience or a "think tank retreat," can have their programming "reinforced" through a lecture or film. The rest of the audience, such as wives and children, will notice nothing out of the ordinary.

Upon completion of Level 4, the subject who has been chosen to become a "programmed sleeper assassin" is fully prepared for Level 5.

Level 5

At Level 5, the "trigger" which activates the program is inserted.

At Level 5, very carefully, a code word, sequence of numbers, or a voice imprint is "etched" into the subject's brain. This is commonly known and referred to as the "trigger" which will activate the subject into action. At this time, the subject will also be implanted with a coded tracking device so that his location will always be known.

Once Level 5 programming is complete, the subject is released to live a very normal and sometimes useful life. The subject will have no memory of being involved with the intelligence community, and will have no memory of the hypnosis sessions.

The "sleeper" who has been given a complete new identity will have no memory of his "former" life, therefore he will never question who he is. The subject will live a normal life as a doctor, an airline pilot, a politician, an eccentric loner, or a movie star until the subject is required to perform the missions for which he was created.

These missions or programs were implanted/written into Level 4 hypnosis. Once the Level 5, programmed "sleeper" assassin is finished with the programming, he is referred to as a "Clear Eyes." A "Clear Eyes" is a "sleeper assassin" who is capable of being triggered, i.e. activated.

Once a "Clear Eyes" is "triggered," accidentally or on purpose, the subject is beyond recall. A Level 5 "Clear Eyes" can only be approached after he carries out his program or operation.

Because of the programming, the subject will not be able to associate with the crime he has just committed. Such a programmed subject is Sirhan Sirhan, the assassin of Robert Kennedy. To this day Sirhan cannot recall anything about shooting Senator Kennedy.

Only psychiatrists trained in our method of sub mental behavior programming, overwrites and overlays, will be able to find any tracks leading to post Level 1 or 2 mind control. In other words, a regular psychiatrist may discover that the subject has been hypnotized in the past, and may even discover the original personality. But a regular psychiatrist will never be able to discover the location in the brain or memory, where Levels 3, 4 and 5 programs are stored.

Without an activation "key," a normal psychiatrist will never uncover the programming unless by accident.

If the programmed subject is told to walk into an armed camp and assassinate an enemy leader, the subject will carry out his program with no regard to his personal welfare, whether he lives or dies, or how he is supposed to escape. In most cases of programmed "Clear Eyes" who commit murders or assassinations, the subject is killed on the spot, either by an innocent bystander who kills only to end the killing, or by an agency operative who is on site to insure nothing goes wrong, in other words, that the subject "self destructs" or is killed.

In some cases the subject is captured and not killed. Due to the type of programming used in "Operation Open Eyes," the subject will not be able to divulge any information. Even if the subject is brutally tortured, he will not be able to remember the actual killing or terrorist act, let alone why he did it. This is because all programming is buried deep within long forgotten childhood memories which were recalled under Level 3 hypnosis. (This is the level where real childhood memories are accidentally destroyed in politicians and other officials who have agendas "overwritten" on their own personalities.)

Even under the 'truth serum" drugs, the subject cannot reveal the truth because his conscious mind has no access to it. Using "Operation Open Eyes," the government can create the perfect assassin, saboteur or terrorist... one who will perform on cue, not be able to remember anything, or self destruct before being captured.

End of Part One.

Five Easy Steps to Create a Manchurian Candidate

Written by Gunther Russbacher from his own Experiences

I have personally witnessed Levels 1-5 programming, and was myself a subject of level 3 programming. In Level 3 programming five different sets of primary aliases were created for me. It takes two years to fully create a new personality. All the small gestures, such as grimaces, laughs, smiles and frowns have to be created, as well as an accent, a specific way of walking and carrying himself... his bearing.

If a subject has a high IQ, around 130-140, the subject is very quick to learn anything fed to him/her during the programming sessions. All major patriot groups, government offices and. government contract corporations have at least one or more "sleepers" attached to them.

The bombing of the Murrah Building was a clear cut case of project "Clear Eyes."

Tom Valentine's radio show as well as *The Spotlight* newspaper are vehicles we have employed in the past to trigger our subjects. In other words, the "Clear Eyes" subject has been given the suggestion to listen to certain shortwave broadcasts or read certain newspapers.

Knowing that the "Clear Eyes" has been programmed to listen, religiously, to a certain radio program, a guest or caller will give the "trigger words" that will activate the "Clear Eyes."

If the subject has been told by his "programmers" to subscribe and read a certain newspaper each day, or week, the "trigger" will be a classified ad or letter to the editor. If the newspaper happens to be an Agency creation or proprietary, the "trigger" word or phrase will be worked into an article. There are some "sleepers" who are kept active by the constant re-enforcement of their programming through key words and phrases that are published in Agency newspapers. These "Agency Papers" are usually publications of new age cults or Christian Identity groups. They usually have a readership of less than five thousand people.

Waco was an "Open Eyes" operation. There were seven "sleepers" in the compound. These seven "sleepers" had been programmed to carry out a specific job. The specific mission was written into their personalities during Level 4 programming. They had not yet received their Level 5 programming, and should not have been capable of being triggered to carry out their the Level 4 programmed mission.

The Davidian group was created to perform a terrorist act similar to the sarin gas that was released in the Japanese subway by the Aum Shin Rikyo cult.

Shortly after the Waco holocaust, attorney Paul Wilcher was briefed on the Waco mind control operation by members of the Delta Force Group that oversaw the programming operation. These men were sent in to neutralize only the 7 "sleepers." Their programming had somehow been prematurely activated, and they were creating a device for mass destruction.

Randy Weaver, of the Ruby Ridge incident, was a control subject that ended up "out of control." (RMNews: Russbacher never gave further information on this.)

Robert Hunt is a sleeper that was put on hold. At some, not too distant date, you will see Bob Hunt performing his true and final role.

(RMNews Editor: Bob Hunt is a Navy SEAL and covert operative who was instrumental in leaking classified documents to Rodney Stich. These documents confirmed that the government operatives who came forward and broke their cover to tell the truth, were indeed who they said they were. Whenever a government covert operative breaks his cover and begins to tell the truth, he/she is either jailed or killed. Robert Hunt is currently in prison.

> *Others, who are listed on the documents he released, are either dead, in prison or in hiding.)*

Gunther Russbacher continues:

"I hope it is becoming clear to you the various levels that are used by the Intel community to get their job done. Remember Jonestown? It was one of ours that went sour because a "Clear Eyes" was in the group.

"When he, the "Clear Eyes," began firing on the runway, it all self destructed. Congressman Leo Ryan, who was killed, knew it was a government operation. The "Clear Eyes" was accidentally, through a lone sequence, activated! There was no way to stop the killings.

All members of the cult were programmed to at least level 3. There were only 3 deaths attributable to cyanide, the rest died of gunfire. Now you know little more about our line of work. I am glad I am out of it."

> *(RMNews: On p. 14 on the September 1996 issue we printed a letter called: Jonestown: The Whole Story, Project Blue, The Guiana Operation. The letter is attached at the end of this article.)*

Russbacher Continues:

How Sleepers are Produced

"The initial stages of hypnosis are derived by subconsciously distracting a person to where he/she does not realize that hypnosis is taking place. If the procedure is done in a doctor's office, or in the emergency room of a hospital, a Level One hypnosis, with a post hypnotic suggestion, to return for another session on a specified day, time and location, can be all be given *in less than five minutes.*

At an emergency room, the doctors have to be far more cautious because of the others (emergency room workers) who are about him. At any rate, a second and far more detailed appointment is made where Levels Two and Three can be attained within a matter of 2-3 sittings.

At Level Two, a light program is already in place that makes the subject pliable to the will of the hypnotherapist. At Level 3, the program is expanded to include specific trigger words; i.e. "stepdown."

A Level Four program can only be attained by completely removing the already altered, conscious state of Level three. This procedure is done under drugs! The needle is inserted into one of the veins of the lower legs, sometimes on the back of the leg. The needle is never inserted in an easily visible spot where it can be seen and questions asked as to where such a needle stick came from.

With the IV fluids of the drugs and the 3 levels already attained, brainwashing takes effect. Complete blocks of intact memory are taken out and removed. The "overwrite" is generally placed next to and/or in addition to childhood memories. The area we choose to attach our program to is pre puberty. It can range from age 9-12. That's where the "overwrite" is placed.

A complete set of instructions are then entered into the void space and are assimilated immediately, by the brain as belonging there–and having always been there. At this point the complete instruction package has been set. It is no trouble at all to create an unspace (an emptiness of several days time–time being removed and rewritten into the main brain.) lasting up to several days or a week. The team, performing the "erase," "new program" and "transfer of data"; at random, choose a period of time where there was no event of special interest to the patient.

The Level Four stage permits the team to go back, one day at a time, in the victim's life. It is an easy accomplishment to find such an ordinary fragment of time where nothing occurred. Remember that the brain assimilates the "rewrite" immediately as its own.

The program entry can be so well covered and truly hidden that if you were to revive the patient-without a level 5 trigger in place to bring the subject to that spot of their lives, the complete program would be lost forever.

Since the brain has continual wave lengths, level 5 is implanted as a trigger command (just like in a computer) to bring that person, instantly (by preplanted hypnotic suggestion) to that moment of their lives where this violent or non-violent program is located. If it is to be a one time mission (with suicide built-in) a complete remake of the victim is made at level 4.

We can take Subject-A, and impose on them all personality traits, customs and beliefs of a person we call subject-B... or reverse them. That means my subject will have to remain in the lab until a complete recycling has been achieved. At that point I can make him believe anything I tell him.

Example: If I tell him that he is a construction worker, and feed him all the data required to perform the job, he will believe just that. If I tell him to take another name, change his entire being, leave his family and become someone else in another town, he will follow through on the command, but only if I insert a level 5 trigger command instructing him to do that when he hears certain words; i.e., a nursery rhyme or any trigger word that I implant.

Certain major corporations and Madison Avenue advertising agencies have a long history of working with the government. Nursery rhymes such as "Twinkle, Twinkle Little Star" can be worked into the advertisements that are played on television and radio. These ads can be targeted to population areas where programmed "sleepers" or "sleeper" are living, thereby activating only certain sleepers without having to have personal contact in any manner.

The other viable alternative, for most of the case subjects under our control, is to implement a "rider package" that will compel him/her to fulfill the functions of our level four programming, by placing an appropriate trigger in his mind. He or she will continue to lead a perfectly normal life until made active by a command from a command file. Any number of unrelated triggers can be implanted hypnotically—just in case the first one has been lost in the deep fog when you bring the subject back to the Pre-Level One stage (state).

We always have a least 300-400, one way mission, Level 5's running about leading relatively functional lives in the different cities where we have placed them. At times a man will leave his wife (or vice versa) and just move away. We don't take into consideration if these men have children. We use them, because they are tailored to a specific task we see coming up in the foreseeable future.

However, please bear in mind that most of our level 5 cases lead very normal lives until they are activated. At that point, the Level Four program takes precedence in the subject's life, above all else, such as family or job

"To fully create a new person; give them a history or something that they can cling to when sad or lonely, it takes a team of lab experts numerous weeks or even months. I don't know the name of the chemicals (several of them) used by the teams but they can hold a subject comatose for a few days to even months. A total transfiguration requires a catheter in the neck, urinary and digestive track, to keep their physical balance. Usually a Level 5, complete transfiguration will require a cover story like a serious automobile accident or something of similar nature. We have never been exposed for any of the Level 5 subjects we created.

Most liable to exposure are level 3 subjects who can remember bits and pieces of their downing after not have been to the "shop" (lab) for a couple of years.

Level 3 Operatives will always know that they have been worked on or modified- -because they sign a document that goes into their personnel file. All case officers and field operatives are Level 3 clan.

The chemical used for Level 4 is not merely a hypnotic drug but also contains proportionate levels of anesthesia. The idea is to keep the subject at the very edge of consciousness during the programming.

One last set of statements about Operation Open Eyes. There are some aspects (areas) of the United States. One, and the first of them, is Project Fallingrock; Project Behemoth; Project Tinyrock; Project Mountainside, just to name a few. All of these projects fall under the auspices of "Operation Open Eyes."

Project and/or Operation Monarch was a completely fictitious series created and released to the public simply to side track serious investigators. You can always judge the authenticity of serious reporters or investigative journals by paying attention to the things they have said about Project/Operation Monarch. This does not mean that the "victims" of Monarch are not real, what it means is that the entire Project was created as a cover story to keep people busy following the Project Monarch leads, while the real work went on in hospitals and doctors' offices around the country.

There are government sponsored investigative journals which are designed to sow misinformation or disinformation. I have been able to spot the newspapers that are putting out bogus information by paying attention to how they treat Operation Monarch.

Afterthoughts from Gunther Russbacher:

The poor guys/gals, who are forced to leave family and all behind in order to fulfill their one way program, sadden me. Although they have a completely new set of memories, they are all usually such bad memories, that they gladly jump from area to area to avoid the direct pain of these memories. They seek company in sleazy bars and are usually limited to one night stands. By day, they work, and by night, they usually sit–frustrated as hell– in front of their TV's. This is why the trigger words presented in television ads are so effective.

More Afterthoughts:

In the event that you have any interest in how my Level 3 programming was done, and how it was found by the therapist here, (in Austria) I'll be glad to give you a run down.

First of all, bear in mind that I went in on my own. I wasn't one of the other cases I have so often made reference to in my letter. They gave me 2-mg. of Valium to calm my nervous system. Then I was hooked up to a polygraph machine, and the hypnotherapist led me to Level One–deep sleep. Then at that stage a color combination pattern was fed to my mind. Then I was dropped to level two. Outside monitors, such as an EEG, were attached to my head. I was fed music or better said, winding jungle rhythms to concentrate upon.

"At that state (Level 2), it was determined that I was patriotic enough to be of use to them. A film, between a good agent and Joe Blow down the street, was played to determine my threshold to cross (under specific orders!) from being a full legal to being an instrument for their causes. All the patriotic nonsense in the world was fed to me at Level 2. Then came the "what if situations."

What if you had to sanction a man because of the good for the country?

"What if it (the order) meant willfully breaking the law in order to do as your employer asks? After hour upon hour of this play, a recall program–reaching me anywhere' a voice could travel–was pounded into my skull. Always, the wishes of the employer had to come first. Then I was covered with the ability to slip in and out of many aliases, during and after doing my job for them.

The Level 3 program consisted of more loyalty bullshit and a number of specific triggers that would activate my mode which made me believe that I was indestructible. I went back for up-dates on the programming every 2-3 years. I was also polygraphed 3 times in the field office, and annually at the main center. Sodium Ambutal was their drug of choice at that time. I would be pulled out of circulation 2 days at a time, when I went in for my annuals.

The hypno-therapist over here (in Austria,) accidentally hit on the entire program because they subjected me to all these color combinations. I began to talk during the session and the key was found quite by accident. They researched up and down this Level 2 stage until I disclosed, under deep hypnosis, the entire program, inclusive of all parts.

The trigger mechanism was less easy to find because it was cloaked by an Oklahoman Thanksgiving party. (Russbacher was raised from age 12 to 17 in Oklahoma) The therapists over here had never heard of such a thing. I talked until they found the mental file that contained all my triggers.

They told me the whole thing, and in a conscious state, I repeated it all to them. They now have a big thick file on what has been done to me, and regretfully, the means to replicate it on others.

I knew a great deal of what had been done to me at the Center. After all, I saw them doing Level 5 work on others. I also know that they had various ways and means to get the job done. I knew all along that I was a Level 3 sleeper. Hell, I signed so that it could be legally done to me. The Agency doesn't employ Level 5 sleepers as Case Officers or Operatives.

Additional Information on Operation Open Eyes

Single words are the designation for a single Project. Two words are the way to title an Operation. See: Operation "Open Eyes" or Project "Behemoth." "Clear Eyes" was an exception to the standard rule of title in our coding a project. All phrases that have two words are ongoing Operations. (This is the reason for the apparent misspelling of Project Fallingrock.)

Project Mirror

An Above Top Secret Project in Mind Control and Assassination

This is a very covert operation. Only 30-40 people know of its existence.

Project name: Mirror (NSA operation number DOM 3416-A-2)

Project priority: To establish/create a force of no more than 30 individuals who are capable of perceiving pre-set, or configured circumstances where certain leaders of nations are rowed according to their specific cause and importance.

Project Order: Liquidate certain individuals according to rowed importance.

Project Assumblage: Seek and find: prediagnosed individuals of various schizophrenic attributes. Gender of individual of no import. Age of subject must range 18-35. Coded for Operation Open Eyes.

Test individuals must meet the criteria as being of good health, and compatible with standard Level (4) preconditioning.

Language: no barrier

Such individual will receive orders to activate upon visually seeing prestated ranged figures on all media accessible to the average citizens of the media country or nationality of the subject.

Subject will follow Level (4) preconditioning, as well as Project Mirror required staunchness of being. Upon such ranged assembly of members of diverse and pre indoctrinated aspects of Project Mirror, "recall" and "discern target" pre-conditioning is "overwritten."

Subject will then be activated to "restore about the 26 tranquility" (or as such described in DOM 3416-A-2) Upon termination of target, subject shall, according to medical advice--return to a rehabilitation center for initial debriefing, or shall in accordance with Level (5) instructions, proceed with self sanction or destruction.

It is imperative that all data retrieved during the case of medical rehabilitation be forwarded, via preordained method to DOM personnel. There shall not be more than 5 prime candidates in waiting, during the course of any fielded operation of stated project.

The remains of self sanctioned personnel are to be cremated upon notification, by local or regional sources

Operations Nu: 6317-ABL-4

Project team leader: DOM 3416-A-2

The Directive to form and proceed with this operation comes out of Ft. Meade, MD. Signatory to the project order was originally Stansfield Turner. Project Mirror is still on the books.

End of Russbacher's Story

Please remember that this article was written by Gunther Russbacher, the SAME man who said he was Atalon. Remember that Atalon used mind control to make Shalma fall in love with him. He also was able to erase or mask the part of Shalma's mind that remembered how much she loved her other half, Xanos.

I LIVED this story... but even for me... the fact that Gunther not only KNEW about our government's mind control projects, but had been part of some of them... and then LOST his memory of ME... just as Shalma... (his new wife Jane), was mind-controlled by Atalon and lost the memory of her love for Xanos... is almost TOO much for ME to believe. But I promise you... to the best of my knowledge and belief, every word that I have written is true... as it was told to me or as I lived it. — Rayelan, 2006

Excerpt from The Wilcher Report

NOTE: Attorney Paul Wilcher represented Gunther Russbacher before both Congressional Task Forces investigating the October Surprise.

Mass Murder at Ranch Apocalypse

"Thursday, March 11th, 1993—12 days after the initial BATF raid on Sunday, February 28th—when I received initial information: (1) That "cult" leader David Koresh had an extensive CIA background. (2) That he was known in CIA circles as a "sleeper"—someone who had been subjected to extensive CIA "mind control" training and programming. (3) That it was not just a mere coincidence that all these events were occurring in or near Waco, TX—since Waco is a major center for such CIA "mind control" experimentation and programming-with much of this activity occurring at the CIA's Leadership Management Institute (LMI) in Waco." *(page 4)*

Paul Wilcher was an attorney living in Washington D.C. As a result of being a victim of Chicago's crooked bankruptcy courts, Wilcher had moved to the Capitol trying to expose the fraud and corruption in the bankruptcy courts around the nation. He sadly discovered there was nothing he could do, alone. He began researching government crimes, corruptions and cover-ups.

Wilcher made contact with Gunther Russbacher, the ONI and CIA operative who was currently in prison. Russbacher claimed he was in prison because the Bush Administration was trying to silence him regarding the October Surprise. Wilcher was the only person to conduct an exhaustive debriefing of Russbacher, which he recorded on 53 ninety minutes tapes.

Russbacher introduced Wilcher to members of his SEAL team. These men and others are the government employees who gave Paul Wilcher the information he put into the 100 page letter he wrote to Attorney General Janet Reno. In the letter he explained, as well as he could, various government mind control experiments. He felt he had to give Reno the background on mind control operations in the Waco area so she could fully understand what was really going on at the Branch Davidian compound.

Wilcher was told that something had gone wrong at Waco. The "sleepers" were waking up from their programming. Not only were they waking up, one or more of them had been accidentally "triggered." The Waco "Sleepers" were programmed to make and deliver a biological or chemical device that could kill everyone in a city the size of Oklahoma City or Houston. Information received by their "handlers" stated that the program had been accidentally triggered and the 7 "Sleepers" had started building the device.

According to information from a government "plant" inside the compound, the device was only days from completion. A CIA/Delta Force team was fielded to go into the compound and "neutralize" the problems. When the BATF learned that a CIA/Delta Force Group was going into the Branch Davidian compound, the BATF decided to raid the compound first. The BATF had no idea why the CIA/DFG team was going in. The BATF had been carrying on an independent surveillance of the compound.

It would not have been unheard of for the BATF to have discovered the mind control project that was going on at the Davidian Compound. Mind control operations are common near the Waco area. Waco was the first major center for CIA mind control schools. No one has ever known if the BATF knew that Koresh and a few others were mind control subjects, or if they had just been tracking David Koresh because he dealt in guns. The Source who provided this information said he had not been able to access the BATF records to discover why the Davidians were under BATF surveillance. Our source commented, "They (the BATF) had no idea what they were walking into."

According to our Source, by the time the FBI got involved, Janet Reno had already been briefed about the device. Her orders to the FBI were to contain and destroy the device. On the day of the Waco inferno, a Delta Group Force was inserted into the compound. Their orders were to kill the seven "sleepers" and disarm the device. The "sleepers" were killed, but the DFG group never had the time to find the device and disarm it.

The compound exploded in flames. The DFG team barely made it out alive. It was their belief that the FBI, the Department of Justice and the Clinton Administration intended to kill them also. This is why they gave their story to Paul Wilcher. In an operation like this, each person is "compartmented" and only told their part of the mission. The DFG team had no idea that Janet Reno knew about the existence of the device. It is not known if she knew about the mind control project or just thought the Davidians were a terrorist group with a device that could wipe out hundreds of thousands of Americans.

When the DFG group briefed Paul Wilcher, they did not tell him Reno knew about the device, because they did not know this. After Wilcher was briefed, he wrote a 100 page letter to Janet Reno. In the letter he described various government mind control projects, and described what had happened at Waco. He made an appointment to hand deliver the letter to Attorney General Reno.

The morning of his meeting with the Attorney General, he was met outside her office by two men who threw him up against the wall and beat him. The 100 page document was taken from him and he was threatened. He disappeared shortly after this incident. His body was found one month later.

Wilcher's good friend, Sarah McClendon, the senior White House correspondent, was the one who alerted the Washington DC police that Paul had been missing for a long time. When the police broke into his apartment, they discovered his body.

The FBI immediately sealed the apartment and confiscated all of Wilcher's research. When they finally returned the computer and discs to Wilcher's family, everything had been wiped from them. There was no record whatsoever of the 100 page document that Paul had tried to deliver to Janet Reno.

Over a year after Paul had been murdered, Sarah McClendon was going through her papers and discovered a bunch of documents Paul had given her. They appeared to be documents he had written when he was helping Gunther Russbacher, the October Surprise pilot. McClendon is a friend of Russbacher's wife, Rayelan. Sarah called Rayelan and asked her if she wanted Wilcher's papers. Thinking they were reports he had prepared for the October Surprise Taskforce, Rayelan asked Sarah to send them to her.

When the documents arrived, Rayelan realized immediately what she had. She knew she had the only copy, outside of the FBI, of Wilcher's 100 page report. When she called Sarah to thank her for the documents, she purposely referred to them as the October Surprise documents. Then she said no more to anyone about them. She didn't even tell her husband, Gunther, what she had. She believed that her telephone lines were still bugged by the government. Gunther was in prison at the time, and she did not dare put this information in a letter and mail it to him.

She hid the document in a safe place and waited for a chance to make copies of it. During the years that she and her husband were trying to expose George Bush for the October Surprise, Rayelan had been followed everywhere she went. At the time she received the Wilcher Report, she was unsure if she was still being followed. She was also unsure if her home was still bugged.

Her schedule was routine and dull at that time. She went to work at the same time, came home at the same time. The only reason she went out was to shop for groceries. Going to a copy shop to make copies of a hundred page document would have been out of character for her at the time. She figured that if anyone was watching her, they would wonder why she was taking a large document to a copy shop.

She waited until an appropriate opportunity arose. And it did. One of her friends mentioned that her husband had just bought a new copy machine for his office. The friend told Rayelan that she was welcome to use it anytime. One afternoon, after lunch, Rayelan and her friend made many copies of the document. Some were left with her friend, and some were put in pre addressed priority mail envelopes and mailed anonymously to people or groups that would copy and distribute the letter.

Rayelan never told anyone she had the original copy of the Wilcher Report until she was sure that there were many copies in the hands of many different people, and the existence of the Report was well known.

Dateline: September 17, 1996

Jonestown: The Whole Story

Project Blue

Operations Directorate of State Department, Section 6

Project Blue was/is the Guiana operation. Project Searchlight was the cover name for Project Blue: Resettlement of 34 Level 4 subjects. Level 4 refers to the degree of mind control that the subject has been programmed to. Level 4 "sleepers" are programmed assassins, the co-called Manchurian Candidate.

Jim Jones was only one of the project leaders. The actual project was headed by Wessley Baker of the Department of State. He introduced Jim Jones to Gary Monroe in the States. Hallucinogenic drugs, supplied by DOS, were put on the consecrated communion hosts. The doses of Trichloral-trimital was fed, in limited form, to the entire church population.

Mass hypnosis and the drug laced communion "hosts" were the primary tools used to determine the candidates for the inner circle. All experiments were produced within the church walls. They used no outside sources or vehicles. The first doctor, flown in, and made a member of the congregation, came from Baltimore, and was a family practitioner of Martin, Delahny and Danvers. The doctor that was sent to be part of the select team was Dr. Danvers.

Danvers was approached by agency personnel in Tran Loc, Viet Nam. (He became one of the first US Army majors to join the Company as a consultant. He was, again approached in 1969 to participate in Operation Strike Back, where he treated RVN soldiers as well as V.C. and sent them back into the field. This too, eventually fell under Operation Open Eyes (the overall name for the government mind control operation) It is still carried on the original Operations page.

Dr. Danvers was a close associate of Jim Jones, and the inner circle of cult members who had arrived, already trained, in part. Each member was assigned a group of three congregation members, whom they put through their paces until complete obedience was achieved. The congregation grew very slowly. The majority of those who went with him to Guiana, came from other church sites.

Programming was only applied to those past the age of eight. The manual that they used to program the children up to age 20 was a book called "Cornflower." It is part of the CIA training manual used in Honduras and Belize. It is still used in San Salvador today.

Project Blue was/is a systematic program used to continue and maintain the level of programming already installed in the small churches, from which the members came, from all over the U.S. and Canada. Then, the DOS sent 65 trained field experts down to oversee the daily programming and training schedule. Leaving the actual number of people on site aside for the moment, there were often 450-500 of our people in the encampment at a time.

Three 10 ml (milliliter) vats of potassium cyanide were delivered from Ft. Meade on a C-123 transport. This amount would have only provided lethal does for 10 men/women.

The actual danger to the camp people, was a self styled chain link fence with shooting platforms. The entire project went sour as some of the "less" programmed began to rebel against Jim. The selection process for membership was faulty, as all congregational members had not received a full dose of Level 3 and 4 programming prior to being brought on site. They rebelled against his "way of life," and wanted to take their young and leave.

No one was permitted to ever leave before they were fully programmed to performed specific tasks. (Ranging from small tasks to tasks of vital importance.) Gun positions were mounted around the entire perimeter to prohibit the flight of any camp member. After two attempts at escape, security was ordered to deal with problems by "fire on sight." Trips out of Jonestown were only permitted by armed escort. No phones were allowed for anyone other than Jim and his closest staff.

The program was monitored closely by DOS. They even sent numerous delegations to "Jonestown," to monitor the process of this mass "type" experiment.

The Project deteriorated from week to week. Soon Jones' own council began to supercede his orders. Jim originally came into our (CIA) hands because of his cocaine and heroin (speed balls) addiction. We didn't clean him up, we merely put a heavy Level 4 program in his head. The Level 5 trigger was to activate programming which would annihilate the entire group through gun fire. Nowhere was potassium cyanide part of his trigger. Task Force 151 supplied the arms, AK-47's and AR 15's with silencers.

The revolt and the massacre took place more than 3 hours before the C-127 touched down in Jonestown. His own council was liquidated the day before–one person at a time-gun shots in the back of the head. The Congressman and his group weren't fired upon as they deboarded. He saw what took place before he was gunned down, and brought by jeep back to the plane. He was a direct representative from Project Blue.

Jones and 12 of his guards were still alive at that time. An Englishman then took the cargo from the plane. 4 pounds of cyanide in plastic. The cyanide canister bore the usual markings and the name of Union Carbide of India. Parts of the shipment were produced by our company called Shalimar (the chemical weapons and munitions part of Shalimar perfumes). The Englishman waved to the crew to take off before dusk set in. All twelve of the shooters fled the country on an English cutter called the M.S. Dunbar. The cyanide kool aid was then put in the open mouths of many of the dead. Cyanide was not -the cause of any death.

Contrary to what has been written, Jim destructed on his own using a .357 Python. At that time Project Blue was canceled. The autopsies were all a big cover-up. That experiment failed, but the data they gathered was integrated into new projects.

The next year Project Phoenix was born. It is the same as today's Contact1 Operation. It was run by DOS (at the beginning, and funded with agency money.) An operations fund of $400,000 was granted to Project Phoenix by the DIA. That's when it changed hands.

Contact/Phoenix books and newspapers contain subliminal type of programs designed to keep the programmed "sleepers" walking the Company line, years after the programming was put in.

The Jonestown experiment was one that had gone sour and had to be terminated. However, enough was learned from the Jonestown experiment to use on other "cults" around the world. Waco was one that was successful, so successful in fact that they were just about to carry out their programmed "terrorist" act, when the government sent in a Delta Force team to neutralize seven "sleepers" who were part of the Branch Davidian Church and had been accidentally "triggered."

Somehow, the NWO part of the FBI and BATF decided that they were going to take over the operation and use it to teach America some lessons. The rest of the Waco story is history now.

The cult in Japan was financed by the same NWO part of the CIA that experimented with Jonestown. The Temple of the Solar Order in Switzerland and Canada were also terrorist sleepers who were programmed to release biological and chemical weapons in targeted cities.

Programmed terrorists are used by the NWO governments around the world to cause the citizens to give up their freedom and demand a police state to keep them safe. Once the police state is in place, the lessons learned from experiments like Jonestown can be used to program and re-educate the population in concentration camps, or as they will be called "Re-education and Training Camps." This is part of the "school to work" legislation that is being rammed through Congress. Those people who have not been indoctrinated in the schools of today, will not be allowed to get a job unless they go back for re-education. The techniques used in Jonestown-like mind control experiments will quickly shape and mold people into good little NWO robots.

If they don't agree to enter one of these re-education camps, they will not be able to get a job, therefore, they will not be able to support themselves or buy food or shelter. If they become homeless they will be forced to enter a homeless camp in which they will be "taught" skills. All the forests and wild lands will have become part of the world's biospheres; there will be no place for dissenting citizens to run.

---

[1]*The Contact* was a "channeled" newspaper used primarily to keep Level 4s and 5s in their programs. *The Contact* grew out of Project Phoenix.

Those citizens who cannot be reprogrammed will "disappear."

Children will be separated from parents, and husbands from wives. You will be sent to whatever area of the country that your skill is needed. Old and useless people will be sent to "nursing" homes, and will "disappear." Families will be split asunder, and as a result of the programming, no one will even notice that they no longer have their loved ones around them. No one will ever be missed.

Jonestown may have been a failure, but what they learned from it has been incorporated into the plan for the One World Government. 1984 should be must reading for everyone these days, because Big Brother is upon us.

The Short Road to Chaos and Destruction

An Expose of The Federal Reserve Banking System
  By Gunther K. Russbacher, CIA, USN
  Edited by Rayelan Allan Russbacher

> *Editor's note: This article was written by Navy Captain Gunther Russbacher in 1992. Gunther is a 29 year veteran of the United States Intelligence Community, (Office of Naval Intelligence, attached to the Central Intelligence Agency). During all of that time he has operated as a deep black covert operative. In 1980 Captain Russbacher flew then vice-presidential candidate George Bush to a secret meeting near Paris in what has become known as "The October Surprise" scandal.*
>
> *In 1989, Captain Russbacher violated direct orders and married, Rayelan Allan, an investigative researcher who was currently working to expose the October Surprise scandal. Captain Russbacher was arrested two days after their marriage and stayed incarcerated until December of 1993... 52 very long and dangerous months. It is evident to all who are familiar with the Russbacher case that he was a political prisoner of the George Herbert Walker Bush administration.*
>
> *The following article was written, in spring of 1992, from his prison cell in the Jefferson City Correctional Center in Missouri. Captain Russbacher has been called the "Company Banker." Because of this, he had to be knowledgeable about the banking system in the United States. Once he began studying the Federal Reserve, its origins*

and its global aspirations, he began to understand how three hundred families control the world. This article was written from memory, with a little help from friends at Langley Center.

The One World Monetary Cabal

The story of my investigation into the one-world monetary cabal begins in the elevator at Langley Center, (Headquarters for the Central Intelligence Agency in McLean, Virginia.) I had just finished a field exercise designed to certify me for further operations status. I had narrowly passed.

On the elevator, a friend invited me to join him and three others for dinner. Knowing that my plane wasn't due out until 0800 hours the following morning, I accepted. I needed a shower, so I hurriedly walked to my car and began the drive back to the city. It was a sweltering day in the Capitol. The air appeared to stand still. Mosquitoes angrily attacked anything that moved on the hot pavement. Little did I suspect, as I drove back to my hotel, that tonight's dinner was going to be more than just a friendly gathering.

After a shower, shave and fresh clothes, I arrived at the restaurant. I arrived early so I could have a drink and check out the place. I made my way through the restaurant, heading for the bar. Hopefully no one noticed my surprise when I saw the group who had already gathered. It was a weekend; the place should have been empty. But it was filled with high level government types, most of whom I knew. My friend from work was already in the bar. Judging from the half-filled drink in his hand, he had arrived early with the same intent in mind. The three others he mentioned this afternoon were with him.

After exchanging the usual, banal forms of greetings, we were led into the dining room. Over hors d'oeuvres I realized that I was in the midst of a serious meeting. The others who were present (with the exception of one man, who was employed by one of the wire services,) were all top echelon government employees. Together we represented the elite of the investigative and intelligence communities. You didn't need to be a rocket scientist to know that something more than dinner was going on here. To slam home the point, a guy from State, (the State Department) read us our evening's agenda. We were apprized that dinner would be brief so we should eat fast. A helicopter would pick us up and take us to a SPECIAL MANUFAC- TURING plant.

Not knowing when we'd eat again, we followed his suggestion and ate quickly, in studied silence. We were soon told that the helicopters were waiting, ready to take us deep into the Maryland countryside.

We left the table and boarded, still not knowing where we were going or why.

The flight was thankfully uneventful and the craft softly deposited us on the lawn in front of the corporate offices of a large manufacturing plant. I offered the guess that the firm was considering an expansion or maybe desired a government contract. Possibly they were looking for government assistance to fund their current projects. At that point, all speculations were pure conjecture.

It was plain to all of us that we were on the scene as representatives of our respective bureaus and agencies. The meeting was to be with various high corporate officials, along with members of a U.S. Senator's office and the mayor's office of a large Maryland metropolis.

After receiving an impressive tour of the facility, one of the members of our group asked why the firm was planning such a major expansion. The corporate official in charge of the tour replied,

"We are one of three companies being considered by the United States Treasury Department to build the printing presses that will print the new U.S. currency."

We all looked at each other. The expressions on our faces said it all. "What new U.S currency?" Not a word was spoken. We were as speechless at that moment as we would have been if we had been lobotomized by the painless methods of chemical ingestion. Here we were, all of us high level government officials, learning about the planned new currency without any warning or introduction. It was almost as if the information had been purposely leaked to us through the grapevine... through a private, non governmental source. The corporate official, when probed about the matter, and unorthodox manner of approach, claimed he didn't know much beyond what he had already told us.

When I returned to my office at Langley the following day, I couldn't help but wonder what last night was all about. I entered the entire proceedings into my Weekly Assessment Report, known within our circles as the "WAR" reports. Over the next several weeks I spent a great deal of time investigating the proposed printing of the new currency and the purpose behind it. I discovered soon enough that others were asking questions as well. (One of those individuals was Congressman Ron Paul of Texas who served on the Congressional committee dealing with the Treasury Department on this particular matter.)

In essence, I had learned that the plans to issue a new currency were international in scope; at least a dozen major countries were planning, or had specific plans, for coming out with new money. They included Switzerland, Germany, the United Kingdom, Canada, France, Italy, Australia, Brazil and several others.

I engaged my network to gather information on these proposed changes. Soon the information began flowing into my terminal. The picture began to clear. Several of the afore named countries had already issued new currencies, in various denominations. Most of these new currencies had two things in common...they had bare spots, about the size of a fifty cent coin, usually on the left-hand side of the bill. Upon closer inspection of these currencies, it was evident that they also contained metallic filament or element strips, enabling special devices to detect the currencies as they passed through airports or across international boundaries.

If the currencies are held over a light, a three-dimensional image (hologram) becomes apparent in the blank spot. The images, barely visible to the naked eye, are seemingly always of prominent world figures, and cannot be reproduced on copiers. The effort to create the "new money" was internationally coordinated.

Rumor had it that these currencies would later receive a common image linking them together in an international monetary system. Several years have passed since I first learned about the proposed new currency. Although it has been printed, and is stored in Treasury vaults, the actual issuance of the currency has, for some unknown reason, been delayed. Based upon my information as a member of the United States Intelligence community, it seems clear that, if we were to enter into a world government in the near future, the first step, from a monetary standpoint would include the establishment of an international currency system.

It must be stated that due to the rapid advances in electronic banking technology and the proven willingness of consumers to quickly adapt to these changes, the chances of by-passing the new currencies and going directly to an electronic (cashless) system are increasing exponentially. If the powers that be perceive the public to be ready and prepared for such a move, I believe they wouldn't hesitate to make this jump all at once, even in spite of the large investment that has already been made in the new currency.

If this were to be the case, the main focus of international finance would, without doubt, shift toward promoting international debit cards, which already are gaining widespread acceptance because of their convenience. Long time antagonists of these cards, such as Austria, Germany and Switzerland, have always believed in a true cash and carry society. They have already, with great regret, lost the battle to the debit card banking schemes.

To make a purchase, the card is passed through a scanning device. After making a positive identification, your bank account or credit account is automatically charged or debited with the amount of the purchase. The willingness of consumers to accept such a single card for worldwide use is already past the test market stage. Even my household has not been spared. We have received the new AT&T card which is being promoted by the intriguing commercial... "One World, One Card." The implications are most clear. Big Brother is at our very door. However, THIS Big Brother, should not be confused with Orwell's; for it is not the Big Brother of our national government, but rather and more ominous...it is BIG BROTHER of world-wide proportions.

Once such debit/credit cards have gained world-wide acceptance, everything would be in place for the next and final step, which would be to force each individual to be tagged with a personal identification code without which he would be unable to buy or sell. The technology for such a worldwide electronic system is already in place, and experiments with such a mark have already been conducted in several countries.

Other developments are underway as well. In the not too distant future, products on our grocery shelves may become labeled with an invisible bar code. The Universal Product Code (UPC), which most of us have complained is an eye sore on product packaging, will no longer be visible. It will still be there, however, only the scanner will be able to read it. Once the transition to an invisible code begins to take place, it will only be a matter of time before humans are tattooed with a similar mark.

Wake up America! The implications to personal freedom are staggering! I emphasize the tattoo in order to bring this discussion down to a personal level. If the globalist cabal has their way, their system will become operational by 1994. To understand how all this fits together, it's important to understand some of the finer points of monetary history.

Recently passed interstate banking laws have made this global centralization possible by allowing "strength and swallow" mergers. I am saying that many of the smaller banks have been virtually eaten by the big ones...at an alarming rate.

Over a 12 state region stretching from New York to the Carolinas, only three New York superbanks control over 85% of all banking assets. The same can be said for the First Interstate System, which is now in place from the Pacific West to the middle of the heartland of America. The writing is on the wall, surely it is finally going to be read.

I had ample opportunity to study the American banking system while serving as an operative for the Central Intelligence Agency's Proprietary Operations Division. After all, we had not only served as members of boards of directors, but more so, held outright ownership of a number of Savings and Loan institutions. I was well in the know, but even I was shocked to realize that I had merely scratched the surface on the national and international banking plot.

I discovered that the SAME forces behind the big bank mergers already controlled the American banking industry, via the Federal Reserve System. This has been the case ever since the Fed's establishment in 1913. Contrary to public belief, the Federal Reserve is NOT a government institution. It is a privately held corporation owned by stockholders. Until a few years ago, however, the names of those who owned the Federal Reserve were one of the best kept secrets of international finance, due to a provision of the Federal Reserve Act which stated that the identities of the Fed's Class A stockholders cannot be revealed.

In our circles it became widely known that the Fed's principle owners, or stockholders, as they prefer to be called, were the ROTHS-CHILD banks of London and Berlin; LAZARD BROTHERS Banks of Paris; ISRAEL MOSES SEIF Banks of Italy, WARBURG Bank of Hamburg and Amsterdam; LEHMAN BROTHERS Bank of New York; and GOLDMAN, Sachs Banks of New York; KUHN, Loeb Bank of New York; CHASE MANHATTAN Bank of New York. These interests own and operate the Federal Reserve System through approximately three hundred stockholders, all of whom are very well known to each other, and frequently are related.

This can be understood better by knowing that a great deal of maneuvering and deception accompanied the passage of the Federal Reserve Act. The original proposal, calling for a central bank operated by insiders and private interests, was presented by Nelson Aldrich, (the maternal grandfather of today's Rockefeller brothers,) and was known as the Aldrich Bill. This bill was narrowly put down, but was soon reintroduced and passed as the Federal Reserve Act, (officially known as the Owens Glass Act.)

Because of the way in which the Federal Reserve System was designed by its founder, whoever controlled the Federal Reserve Bank of New York essentially controlled the entire system. For all practical purposes the Federal Reserve Bank of New York IS the Federal Reserve. Currently, more than ninety of the 100 largest banks in the United States are located within this district.

Class A stockholders control the entire Federal Reserve System by owning the stock of the largest member banks in the New York Federal Reserve Bank. This controlling interest is held by fewer than a dozen international banking establishments, only four of which are factually based in the United States. The rest of the outlaying interests are European, with the most influential of these being the Rothschild family of London.

Each of the American interests are in some way connected to this family. Included among these are the Rockefellers who are by far the most powerful of the Fed's American stockholders. (The Rockefeller holdings in the Federal Reserve are primarily through Chase Manhattan Bank.)

Through their U.S. and European agents, the Rothschilds would go on to finance the Rockefeller Standard Oil dynasty, the Carnegie Steel Empire, as well as the Harriman railroad system. The Rockefellers, who later became intermarried with the Carnegies, would go on to finance many of American's leading capitalists, through Chase Manhattan and Citibank, both of which have long been Rockefeller family banks. Many of these families would also become intermarried with the Rockefellers so that by 1937 one could trace "an almost unbroken line of biological relationships from the Rockefellers through one-half of the wealthiest sixty families in the nation."

Owing much of their wealth to the Rockefellers, these families have become loyal allies of the "family." The Rockefellers, on the other hand, owing their enormous fortune to the Rothschild banking empire, have for the most part remained true and loyal to them and to their European interest. As a direct result of this chain, much of America's corporate wealth is ultimately traceable to the old money of Europe and the ONE-WORLD INTERESTS of its members.

In order to bring the reader up to speed, and make the connection between the new currency, the international debit/credit card, the Federal Reserve System and the New World Order, it is imperative to present a little American History within this report.

In 1911, the Supreme Court of the United States ruled that Standard Oil had in fact, long been in violation of the Sherman Anti-Trust Law. However, the problem goes back all the way to 1890, where Standard Oil of Ohio, owned by John D. Rockefeller was refining more than 90% of all American crude oil and was well on its way to international expansion politics. Although J.D. and his family were the repeated subjects of congressional investigations for anti-trust violations and criminal conspiracy, the investigations had little or no effect on the family's business or progress. They always managed to stay a step ahead of the federal government. The law was not able to thwart such illicit maneuvering. The American peoples' hands were tied.

It is worth noting that the 1911 action did indeed cause the Rockefeller family empire a certain amount of legal difficulties. It brought them into the United States District Courts. A verdict was found in favor of the government. The firm had to be split and many of the peripheral firms sold off. The holding company was dissolved, its shares distributed among thirty three companies in an attempt to break up the monopoly. However, it soon became evident that all of the new companies were owned by the same people (J.D. Rockefeller had 25% of stock in each of the new firms), "and that there wasn't a shred of competition among ANY OF THEM!"

Offshoots of the original Standard Oil Trust included Standard Oil of New Jersey (today EXXON), Standard Oil of New York (today MOBIL), Standard Oil of California (today operates under its name and Chevron), Standard Oil of Indiana (DX-BORON), Standard Oil of Ohio (SOHIO), Standard Oil Company, Phillips 66, and many lesser known others.

In 1966 (data supplied from my "company," as a result of congressional investigation headed by U.S. Representative Wright Patman of Texas,) it was discovered that four of the world's seven largest oil companies were under the direct ownership and/or control of the Rockefeller family. According to an earlier Operations Reports, the largest of these, Standard Oil of New Jersey (EXXON), alone controlled 321 other major corporations, including Humble Oil and Venezuela's OREOLE Petroleum; themselves among the largest oil corporations in the world.

By 1975, the Rockefellers had gained control of the single largest block of stock in Atlantic Richfield (ARCO) and were believed to be in control of TEXACO as well. (Therefore, it must be assumed that the extremely large suit and judgment against Texaco was merely a put-on for the public, and not a true verdict. Consider the true premise of a parent company bringing suit against its darling daughter.) It was further noted that the Rockefellers were operating major joint ventures with Royal Dutch Shell, which was already in the hands of European one-world interests. I am specifically referring to the Dutch Royal Family. It was Queen Juliana who was the sole owner of Shell. Upon her daughter's (Beatrice) marriage to Klaus (Germany), she divested herself of the interests in Royal Dutch Shell. Substantial interests were offered and sold through Credit Anstalt Bank Verein, as well as Union Bank of Switzerland.

However, our article deals with global strategists from both sides of the Atlantic. It should have seemed obvious to any American that major problems were to be encountered with the continuation of the Fed System. Ever since the founding of the Federal Reserve, consistent efforts have been made by conservatives of both houses of Congress to have their leaders put a stop to the Fed and to the dark forces behind it. With the passing of each decade, there was at least one valiant attempt to expose the already well known conspiracy.

Congressman Charles Lindbergh, Sr., the father of the famous aviator, was among those who fought the passage of the dark Act and later managed to raise an investigation into the cartel. His life was made extremely difficult as a direct result of crying for such investigation. Lindbergh had openly yelled his warning to Congress and to the American people. It was all to no avail. No one would hear his cry in the wilderness.

It must be noted that Lindbergh's efforts to expose the plot were followed by those of Congressman Louis T. McFadden, who chaired the House Banking and Currency Committee for a ten year period. During his tenure, three attempts were made on his life. First, he was shot in Washington, D.C., then his food was poisoned. The third attempt was unfortunately successful. His mysterious death occurred while on a visit to New York City. The cause of death, as listed on the death certificate, was given as "heart failure," although more than enough evidence pointed to poisoning. It is my proffered opinion that Mr. McFadden was poisoned by members of the cartel. Without proper court orders demanding the exhumation and forensic pathology tests, we shall never know the true story.

During the 1950's, Congressman Carroll Reese of Tennessee headed what became known as the Reese Committee. The Committee was charged with conducting a thorough investigation of the (then) major tax-exempt foundations linked to the international money cartel. The investigation centered on those foundations and trusts actually owned and controlled by the Rockefellers, Fords and Carnegies, and well as the Guggenheim foundations. The findings regarding the wealth and absolute power of these foundations were so traumatically overwhelming that many in Congress found the information difficult to believe. That disbelief, was the door opener for the continuation of the Machiavellian machinations within the money industry.

The disbelief and resultant inaction was also indirectly responsible, for allowing Agency personnel to defrock the already threatened Banking and Savings industry. The implementation of this defrocking, thanks to Congressional Oversight Committees, was easily attained. Please bear in mind, though, that the raping of the American financial institutions began long before the Agency entered the picture.

During the 1960's and 1970's, Congressman Wright Patman of Texas also investigated manipulations by these foundations, trusts and the Federal Reserve. Using his influence as Chairman of the House Banking Committee and later as the Chairman of other important committees, he repeatedly tried to expose the so called "One World Plot" by calling for audits of the Federal Reserve, and even trying to have the Act repealed. However, the findings of each of his committees, for some strange reason, were unable to attract any attention from the media. Patman, and others who have gone after and before him, frequently stated and vented his frustration over this lack of press and media coverage. On one occasion he stated, "Our exposes of the Federal Reserve Board are shocking and scandalous, but they are only printed in the daily Congressional Record, which is read by very few people."

In the 1970's and the 1980's, Congressman Larry McDonald was the one who spearheaded the efforts against the Bush version of the allanNew World Order. In 1976 he wrote the introduction to the "Rockefeller File," a book exposing the Rockefeller's financial holdings and secret intentions. The book supposedly revealed that the Rockefellers had as many as two hundred trusts and foundation type organizations, and that the actual number of such foundations controlled by the family might well number into the thousands. Such control IS possible because Rockefeller banks, such as Chase Manhattan, have become the trustees for many other U.S. foundations as well; possessing the right to invest and to vote the capital and common stock of these institutions through the trust department of the bank.

McDonald did everything in his power to warn the American public. However, as usual, the attempt was to no avail. He stated unequivocally, that the Rockefeller intended to control "—first our own country, and then the world!" He went on to state. "Do I mean conspiracy? Yes, yes I do. I am convinced there is a plot, national and international."

McDonald's warning was written on legal congressional letterhead and was dated November, 1975. During the ensuing years, frustrated by the media's refusal to report his findings, he began, like others and myself, to take his message to the streets by speaking out against these forces publicly to anyone who would listen to him. McDonald's coura- geous efforts came to an abrupt end on August 31, 1983 when he was killed aboard the Korean Airliner 007 flight, which "accidentally" strayed over Soviet airspace and was "accidentally" shot down.

Today, as with many other true patriots, very little remains of his fight for freedom. Critical information *does* kill the holder.

The chance of a U.S. Congressman being aboard a commercial airliner shot down by the Soviet military is less than one in a billion. Depending on the variables entered into the equation, the numbers may very well be higher and greater still. You, the public, are expected to believe that it was pure coincidence, just as we are supposed to believe that the recent (1991) deaths of Senator John Heinz and former Senator John Tower, in two separate crashes were "pure" coincidence as well.

Tower had been an outspoken critic of the "Eastern Establishment" (a euphemism for ONE WORLD ORDER), even though he had himself been associated with such organizations. He had a very strong sense of right and wrong, particularly on matters concerning national security. He was well known for "bucking" the tide. This backfired on him with deadly results when certain members of Congress, loyal to the Regan (Reagan) and Bush faction of the Intelligence Community (Faction #1), banded together against him in a smear campaign which resulted in the denial of Tower's confirmation as U.S. Secretary of Defense.

Outraged over the undocumented allegation made to slander his name, Tower began the book writing process so feared in Washington circles. His controversial book heavily criticizes his old crony pals in Congress. His death in a plane crash on April 5, 1991 came very shortly after the book was released.

One day earlier (April 4, 1991), Senator John Heinz died in a blazing plane crash near Philadelphia. The official reports state that the plane's landing gear had suddenly malfunctioned. A helicopter was sent up to check out the gear, only to end up (allegedly) crashing into the plane itself. We are really stretching the "coincidence theory" when we state that two freak accidents occurred in One! First, the landing gear fails, and then the rescue aircraft slams into the plane. No one should make book as to the veracity of such obviously slanted and untrue reports.

Heinz and Tower had both been members of a prominent One-World society known as the Council on Foreign Relations, the CFR. Both had served on powerful Senate banking and finance committees, and had known a great deal about the matters discussed in this article. I suppose the obvious question must read... "could they have known too much?" I submit that they in fact...knew too much! Both were very astute when it came to matters of monetary policy and the implementation of foreign policy. Yes, without doubt, they knew too much. Although accidents do happen, how much longer are we supposed to believe that all of these "so called" accidents are mere coincidence?

Since the earlier death of Congressman Larry McDonald on KAL007, *(Editor's note: There are some who believe that Congressman McDonald is still alive and living under Russian protection until the time is right for him to return to denounce the Federal Reserve.)* Senator Jesse Helms has led many efforts to expose the plot. Although Mr. Helms has recently been required to undergo extensive cardiovascular surgery, nothing appears to have happened to him, YET! I am quite certain that Mr. Helms would appreciate the combined prayer of Americans who are concerned for the truth as well as his safety.

The vivid remarks and statements of Senator Helms, like those of his predecessors, have been entered into the Congressional Record, without receiving any network coverage. Regretfully, the only attention Mr. Helms manages to garner in the press is in the form of public ridicule over his conservative voting record. It must be noted here, that the major threat to the American way of life transcends labels like Conservative and Liberal. Those who valiantly try to protect the way of life that Americans love and cherish are the new American patriots. They come from all backgrounds, Republican, Democrat, Liberal and Conservative.

The American people must wake up immediately and realize that the "Labels" applied to them are merely a way of dividing and conquering. One has only to remember the 1992 republican convention and its blatant attempt to divide and conquer the American people with obvious divisive and untrue statements. Wake up America and understand why the "One World Elite" needs to label groups. As an example, when the women's movement began to gain momentum and presented problems to the entrenched elite, a way had to be found to neutralize the power of the women's movement. Women who join together and fight for common causes such as child care, health care and education are a formidable force. To keep such a powerful force from taking over government, the "think tanks" created the solution...divide and conquer. Turn women against each other and they will never be able to become a powerful political force. The method they chose to divide and conquer the growing women's movement was abortion. Other methods are employed in other areas...first label, then divide, then conquer. My lengthy digression can be summed up in one sentence: Forget all the old labels, become American patriots...it's the only way to save America.

* * * * *

During the 1960's and 1970's, thanks to the efforts of Congressman Wright Patman, Larry McDonald, and others, the message of a "One World Conspiracy" had begun to reach the "reading" American people. The usual action groups were formed by various citizens in an urgent attempt to get this information into the hands of the public. However, as usual, without coverage from the major media, their efforts have had only limited results. These groups have had to rely on self-published newsletters and books. Numerous radio appearances also were used to spread the word. The task of educating the American public is not a simple one, but rather and more so, based and predicated upon numerous unpublicized speaking engagements in order to get the word out. Such is the stress associated with an active grassroots campaign.

Lt. Col. Archibald Roberts is one of the individuals who has made significant impact. As Director of the Committee to Restore the Constitution, he began testifying before state legislatures, informing our elected officials, at the state level, about the deception surrounding the Federal Reserve Act. His campaign, urging state legislatures to repeal the Federal Reserve Act was, according to Agency records, launched on March 30, 1971, when he testified before the Wisconsin House of Representatives. The text of Roberts' address was subsequently entered in the Congressional Record on April 19, 1991 by Louisiana Congressman John Rarick.

As a result of Roberts' work, by the mid 1980's, approximately twenty states had taken some form of action to pass legislation, calling either for an audit of the Fed, or for the repeal of the Federal Reserve Act. However, there has been virtually no media coverage, and the American public is still largely unaware of the intense battle going on behind the scenes of the Washington Establishment.

During June, 1989, the battle waged at the state level had once again reached Congress. Representative Henry Gonzalez, of Texas, introduced House Resolution 1469, calling for the abolition of the Open Market Committee of the Federal Reserve System. He also introduced House Resolution 1470, calling for the repeal of the Federal Reserve Act of 1913. During the same session, Representative Phil Crane of Illinois, introduced H.R. 70, calling for an annual audit of the Federal Reserve. However, all of these efforts, like those of others before them, failed.

We have personally come to know that it is far more than merely difficult to get the public behind a legitimate cause or issue, if the media refuses to cover it. Obviously such coverage is necessary in order to get the public to put the kind of pressure on Congress that will lead to action. This is particularly true of a Congress in which One-World interests now hold the upper hand, and own the media.

When I was asked to write this article, I made my way back into the dark corridors and lesser known places inside Agency Headquarters. Some of my old friends and associates were still willing to hear from me, even though several years had passed. They not only talked with me, but were gracious enough to accept my collect calls from prison. We pulled files, read numerous articles, and reviewed stymied legislation. The information you have been made privy to is a result of cooperation with the "so called" unspeakable, and unclean element from the CIA Center. We have come a long way in tracking the specifics of this money trail and how One World money is being used to influence our society. Our distaste must seem obvious to the reader. These one-worlders have invaded every aspect of American life and not only threaten the well being of the nation, but have virtually managed to secure a strangle hold upon the physical bodies of each and every one of us.

It must be stated, for the record, that each year billions of dollars are EARNED by class A stockholders of the Federal Reserve. These profits come at the expense of the U.S. Government and American citizens, who pay interest on bank loans, a portion of which ends up going to the Federal Reserve. Much of this money, along with the annual profits stemming from hundreds of corporations and banks owned and operated by these same interests, is then funneled into tax-exempt foundations where it is then reinvested into American and foreign corporations, and used to influence our thoughts and our economy. In this fashion, a small group of people, dedicated to the establishment of a strong type of world government, has gained considerable influence over global activity and therefore your life.

It is NO coincidence that the forces responsible for the founding of the Federal Reserve were also responsible for the passage of laws permitting the creation of tax-exempt foundations. Such private foundations were specifically intended to serve as tax shelters to stow and hide the enormous wealth generated by the international banking cartel. It might be significant to note that they have also been most cherished for the purpose of funding major think-tanks, which influence virtually every aspect of American life.

AUTHOR'S ASSESSMENT AND CONCLUSIONS
REPORT FORMAT
(Personal opinion included)

At the close of research and investigation for this article, the writer must conclude that the influence of one-world foundations in the areas of social science, education and foreign policy has only accelerated; thereby accomplishing great strides due to minimal opposition from opposing foundations.

It must be remembered that it was the One-World cabal, (Rockefeller, Rothschild etc.), who pushed for the legalization of tax-exempt foundations, and were therefore the first to establish them. They were able to successfully get off to a head start. Even if a sizable foundation-sponsored opposition were to develop, it would be on a small scale and of rather insignificant result, compared to the massive efforts exerted by the One-World Cabal's mega-foundations.

The One World Cabal will always have more power in the world because of the devious strategies it is willing to employ in order to accumulate money and manipulate the rest of us with it. Clear cut, and decisive action is required immediately. Otherwise, it is this writer's opinion that we will very quickly lose the freedoms our Constitution guarantees for us. In short, our Constitution will be superceded by a One-World document, in fact it already has.

It is important for the reader to begin to think about what the world will be like if the One-Worlders succeed. Because this is a short article, all the possible ramifications and changes to your lifestyle cannot be covered. But one possible negative outcome could be a return to a feudal system with 98% of the people shackled to some major corporation in the same way that serfs lived by the whim of their overlord. This is just one of many possible scenarios, all equally black.

That being said, the ball is squarely in your court. You are part of a select few who have the education, intelligence and desire to even care about such things. In other words, it is up to you. You are part of the last classically educated free-thinking generation in this nation. If you wish to preserve your country for your grandchildren, then get busy. Write letters, form groups which will inform your family and friends. Buy shortwave radios, and create radio networks which will get together and decide how to create an informed voting block that will take back your country.

The Art Of Global Politics
By Gunther K. Russbacher
Edited by Rayelan Allan Russbacher

This article is the follow up article to The Short Road to Chaos and Destruction, Gunther's Expose of the Federal Reserve Banking System. "The Art of Global Politics" was written in 1992, while Gunther was in prison in Missouri.
—Rayelan

In order to understand and be able to identify the various factions at work in and during the previous administrations, it is desirable to find the common denominator, linking the various factions ... watching as they form a cohesive relationship within the historical framework of the story of panglobalism. The diverse information available for scholars of today is magnificent compared to the sum total of knowledge of the years gone by.

During the course of my research into this subject matter, I received a list, a rather long and extensive list, showing the relationships between the European branches of Secret Societies, and their American counterparts. The list furthered MY understanding that these so called factions actually were not singular units, scattered throughout Europe and America, but rather that these societies all shared a common history, and were therefore, one and the same, regardless of their respective names or agendas. Of course, even within and among these societies, considerable internal differences manifest themselves with regard to ultimate goals or agendas.

The list of members reads like a Who's Who of American leaders, including numerous members of government, private industry, education, most of the press and media, as well as the military, and the cream of the crop of high finance. It included a good many names I had seen earlier, during the research phase of the first segment of this article. There seemed to be a common denominator—everyone on the list was either a member of the Council on Foreign Relations or the Trilateral Commission, with some members belonging to both organizations.

In order to bring these matters into proper perspective, it becomes necessary to bring forth these secret organizations, and shed a little light into their dark and hidden nature. As the organizations had to present a beginning for comprehensive research, I shall choose to begin with the secret order of the "Illuminati."

The Illuminati

The Illuminati was a secret order founded and established in Ingolstadt, Bavaria (Ingolstadt, landkreis Bayern) on or about May 1, 1776. It was known to be a Luciferic Order. The founder was none other than Mr. Adam Weishaupt, a prominent Freemason of his time. He was a lodge member in Ingolstadt. For the sake of the readers it must be known and most seriously stressed that the name Illuminati, or the Luciferic Order, does *not* (in this case) refer to Satan or Lucifer. It specifically refers to the state of the enlightened membership. The term "Luciferic Lodge" originated in the pre-Christian Egyptian mystery schools. At that time there was a belief in a dualistic material plane comprised of good and evil. Neither was elevated above the other. They were viewed as two sides of the same coin, two paths that must be walked to complete the earth experience. The designation, "Lucerfic Lodge" denoted a group of enlightened beings who came together and attempted to educate and enlighten humanity so that they could take their place in the universe next to their God.

Even though the Illuminati referred to themselves as a "Luciferic Lodge," it will soon be seen that their aims were anything but enlightening. They usurped the label "Luciferic" from the lodges who were genuinely concerned with the education and uplifting of humanity. It will be noted at various times throughout this article, that something which started off having as its purpose, "the good of humanity," was usurped and perverted by the Illuminati and those who carry their banner in today's world. This was done for several reasons. The first and foremost reason was to hide the nefarious nature of their real purpose, the second reason was to ensnare innocent spiritual seekers and pervert them to their path.

The Illuminati established itself as an extension of high, or Illuminized Freemasonry, existing as a special order within an order. Its operations were closely connected with the powerful Grand Orient Masonic Lodge of France. The order's name translated literally as "the enlightened ones." This signified to all who were familiar with such secret Orders that the members had been initiated into the secret teachings of Lucifer, not to be confused with the Lucifer of the Bible or with Satan. It must be remembered that these teachings came from a time that preceded Jesus and Christianity.

In the Egyptian mystery schools Lucifer was seen as the brightest and best among Gods angels or messengers to earth. Lucifer gave mankind the tools he needed to cast off the dark cloaks of ignorance and climb the ladder to enlightenment and finally return to God. Lucifer, the "light bearer" was seen as the source of enlightenment, according to the early doctrines of Illuminized Freemasonry. His fall from grace came after these teachings.

It must be stated that while the origins of the Masonic Order in the distant Egyptian past were benign, over the centuries the order was taken over by men who perverted its teachings to further their own evil ends. The Illuminati Order was made up of such men. The Illuminati was designed for one purpose: to carry out the plans of High Freemasonry. These plans included creating a New World Order which would be ruled by the Masons. In the original concept of five thousand years ago, the only purpose for the World Order was to educate and enlighten. However, down through the ages the true purpose was lost to the masses, and unenlightened Masons innocently flocked to the Illuminati and helped Adam Weishaupt gain a foothold in the key policy making circles of Europeans governments.

From within these circles, Illuminati members were able to influence the decisions of Europe's leaders. This technique has-been carried down to the present time. In reference to the various governmental leaders, which the Illuminati had targeted for subversion, Weishaupt remarked:

"It is therefore our duty to surround them (the leaders) with our (The Illuminati) members, so that the profane may have no access to them. Thus we are able most powerfully to promote its (Illuminati) interests.

"If any person is more disposed to listen to the Princes than to the Order, he is not fit for It (the Illuminati), and must rise no higher. We must do our utmost to procure the advancement of Illuminati in all important civil offices,

"By this plan we shall direct all mankind. In this manner, and by the simplest means, we shall set all in motion and in flames. The occupations must be so allotted and contrived, that we may, in secret, influence all political transactions."

For the Order's strategy to succeed, its activities and the many names of its members had to remain absolutely secret. Initiates were therefore ordered and sworn to secrecy, taking bloody oaths which described in detail the brutal and specific, way they would be punished if they ever defected from the order or revealed its plans. As another measure of internal security, the Order and its correspondence would be conducted exclusively through the use of codes, symbols and pen names. Mr. Weishaupt's alias and pseudonym, for example, was Spartacus.

The Order was given a tremendous boost at the Masonic Congress of Wilhelmsbad, held on July 16, 1782. This meeting "included representatives of all the Secret Societies—Martinists as well as Freemasons and the Illuminati, which now numbered no less than 3,000,000 members all over the world." It enabled the Illuminists to solidify their control over the Lodges of Europe, and to become viewed as the undisputed leaders of the ONE-WORLD movement.

It was decided at this Congress that the Headquarters of the Illuminized Freemasonry should be moved from Bavaria to Frankfurt, as Frankfurt was already becoming the stronghold of the Rothschilds and the international financiers. The ensuing cooperation between the Rothschilds and the Illuminati would prove to be mutually beneficial to each. By cooperating with each other, the two groups were able to geometrically increase their influence throughout all of Europe.

Approximately ten years after the Order's founding, it was discovered and exposed by the Bavarian government as a result of specific tips received from several of the Order's initiates. The leaders of Bavaria moved quickly to confiscate the Order's secret documents. These original writings of the Illuminati were then sent on to all leaders of Europe in order to warn them of the exposed plot. However, some of these leaders had already fallen under the influence of the Order and the warnings fell on indifferent ears. Some of those who had not succumbed to the enchantments of the Illuminati, found its plans to be so outrageous that they didn't take the warnings seriously. These leaders simply could not believe that anything as outrageous and all encompassing as were the Illuminati plans, could possibly be serious.

Their naïveté and disbelief would become their undoing. Disbelief remains as the single biggest factor working in the Illuminati's favor, even today. Decent people tend to find it somewhat difficult to believe that there could be individuals so evil in nature as to actually wish to take control of the whole world under conditions amounting to theft, slavery, brutality and to have as their goal, the imposition of a world totalitarian dictatorship. To the reader this should sound a theme more fitting of a James Bond or George Orwell novel than real life. However, difficult as it may be to believe, this effort at world usurpation and the intent to create a New World order based on enslaving the masses, was and is, for real ... to the point where one could conceivably bet their very life on its strategy and intended outcome.

Although several members of the Order were ultimately persecuted by the Bavarian Government, most of the initiates managed to get away and were taken in by various European leaders. Weishaupt, for example, took up refuge with the Duke of Saxe-Gotha where he remained until his death in 1811.

By the time the Illuminati became exposed, its efforts had already spread into more than a dozen counties, including the fledgling United States. Since 1776, at least three U.S. presidents have warned the public of the Illuminati's activities in this country. One of these presidents was George Washington, himself a Mason, but an early member whose Lodge had not been infiltrated and perverted by the Illuminati. Washington stated and wrote:

"I have heard of the nefarious and dangerous plan and doctrines of the Illuminati. It was not my intention to doubt that the doctrine of the Illuminati and the principles of Jacobinism had not spread to the United States."

Washington went on to denounce the order in two separate letters written in 1798, and would once again warn the people of the United States of America against foreign influence in his farewell address to the nation. Concerned that the American people might fall under the sway of corrupt powers, Washington stated:

"Against the insidious wiles of foreign influence (I conjure you to believe me fellow citizens), the jealously of a free people ought to be constantly awake; since history and experience prove that foreign influence is one of the most baneful foes of republican government. But that jealously, to be useful, must be impartial, else it becomes the instrument of the very influence to be avoided, instead of a proper defense against it. Excessive partiality for one foreign nation and excessive dislike for another, cause those whom they actuate to see danger only on one side, and serve to veil and even second the arts and influence of the other. Real patriots, who may resist the intrigues of the favorite, are liable to become suspected and odious; while its tools and dupes usurp the applause and confidence of the people, to surrender their interests. The great rule of conduct for us, in regard to foreign nations, is, in extending our commercial relations, to have with them as little political connection as possible. So far as we have already formed engagements, let them be fulfilled with perfect good faith. Here let us stop."

If only this great country, America, had listened to President Washington's sound advice to a fledgling nation.

Illuminized High Freemasonry

Although the Illuminati officially ceased to exist after is exposure in the 1780's, the continuation of its efforts would be ensured through the Grand Orient Lodge of France. Working through the Grand Orient and the network of Illuminized Masonic lodges already put in place by Weishaupt, High Freemasonry would continue with its plans to build a allanNew World Order.

One of the factors working in Freemasonry's favor is that it rarely, if ever, does anything covert or openly evil under its own name. In order to advance its respective agenda, it establishes other organizations, to which it gives its special and oftentimes dangerous assignments. All of which are carried forth in an extremely covet manner. The advantages must appear clear, for in this way, if anything goes wrong and the operation gets exposed, Freemasonry remains relatively unscathed, claiming it had nothing to do with the matter. This technique is one that has been employed numerous times in recent history by groups who have been well schooled in the arts of deception.

Throughout the late 1700s and all of the 1800s, Illuminized Freemasonry would continue to operate in this fashion, creating new organizations to carry out the tasks begun by the Illuminati, frequently still collectively referred to as the Illuminati by many Agency Operations Divisions.

The first major "accomplishment" of Illuminized Freemasonry was to incite the French Revolution through the Jacobin Society and Napoleon allanBonaparte, who was groomed by them to initiate and bring about the beginnings of the New World Order. (The revolution that began in France in 1789, overthrew the French monarchy, and culminated in the start of the Napoleonic era in 1799.) Illuminized Freemasonry would also receive help from Voltaire, Robespierre, Danton and Marat; all of whom were prominent Masons. The Jacobin Society's motives and connections were revealed when it named Weishaupt as its "Grand Patriot."

To continue the presentation of the issues it is imperative to fully understand that the United States had barely declared its independence from England when the same European forces began efforts to bring America's young banking system under their control. Alexander Hamilton, believed by some to have been an Illuminist agent, was at the forefront of this drive. President Thomas Jefferson, all too well aware of the plot to gain control of our banking system argued:

"If the American people ever allow private banks to control the issue of their currency, first by inflation and then by deflation, the banks and the corporations which will grow up around them, will deprive the people of all property until their children wake up homeless on the continent their fathers conquered."

During the mid 1800s, Illuminized Freemasonry would be partly responsible for inciting the Great War between the states. Charleston, South Carolina; where the Secessionist Movement began, also happened to be the American headquarters of the Scottish Rite Freemasonry, at the time, a little known fact which

TheObergon Chronicles

Freemasonry has successfully kept from the unsuspecting public. The headquarters of the Scottish Rite were later moved to Washington, D.C., where they remain to this day. Others also spoke out quite strongly, urging the people to resist these coup attempts. Abraham Lincoln strongly resisted efforts by Illuminist forces to establish a privately controlled central bank. His foresight and wisdom (as I choose to call it) would prevent the establishment of such a system for another forty-eight years.

Just days before his assassination, President Lincoln warned:

"As a result of the war, corporations have been enthroned and an era of corruption in high places will follow and the money power of the country will endeavor to prolong its reign by working on the prejudices of the people until wealth is aggregated in the hands of a few and the Republic is destroyed. I feel at this moment more anxiety for the safety of my country than ever before, even in the midst of – r.11

Colonel House ands The League of Nations

In 1913, the persistent efforts of Illuminized Freemasonry finally paid off with the creation of the Federal Reserve System, insuring European illuminists a permanent role in America's finances, along with giving them more money with which to further their particular cause. Some of this money would eventually go toward financing the Council on Foreign Relations, whose formation was influenced by a man named Edward Mandell House. (House's father, Thomas P. House, was a Rothschild agent who amassed a large fortune during the Civil War by supplying the South with essentials from France and England.)

Colonel House, as he was called, was an Illuminist agent committed to the one-world interests of the Rothschild-Warburg-Rockefeller cartel, serving as their point man in the White House. He apparently gained national prominence in 1912 while working to get Woodrow Wilson nominated as president. After the election, and subsequent win for Wilson, he became the president's most trusted personal advisor. House was to Wilson what Henry Kissinger would later be to President Nixon; he was without question, the dominant figure in the White House, exerting his influence particularly in the areas of banking and foreign policy.

His numerous accomplishments as Wilson's chief advisor were diverse and many. Among some of the things, he successfully persuaded Wilson to support and sign the Federal Reserve Act into law. Later, realizing what he had done, President Wilson remorsefully replied:

"I have unwittingly ruined my country."

During World War I, which began within a year after the Act's passage, Colonel House would undertake secret missions to Europe as Wilson's chief foreign diplomat. It didn't take very long before he managed to drag the United States into the war in Europe (April 1917). As the war came to an end in 1918, House worked ever so diligently to help plan the League of Nations. Funded in part with Rockefeller money, the League of Nations was to serve as the first political step toward the forming and implementing of a world government.

President Wilson, as a result of House's counsel, would become the leading spokesman for the League of Nations, publicly viewed as the League's chief architect, in spite of the fact that it was House who really was the one who was in charge.

However, much to Wilson's dismay and real embarrassment, he could not even persuade his own country to join the newly founded organization. The American people strongly resisted this move toward globalization, placing increasingly heavy pressures on Congress to reject the absurd treaty thereby keeping the United States out of the League of Nations.

The Council on Foreign Relations

In order to properly receive the following information, it would seem prudent to bring forth a little of the actual history of this infamous Council. It is an organization, deeply entrenched into our political system. No one has been spared; no party has been left out, as the greed of a few has forced this organization down the throats of the many Americans who stridently believe that we should not permit ourselves to get involved with monetary and governmental globalism.

Later in this expose, I shall cite a number of articles, verbatim, as they appear in their organizational charter. The following excerpt is taken from the Handbook of the Council on Foreign Relations, and gives a number of details pertinent to their establishment.

"On May 30, 1919, several members of the delegations to the Paris Peace Conference met at the Hotel Majestic in Paris, France to discuss setting up an international group which would advise their respective governments on international affairs. The United States was represented by General Tasker H. Bliss (Chief of Staff, U.S. Army), Colonel Edward M. House, Whitney H. Shepardson, Dr. James T. Shotwell, and Professor Archibald Coolidge. Great Britain was unofficially represented by Lord Robert Cecil, Lionel Curtis, Lord Eustace Percy, and Harold Temperly. It was decided at this meeting to call the proposed organization the Institute of International Affairs. At a meeting on June 5, 1919, the planners decided it would be best to have separate organizations cooperating with each other. Consequently, they organized the Council on Foreign Relations, with headquarters in New York, and a sister organization, the Royal Institute of International Affairs, in London, also known as the Chatham House Study Group, to advise the British Government. A subsidiary organization, the Institute of Pacific Relations, was set up to deal exclusively with Far Eastern Affairs. Other organizations were set up in Paris and Hamburg, the Hamburg branch being called the Institut fuer Auswaertige Politik, and -the Paris branch being known as Centre d'Etudes de Politique Etrangere."

Baron Edmond de Rothschild of France dominated the Paris Peace Conference, and each of the founders of the Royal Institute ended up being men who most certainly met Rothschild's approval. The same was true for the Council on Foreign Relations, which was not officially formed until 29 July, 1921.

Money for the founding of the CFR came from J.P. Morgan, Bernard Baruch, Otto Kahn, Jacob Schiff, Paul Warburg, and John D. Rockefeller, among others. Obviously this was one and the same crowd of moneyed men who were instrumental in forming the Federal Reserve. The Council's original board of directors included Isaiah Bowman, Archibald Coolidge, John W. Davis, Norman H. Davis, Stephen Duggan. Otto Kahn, William Shepard, Whitney Shepardson, and Paul Warburg.

It must be mentioned, for the record, that numerous well known American politicians (I shy away from the term Statesman) have served in prominence on the Council's board. Some of the more prominent, who have served in the capacity of director, since 1921, include Walter Lippmann (1932-37), Adlai Stevenson (1958-62), Cyrus Vance (1968-76), Zbigniew Brzezinski (1972-77), Robert 0. Anderson (1974-80). Paul Volker (1975-79), Theodore M. Hesburgh (1926-85), Lane Kirkland (1976-86), George H.W. Bush (1977-79), Henry Kissinger (1977-81), David Rockefeller (1949-85), George Shultz (1980-88), Alan Greenspan (1982-88), Brent Scowcroft (1983-89), Jeanne Kirkpatrick (1985-present), and last but surely not least, Richard B. Cheney who has served from 1987 through 1989. Obviously a number of these people served more than one master!

It must be noted that most of the above mentioned occupied—in some form—Cabinet Posts while actively engaged with the Council on Foreign Relations. Such an act is at least questionable, in that it goes beyond the borders of Law and Ethics. However, that is not to infer that the persons mentioned herein are anything but good, decent and hard working Americans, out to do their very best for their Masters!

Please take several deep breaths of air in the event that you feel that you and your country have been sold to foreign interest groups!

No decision as to why, what or how to deal with the issue must be made at this time. We can well not avoid facing the issues which demand to be heard. However, before the reader determines what must be done to protect American interests from Pan-Globalism, it behooves us to know a little more about the nature of the beast with which we must do battle. A little further discourse on the subject appears called for.

The CFR: Funding and Members

The most powerful man in the CFR during the past two decades has been David Rockefeller, the grandson of John D. Rockefeller. Along with being a Council director for thirty-six years, David served as chairman of the board from 1970-85, and remains to this day, the organization's honorary chairman. During this time, David was also the chairman of Chase Manhattan Bank. Such actions surely must reek of collusion and worse.

Permit me to state that in my professional opinion, the Rockefellers are in no great danger of losing control of the CFR any time soon! Another generation of family members is being groomed to continue their tradition. David, Jr.; John D. IV; and Norman C. Rockefeller are all current members of the Council on Foreign Relations.

As mentioned somewhat earlier, the Reese Committee found that the CFR was being financed by both the Rockefeller and the Carnegie foundations, and investigated it as well as its sister organization, the Institute of Pacific Relations, stating that the CFR "overwhelming propagandizes the globalist concept."

In order to determine from whence the funding came, it became necessary to call upon my "so-called" ex-associates in Langley, Virginia. The response was overwhelming. I never doubted that they would feed me a morsel or two. However, it soon became quite clear that they intended to inundate me with far more research material than I was capable of dealing with. After sorting through a virtual panacea of secrets, I did determine it to be necessary to divulge the names of many sponsors to the organization. They didn't merely contribute; they matched contributions and grand gifts during the early years of CFR's existence.

The areas of concern are actually a little more recent. We are dealing with contributors, gifts, and matching funds received between the years 1987 and 1991. These were received from leading organization men, corporations and individuals. They are deemed to include, but are not limited to Chemical Bank, Citibank/ Citicorp, Morgan Guaranty Trust, John D. and Catherine T. MacArthur Foundation, British Petroleum American, Inc., Newsweek, Inc., Reader's Digest Foundation, Washington Post Company, Rockefeller Brothers Fund, Rockefeller Family and associates, the Rockefeller Foundation, and David Rockefeller.

During the same period, the CFR received major grants from other major corporations and foundations, including (partial list) the American Express Philanthropic Program, the Asia Foundation, the Association of Radio and Television News Analysts, the Carnegie Corporation of New York, the Ford Foundation, the General Electric Foundation, the General Motors Corporations, the Hewlett Foundation, the Andrew W. Mellon Foundation, the Alfred P. Sloan Foundation, and the Xerox Foundation.

Presently, the Council currently numbers 2,670 in active member-ships; of whom 952 reside in New York City, 339 in Boston, and 730 in Washington D.C. Its memberships, as you the reader shall see, reads like a Who's Who in America, including most of the nation's top leaders in government, business, education, labor, the military, the media, and of course, in banking. In addition to its headquarters in New York City, the CFR has thirty-eight affiliated organizations, known commonly as Committees on Foreign Relations, located in major cities throughout the United States.

Attempts to Warn and Educate Re: the CFR

Rear Admiral Chester Ward, a former CFR member for sixteen years, issued a decisive warning to the American people as to the organiza-tion's intentions. For information purposes I shall cite an excerpt of his warning:

"The most powerful clique in these elitist groups has one objective in common: they want to bring about the surrender of the sover-eignty and the national independence of the United States."

A second clique of international members in the CFR ... comprises the Wall Street international bankers and their key agents.

Primarily, they want the world banking monopoly, from whatever power ends up in the control of global government."

Dan Smoot, a former supervising member of the FBI headquarters staff in the Washington Office, and one of the first and primary researchers into the CFR, summarized the organizations purpose as follows:

"The ultimate aim of the Council on Foreign Relations ... is ... to create a one world socialist system and make the United States an official part of it."

This of course would all be done in the name of democracy.

Congressman John R. Rarick, deeply concerned over the growing influence of the CFR, has been one of the members in Congress making a concerted effort to expose the organization. Rarick warns:

"The Council on Foreign Relations—dedicated to one world government, financed by a number of the largest tax-exempt foundations, and wielding such power and influence over our lives in the areas of finance, business, labor, military, education, and mass communication media-should be familiar to every American concerned with good government and with preserving and defending the U.S. constitution and our free-enterprise system.

"Yet the Nation's right-to-know machinery—the news media— usually so aggressive in exposures to inform our people, remain conspicuously silent when it comes to the CFR, its members, and their activities. And I find that few university students and graduates have even heard of the Council of Foreign Relations."

The CFR is *the establishment*! Not only does it have the influence and power in key decision making positions at the highest levels of. government to apply pressure from above but it also finances and uses individuals and groups to bring pressure from below, to justify the high level decisions for converting the United States from a sovereign Constitutional Republic into a servile member state of a one world dictatorship.

In the event that I had any doubts remaining over the real intent of the CFR they were removed after becoming aware of the state- ments made over the years by the CFR itself, advocating world government. For example, on 17 February, 1950, CFR member James Warburg, testifying before the Senate Foreign Relations Committee, stated,

"We shall have world government whether or not you like it—by conquest or consent."

On another occasion, in the April 1974 issue of the CFR journal, Foreign Affairs (p.558), Richard Gardner stated that the New World Order "will have to be built from the bottom up rather than from the top down. It will look like a great booming, buzzing confusion...but an end run around national sovereignty, eroding it piece by piece, will accomplish much more than the old fashioned frontal assault."

Study Number 7, a CFR position paper, published on or about November 25, 1959, the CFR stated that its purpose was to advocate the "building (of) a new international order (which) may be respon- sible to world aspirations for peace (and) for social economic change ... An international order ... including states labeling themselves as Socialist (Communist). (Obviously such maneuvering has already taken place among the new republics of Eastern Europe, the former Soviet Union, and the numerous, small but ethnically tormented Balkan States. No one appears willing to embrace this "so-called" New World order!)

The New World Order

The term allanNew World Order (or New International Order—as possauned by the communists since 1917) has been used privately by the CFR since its inception to describe the coming world government. However, since the winter of 1990, and spring of 1991, CFR members have, for the first time, begun using the term publicly to begin the conditioning process in order that the unsuspecting public might brace and prepare themselves for what lies ahead. It is their opinion that if the American people hear the term often enough, on a daily dose basis, that they will be less likely to resist or feel threatened by it when that fateful day arrives.

The New World Order, it should be explained, is an expression that has been used by Illuminized Freemasonry since the days of Adam Weishaupts to signify the coming world government. One of the symbols portraying the message of "allanNew World Order" was placed on the back of our one dollar note during the administration of Franklin D. Roosevelt. It consists of a multipart message. One of the parts of the message is the pyramid, containing the eye of Osiris. Under the pyramid is the writing "Novus Ordo Seculorum" Translated from the Latin text to the English language, it means ... New World Order! It must be mentioned that this symbol was designed by freemasons... or better said, Masonic Interests, and became the official reverse side of the Great Seal of the United States in 1782.

To this day, most people have never given a second thought to this Latin phrase or the meaning contained therein. Some unusually astute people did recognize the seal and the meaning contained therein, and began exposing it, in context to what it really represented.

The reader should also note that at the time the seal was designed, the allanNew World Order was a fledgling, in the early stages of being built, and was not yet complete. This is symbolized by the capstone (of the pyramid) being separated from the rest of the pyramid.

However, once the New World Order has been built and the one world government is in place, the capstone will be joined to the rest of the pyramid, symbolizing the completion of the task. One must remember that the Illuminati usurps names, ideas and symbols and perverts them for their own use. There are some who believe that the symbol was created by the Founders of our country as a message of what a democratic republic can do once it has spread throughout the world—educating and enlightening men who will join together and establish a world government based on liberty and justice for all. But from the research I have done, it appears as if the symbol has become a sign–almost a secret codeword–for the domination of the world and the subjugation of her peoples.

As I continued my reading and research, I discovered that the CFR had far more in common with the Illuminati than a mere use of the same terminology. The facts of the conspiratorial plot are known to us. The question in my mind remains unanswered as to whether we can thwart their well placed efforts.

One of the reasons you have heard so little about the Council on Foreign Relations, is because its rules, like those of the Illuminati, require that important meetings of the membership remain an eternal secret! Article II of the organization bylaws contends that:

"It is an express condition of membership in the Council, to which condition every member accedes by virtue of his or her membership, that members will observe such rules and regulations as may be prescribed from time to time by the Board of Directors concerning the conduct of the Council meetings or the attribution of statements made therein, and that any disclosure, publication, or other action by a member in contravention thereof may be regarded by the Board of Directors in its sole discretion as ground for termination or suspension of membership pursuant to Article I of the Bylaws."

Page 182 of the CFR's 1991 Annual Report further states that "it would not be in compliance, with the organization's non-attribution rule for a meeting participant ...

"(i) to publish a speaker; his statement in attributed form in a newspaper; (ii) to repeat it on television or radio, or on a speaker's platform, or in a classroom; or (iii) to go beyond a memo of limited circulation, by distributing the attributed statement in a company or government agency newsletter ... A meeting participant is forbidden knowingly to transmit the attributed statement to a newspaper reporter or other such person who is likely to publish it in a public medium. The essence of the Rule... is simple enough: participants in Council meetings should not pass along an attributed statement in circumstances where there is substantial risk that it will promptly be widely circulated or published."

Well, so much for the freedom of the press! What could be so important that such secrecy is required if the purpose of the CFR is not to influence U.S. policy in the direction of world government ...

a world government that does not take into consideration the welfare of its citizens?

In order to accomplish its mission of leading the American people in a New World Order, the CFR has been using a strategy very similar to the one employed by Adam Weishaupt. It was designed to surround leaders in high places with member of the Council, targeting especially the key advisory positions in the executive branch of the U.S. government, until the Council's members were in absolute and complete control of the nation's presidency. In furtherance of their goals the tactic would also be used and applied to the fields of education, the media, the military and banking, with CFR members eventually becoming the leaders in each of these fields.

The goal of the CFR, quite simply put, was to influence all aspects of society in such a way that one day Americans would awaken to find themselves in the midst of a one-world system whether they liked it or not. Their hope was to get Americans to the point where entering a world government would seem as natural and American as baseball and apple pie. Although this scenario might seem preposterous to many, I respectfully suggest that the reader entertains the scope and concept of how far the CFR's plans have already come. To implement such "Order" does require some time for planning, execution and on line bringing of such new regime.

Using illuministic tactics and with the backing from the major global foundations, the CFR has been able to advance its agenda rapidly and with relative ease. During the 1920's and 30's the organization made significant strides toward control of the Democratic Party, and by the 1940's had managed to establish a foothold in the Republican Party as well. Since the early 1950's the progress has been more than merely significant. Today, the Republican Party is saturated with members of the CFR; members who propagate the idea of a New World Order. It must be stated that there is very little difference between these parties, since the advent of global communications and shortened distances. Both parties are controlled by the CFR and it various sister factions, all operating for the common goal of the CFR.

Numerous historical antecedents not only exist but have been followed to the letter while building the CFR into a power to be reckoned with. With the start of World War II, the CFR, thanks to the superb help of Franklin D. Roosevelt, managed to gain control of the State Department, and therefore, our foreign policy. Even today, this department as well as others remain firmly under the control of the CFR. Recent foreign policy directives toward the warring factions of the Mid East more than prove this point. The involvement of the United States, the United Nations, and the Arab League in the affairs of Iraq adequately verify the writer's contention that the war waged between the Coalition forces/Kuwait and Iraq show a greater goal was at stake.

It was not merely the issue of Mid East oil. It was one dictator's will against the will of a larger and more powerful one. Oil played a significant part but it was not the only cause for the hostile action. The reader must bear in mind that Kuwait, only recently, was a part of the state of Iraq. It was through United Nations Decree that Iraq was forced to give up its territory, and cede political government in the region once known as a province of Iraq. No one considered the will of the Iraqi people. It was done in a covert and underhanded way. All signs point to the infiltrated Department of State. It was a CFR member who voted that such action was compatible with the furtherance of the New World Order.

Rene Wormser, a member of the Reese Committee explained so well how the United States permitted itself to be drawn into and accept the CFR. Such history dates back to the Second World War. Wormser stated:

"[The] organization became virtually an agency of the government when World War II broke out. The Rockefeller Foundation had started and financed certain studies known as THE WAR AND PEACE STUDIES, manned largely by associates of the Council; the State Department, in due course, took these studies over, retaining the major personnel which the Council on Foreign Relations had supplied."

A Closer Look at the CFR and The United Nations

CFR control of the State Department would insure U.S. membership in the United Nations following World War II. In fact the Council on Foreign Relations would act through the State Department to establish the U.N. These details, long known by Consular Operations and Central Intelligence personnel, were finally revealed in 1969 during a debate between Lt. Colonel Archibald Roberts and Congressman Richard I. Ottinger, Director, United States Committee on the United Nations. During this somewhat spectacular debate, Col. Roberts testified:

" . . the United Nations was spawned two weeks after Pearl Harbor in the office of Secretary of State, Cordell Hull. In a letter to the President, Franklin Roosevelt, dated 22 December, 1941, Secretary Hull, at the direction of his faceless sponsors ... recommended the founding of a Presidential Advisory Committee on Post War Foreign Policy. This Committee was in fact the planning commission for the United Nations and its charter."

Col. Roberts went on to identify the people who made up the Committee, besides Secretary Hull. The list included various department advisors and staff members, CFR officials, and leaders in education, the media, and foreign policy research.

These are the real founders of the United Nations. Altogether, ten of the fourteen Committee members belonged to the CFR. As Roberts pointed out, "Each member of the Committee ... was without exception, a member of the Council on Foreign Relations, or under the control of the Council on Foreign Relations.

In 1945, at the founding conference of the United Nations, forty-seven members of the CFR were in the United States delegation. Included among these were Edward Stettinius, the new Secretary of State; John Foster Dulles; Adlai Stevenson; Nelson Rockefeller; and Alger Hiss, who was the Secretary General of the U.N.'s founding conference.

To make certain that the United States would not back out of joining the United Nations, as it did with the League of Nations, the international body would this time be located on American soil. Such a gesture, it was determined, would make the American public less resistant to the move. The land for the United Nations building was "graciously" donated by John D. Rockefeller, Jr. The land had been a slaughterhouse and the soil where the U.N. buildings now stand had been fully saturated with the blood of the slaughtered animals. Knowing what I do about the purpose of the United Nations, I can think of no place more fitting.

By getting the United States to join the U.N., which represents a limited form of world government, the Council on Foreign Relations had accomplished its first major objective. Using its influence in public education and the media, the CFR would now proceed to cast a favorable image for the United Nations among the American public, eventually leading step-by-step to U.S. participation in a full blown system of world government. This, it was realized, would take some time.

Had the CFR attempted and tried to bring the United States into a world government all at once, the effort would have failed. The American people would have reacted full force against any such attempt. The immediate purpose of the U.N. was therefore merely to warm Americans up to the idea of global government. You may rest assured that it was a well constructed conditioning plan.

Since the United Nations was founded in 1945, two of its main leaders have been guilty of outrageous actions. Alger Hiss, for example, was exposed as a Soviet operative and Spy. Secretary U Thant praised Lenin as a leader whose "ideals of peace and peaceful coexistence among states have won widespread international acceptance and they are in line with the aims of he U/N. Charter."

Secretary General Kurt Waldheim was regretfully and erroneously targeted and smeared by factions who were not able to exercise any degree of control over him. They branded him as a Nazi Foot Soldier, and smeared his honest name throughout the world. It was the largest slime and smear campaign ever undertaken by the United States Department of State and the CFR in its entirety. All America is aware of the atrocities attributed to Waldheim, having heard about them or read about them in the international media.

Yet in spite of these revelations, most Americans today continue to view the U.N. as a "good organization." It is truly amazing what a media publicity campaign can accomplish. It can cover the misdeeds of many and destroy the very honor of the one man who was totally dedicated to promote good will among men. One of the oldest tricks of the Illuminati was to label their enemies as having the black hearts and evil motives that were actually their own. In this way, down through the ages, they have branded and burned their enemies, and turned the gullible public against their adversaries.

Along with being responsible for the United Nations, the Council on Foreign Relations would go on to serve as a mainspring for numerous spin-off groups, such as the Club of Rome, the Trilateral Commission, and with some error, the Bilderberger society. All but the Bilderbergers were designed to carry out a specific task within the broader mission of establishing a allanNew World Order. The creation of these organizations represents a restructuring of the one-world political hierarchy. This hierarchy is always changing, revising, and adapting itself to current situations. This must be done so that it can more successfully and effectively further its agenda.

The hierarchy, among other things, had called for world government to be achieved in stages through the forming of world administrative regions. This was in accordance with the U.N. Charter, which encourages the implementation and administration of world government on a regional basis. [According to chapter 8, Article 52 (2-3) and 53 (1) of the Charter, under "Regional Arrangements.]

The strategy was really quite simple. The countries of the world would first be merged into several regions. This would serve to break down the long standing concepts of national sovereignty, then, region by region, they would be merged into a system of world government. The idea was grand, but national politics were not counted upon. All one has to do to understand this is look at Europe as it tries to ratify the Maastricht Treaty or look at the doubt within many American workers as their plants move to Mexico because of NAFTA. (North American Free Trade Agreement.)

However, as previously indicated, with emphasis placed on nationalism, it was soon realized that regional government would be next to impossible to achieve politically because of resistance to the idea from the world's people. That's when the powers-that-be decided to divide the world into primary economic regions first, hoping to pave the way for later political unions based and predicated on the same geopolitical boundaries.

The Bilderbergers

In order to accomplish this feat, several special task organizations were established to oversee the creation of regional trade associations. The society responsible for Europe's economic integration would be the Bilderberg Group, here known better as the Bilderbergers.

At first it was assumed that this society would form a complimentary relationship with the U.N., the CFR. The Club of Rome, the TLC and numerous other sister organizations founded to promote a singular one world order. This was not to be the case as the members of the Bilderbergers Society were (are) members of Europe's old hard line aristocracy. They were more nationalistic than the entire global cabal combined. They began to break away from the CFR gang, and forge their own New World Order, based on freedom and equality for all citizens.

The present day and public name for the group was derived from the Bilderberg Hotel in Oosterbeck, Holland, the site of the association's first meeting in 1954. The present day group consists of approximately one hundred power-elite from the member nations. Most of them are members of the North Atlantic Treaty Organization. However, Austria and France were admitted because the organization originally appeared within their respective borders. Many of these Society members have come from a long heritage of Templar Knights. Many of their ancestors served as Knights Templars as well as Crusaders throughout the wars in the Holy lands. Today's leadership is at relative ease with the Council on Foreign Relations.

The express purpose of the Bilderberger Society was to regionalize all of Europe. This goal was revealed by Giovanni Agnelli, the head of Fiat and one of the leaders of the present day Bilderbergers. Agnelli stated:

"European integration is our goal and where the politicians have failed, we, the old world elite, intend to succeed."

The original seat of the prior Bilderbergers was Schloss Bilderberg, in Passau, Germany. Here they met for hundreds of years to promote commerce between the many fiefdoms along the riverways of Austria, Germany and France. These Dukes ruled their lands with fists of iron and wills of steel.

George McGhee, the former U.S. ambassador to Germany, revealed that "the Treaty of Rome, which brought the Common Market into being was nurtured at the Bilderberg meetings." In other words, today's European Economic Community, which is soon to become a political reality, on December 31, 1992, is indeed a product of the Bilderberg Group.

Although the Bilderbergers share some of the goals discussed earlier in this article, they differ considerably as to what the average citizen stands to gain in giving up his nationality to further a United States of Europe. It is common knowledge that most, if not all of Europe, presently has adequate housing, food, clothing, and most important, medical care for all of its citizenry. No one lives in a slum like environment. Children receive free education, only subject to the students obtaining and holding a passing scholastic grade. Although money is an object, or better stated... the piece d'resistance, the food of the buerger is deemed to come first. It is the contention of this writer that the goals expressed by the Bilderbergers merit closer examination.

As my friend Dave Emory puts is so well ... "its food for thought and grounds for further research."

For lack of space, the rank and file of the Bilderbergers shall not be discussed in this article. A larger and more informative expose is being planned for the next installment.

Therefore, the focus of the next installment shall be directed to exposing as well as discussing the negatives and positives of the Bilderberger Society, and its impact on the rest of the here to fore named organizations. As alternate topic the Tri-Lateral Commission, its history, agenda, and opportunists growth patterns shall be scrutinized. Exposure of these organizations can not harm the American Will to survive. It merely gives us the much needed ammunition to fight a war for which, by virtue of our large and demographic landscape, we are ill equipped to wage.

Afterthoughts

A lone and single thought, nurtured and brought to action on our common behalf is a round fired for freedom. Let us not permit this chapter of history to be written without our input for proposed change. Never give in to these Globalists. Remember the battle cry of John Paul Jones ...

"I have not yet begun to fight ...

I urge each and every one of you to shout with me, the new cry for battle ... the pledge we learned in grade school; the Pledge we grew up with, and learned to honor and revere ... Ladies and gentlemen, I am referring to the pledge upon which this country's way of life is based... I am referring to

THE PLEDGE OF ALLEGIANCE TO THE FLAG OF THE UNITED STATES OF AMERICA!!

This short pledge says it far better than I could ever dare. It speaks not for the Globalists; it speaks not for a New World order. It speaks of the flag of these United States, and not the flag of a United Nations. It speaks of One Nation under God, with liberty and justice for all. This was the dream of the Founders of the United States of America. While they may have dreamed of taking their dream to the whole of the world, they never in their wildest nightmares imagined a one world government based upon the enslavement of its peoples.

We cannot let this country be lost because her citizenry cannot see what the global masters have in store for us. We must form a figurative chain, interlocking arms to show our national pride and unity. This must be done immediately, before they manage to separate and divide us. Their tactics include clever plans for dividing and conquering a people. If you are made to believe that you are separate and apart from other Americans, you won't mind when their rights are taken from them. And slowly one by one, with the same tactic known in prewar Germany as "the salami tactique," you will suddenly realize that you have given up all your rights and you too will have become a slave of the new world order.

We have a covenant, signed and sealed with the blood of those who came, lived, fought and died for liberty and freedom long before we were born. You live freely because of their commitment to an ideal of self-determination, liberty and justice for all. The thread of their dreams that reach from them to you will surely whither and die if you do not pick up their ideal and carry it to its completion. Fight for your freedom... fight with everything you have. Let the united will of the American people preserve our way of life and our ideals for those who shall, God willing, come after US.

Lastly, let us proudly tell the world that we are Americans ... we have a history ... we have a purpose ... we stand as a beacon for the rest of humanity of freedom, liberty and justice. We will not be swallowed up by global masters who wish to exploit us for their own economic gain. We will march forward with our arms interlocked and proclaim to the world that we only pledge allegiance to the flag of the United States of America ... and we're damned proud of it!

A Final Word of Warning...

If you do not take personal responsibility for your country and your way of life right now ... you will only have yourself to blame as your liberties erode. Get involved ... get informed and then get started informing others. We must reject the one world government, we must reject the U.N. troops on our shores, we must reject NAFTA, GATT, the WTO...

Wake up and take back your country!

If not you ... who?

If not now ... when?

The Templar Charter

Note from Rayelan: When Gunther and I were in Austria in 1994, I was shown numerous documents. One of them was the original charter that formed the Knights Templars. It was written in a language I couldn't read. I think it was Latin, but the manuscript itself made the language hard to identify.

The man who showed the document to me translated it for me. In 1996, when Gunther was writing articles for the print version of Rumor Mill News, I asked him to send me a copy of the document. He said he was not allowed to send a copy, but he could translate it and send me the translation in his own handwriting. The following is what I received:

"On a rain swept, desolate day, at Larambique, in the foot hills of the massive Mt. Blanc, a group of dedicated monks and their worldly brothers gathered on September 24, of the year of our Sovereign Lord, Jesus Christ.... we are writing the year Anno Domini 938.

"They gathered to form a New Order to keep alive the words which God had granted Solomon, in a dream.

"Although the drenching rains continued, a large beam of light filtered down to the statue of the Christ child, securely carried in the hands of his Godly Mother, Mary. The fright and silence were awesome as those gathered beheld the sight. All present began to speak at the same time, each in the language of his birth. Within minutes the babble ceased and they began to work on the plans to form a new charter, granting that each living being had diverse basic rights. When they were finished, they had created the following charter:

"Each living being possesses basic divine rights. The most basic right is the right of self determination. Each and every being upon Earth is divinely given the right to control his own life. Other inalienable2 divinely granted rights include food, shelter, clothing and fair compensation for work well done."

---

[2]"in-a-lien-able," meaning incapable of having a "lien" placed on them. Look up the words 'alienable" and "inalienable" in your dictionary.

Gunther and the Philippine Gold Transfer

In December of 1993, shortly after Gunther was released from prison in the United States, a man came to visit us in St. Louis. This man told Gunther about large amounts of gold that have been hidden in the Philippines for an undeterminable about of time. Most people believe this gold came from the Japanese, but Gunther told me that the history of the Philippine gold goes back to Lemuria, South America, and King Solomon's Temple. — Rayelan

The Philippine Islands are the last traces of the continent of Lemuria. Gunther believed that the Philippines are the key to the future of the planet. He told me that under the Pacific Ocean, near the Philippines, is an underwater city. He said that his Faction, (Faction Two) has a private Navy which is mainly made up of submarines. He said that he and others who are close to him have been to the underground city many times.

One of the Admirals who used to visit me told me that they use light emitting 'sea creatures' to light the area. The 'sea creatures' are held in some kind of emulsion on the walls. The Admiral said that when you enter a room, you 'flick your bic' and the 'sea creatures' compete with each other to see which one can make the brightest light.

Gunther also told me that when the Templar Order was destroyed by the King of France and the Pope, that the Templar fleet transported the Templar gold to several places. One was on Oak Island, but that gold was eventually transported to a cave in Utah. The major part of the Templar gold was taken to the Philippines. The surviving Templars created a priesthood among some of the Philippine natives.

The Templars took wives from the Philippine royal line. This line was descended from Lemurian royalty. The Templar priesthood was set up to protect the gold that was hidden there. It was also set up to protect the Lemurian treasures that are there.

Over the ensuing centuries other members of secret orders transported sacred texts from all over the world to caves in the Philippines. The texts that were transported to these caves were made of gold or stone. Texts from papyrus, leather or paper were taken to the salt mines near Salzburg, Austria.

After World War Two other treasures were hidden in the Philippines. These treasures were hidden there to keep them safe for the people of the world. Those who hid them understood what the New World Order had in store for the people of the world. The treasures that were hidden in the Philippines were put there to provide an economic future to the people of the world after the NWO had economically collapsed.

Here is the story that Gunther wrote regarding his involvement in the gold transfer. He sent this information to me while he was "supposedly" in prison in Austria. He was imprisoned for not paying a hotel bill. The hotel bill had already been paid by General Shelton who had called and re-activated Gunther due to the war in Haiti. I was so angry with Gunther for going back to work for the CIA and Navy Intelligence, that I left him in the hotel and caught a midnight train out of Vienna to Frankfurt. From there I caught a plane back to California.

Within a few hours of arriving home, I received a call from the Vienna police. I was told they had arrested Gunther for failure to pay his bill. No matter what I said or swore to in affidavits, R was convicted. He was sentenced to two years in an Austrian prison. During these two years my contacts in the Philippines told me that he and Austrian President Kurt Waldheim were in the Philippines finishing up the gold transfer.

The reason I am including this information in the Obergon Chronicles is because I find it an amazing coincidence that Atalon needed gold for the biosphere that surrounded his palace on the planet Obergon. Sitchen talks about the Annunaki that arrive every three to four thousand years to pick up the gold that has been mined, and Gunther and the Templars have a stash of gold in the Philippines that is *far* in excess of the total amount of gold that the bankers claim exists on earth.

The following information comes from an article written by R. G. Blair for a newsletter. It is published in its entirely on Rumor Mill News at this link:
http://www.rumormillnews.com/cgi-bin/archive.cgi?read=908

A Worldwide Gold Standard

Gunther Russbacher became the central figure in the transfer of a huge amount of gold from the Philippines to Austria. Russbacher and his wife, Rayelan, were told that the gold would be used to create gold backed currencies for all of the world governments. The gold returned to Europe in November of 1994. It went into a refinery in Greece where the bars were melted down and the Swastika was removed. The gold was then distributed to the countries whose treasuries had been looted by Hitler. There is enough gold to put every country in Europe on a gold standard, with some left over for other countries. When the gold based currencies go into effect, this will mean the end Federal Reserve System, the age old enemy of the royal bloodline.

Operation White Robe

The Gold Transfer

From his home in California, Russbacher orchestrated the transfer of the Philippine gold, code named White Robe, to Austria. Once he had secured "the firm offer to sell" from the Philippines, the deal came to the attention of his enemies within the banking world, and two attempts were made to kill him. His health had suffered under the stress of the recent open heart surgery as well as his confinement for the last four years. His liver was swollen, his pancreas was failing, and his kidneys were shutting down.

He was afraid to go into an American hospital. He felt he would be killed. Several men, who were involved in the gold transfer, accompanied him to Austria. He was arrested for entering on illegal documents. During the arrest, he suffered a heart attack. He was taken, via helicopter, to a hospital. The charges were eventually dropped and he proceeded in the completion of the gold transfer.

What had appeared to be a done deal while he was in America, soon became a nightmare of tangled threads that stretched from the gold mines of King Solomon, to the gold teeth of Hitler's holocaust victims. Russbacher was impeded at every turn. He was told by representatives of the Austrian government that the Jews felt all of the gold that Russbacher was trying to bring back into the country came from the teeth of their grandfathers. Russbacher had been told that the gold he was bringing back... in the first transfer, was Austrian gold that had been stolen by Hitler in 1938. He had been told that the symbol for Austrian gold, a fox, was still stamped on all the bars. But he wasn't told that the bars also had HH and the swastika stamped on them. (The HH stands for Hitler Helvetia. Helvetia is a Latin name for Switzerland. The Swiss were Hitler's bankers.)

To Save the Gold Transfer Russbacher had to Give it Away

After betrayal, intrigue, lies and disinformation, Russbacher found himself growing weaker and sicker. The heart pain was unbearable. To stop the pain, he started drinking. His pancreas had shut down. The alcohol went directly into his blood stream. In that condition he could do nothing to complete the gold transfer.

After weeks of put-offs from the Austrian National Bank, Russbacher finally realized that if he were to ever accomplish what his ancestors have been trying to accomplish for hundreds of years, then he had to let go of everything. The commission on the gold deal would have made him and his wife two of the richest people in the world. Because of the way they had been treated at the hands of an out of control government, they already had plans for publishing and film companies that would begin to educate the world in the conspiracy to enslave it.

It was hard to let go of the dream of awakening the world, but there was no other way. On a train from Salzburg to Vienna, Russbacher finally decided that the only way to save the gold deal was to give it away—everything, including the commissions on which he had planned to build his new life with his wife, Rayelan.

He called the man who had been instrumental in keeping him alive during his years in prison. Kurt Waldheim was the president of Austria while Gunther was incarcerated in the United States. Now he was the head of a non governmental organization called The League of the United Nations. Russbacher and his wife went straight there.

Waldheim was with the King of Denmark as the Russbachers entered the outer office. They were told to wait. The King soon left and they were ushered in. In a few sentences Russbacher explained what was happening. Waldheim gave him the name of a man within the Foreign Ministry and arranged for them to meet. Waldheim then showed them out, introducing them to Helmut Kohl, Chancellor of Germany, as they left.

Russbacher turned the gold deal completely over to Waldheim, including all the commission. When his American partners, who had financed the deal, for a share of the commission, discovered what he had done, they stopped funding him. The Russbachers were broke on the streets of Vienna. Gunther called the American Embassy in Vienna, where he had been CIA station chief in the 70's. He asked for help. They told him due to the Haiti crisis, he had just been reactivated into the Navy. He was told an airplane would come to take him and his wife back to the United States.

Rayelan felt another set-up coming on. She knew her husband had been on probation when he left the United States, and he would be arrested if he returned. She could not make him see what was going to happen. In anger she told him that she was not going to stand by and watch him end up in an American prison again. She caught a midnight train, from Vienna to Frankfurt, and took a plane home to California.

By the time she arrived home, Gunther had been arrested for not paying his hotel bill. Within weeks, Gunther was back in an Austrian prison, serving two years for defrauding a hotel.

The "gold deal" continues to move forward in transfers from the Philippines and other countries. It is not known how quickly the world's governments will see their currency replaced with gold-backed currencies. But from the headlines in current newspapers, the whole world is suddenly focusing on Nazi gold.

Russbacher and his wife concluded their part in the gold transfer in 1994. They were to be paid a 1/2 percent commission. To this day, they have received nothing from the transfer. The Swiss, the Swedes and the French surely wish that they had never heard of Nazi Gold. Israel demanded that Austria share the gold. Austria refused and told Israel if they wanted to look for Jewish gold they needed to investigate Switzerland, Sweden, France, and Liechtenstein.... plus all 26 international bankers who make up the Federal Reserve. Major investigations into Jewish bank accounts in all three countries have discredited the once noble reputation of Swiss, French and Liechtenstein banks.

A quick reading of any major newspaper archive from December of 1996 will show you that Israel followed the advice it was given by the Austrians, and are forcing Swiss and Swedish banks to finally turn over Jewish gold. Soon, Israel will take on Liechtenstein. But it is doubtful that they will ever ask the Federal Reserve member banks to turn over their Jewish gold.

In a letter that Russbacher wrote to his wife on November 26, 1994 he gave the partial history of the gold transfer3 which was code named Operation White Robe:

"Let me give you a bit of background for Operation White Robe. (This was the code name of the gold transfer.) "It begins with the U.S. government imposing an embargo against the Swiss in WWII. They (the Swiss) had been making deals with the Nazis. They allowed them to use their rail systems to bring war materials to the German troops of Italy. In return, the Swiss were the true bankers of the Third Reich.

"To further the true meaning of hypocrisy, the Swiss received coal from Germany. (the Swiss have none of their own). The U.S. government went straight for the jugular and imposed an all out food embargo. Almost 60% of Swiss food was imported from other European markets. The Swiss told the U.S., in 1944, to go to hell and they began importing food stuffs from South America. The vessels flew Liberian and Swiss flags. The U.S. put a halt to that in December of 1944.

---

[3]See www.rumormillnews.com for documents

The Swiss had almost all of Hitler's gold, which he had seized from Jews, the National Bank of Austria, Belgium, France and numerous other countries. The gold was a real sore point for the U.S. They wanted it in their hands. The Swiss, operating on orders from Hitler's men, began the long and worrisome transport of the metal to Argentina and Paraguay. After March of 1954, the gold bars and chunks of used gold, were shipped to a remote area of the Philippines.

"There it has remained until we (meaning Gunther, Rayelan and the group they worked with) entered the picture. Only a hundred or so people knew about this horde of precious metals. The White Robes (The Knights Templars) became involved because great gold monstrances (crucifixes) as well as solid gold chalices and coins were robbed from many churches (Catholic of course). It became a brand new quest for about 30 of us. Most of these men were my seniors and have long since died without fulfilling their cause. With the deaths of my two best friends in Laos this February, (1994) I was the only one left who was empowered to move the gold.

"Even though it looked to you that I was a recent player in the gold transfer, the truth is, I have known about it my entire life, and I knew that eventually the gold would return to Austria. It will return to Austrian in 1995, 50 years after the end of the war."

This article can be read in full by using this url to pull up the entire article:

GUNTHER RUSSBACHER, POLITICAL PRISONER OF THE NWO
http://www.rumormillnews.com/cgi-bin/archive.cgi?read=908

Part V

A Message from Odon

Atalon and Raelon's Father, Odon, and Some of His Friends Speak to ALL of us!

It has been a long time since we have spoken with you. We use the royal "we" because as we speak to you, both parts of our being are fully present. We are referring to the part of us which has incarnated upon the earth and the part of us which has never known physical incarnations. Both parts are here and speaking with you. Thank you for joining with us on this day. I am the Master you know as Metatron. You are in my ashram. Being in my ashram means that you are my student... I am your teacher.

On Terra you know me as Metatron. On Obergon, the home planet, you called me Father. Throughout the combined universes I am known as the Great Lord Odon. All aspects of our being are fully present with you at this time. In ancient days when advanced souls incarnated in positions of power, their full soul natures surrounded them. This is why the kings and queens of old used the term "We" when they spoke.

Once a ruler sat upon their throne and placed the crown of power upon their heads, their crown chakra opened up and they were able to blend their consciousness with the full essence of their soul being. They were also able to solicit outside help from other wise souls. And so, the custom of using the royal "we" began when humans could still experience their true soul nature. It was carried on as custom by succeeding monarchs who had completely forgotten that at one time, there was a meaning, to the royal "We."

From the beginning of your stay upon the planet Terra, you have been in my Ashram.

However, recently, at a soul level, you asked to be transferred to the ashram of the Master Melchizedek. Your request was heard and the transfer was honored.

It is important for you and for others to understand why the transfer can be granted in this lifetime. After many thousands of incarnations in Terran bodies, you have approached a point in your evolution where it is possible for you to awaken your full memory while in your Terran body. Once you are able to awaken your memory, you will be able to share with others the secrets of awakenings.

Master Melchizedek is the teacher of the Chronicler souls. These souls remember the secrets of Awakenings. Let us try to help you understand why it is necessary to regain your full memory.

Sanat Kumara, an older and wiser being from a different evolutionary soul family, was chosen by the regents of our area to be the one who accompanied all of you to your new home. You and several of your brothers and sisters were sent ahead as scouts. Then you returned home and lived in Shamballah for many eons. Shamballah is the school which was set up to educate the souls who were the first to individuate. These souls were the offspring of all the Great Lords and Ladies who make up this universe. The first children to individuate spent an incredibly long time alone, and so we parents decided to create a school where the first born could study together and have companionship.

Shamballah was never physical. It still exists behind the star you know as Sirius.

Even though it was created as a school, it long ago outgrew this purpose. Now it serves as Universal Headquarters. One of its main functions in regards to Terra, is overseeing the breeding experiment.

There was much to be done upon the planet Terra to prepare it for the eventual housing of the souls from Shamballah. The scouts from Shamballah, who chose to stay were in charge of the breeding process. These early scouts came in their Obergonian bodies, which are denser than Shamballan bodies. they did this in order to bring with them the DNA of Obergon. This was probably the most important part of the preparation stage, next, of course, to the preparation of the planet itself. If the proper combination of chemicals and minerals are not present upon the planet, then it would be impossible to create the bodies that are needed to house the souls from Obergon.

Many souls decided that they could best serve their brothers and sisters by remaining on Terra from the very beginning of our colonization and development period. These souls helped prepare both the physical aspect of the planet, as well as the individual bodies. The Obergonian body lived in the Terran atmosphere for hundreds of thousands of years. In the beginning, the only way that a body would die would be if the soul using it decided it had finished its mission upon the planet.

Some of these early settlers lost contact with Shamballah at an early stage. They forgot why they had come to the planet. They became blind. The earth plane causes many to lose their memories. This is what happened. Some of the Terran settlers lost their memory just by being in the Terran atmosphere. Others lost their memories because they had fallen under the spell the traders and travelers from developed planets. These beings had come to exploit the developing bodies and evolving souls of the earth inhabitants.

Some of our people could resist the powerful mind to mind melds that these invaders used to enslave our people. It was these strong souls who called in reinforcements in the form of a visit by my daughter, Raelon. It was her duty to go to the planet and free those souls who were encased in the early versions of the human body.

These souls had been enslaved by the invaders and also by members of their own family from Shamballah, who had joined with the invaders, and set up a kingdom of rich and fat owners who lived upon the labor of the slaves, the little people who were still undergoing evolutionary growth.

When Raelon came onto the earth plane she did so in the body she wore at Shamballah. The vibrations carried by this body were enough to awaken all of the souls that were housed in the tall bodies which were originally transplanted to the earth from Obergon, the home planet. These original bodies were transported to earth so that their DNA could be mixed with the developing life upon planet Terra.

It is important at this time that you realize that there were no other souls using the planet. Terra had been a school many millions of years before, but it had closed because all its students had graduated. Even the soul that carried the light for the planet had graduated and the planet was a dark planet without any life at all.

It was decreed by the Planetary Council in charge of developing souls, that the earth in the orbit of the sun Sol, would be the most likely planet to turn into a replica of the home planet on which many of these souls had begun their training. And so… early expeditions were sent to the planet to prepare it for the eventual coming of these souls.

In addition to using Terra for the Obergonian School, the Planetary Council decided that while Terra was in the evolutionary phase, it could be utilized as a home planet for some of Great Lord Michael developing children. Michael's children had never lived in physical form before. And so, as the planet began recreating itself in a form which would be suitable to the children of Odon, Michael began bringing his young souls to school.

Before any school could be established upon Terra, certain things had to be done. First, the energy of the planet had to be held together. Two great beings were assigned this task. In actuality the great beings are one, but as yet they are still unjoined and so they are two. They are Sanat Kumara and the entity you know as Terra. The two came to the earth plane bringing with them the two energies that are needed for the development of the souls upon the planet.

There will be more on Terra later, but now we must return to what we were saying about the Shamballan or Obergonian souls which were housed in the original bodies which had been transported to the earth plane for the specific job of bringing their DNA.

Some of the Shamballan souls had forgotten who they were and had joined with the invaders from other worlds. These invaders were immature beings who just wanted to have a good time upon Terra enslaving and misdirecting the little people who were part of the breeding experiment.

The soul of Raelon was dispatched to the earth to free the little people from their cruel slave masters. She was also sent to restore the memory, of who they are, to the souls who were trapped in the original Obergonian bodies. These souls were trapped inside the bodies because they had forgotten who they were. Most were tricked into forgetting by powerful hypnotic mindmelds used by the invaders from other worlds.

As was said earlier, Raelon came to Terra in her Shamballah body. This is very easily accomplished by us. We can travel anywhere we wish wearing the Shamballah body. We know how to adapt them to whatever condition we discover upon any planet. At times we are required to wear protective clothing for extended stays.

In the case of Raelon, her first visits to Terra were so brief that she was able to live upon the planet without protective shields. This was accomplished with the help of the ship that hovered near her at all times. When those on board saw that her body supplies were running low, she was transported back aboard the ship and her system was replenished. It must be remembered that the ship still hovers nearby, and all of the Children of Obergon can request permission to be brought aboard to be replenished.

In Raelon's case, these minitransporatations were so quick that the Terrans did not even know she was gone. She would simply disappear and reappear at another point. It was thought by those upon Terra that she was merely showing off, or showing her power so that none would doubt her. In fact she was replenishing herself so that she could continue her work upon Terra.

Because she chose to wear her Shamballah body instead of incarnating in a Terra body, she was able to change the illusion of the Shamballah souls immediately. There were no Obergonian souls upon Terra who had not attended the Shamballan School. Once a soul graduates from Shamballah, it is referred to as a Shamballan soul. This is used to differentiate between Obergonian souls who are still unevolved and those who have studied the mysteries of Shamballah as well as Obergon. The energy that is carried by a Shamballan body can immediately restore to balance any Shamballan soul, no matter what kind of body it is in. Raelon understood this and chose to come to Terra wearing her Shamballan body.

I use the terms Obergonian body and Shamballan body seemingly interchangeably. Let me explain the difference.

The two bodies were so similar that there was hardly any difference. In the case of Raelon, her Shamballah body was slightly more ethereal than the one she wore on Obergon, but for all practical purposes upon the earth, the two bodies were identical. You see, there is still no way upon the earth that we can explain to you the fact that all the same atoms make up a dark body and a light body, it's just a matter of density. In other words the atoms become lighter on certain planets or certain headquarters, and this makes the bodies seem different. The main difference between the two bodies was that the Obergonian body could reproduce with Terrans. The Shamballan body was asexual. When more Shamballan bodies are needed they are created in a laboratory in a process similar to cloning.

When Raelon transported down to planet earth to free the souls from the enslavement they had been enduring, she performed her job rather quickly and then returned home for further orders. Her orders required her to go to the Pleiades to help establish the Court of Justice in that developing system. The Pleiades were rapidly developing extreme intelligence and so it needed a system which would fairly insure that all rights to all souls.

Raelon chose to work with another from Shamballah named Fanra. Fanra was the first born son of Vestran. Great Lord Vestran had reached the level of Solar Lord and had agreed to hold the energy in stars which were not large enough to become black holes. The star Sol is in the Vestran Protectorate, as is the star Atreus around which Obergon, both sun and planet, was orbited. More will be said about this later, when Vesta and Celeste enter our story.

Raelon and Fanra were transported to the Pleiades and there with the help of many others they established the Galactic Judicial System of the Pleiades.

However, while upon the Pleiades, Raelon received a transmission regarding her sister soul, Sharlon. She was told that Sharlon had forgotten who she was and needed help upon Terra.

Fanra, Raelon and Fanra's brother Andron, quickly incarnated upon Terra. When they arrived, they discovered that the souls who had been awakened by Raelon's earlier trip to the planet were once again caught up in the maya of Terra.

Living in a physical body on Terra can sometimes lull you into a sense of peace and forgetfulness. This happens when conditions are so wonderful that the soul simply sinks into the beauty and bliss of Terra and enjoys the physical sensations. Terra can be similar to the old stories of fairyland where humans enjoyed the good feelings so much they simply sleep and enjoy. That is what was happening on the planet.

Sharlon had led the little people and the surviving Obergonian bodies to a part of the African continent which was very hot and tropical and lush. The food was plentiful and the life was easy. Most of them chose to sleep and enjoy the lovely sensations their bodies gave them.

Sharlon still wore the body of one of the early Obergonian settlers. She had stolen it from the soul who had been using it up until Sharlon arrived and used her authority as high priestess from Obergon to usurp the body. The original Obergonian bodies were tall and white and covered with fine golden hair, very similar to the body hair upon most humans now only slightly more plentiful.

When Raelon and Fanra returned from the Pleiades, they chose to incarnate in little people's bodies. They incarnated as part of the priesthood of Melchizedek and as such, they retained their memories. With their wisdom in tact, they rapidly rose to priest and priestess level.

Andron was fascinated by Sharlon and chose to incarnate in a body produced as an offspring of two early settlers. Obergonian bodies do not require the usual childhood growth period. Within a few Terran years he had grown to adulthood and became the consort of Sharlon.

Their misadventures are the subject of another tale. The purpose of this transmission is to explain to the soul of Raelon and to others why they need to join the priesthood of Melchizedek.

There are many priests and priestesses of Melchizedek upon the planet. These are the souls who had chosen to stay from the very beginning. They could be called the early historians or Chroniclers of the Terran Mission. In addition to the Chronicler part of their mission, they served as examples to the little people of what living a pure life could be. They also passed on the oral tradition. These souls have populated the planet ever since the reconstruction phase some 20 million years ago.

When Raelon and Fanra returned to earth they joined the ranks of the Chronicler souls, because these souls were ones who had the power. Sharlon felt that the power was with her... but she had lost her memory. Without the full memory of who you are and why you are here, you can have no real power. Therefore, it must be remembered that the real power lies with those beings who retain or regain their memory. Remember this!

The real power is with those who have their memory!

Sharlon and Andron were the rulers and protectors of the little People, the ones you now call humans. Sharlon had stopped the breeding experiment because she could not bear the thought of joining her body with, what she called, the ugly bodies of the little people. Their skin was darker and their bodies were smaller. Because they did not appeal to her esthetic senses, she chose to mate only with Obergonian bodies. As much as she disliked young Lord Atalon, she acted just like him.

Sharlon and Andron had many children. However, because Sharlon had forgotten her original orders, the children she bore merely perpetuated the line of settler bodies. The new souls could NOT remember the missions they came to perform. The new souls took their direction from their mother, Sharlon and father, Andron. Sharlon and Andron set down many rules and laws, but neither of them remembered their original missions, therefore, nothing they taught their children had anything to do with the wishes of Sharlon's father.

The settler bodies lived a longer time upon the planet than did the bodies of the little people. This was because certain genetic changes were made in these bodies before they were sent from Obergon. It was known that they must survive long enough to finish their original mission. It was not foreseen that the souls inhabiting the bodies would be loath to give them up and the bodies would live upon the earth for thousands of years after the original mission had been forgotten.

So in the length of time that Sharlon and Andron ruled the encampments of little people, Raelon and Fanra incarnated hundreds of times in the bodies of the little people. Finally they realized that they could do little against Sharlon and her tyranny while living in the little bodies, and so they incarnated in the bodies of Sharlon's offspring. From this position of privilege it was felt that they could get Sharlon's attention and restore her memory to her.

It would have been easier for these two dedicated souls to have simply returned home to Shamballah and gone to Terra again in their Shamballan bodies. If you will remember, the energy of a Shamballan body would have simply restored her memory by being in her presence. However, the plan was not very well thought out by these two. You must remember that both Fanra and Raelon are developing souls. This mission was one of the first that they had performed on their own. It was left up to them to decide how best to correct the situation.

For hundreds of years both Fanra and Raelon remembered who they were, but after they incarnated in Obergonian bodies and out of the Order of Melchizedek, they began to lose their memories. Soon they were no better than Andron and Sharlon.

It is here that the story of Raelon and Fanra and their help in the breeding experiment ends. After they lost their memories they were no longer able to help create the evolutionary bodies which would house the influx of Obergonian souls that were scheduled to study on Terra.

Now it is understood, why it is time for the transfer from the Ashram of Metatron to the Ashram of Melchizedek must be made. The Priests and Priestesses of the Order of Melchizedek remember who they are. The memory in one of the Raelons is about to awaken. Because of this, it is time to transfer her to another Master so that he and his ashram of workers upon the planet can carefully work with her while her memory returns. What is currently happening to one of the Raelons will soon be happening to many of you.

There are several Raelon units upon the planet at this time. Remember that when the original souls came to earth they had the choice to remain whole or to split. Some of the souls split into millions of pieces, some only into hundreds. In the case of Raelon, she split into thousands, but most of the pieces have been gathered back together and there are just a few upon the planet at the moment. The other pieces have returned to the original soul body which overshadows and influences the remaining Raelons.

The transfer from the ashram of Metatron to the ashram of Melchizedek was made for another reason. By being a member of the ashram of Metatron, or Odon, Raelon learned the skill of communication. It is now time to combine her skills in communication with her skills at leading the people in the way of the light. And so the transfer was granted and the order of Melchizedek has now officially accepted her into its ranks and she will soon be assigned certain helpers who will remain with her and assist in the work she will be doing.

Master Mel, as we call him, is the spokesperson of the goddess. The original priesthood was of the goddess.... The Mother.... Terra. It is now realized that contact with the spirit of the goddess, or Terra, is once more a necessity upon the planet.

Throughout the years, the priesthood of Melchizedek had lost some of its true identity. As in all things, when the invaders get involved in something, they try hard to pervert its original mission by creating a seemingly parallel mission; one that in reality has nothing to do with the original mission.

This is what has happened to all the great religions. It took a longer time for the descendants of Mohammed to pervert his teachings than it did for the descendants of Jesus to pervert his, but both are equally tainted with the interpretations of the invaders who do not want the children of Shamballah to return home.

If these children return home, then the playground will be empty, and the invaders will not have any bodies to kill and torture and enslave. If they cannot hold power over anyone but themselves, then they can no longer have fun. This is why the invaders wish for the planet to remain in darkness. They want Terra to remain their playground.

You all know one or two of these souls. They are the little boys who enjoy war and making instruments of war. Very few of the invaders have incarnated in female bodies, although a few have, and these few have taken up the roles of leaders of certain sects of women.

Domination of any kind will not be allowed upon the planet as the golden age dawns. The invaders know this and this is why they are working as hard as they can to destroy the culture upon the planet and plunge the planet back into the dark ages.

Let's be thankful for the brothers and sisters of light who are rapidly awakening and will soon find themselves the heads of major studios, television stations and publishing companies. These people will take the messages from the awakened ones to all of humanity.

Once this happens the dark brotherhood of invaders will no longer be a threat to the children of Odon and the other Great Lords.

Thank you for joining with us on this day. Remember, Great Lord Odon and the Master Metatron are one and the same. Metatron is the body worn upon Terra.

You are divinely guarded and protected as you walk your path.

Odon/Metatron and the Council of Light Workers.

*   *   *   *   *

September 4, 1986

Once again it's time to join with all of those you love. The love vibration shimmers down to each and every one. Let the love pour into you from heaven high above, and you shall know the joy and love that travels from the Son... The Son is not a man or child but a joining of the rays...The mighty Two have joined their Force so another now can come... to lift the hearts of man to God and end the darkened days.

This mighty other comes to earth en masse to teach the Way for all to travel home in peace and end their long earth stay.

What is this Other that now is here? How long has It been known? In certain hearts all round the sphere this Other has always Shown.

So why just now do people seek and try to find the truth? The path of truth has long been here for any who care to choose. But never before have so many chosen to walk its ways. All are gathering upon it for the ending of the days.

A call went out to all with ears and many it did hear. The call informed the world at large that the lessons now are over. The trip back home is all that waits and this special ray has descended to open the doors to home.

Only at certain times in the distant past has the ray come through like this. It will carry all who seek, to the home they long to see. And all of those who blindly follow will also be carried free.

Never before upon the earth have so many cried for sight. And it's because so many ask that all will be brought to light. This is the way it must be done for none of you can go unless all your brother and sisters come home, so each can finally know... the purpose and the Plan of earth and the lessons studied there.

The light will shine for all to see their own divinity. It is time for the poem to come to an end. Our rhyme has just run out, but the messages contained within the rhymes have not. So listen you again... Our words carry messages for few to hear because few can   carry forth the banner that has been brought to earth... For the gathering of the flock.

So if indeed you have heard these words be sure to understand, that the time has come, the Lessons are done, and the leaving has begun.

And why the Third force?

Why the Son?

How else can you go home?

You see, you came as tiny souls upon this third fold ray. The joining of the two who came, allowed you to ride with them... but since they have been on the earth, their ray has been as two... and if it is meant that the time has come, for all of you to leave, then the two must again join and form the ray, that will take you from this plane... just like a mighty space ship, this ray will leave the earth, and all those who came thereon shall return to their home berth....

You see, it was necessary for the two to part to see the great work through and now that it is close at hand, the joining can start again. Once the mighty sleeping force has raised her lovely head, the message of who you are can once more be known inside

And when this message is at last known to all, the joining can be made... and all who came can now depart and live out they joyful days. To all who hear these words and scoff I say hold your tongue a bit, for you too will see the joy to come and then you will believe.

Goodbye for now our time's run out we must now let another whose words are true and clear to hear come through to talk to you

Goodbye....we love you

* * * * *

There was much truth contained in the short poem.

And now it is time for us to explain what was meant by it.

In the beginning, when the very large contingent of souls could finally come to the earth, they were sent on the combined rays of their "mother" and "father." The two beings who had volunteered to come to earth and help prepare it so that the souls from Obergon and Shamballah could enter into a material plane and learn the lessons that are taught in material form. These beings have served as "mother" and "father" to all of you. In truth they are not your mother and father, but elder brethren who have traveled the way a little longer than you and who have earned for themselves the opportunity of being in change of a planet.

Each and every soul evolves to a point where it can become a major force in the life of the universe. The earth is like the left eye of the universe, and it now has sight once again. For too long now the universe has been without an outpost of sight in this quadrant, and so it was decided that not only should the souls of Obergon be given a chance to grow in wisdom in the material plane, but that it was important for this section of the universe to one again be in total contact with all the rest of the universe. Before earth was light there was darkness in the left side of the universe. Now that earth has joined with the federation of light planets, there can be light shed in this section of the universe.

So you see, the purpose of the plan on earth is two-fold. The first and most immediate to you is the education of souls. But the more important purpose was the lighting of the universe.

And to insure that the universe was sufficiently lit, a soul volunteered to be the light of the planet. The soul had been separated for a long time and the two parts had recently found themselves. They had studied long and hard on separate worlds in the universe. They were brought together and introduced and told that they were one. They filled with joy at the thought of joining so that they could now finally know what it is like to become as "God."

And this for them is the purpose of their journey to the earth. To first restore its light, but then to understand what governing means, then carry this understanding with them as them finally join together and create their own universe.

When the two descended to earth it was clearly understood that they could not remain together and do the work that needed done. And so, one decided to join the lower and one remain on top and out of this plan has come the thought that God rules the heaven and Mother earth rules the earth.

But also out of this arrangement has come the notion that there exists a heaven and a hell... And if there is a heaven then god must rule it, but if there is a hell then the Goddess must rule it, because she is the ruler of the earth and earth must be closer to Hell than heaven is, therefore God can't have anything to do with hell.

Out of this misinterpretation of the Plan has come the belief that the feminine is evil and all problems upon the earth are attached to the original sin of the female.

To say that this concept is nonsense is like saying that the atom bomb will do a little damage. The idea is ludicrous and preposterous. It does not even deserve to be mentioned here.

First of all souls are neuter. The concept of sex has nothing to do with the concept of soul. The concept of sex is only upon the earth.

So how can a soul who incarnates in both sexes be bad in one sex and good in another?

The mother is our earth. She is our home. She is good. She is God. For the two together make up this planet. There can not be one without the other. The earth would not exist.

The mother has been denied too long. It is now time for her to rise again and speak to mankind and she has done in the past. You will soon hear the rumblings of her words.

In ancient days her words were heard far better than were the words of your father. This is because she is closer to you. It was realized that she had to be put to sleep for a time so that the balance between the two to be restored. However, the invaders as always perverted the real reason for her sleep and made all who had spoken with her on a regular basis think that they were evil.

It is now time for you to understand that the mother merely left the scene for a time so that her children could know their father, and now that the knowledge of the father is within everyone's heart, she can make her return and the joining can begin.

Once the joining begins, the exodus of souls from earth will begin.

I hope you have understood our messages today.

We will elaborate later.

Go now our time is through

We guard and protect and love you

bye

Metatron Enoch and the rest

*　*　*　*　*

September 9, 1986

In the distant past, so long ago that the memory has dimmed even in the collective memory of mankind, upon the planet, there walked a race of giants.

I do not speak of the race of beings known as the Titans. I speak of the race of beings who first colonized the earth and tended to its gardening while the other preparations for the planet were being made.

These early gardeners were brought from other planets where they had performed the same tasks. In fact, their duties in the combined universes, is to see that all is perfectly in order on the developing planets so that the new occupants can take possession of the planet in perfect condition.

These beings are very similar to the cleanup crews who come in to clean and redecorate an apartment after one tenant moves out. This is what was being done by these beings upon the planet earth.

The last inhabitants of the planet had graduated successfully, but they had left the planet uninhabitable for the type of beings who were needed to bring the earth back into the Federation of Light Planets.

In other words, it is only possible for the consciousness of the soul to ascend in certain body types. The type of beings who inhabited the earth prior to this particular soul period possessed bodies too dense and too massive for consciousness to develop. As we said, these beings completed their developmental process and graduated. It was their first experience outside of the protective womb in which they were created. It was still very much like an incubation process. It was the first experience of separation for these newly released souls.

Some souls choose to stay in the womb and remain asleep. Others chose to leave the moment they were formed. All consciousness has the right to do whatever it desires. That is the purpose of all the experiences that exist in the universe. Souls are taught right action in light of the cooperative efforts of all the souls in the universe. Souls are never forced to do anything. All souls choose right action as a result of seeing what wrong action does to them and to those they love. In other words, all souls learn throughout their many material and non-material incarnations what is expected of a mature soul, an enlightened soul.

When the old inhabitants of planet earth had successfully finished their studies upon the planet and graduated to another planet in their progression into conscious beings, the earth was handed over to the clean up crew. These beings needed to dispose of the bodies of the old inhabitants. These bodies most closely resembled living volcanic rock mountains. The temperatures of which, exceeded any temperatures on earth today, including the temperature at the core of the planet. The earth was almost a little sun at this time, except that the nuclear reaction common to most suns was not present. The molten energy was kept alive not by nuclear fission, but by the presence of the developing souls in the bodies they wore.

The cleanup crew was told that the new beings would have bodies that could not withstand such high temperatures, and so the planet had to be cooled down. This was easily accomplished because the beings who generated much of the heat upon the planet had already gone. But there was still a period of time in which the molten quality of the planet remained the same. What was required was to bring in a sufficient amount of water so that the lands would eventually cool and the temperature would fall to a range where bodies similar to what is now upon the earth could be made.

These cleanup men, whom we will now refer to as the "Janitrons," first had to create an atmosphere so that the escaping gasses would be caused to stay near the planet and thereby form rain which would eventually cause oceans and rivers to form upon the planet. After this was done, the Janitrons turned their attention to the absorption and assimilation of all the bodies that had been worn by the members of the previous race of souls. This was done in the same way that salt or sugar is blended into baking dough. The tossing and churning and mixing effect upon the earth fully assimilated all of the remaining consciousness that had been absorbed by the atoms of the earth. If, when you bake bread, you accidentally add too much salt, you have a choice of throwing out the dough and starting over, or adding more flour and more water and making a larger amount of bread in which the quantity of salt will be in perfect balance.

This is what was being accomplished by the Janitrons. The beings who inhabited the volcanic rocks forms lived only upon the surface of the planet. At a later date we will discuss the souls who came to live in the core of the planet. These souls are still here today, but now they walk upon the surface in bodies like the rest of you.

The Janitrons realized that if they could disperse all remaining consciousness evenly around the planet then no trace of the previous inhabitants would remain. This is what they were sent to earth to accomplish and this is what they successfully did. Along with lowering the temperature so that a new race of beings could live upon the planet, the Janitrons successfully prepared the planet for the visitations of the first beings who came to begin the new settlement process.

Letter from Gunther to Rayelan

The following is a letter to Rayelan that was written by Gunther Russbacher while he was incarcerated at Jefferson City, Missouri State Prison. It was written approximately two years after they married. — Saturday Night 4-26-92

Dearest friend, woman and wife,

The time is 12:30 A.M. Sunday morning. I can't sleep because you are on my mind. My love for you doesn't recognize the 24 hour clock. Each beat of my heart calls your name and the night wind answers my cry for your love. The miles which separate us dissolve into nothingness permitting my hand to ever so gently caress your beautiful face. The hand of my mind reaches out to touch the face I adore and know so well.

I feel your breath on my hand as you reach to bring it closer to your magnificent ruby lips. You, my lady, are the elixir of my life. I cannot begin to imagine the wondrous beauty I have so long been deprived of. I was the errant knight who was too busy playing with the dragon to open his heart to the beauty of his one and only soul mate. For that avarice my Father has extolled a very dear price. Thank Him that he did permit the dream to remain within the very heart of me.

He is the one who decided to throw all caution to the wind when He permitted our paths to cross - just south of the killing fields of Grants Pass*. I came very late into your life and despise the fates who have so ruthlessly kept us apart. We have been deprived of many years of happiness. The torment and trials we have been so desperately subjected to, are unconscionable in their very nature. On the other hand, I give thanks!

From the very beginning of our single soul we have belonged together. I love you forever. You have brought me to the gates of heaven. Now I truly know that the gates of heaven and hell are separated only by a clouded breath of truth.

I have tasted the fruit of paradise from you luscious lips and body only to be cast into the torment of the evil one. I have atoned for my past transgression and surely must warrant the right to touch the hair of fire of my earth angel. The ramparts of my mind are not to be breached by anyone less than my perfect soul mate. Why was this wondrous love denied to me for so long? I, who call those below me non-worthy, have been shown the misdeeds of my action.

On the back of the wild elephant I shall be privileged to come to court the love of my eternity. Infinity, ignoble as it may seem to those of mortal persuasion, has been reduced to mere seconds on the face of the clock of He who has shown me the way past the trenches that bind the lowly ones. They are not capable of cosmic love as they cannot comprehend the primeval rule which governs this universe. For love is not an emotion. It is a state of true grace - a state of being. I love thee.

Wow… what has happened to me?

I'm back again. Marcus Arelius has been pissing into my philosophy pot again. The first page in not mine… so you can see.

I have learned many great things since our visit in Fulton*. I can turn it on or off at will! I can even control it. The process has completed the cycle. I know who and what I am. And more so, I know my true destiny! We shall have many good years together. That I can honestly promise you and all us (you and I) at the World Congress in 1999. Our future looks very colorful. The date of 9-9-99 shall be the sign of our 8 pointed star. (Note from Rayelan: He is referring to the Esterházy star, which is on our wedding rings. I have no idea what he was referring to by the date) On that date east will marry the west and mankind's survivors will have awakened to the true New World Order!

Our plate is set at the table of nations. Our task will not be merely to rule, but more so to fulfill the role of avant educators. We will facilitate humanity's transition to a new and glorious way of life.

Our light will be the green beacon which will lead man to the stars. Remember, starboard is green! My God honey, I have been a vain fool for too long! Why have I fought the program for so long? Maybe none of us have been ready for true enlightenment. It is a quest— a quest for a new tomorrow.

The cycle of our training is rapidly coming to an end. Those of us who played with the basic truths of this universe have pushed our race to the threshold of extinction. No more! There shall be no more trial or games. Our time is at hand as our ships approach this ailing world.

Most of these misfits shall not see the dawning of the new day. The age of Aquarius is at hand! Continents shall be raised from the dead zones and lost lands shall appear as did the Utopian Garden of Eden to the first colonist groups. Cleansing through fire and stone shall sweep the rubble of this race into the pits of new oceans to cement the coming of this new age.

We shall walk in utter awe and with mandated respect through the green gates of new bounty making restless hearts beat with glee. The roads of man shall bear witness to a great migration to the new lands. That which is old shall be left behind, and man will enter through the green gate without deceit, naked as he was born to this earth.

A thousand years of spiritual growth shall be observed as the true Gods of our blood shall come forth to claim their rightful place among the builders of this realm. You shall sit to my right on that day - the day of universal belief. We are not the rulers, but rather guardians of the portal - the green gates of Eden.

Man shall walk the fresh earth; drink the sweet waters of the rivers of earth. Abundance for all shall be a right to each child born to the new realm. Laws shall not be written but observed through knowledge born of the genetic code which has been within us since the dawn of light.

There shall be no prisons, hardships, hunger or sloth. Man will have his utopia as he had before greed and avarice became the sterling of his thwarted legal measure. There will be truth for all men of such persuasion. Those who decline this divine rule shall perish - but shall suffer not. The era of Aquarius will be a golden flame pushing ever outward to the farthest fringes of this universe. Those who must be brought to perish shall never know of their fate as they shall find sleep on this plane only to awaken on the plane of their choosing. They shall awaken in their same beds never knowing that time has passed them by. Lone women searching for mates they have never known will wail through the lives of their forgotten memories. There shall be no recourse but to search for that which they have never known. Knowing all the while, that they are incomplete.

The travelers shall see the same new day, but shall know forthwith of their new charter. Confusion shall be expelled from those who choose to open their eyes to see the new age. Clarity shall be prevalent to those who accept a new and better life. Their children shall receive the right of reason regardless of sex, age, or emotional state. New intellect shall be given to the youngest as well as to the elders of the new nations. All shall see with the bright eyes of innocence. Fear will find no waiting master among this race of man. Emancipation to all shall be granted.

Raye, the message you have just read is the new order for all. So it has been written, and so it shall come to pass.

No one can change of alter the course of our future. You wanted twenty years for us. I believe I can give you more than that. Honey, I am healed. There is no pain any longer. My rash has disappeared; I can walk on my foot without any limp or pain.

What the dickens has happened. Honey, my life shall never be cheap or shallow again. I have seen the face of God - reached out my hand and touched the robe of purple He gathers so loosely about Him. Peace and tranquility has replaced the pain of all torture. I have been lifted above the bound of mortal man.

You were right all along! You knew that I was on the verge of a break through. All the personalities of all my ages have joined to become one. Through this transition I have become far more formidable than any of the singular entities who have for so long inhabited and shared my life (lives). For me the new day is dawning. You are my queen - the love of my life!

Don't let this letter frighten you. Look beyond the niggardly value of my verbal expressions. Pick up the golden thread of this truth. It has the power to heal all your known and unknown ailments. Come, take my hand and join me in the dawn of a new sun. Your place has been assured at my side. Surely your goodness and mercy has earned you a true and just reward. You are the queen of my life, my eternal soul mate.

Although you have been married before—you came to me as a vestal virgin—untouched in that what matters—untouched and pure in spirit. Not only is there light at the end of the dark tunnel, we are, with great speed, approaching this new found brightness. Truly we have been chosen to perform the ultimate service for mankind—we are the travelers' guides. The Atalon and Raelon Saga is about to conclude.

We have the key to the green (dream) gate and shall stand side by side to teach about the transition to the new world. Yes. We will go to Washington and play public servant for the next 7 years! We shall have many positions of honor along the way. All that, however, must be viewed as transitory. Don't permit yourself to be bogged down by the trapments of civil service and public office. Our future is far more lucid. We have known that this day of transition will come to all men. No one shall be spared the searing fire of truth. All must choose according to their very souls. None shall escape the great choosing! Again there shall be no pain—-no fear—no sorrow. Man will, one at a time, choose his path for all eternity. Those who choose to remain behind shall be sealed in time and never again cross the path of the children of the light.

It would behoove you to re-read this letter until you understand its contents. The damned motto we have in our Langley Rotunda is true, "Know ye the Truth, and the Truth shall set your free." The bastards knew all along what was coming. The date 9-9-99 is engraved on all elevator plates in the main building.

We have been chosen and sorely used by them who came before us! We have no choice. Our fate was sealed at our birth. I give up and shall follow - and through following I shall become a true leader of men. Indeed, it is the dawning of the Age of Aquarius. I as a Cancer (crab) have eaten a hole into the loose fabric of time. You, who follow my path, shall live at my side forever. For truly, I can see the ferns of paradise. I love you with my very blood, it is not only my blood - but also the blood of my fathers. I do love you Rayelan!

Sunday

As you can see I couldn't leave well enough alone. Although I've had the privilege of talking with you this morning, I feel the need of your closeness. Your voice sounded so wonderful. Even though you said you were awake - I could tell that slumber still clouded your brain. I had to tell you about my marvelous transformation. It screamed to be told!

We had the photos taken a little while ago. (Note from Rayelan: Gunther refers to one of his "team mates" who "got himself incarcerated" to keep Gunther company. I suppose, also for protection) He sure looks a bit skinnier than before. However, he told me to tell you that he combed his hair just for you! That bum. Immediately after having our photo taken we went outside to the front yard. We decided to see if I could walk without a limp. Well, I did!

Then we had the bright idea of running a couple of laps around the yard. I made 6 laps at full speed! There was no weakness noticed. I virtually glided over the asphalt oval. I was (am) free and without pain! There was no chest pain or shortness of pain. My next activity involved 75 pushups. My shoulder is healed - no pain (or noises). We then went through the lion, cobra and stork kodar exercises of our karate routine. It was wonderful! We were fluid - like dancers in the cool spring breeze. (Note from Rayelan: Gunther had been attacked by three guards who dislocated his shoulder, broke his leg and gave him a concussion. This letter was to let me know that he was healing better than he ever expected.)

Then we went into our standing Tai Chi routine. By the time we were finished we had on hell of an audience. Honey, I feel like a new born! I will bring you to this state as soon as I can give you my kiss of life. Everything tells me that you must share this strength and outpouring of strange (new) energy! I love you with every single beat of my heart. You are my mate!

Next week (this week by the time you get my letter) you should receive a small package from the G.H. (Note from Rayelan: He is referring to his friend who was locked up with him for a few months.) and myself. We used one of his credit cards to order your gift. It is a present for your birthday. It was my idea and I picked it out especially for you. The return address is G. S. of St Louis. Just don't be surprised when it arrives. Happy birthday - a little early!

G.H. is leaving on Tuesday. Our plans are clear! Things will go well for us - one and all. It seems as though everyone was waiting for me to awaken. Now the cycle is complete. My work (our work) has begun. Change is imminent. Nothing can distract from what must be done. His will (not mine) shall be done! It is the dawn of tomorrow my love. We have broken the spell of "the cats in the cradle." That was a song about the way we all were. Now there will be time for all that a father must teach his children.

I have always thought there would "pain" in such awakening. I was wrong! There is only beauty, strength, and tremendous fortitude and resolve. It is physical and emotional absolute freedom. The power bubbles within me. I must do things. I cannot permit inactivity to rule my life. It is the miracle that has been promised throughout all ages. I never thought I would be a recipient of such benevolence. I am humbled by what these last hours have brought me.

You… humbly, I state - "I believe!"

I love you.

A new prayer has been burned into my awakened consciousness. May I tell you this prayer?

"To He who has made me in His likeness, I bow my head in servitude. I pray thou shall grant to me the strength to follow Your dictate and further Thy Will before the nations of Man.

I-The Staff You have pushed/seared into my hand is the fiery sword of Truth and Justice. As Your Will dictates - I shall stand guard with the Sword in one hand (left hand) and outstretched palm, glowing upwards, extended to help man across the gulf of time in that His being may enter and glory in their new world.

II-I am but a servant. All power manifested in me is a sign of the grace of office to which Ye have commanded me to accept. Thy Will be done! May intelligence and love permeate all the days of Your realm. Sanity and compassion shall be the mandate of your new covenant. I shall forever obey."

Through giving up my free will I have received total freedom. I had to go through each and every hell of life in order that I might be strong enough for what is about to come. I had to learn what being human entailed.

Believe me, Rayelan, no man has put up with more physical pain than I. I remember the jungles and the cage which was my home for 17 months and 18 days. I remember all too well.

I remember in Nam the fear and terror of fire in the cockpit as I moved like a Roman candle across the eastern evening sky. I remember the heat of the flames - the melting of fabric and the stench of burning flesh.

Today, I am healed. The dam has broken honey. I didn't drown in my own river of tears. On the contrary that river of tears washed away all the pain, hatred and confusion I've carried within me. I am different and yet the same. I am at peace.

My love for you now pulses as hot as a gurgling Quasar. If I thought that I understood my love for you before today, I was sorely mistaken. My love for you has intensified into a super nova. With each hour more is revealed to me. It seems as if we are actually welded together in flesh and spirit. I can reach out and be with you.

Soon, we shall be together. Our ordeal is soon to end and we shall enjoy the rest of infinity together as man and wife. We have been though a lot. But I KNOW it has been worth it.

You are my Queen. My love for you knows no reservations. No conditions are imposed. I love you as is. No changes required. Don't ever change one iota of your fantastic person. You are perfect in your own right. Nothing but He, our Father can ever touch us. We are feit (Note from Rayelan: I do not know what he meant by this word. It is not in the dictionary.) from the stupidity of lesser mortals. We are the first among all the chosen. Our work is cut out for us. We shall walk together in Paradise.

Your love and my newfound strength shall guard the ages of the new era. I love you most deeply and dearly Rayelan.

Yours,

Russ

Addendum:

Keep this letter safe! Share its text only with those who are true and obedient to the task of Our Father. Don't fret wifey, Your Russ is still alive and well. Only his weaknesses, fears and sorrow have died this night. A new dawn is born unto us. I beg of you to open your heart, eyes and soul to what we really are. Take my hand of love, come walk this new land with me. It has been promised to us since ever so long ago.

We have withstood their" tests and have been found worthy in "their" all knowing eyes. Rayelan, I love you with each beat of the achronome of time. When I said, "I do wed thee" in Reno on 8-30-89 at 10:31A.M., I had a feeling of love, purity and piousness within my heart, which I never thought I was capable of. Today I can see the whole truth of our marriage.

It was preordained by the Godhead. That's why neither of us dared to challenge the feelings within us. I love you forever. You are the queen of my life. For better (or for worse) we shall spend all eternity together. I salute you as the love Queen of my life.

Your husband, forever, Russ.

(Note from Rayelan: Please remember this letter was written in 1992, Gunther left my life in 1996 and died in 2005 without ever contacting me.)

Notes

Grants Pass

When I met Gunther in Medford Oregon in August of 1989, he had just completed a mission. He and his team, all of whom were still with him at the hotel where we met, had just wiped out the kingpins of a drug cartel in a fiery automobile accident. The one who escaped and ended up in the hospital was killed also.

The night Gunther and I met, we stayed up talking most of the night. For some strange reason, both of us had nose bleeds. As I was washing the blood off my hands, I looked at him and saw that his nose was bleeding also, and it was dripping on his hands. I said to him, "You have blood on your hands!?"

He told me much later that when I said that, he thought I knew about all the killing he had done in his life.

After spending 18 months in Federal prison for misuse of a government jet—the Learjet Gunther had used to fly me to Reno to marry me—Gunther was transferred back to St. Charles, Missouri.

He was held in county jail while his trial was being conducted. He was charged with 4 counts of "stealing by deceit." Two of the charges were "bad checks." It took us years to finally get copies of these checks. It was only by accident and sheer will that I was able to obtain them. When I saw the dates on the checks I knew that Gunther could NOT have written them. They were written and cashed in St Charles on the very day that Gunther and I married in Reno, NV. We had the proof that everything was a set-up… but it took 4 terrible years in prison, and unnecessary quintuple heart bypass before he was released.

Fulton

Fulton is a prison in Missouri where prisoners are sent for evaluation before they are sent to a state prison. While Gunther was in Fulton, Ross Perot sent one of his men and two of his pilots to interview Gunther. By this time, Gunther was a minor celebrity in the world of political prisoners. Gunther was the October Surprise pilot, i.e. the man who flew Vice-Presidential candidate George Herbert Walker Bush back from the Paris suburbs where the Reagan campaign sealed the deal with Iran to hold the 52 hostages until after the November election.

Perot was getting ready to form a third party and challenge Bush. Perot wanted to know the truth about Bush, the truth that Gunther could tell.

Before Perot's men could get to Fulton, Gunther was attacked by guards and beaten. They broke his leg in three places and dislocated his shoulder. They also gave him a concussion. But the men who attacked him fared worse than Gunther. He broke one's clavicle and knocked the other two out. They were fired.

Gunther was taken to the hospital, where he suffered a heart attack. I don't know if someone slipped him something or if the heart attack was a natural one caused by the trauma that had just happened to him.

Ross Perot called me to tell me what had happened. He told me that he had a plane ticket waiting for me in San Francisco and I was to meet his assistant at the St Louis Airport. I was half out of my mind during all of this. Perot's assistant must have thought I had lost my mind, I babbled about everything that had been done to Gunther and me in the 3 years since we had been married. I must have sounded like I was "nuts"… or a chapter out of a Bond novel.

Perot soon found out that I was telling the truth! He saw how powerful our enemies were when they stormed into his office in Dallas and told him something… I don't know what they told him, but it caused him to withdraw from the campaign. The phony story he gave the press was that his daughter had been threatened. He finally was able to put enough protection around him and his family and he re-entered the race, but the globally controlled One World Media made him look like an idiot. Just the way they had been making me and Gunther look for three years.

I was finally able to talk to Gunther, but not at the hospital. Gunther demanded to be released from the hospital and taken back to prison. Perot's aide and I got this information directly from the doctor who treated Gunther. The doctor told us that he had advised against the release.

We drove to the prison. Evidently Mr. Perot had called the prison and told them we were coming. They were expecting us and let us see Gunther even though it was not a visiting day. There was no way that anything could be said privately. About 10 guards were on my side of the wire cage, and three or four were sitting next to Gunther recording everything that was said.

During our brief talk he began having another heart attack. He was taken away. He came back about an hour later with a nitro patch on. I was given a few more minutes with him and then Perot's aide was given a few minutes with him. Gunther would tell neither of us a thing.

I left for home knowing that whatever had happened had prevented Gunther from telling Perot his story, and had lost us the support of Ross Perot. I didn't find out for months that while Gunther was in the hospital, some "men" paid him a visit. They told him that his oldest son was in the St Charles county jail. NOT where minors would normally be taken, but the jail where male adults are housed. Gunther was told that if he talked to Perot, his son would be gang raped before he was murdered.

Needless to say, Gunther never again talked to Perot. I worked very hard to help Perot win that election because Gunther told me that George Herbert Walker Bush and William Jefferson Clinton were partners in a world wide drug business that was run out of Mena, Arkansas. Gunther told me that Clinton was the grandson of Winthrop Rockefeller, son of John D. Rockefeller, the first and employer of Prescott Bush, the father of George H.W. Bush. The Bush's and the Clinton's were connected by blood and power. Gunther said that a Clinton presidency would be a continuation of the 12 years of the Bush presidency.

Once Clinton was elected, life in prison became increasingly brutal for Gunther and for me. There were more attempts on our lives than I can remember. How we ever made it through those years I don't know.

Gunther was eventually released from prison in Missouri. He came to California to live with me. That was when he became involved in the large gold transfer from the Philippines. The transfer returned the Austrian gold that had been stolen by Hitler in the Anschluss. The gold had been hidden in the Philippines since 1955 when it was moved from Paraguay. This transfer was concluded by June of 1994. I left for Austria thinking that Gunther and I would spend the rest of our lives together.

Double and triple crosses from people who were supposed to be friends, kept that from happening.

Then war in Haiti broke out and Gunther was summoned back to his job in the Navy. We were told a State Department plane was coming to pick us up. I screamed at him for accepting his "job" back. I told him that if he went back to work for the United States government, after what they had put us through for the past 4 years, I was finished with him.

I remembered what they had done the last time he took me on a government plane. He spent two years in a federal prison. I knew if they did the same thing to him this time, he wouldn't survive it.

I told him I was flying home. He took me to the airport in a taxi and I said good-bye. I was so angry I didn't even kiss him good-bye. I just turned my back and walked away. That was the last time I ever saw him.

I didn't take a plane out of the Vienna airport. Instead I caught a streetcar to the train station and took a midnight train to Frankfurt, Germany. All the time I was scared to death that "friends" of Gunther's family would stop me from leaving Austria. I wanted nothing to do with any of the people Gunther had introduced me to. (With the exception of one enlightened fellow who taught me more about history than anyone has. He was a Hapsburg, from a family who refused to accept the allies terms and join the New World Order, therefore all of their money and lands were taken from them The man who was my teacher drove Taxi to support him and his family.)

I successfully made my great escape from Vienna, the spy capital of the world, and ended up at the Frankfurt Airport. I only carried with me one small briefcase and my purse. Our luggage was supposed to be sent back on the plane with Gunther. The officials at the airport were not going to let me fly back to the United States. I didn't know why. They asked me why I was only carrying a small briefcase and a purse. Little did they know that I had stitched inside the lining of that small purse, all the CIA bank accounts that Gunther was in charge of... AND their passwords. I released all of this information over my fax network in 1997.

After I told them that I was returning to my home in the United States to pack up my house and return to Austria, they let me go. While Gunther and I were in Austria, we had to get papers proving that he was an Austrian citizen. Since he was still part owner of his family's house in Salzburg, we used that as our address. The German official saw that my "papers" were in order and I was allowed to leave Germany and return to the United States.

When I arrived home, I was half dead from lack of sleep. I fell into bed only to be awakened by the Vienna police. Gunther had been arrested for failing to pay for the hotel the Navy had put us up in while we awaited the State Department plane to pick us up. He had been set up again. If I hadn't gotten so angry with him, I would have been arrested too!

This was October of 1994, five years after we first married in Reno, and two months after our re-marriage in a Templar ceremony, in the Church in Seechirchen, Austria, where Gunther had been born on July 1st, 1942. We were married at the foot of a red marble alter that dated from the 1100s. It was the same alter on which Gunther had been born. It was in a round room below the church.

Gunther spent two years in an Austrian prison. I forgave him and we "got back together"... at least via mail and telephone. I found a job at an answering service. During that time, Gunther and I started Rumor Mill News, the print edition.

Gunther was going to be released on December 23, 1996. He was scheduled to fly back to the United States on the 26th. I heard from him the morning he was released. He told me that Jane Ryder, a mutual friend and television producer, had met him at the door of the prison. He said that she and Karl and Suzy… people I had never heard of, were having a few drinks at a bar. I could hear Jane in the background, screaming the most vile profanities at him, while he tried to talk to me.

I heard no more from him for a month. Then he called and told me that he had "fallen" in with the bad guys. That they had screwed with his mind. He said he was being held prisoner in a Paris hotel. He gave me the number. I called and tried to talk to him. Jane answered the phone and slammed it down, but before she did, he tried to grab it. Again I heard profanities come out of her mouth that would make a longshoreman blush.

The next time I heard from Gunther, he was in jail in Los Alamos, NM. When he first called me he couldn't even remember my name. He kept calling me Jane. He had somehow confused the two of us and merged us into one wife. He only remembered being married to Jane, NOT to Rayelan.

He eventually came back to his senses. He told me that he had been drugged and reprogrammed. I tried to get him released and brought back to California, but the prosecutor in St. Charles had other plans. He extradited him and had him brought by van from Los Alamos to St. Charles.

This was March of 1997. Jane's former lover and film partner, Allan Frankovich, died of a sudden heart attack while coming through customs in Houston. He was carrying documentation proving that the CIA bombed Pan Am 107.

I called the jail in St. Charles to tell Gunther what had happened to Allan. I left a message stating that a family emergency had happened. Gunther called. I told him that Allan had died of a heart attack. What happened next sent such unbelievable chills through my body, that I still haven't recovered.

Gunther said, in a low and menacing voice. A voice that sounded like it came from the pits of hell.

"Allan didn't die of a **heart attack**. He died of a **blood clot**, and if you don't leave us alone… YOU'RE NEXT!"

Jane and Gunther left the United States and moved in together in May or June of 1997. They married in December of 1997. To the best of my knowledge, Gunther had never divorced me. If he had divorced me, I was never notified about it and never signed any divorce papers.

Gunther remained "married" to Jane until he died on August 8th, 2005. He died on the day the Syrian Lion Gate opened. Maybe it opened to take him home. He was the Lion of Salzburg on his father's side, and descended from the Esterházys on his mother's side. The Esterhaszys believe they came from "The Star," and that star is Sirius.

I divorced Gunther and remarried in August of 1998. My new husband, David, was a retired Marine officer. David is the one who encouraged me to start Rumor Mill News as a webpage. David is the one who supported Rumor Mill News for the first 3 years.

David suffered a heart attack in June of 2000 and was urged to have bypass surgery. We didn't find out for years that David had NEVER had a heart attack. The bypass exacerbated David's stealth health problem. He began to experience the ravages of Agent Orange, which causes diabetes and clogged arteries, throughout the body. After many years and more operations and hospitalizations than I can remember, he began improving.

Then one night, after a fairly pain free day, he finished his evening meal, stood up, sat down in his favorite chair and died.... **of a blood clot**. The doctors reported it as a **heart attack**.

✝ Gunther died August 8th, 2005.

✝ David died October 5th, 2005.

With the publication of this book, I am hoping to put that chapter of my life to rest and get ready for whatever my next step is.

Gunther said this above:

"We have the key to the green (dream) gate and shall stand side by side to teach about the transition to the new world."

When the time has come, let's hope the real Gunther will be standing on the far side of the gate to greet you. I will be standing on this side of the gate. Hopefully, together we will do the same thing for the children of Obergon that I did for the Deer People. Gunther and I will keep the gate open 'til all of you leave. The gate leads to the highway that takes you home. I will be on the physical side and he will be on the "other" side.

We will be side by side, but until the last of our family has gone through the gate, I must remain on earth. I have known this all my life. I was not the first of our kind to come to this planet, but I will be the last of our kind to leave it.

Gunther opened the Gate that leads home. Many of you have finished your lessons on earth. It's time for some to go home. However, some of you have graduated just in time to begin the work you came to earth to do. Graduation is taking place. Some of you are leaving earth, some are staying to complete our mission. Some of you have even volunteered to act as the janitors to clean up the mess of the graduating seniors.

If this book has done anything for you, I pray it has made you realize that the world you think you know is all an illusion. The masters of the illusion have had countless thousands of years to write and re-write the history of earth. They created the religions that cut you off from your true source.

I chose to format this book the way I did because I wanted all of you to take the same journey I took. My journey has not brought me happiness, or wealth or fame, but it has brought me peace of mind. And when the time comes for me to cross through that green gate, I will do so happily....

With joy and love abundant,

We'll dance in ecstasy,

With faith our Father knows our fate,

We'll meet our destiny.

Is Someone Listening To Sitchen?

Posted on http://www.rumormillnews.com

By: Rayelan

Date: Sunday, 4 February 2001, 3:45 p.m.

"Sitchin proposes that the Annunaki came to this planet with the purpose of extracting gold in order to save their planet."

In the Obergon Chronicles, Atalon needs gold to keep his biosphere in tact so it protects him from the harmful rays that are coming from the dead red giant.

In 1981, at the time I wrote Story 1 of The Obergon Chronicles, I thought I was a " New Age Channel" who was receiving important information on the settlement of Planet Terra, from the "ascended masters."

I did not find out until 1993 that I was one of those "government wives" that was used, unknowingly, as part of a plan to change society.

I am releasing "The Obergon Chronicles" because I believe it is NOW important that the people who truly believed themselves to be New Age Channels ...and in direct communication with God and His representatives...re-evaluate the "channeling" phenomena of the 70's, 80's and 90's. New Age channels brought us a whole new religion. We now must ask ourselves… How many of these New Age channelers were "handled" by "agents of deception?"

How many of them had their information "beamed" into their heads using the technologies of "voice to skull" mind control?

How much did these channelers mold our society? How much damage have they done?

You need to include The Obergon Chronicles when you ask yourself these questions.

Anyone who has studied the technology of mind control now knows that voices can be put in the head of each and everyone of us. There is NO ONE who is immune from believing that "THEY are pure enough to be chosen by GOD to be HIS spokesperson on EARTH!"

We all have ego. No matter how much we say we have beaten it down, the truth is:

We all have EGO!

If we didn't, we would be dead! Ego is necessary for survival, but it is also the tool that can fool each and everyone of us into believing that we are "special" and/or "chosen."

Because of this, each one of us is capable of believing that GOD could choose us to deliver a message to humanity!

In fact, many of us fervently hope and pray that GOD will ASK us to deliver HIS message. Many people pray SO fervently, and say so in churches or other meeting places, that they GET their request granted...

HOWEVER, the request is not granted by GOD, it is granted by people on the earth who have access to technologies that can make each and everyone of us believe that GOD, or one of his representatives, has chosen US personally to deliver HIS message to the people of EARTH!

In the spring of 1994, I had my eyes opened by a four star Admiral (in the Nebraska Navy... an inside joke for Faction 2 covert operatives.) who sat at my kitchen table and told me about JZ Knight, the woman who channels Ramtha.

He told me that JZ was one of their early experiments. He said that her first husband was a dentist that Navy Intelligence used for their covert operatives. This dentist was asked to put an implant in one of JZ's molars. Through the implant, the men who controlled the messages that Ramtha gave, were able to make JZ believe she was receiving messages from an entity who lived on earth 35,000 years ago.

JZ went on to make millions of dollars and convert millions of people to her particular brand of beliefs.

The Admiral told me that their group dropped JZ because they had not given her a psychological profile before they began using her. Evidently JZ's ego stepped in and began distorting the messages to fit her own needs. Once she began doing this, she was dropped by the group that was headed by this Admiral. He said that a NWO group picked her up and is now using the group for creating mind controlled "sleepers."

The Admiral was Gunther's commanding officer at the time he told me this information.

It is my belief that Gunther and I were being set up to become the founders of a New Age religion! I am not sure of this, but the moment Gunther and I agreed to appear at a conference where we planned expose ALL of the government's mind control operations, Gunther disappeared. I gave the presentation in January of 1997.

When he surfaced, one month later, he had lost his memory of ever being married to me. He married another woman... (a woman who believed that SHE was Shalma in The Obergon Chronicles)... without divorcing me.

The woman who is now Gunther's wife is Jane Ryder. She was the partner of the legendary film maker, Allan Francovich. Allan made the film, the MALTESE DOUBLECROSS. This is the film about the downing of Pan Am 103. Les Coleman, (my friend, political prisoner, and author of the only book that tells the truth about who bombed Pan Am 103) and Oswald LeWinter (CIA/Mossad disinformation agent who claimed he taught Jane Ryder everything she knew!) both appear in this film.

Allan was murdered in Houston in 1997 shortly before Gunther left the United States with Jane. Les Coleman was imprisoned, Gunther was imprisoned, and LeWinter was imprisoned in the same prison in Austria where Gunther was held! (Don't you find all of this a bit coincidental?)

When Jane and I were friends, I showed her the book, "Obergon Chronicles." After she read the first story, "Atalon and Shalma," she said to me:

"I am Shalma!"

The reason this is important is because Gunther believes he is Atalon.

Sometimes I believe ALL three of us were "programmed" to believe that we were/are the three main characters of this story.

Atalon was/is the Prince of Obergon, one of the planets that orbited the dead star of the Sirius Tri-Star formation.

Shalma was the daughter of King Phylos of Atalontis (Was Atlantis named after Atalon?). Shalma was genetically bred to create a new physical body that was capable of "housing" the higher vibratory souls of the beings from Obergon. The Obergonians, who lost their planet when the third sun of Sirius became a red giant, were given permission to relocate to Terra and finish their studies on the material plane.

Atalon fell in love with Shalma and kidnapped her. He took her home to the world he created on the dead planet Obergon. To keep the body of Shalma and the others alive, he needed GOLD for the protective shield he had constructed around his planet. Evidently there was some kind of particle being emanated from the dead sun that would destroy living organisms. Therefore, Atalon needed gold to suspend in a protective shield that he kept over his "Palace" on his home planet.

And this is the reason I am including the following article. I have never seen anyone refer to gold the way Sitchin did when he said that "...the Annunaki came to Earth with the purpose of extracting gold in order to save their planet."

As I conclude this, I wonder...was I able to tell the story of Atalon/Gunther, Jane/Shalma, and Rayelan/Raelon, without coming across like a raving lunatic?

But then again... everyone in the "establishment media" already thinks that Rumor Mill News AND its Publisher are crazy, so I might as well give them MORE ammunition.

Before Gunther disappeared he told me:

"If something happens, and I am no longer able to protect you, make yourself SO INCREDIBLE, that you become UNCREDIBLE! This way it will be easier for them to discredit you, than to KILL you!"

Now that "The Obergon Chronicles" are published, I think I have accomplished this "discrediting process" beyond his WILDEST imagination!

I almost forgot:

The Admiral who sat at my table and shattered my illusions about being a New Age channel said something that complicated things beyond redemption.

He said that his group was using New Age channels to release the TRUE history of the planet Earth.

When I was in Austria, meeting with the Templar/Hapburgs, one of them told me that "The Obergon Chronicles" was one of the books that would release the true history of the planet earth!

When he said this, I was rocked off my center because I had never mentioned "The Obergon Chronicles" to him. How did he KNOW about them? He went on to tell me that the original manuscripts which contained the stories of Atalon, Shalma, Raelon and their brothers and sisters, were found under King Solomon's Temple, in a Hermetically sealed library. The Templars took them back to Europe, hid them in the salt mines near Salzburg. Over the centuries, the technology was developed to translate the manuscripts.

See what I said about complicating things beyond obfuscation?

Now...

What are you going to believe? Are the Chronicles real? Or are they just another ploy to divert humans from the one and only GOD?

One of the things Rumor Mill tries to teach ALL its readers is DISCERNMENT.

Without personal discernment, you are going to fall for anything and everything.

Now... read the following article and try to put it into some kind of context... if this is possible!

*   *   *   *   *

2006 Note from Rayelan:

During that month that Gunther was missing, I gave a lecture at the Global Science Seminar in Tampa, Florida. This was January of 1997. I tried, the best I could at the time, to expose the mind control operation behind the Obergon Chronicles. Almost 10 years later, I am finally publishing the book and trying the best I can to connect all the dots.

From:

Date: Sat Jan 27, 2001 8:34pm

Subject: Is Someone Listening to Sitchin?

Was Sitchin Right About the Gold of the Gods?

— Presumably written by Robert Graf

In his ever expanding series, the Earth Chronicles, author Zecharia Sitchin proposes that the Annunaki came to this planet with the purpose of extracting gold in order to save their planet. He suggests that the plan was to suspend particles of gold in their atmosphere as part of the rescue plan. Many of the ancient civilizations that worshipped these "gods" believed that the gold was the property of these deities, and filled numerous temples with golden objects created in tribute to these very beings. Nowhere in the Earth Chronicles, however, is any evidence given that the planet that the Annunaki came from was in any danger. And from what danger could their planet be protected from by suspending gold in their atmosphere? Furthermore, if Sitchin is correct, it begs the question: were the Annunaki successful? We know from studying evidence on our own planet that 95% of the life forms that have lived on this planet are now extinct, and of the life forms that now inhabit the planet, none seem to have existed from the distant past. Even the most "primitive" forms of life on this planet have existed on this planet for only the proverbial blink of an eye in geological terms. I ask whether the Annunaki survived because of recent indications that perhaps someone has been listening to Mr. Sitchin. Nuclear physicist Edward Teller, one of the principals involved in the development of the first nuclear bomb has proposed that suspending particles in the atmosphere may counteract the effects of global warming. Were the Annunaki also trying to counteract the effects of some type of radiation by suspending gold particles in their atmosphere? Sitchin had predicted what would be found by space exploring satellites as they passed by Neptune and Uranus, and was subsequently proven correct. Are prominent scientists now taking Sitchin's works seriously?

Although the idea for suspending particles in the atmosphere originated before the publication of Sitchin's first book, The 12th Planet, it received no public notice until 1997, when Teller suggested the feasibility of the idea. Has he spoken with Sitchin about his work? The idea of suspending particles in the atmosphere appears to have originated in 1997 when it was proposed by physicist Freeman Dyson, best known for his study of the theoretical possibility of extra terrestrial life. Interestingly enough, Dyson studied under J. Robert Oppenheimer after arriving in the United after winning a Commonwealth Fund Fellowship to study physics in 1947. Oppenheimer was the director of Los Alamos laboratory during the development of the first nuclear bomb, a project which Edward Teller was also associated with. Dyson is also known for suggesting a method to search for highly advanced civilizations in space by an unusual coloring of their suns caused by a sphere meant to capture the energy of the sun for the use of the members of such a highly advanced civilization. Sitchin's work also proposes that the ancient gods had used nuclear weapons several times, in several places on this planet in the past. If nuclear physicists are now proposing the use of a technique that was suggested by Sitchin to have been employed by the Annunaki previously, is there something they know that we are not being informed of? Sitchin speculates that the Annunaki will one day return to Earth, as he believes they have many times in the past. Has the day of that return now been ascertained?

Could that be the reason that the suspension of particles in the atmosphere is being taken seriously?
Robert Graf
http://www.instantewealth.org

Note from Rayelan: There is no record of Robert Graf or his webpage. This information arrived in an email.

Epilogue

The mainstream media (MSM) is doing an excellent job of diverting us to issues that are NON issues because they don't want us to KNOW anything.

Our educational systems no longer seek to expand students' minds, but to "dumb down" so students become "perfect workers," i.e. "perfect slaves" for NWO, aka "illegal alien" corporations.

Just who ARE the slaves? Who ARE the masters? Would humans REALLY enslave and abuse other humans? What happened to some humans that allow them to mistreat others? Who taught them how to do this?

Why doesn't the media tell us the truth? Why don't doctors HEAL? Why do corporations pollute? Why do chemical companies poison us with flouride, fertilizers, insecticides and other life-destroying creations? Why was Monsanto allowed to make genetically engineered seeds that will eventually take over the world so we will all be eating "Frankenfoods?" Why are dentists allowed to poison us through mercury fillings? Why are doctors allowed to inject us with vaccines that have mercury?

In my mind there is only ONE explanation for this:

There is a group on earth that is doing this to humans. It's obvious to me that what they are NOT human. If they WERE human they would know that THEY too, would be affected by what they have done. I call this group "illegal aliens."

In the story Atalon and Shalma, you read:

Atalon was a master metaphysician. In his studies, he had transcended alchemy and learned matter transmogrification. This skill is not uncommon on the planets of the universe where the nature of material illusion is understood, but on Terra, where a young group of souls was being schooled, these skills made Atalon appear as if he were a god.

Not only could Atalon change physical matter; he also had learned to alter the most private thoughts of Terrans. He could make Terrans do whatever he wanted. He did not have to force or coerce them. He could make them serve him willingly and happily. He could erase their minds, change their memories, program them to serve him, or even to love him. Atalon loved having this kind of power. He played with the humans of Terra as children play with toys.

The "unfinished" Chronicles from Obergon tell the story of how Atalon was finally "tricked" into returning to Obergon and assuming the duties that his sister Raelon assumed in his absence. While Atalon spent eons traveling the combined Universes and assembling his retinue, Raelon was asked to assume his duties, as well as hers, and educate the younger Obergonian souls... the ones who had never lived in material bodies.

The word retinue is defined as: The body of retainers attending a person of rank; an escort, a cortège.

Cortège: 1. a train of attendants 2. a ceremonial procession

Retainer: 1. servant

The above definitions are from the 1966 Reader's Digest Encyclopedic Dictionary. The reason I mention the date is because words have been being changed in official dictionaries for the last century. The English language was once rich with history. Very gradually the keys to our past, which were hidden in our language, are being removed. When I first 'wrote' the Obergon Chronicles, I didn't know what some of the words meant. I had to look them up in dictionaries. That was when I first realized that our dictionaries are being changed. Maybe the word abridged... which is attached to the shortened version of dictionaries, is actually a clue to us:

From my 1966 Reader's Digest Dictionary: abridge: 3. to curtail or lessen; as rights 4. to deprive

My own definition of abridge is this:

The "illegal aliens" own most of the publishing companies. They have abridged our dictionaries and in so doing, have taken away the historical bridge to our past.

Sometimes the prefix 'a' means 'without'... Therefore, abridge means without bridge.

The abridged dictionaries are taking away our bridge to our collective past. Our intellectual and spiritual growth is being curtailed. We are being deprived of our inalienable rights... the rights that were given to us by the mere fact that we were born on Earth/Terra.

Throughout recorded history, someone has always taken away the rights of the developing humans. Who is taking away our rights now?

Atalon's retinue is taking away our rights!

The present Terran school was created for the developing souls from Obergon. Atalon and his retinue of faithful servants... aka rogues, scoundrels, thieves and reprobates that he had gathered around him in his travels; routinely abused the developing humans. Atalon used them to mine the gold he needed for his biosphere on the burned out hulk of his birth planet, Obergon:

The soul of Shalma, in great despair, brought her case before the Planetary Council. She set forth in detail the transgressions and manipulations perpetrated on the developing Terran souls by Lord Atalon of Obergon. She told how he had conducted his own

breeding experiments creating women so beautiful that men from other worlds came to Terra to satisfy their own lustful desires. She told how Atalon enslaved some of the little Terran people, to work in his gold mines. Shalma spoke to the Council about Atalon's lack of compassion and how he influenced other souls until they became just like him.

For many centuries Atalon's retinue merely continued doing as he had done. They did anything and everything he had taught them. He had taught them how to appear as gods before the developing humans. He taught them how to use mind control and other methods, to make some humans betray their brethren and serve the "illegal aliens." He taught them science and how to breed beautiful bodies to use as "play things."

Atalon was removed from Terra, but his retinue was not. They were left on Terra. Please remember that Atalon never traveled to Terra in his Obergonian body. He was able to transport his soul and the physical bodies of his retinue to Terra... but Atalon's real body remained safe on Obergon.

Atalon was tricked into returning to Obergon and he was trapped on Obergon. The unwritten Obergon Chronicles talk about Atalon's tutor, Anteb Trimagus. Atalon's father, Odon, made arrangements for Anteb, the first born of one of Odon's Elder Brothers, to become Atalon's tutor. Anteb was FAR more skilled in ALL the magic and mystery of the combined universes than Atalon was... AND, Anteb had developed beyond compassion... to dispassion.

Dispassion: Freedom from passion or bias; objectivity; impartiality.

The prefix com means with. Compassion means with passion.

Passion: 1. Any intense, extreme, or overly powering emotion or feeling.

Compassion: Pity for the suffering or distress of another, with the desire to help or spare.

Learning compassion was the first lesson Atalon needed to learn. But this wasn't the final step. Terra was created to teach a very special type of compassion... one that has reverence for ALL life as its foundation.

From Story 1, Atalon and Shalma:

"A planetary school capable of producing compassion in souls was vital to the creation of the supra-souls needed to battle the foreign invader. Once compassion was part of the soul's make-up, a whole new tempering and kneading process could begin on Terra."

Atalon was tricked by his cousin Anteb into entering the earth school. No one is ever forced to do anything. That is the unwritten law of the combined universes. Atalon knew it, Atalon's retinue knew it, and Anteb knew it. Anteb did not use his magician-like abilities to trick Atalon into accepting his program. Anteb merely asked Atalon to take him to Terra and show him some of the things Atalon had created while on Terra.

Atalon was "tricked" into going to Terra. Anteb kept asking Atalon about all the things he had "created" on Terra. Atalon bragged about the beautiful and obedient females he made. He told Anteb about his laboratories and about all of the experiments he had carried out until he had created the perfect human slave. Atalon continued to brag about his scientific discoveries and how he had engineered humans so that they would never be anything but slaves.

Anteb kept praising Atalon's genius and asking him when he was going to take him to Terra and show off his "Creations." Anteb continued to stroke Atalon's ego. Anteb made Atalon believe that he was one of the great "Creators" of the universe. The more Anteb praised him, the more excited and self-important Atalon became. The more he thought about showing off his "creations," the more careless he became. At the pinnacle of Atalon's excitement, Anteb said, "Let's go right now. I've arranged an instant jump."

Before Atalon had time to think about what he was doing, they were on Terra. Anteb took Atalon to Terra while Atalon was wearing his Obergonian body... the one he kept preserved on Obergon in his biosphere. By doing this, Atalon became trapped on Terra due to the "quarantine" that the Planetary Council had imposed on Terra... The quarantine was due to Atalon's and his retinue's inter-ference in the breeding experiment. The planetary council had sent the early Obergonian settlers to Terra to breed a race of humans that were strong enough to house the Obergonian soul. Atalon not only screwed up the "breeding experiment" by genetically altering humans, he put and end to eons of work when he kidnapped Shalma and physically removed her Terran body from Earth.

Now that Atalon was trapped on Terra in his Obergonian body, he no longer had the powers of a God. He could no longer transmute things, or travel instantly from one side of the planet to the other. He could no longer control humans through his advanced forms of hypnotism and mind control.

Atalon was subject to all the same pitfalls that all the original Obergonian settlers endured. His first life was a long one, but the older he grew, the less he remembered about who he was and what he had been able to do when he was the Lord Atalon of Obergon. When his first body wore out, his soul incarnated in another Terran body. At first he had brief glimpses and remembrances of who he was. But the history and teachings of Terra were nothing like what he remembered and gradually after many lifetimes, Atalon completely forgot who he was. Anteb returned home.

Atalon has NOT been leading his retinue of faithful followers for eons.

For eons Atalon's retinue to behave just like him. They continued to enslave humans. They continued their own breeding experiment. But one day, a visitor from another world arrived on Terra. No one knew he had come. His visit was brief, but he was able to accomplish his mission quickly and rapidly. This visitor had permission from the Planetary Council to come to Terra and undo what Atalon had done to the genetic structure of humans.

This visitor modified the genetic code and gave Terrans the ability to become gods. Terra is scheduled to become a doorway into a new universe. This new universe will be Odon's Universe. Odon and his children will create it, thereby continuing the outward expansion of the universe and the growth of new souls and new universes.

Atalon's retinue soon realized that these altered humans had capacities that THEY didn't have. If the Retinue wanted to remain in power, they had to do everything in their power to keep these altered humans from realizing the truth about themselves. Terrans were rapidly catching up to the "illegal aliens" in knowledge, intelligence and spirituality. But Terrans had something else, something the "illegal aliens" couldn't understand. Because they couldn't understand it, they feared it. Because they feared it, they decided to stunt the growth of all humans through a variety of different methods.

* * * * *

In 2003 I wrote the following article for Rumor Mill News:

Stargates in Iraq and Their Connection to Chemtrails

Is an Alien Race Genetically Re-engineering Humans to Return them to their Original Status as Slave Workers?

Did Another Alien Group Intervene on Behalf of the Humans Tens of Thousands of Years Ago? Did this Group Genetically Alter Humans and Free them from their Slave-like "Borg" Existence?

Are the Modifications these Aliens Made NOW being Undone via Chemtrails, Genetically Modified Food, Vaccinations and other Diabolical Methods?

Will the "Good Aliens" be Able to Intervene and Restore Their Plan for Creating A Race of Humans that not only is Equal with Other Races in the Universe....

But Surpasses All of Them?

Recently an old friend called. This friend has supplied me with bits and pieces of the puzzle over the years. He is one of the people who was involved in the original gold transfer from the Philippines to Austria. Like many of us, he was one of the ones who DIDN'T get the commission that was promised to us for arranging the gold transfer.

He still has his sources... both in and out of governments around the world. When he called the other day, I mentioned to him, that there hasn't been the usual number of chemtrails being reported. The information he passed on due to this comment is so complicated and spans so many different levels, that I don't know how to begin.

The subjects my friend discussed are so complex and so SEEMINGLY unrelated, that it seems to be an impossible task for me to try to condense a one-hour conversation into one paragraph. But I am going to try.

The essence of my friend's conversation goes like this:

Earth was started as a slave colony. I believe he said the Dracos were the ones who created the first slave race? AKA Adam. He compared Jehovah and Yahweh to Enki and Enlil. One being the harsh slave master and the other being a God who genuinely loved his creation and stood by them, guarding them as they genetically grew into beings who not only would equal other races in the universe, but who had the ability to surpass the other races.

My friend stated that the new race which is being created on planet earth would have the ability to create with their minds all the things that other races need technology to create. In Story One, Atalon and Shalma you read this sentence:

"Atalon was a master metaphysician. In his studies, he had transcended alchemy and learned matter transmogrification."

Story One does not elaborate on this, but in subsequent stories it is explained that Atalon had the ability to create anything he wanted, just by thinking it into existence. My friend said that the Dracos wanted to keep Earth a slave race, but another soul group from Sirius wanted to allow the human race to evolve into a race that would surpass all races. (My friend has not read The Obergon Chronicles.)

He said that the Dracos and the Sirians had been allies in the past, but now the Sirians realize that it would be far better to ally with the developing humans on earth.

It is the opinion of my friend that the reason for chemtrails, genetically altered foods, the AMA, western allopathic medicine and big pharma, is to deprive the human body of the nourishment it needs to evolve.

My friend also believes that in spite of the attempts during this century, to keep the human race as a slave race, the human race was evolving too quickly. This is why our atmosphere is being contaminated with chemtrails. (This is not saying that chemtrails are not also being used in junction with HAARP, but that is for mind control, not contamination.)

Reports, from different areas of the US and Canada, have stated that chemtrails contain bacteria while other reports show no bacteria but high aluminum content... different uses in different places could explain this.

The theory my friend was putting forth is that the recent incursion into Iraq had to do with finding the ancient alien technology and either destroying it or stealing it so they could use it themselves. According to my friend's theory, this signaled the Sirians that their intervention was needed on earth to ensure that the human race survives.

My friend believes that the Sirians have intervened and told the Dracos to knock off their plans to genetically dumb down the human race so they, the Dracos, could return humans to the slave race they created originally.

If my friend's thesis is correct, and the Sirians have intervened, then there are many things we should see in the near future.

o One is the secession of chemtrails.

o Next would be a ban on frankenfoods. Companies like Monsanto would face bankruptcy due to lawsuits and the legally mandated clean up of our environment.

o A change in our court system would be mandatory! We need an honest court in order to do these things.

This process of change is bubbling to the surface right now in California. Soon all states will look to California and realize that THE PEOPLE REALLY DO HAVE THE POWER. The people can take back their governments and their courts. All they need is a few people with vision and money to back their efforts and all crooked politicians and judges will be forced out.

The California Recall successfully collected the signatures it needed to force a special election to Recall Governor Davis. If the people of California, with a few hundred thousand dollars in start-up money, from Congressional Representatives:Congressman Darrell Issa, can force the removal of a politician who has ties to some of the most corrupt people and groups in the world, then it means that all people in the United States, and maybe in Canada, the UK and Australia can unite and force their crooked politicians and judges out of office.

Once the crooked politicians are forced from power, the people need to go in and revise the election process and the political money contribution process. The corporations are funneling both to political campaigns AND to non profit activist groups that make and distribute political ads and organize protests against politicians they want removed.

In other words, the activist groups are unknowingly being used by the very corporations they say they hate!

If our political system is left the way it is, only the servants of the corporations will be elected. It doesn't matter which party, the corporations support and own politicians from all parties.

The two party system in the United States was only designed to divide and conquer the ignorant and uneducated. Remember, educated people CAN still be ignorant! The colleges and universities that are run by the INTERNATIONAL ELITE. Their motto is: IGNORANCE through EDUCATION!

Returning to 2006:

The friend who gave me the information above had not read the Obergon Chronicles. I believe the beings he referred to as Dracos are Atalon's Retinue.

I believe the Sirians, who my friend believes are now entering earth/Terra, are the elder brethren of the souls from Obergon.

I believe that many of the Obergonian souls who have been studying on Terra, have now completed their lessons and they are either going home or to other schools.

My friend compared Jehovah and Yahweh to Enlil and Enki. Jehovah/Enlil were the harsh slave masters. Yahweh/Enki were the God who genuinely loved his creation and stood by them. Who were Jehovah/Enlil and Yahweh/Enki? I have often wondered if Atalon was the prototype for the Jehovah/Enlil god model and Anteb was the prototype for the Yahweh/Enki model.

As I have said many times…. I don't have the answers to all your questions. I have as many questions as you have. But since I have the background of the Obergon Chronicles, and few people on earth have this background, there are some things I believe.

I believe Atalon's Retinue has been dealt with. I believe these "illegal aliens" are now in the process of being deported.

However, over the eons, The Retinue of "illegal aliens" created many "willingly slaves." These willing slaves are now in power all over the world. They are human, but they have been programmed to believe that they are superior to other humans. This programming has been passed down from generation to generation. Eons ago, some bloodlines of the more powerful "willing slaves" were genetically altered. Humans were forcibly bred with "illegal aliens" in order to create a race of "willing slaves."

The "illegal aliens" are almost immortal... but not quite. They think they cannot be killed, but many of them have been killed. The "illegal alien," population dwindled, and over the eons, the alien DNA has been diluted with human DNA... almost to the point that these "willing slaves" are almost 100% human.

But even in spite of being almost 100% human, these "willing slaves" are still operating on the original program that was put into them genetically, by the "illegal aliens." This is because when a soul incarnates in a material form, it absorbs the lessons that were studied. That's how a soul grows. When a soul incarnated in a bloodline that was contaminated with the "programmed" DNA, the soul absorbed the "program" that was created by the "illegal aliens" and carried it on to the next incarnation.

Even though most of the "illegal aliens" have been evicted, their "willing slaves" continue the "program" as if their masters were still around. Their programming probably would have held forever, if highly evolved souls had not chosen to incarnate into these blood-lines. These highly evolved souls know the secret of transforming the DNA and transmuting all programming that was in the genetic code.

Not only can the highly evolved souls transmute the DNA programming in their present bodies; but using a process which is an ascended version of "morphogenic fields," these highly evolved souls can transmute the DNA programming of all the souls from which they are descended. In other words, the highly evolved souls that some refer to as the Indigo Children, are freeing all Obergonian souls from Atalon's Retinue's "programming."

It is possible that a few of the Retinue, aka, "illegal aliens" have escaped detection by the Planetary Council and are still hidden in their underground palaces, but "illegal aliens" no longer control Terra... their "willing slaves" are the ones who are in control.

Within a 100 years or less, I suspect that all of these "willingly slaves" will be released from their DNA or soul programming.

One of the lessons that Atalon needed to learn was what it felt like to be mind controlled, and NOT in charge of his own life. If Gunther Russbacher really was Atalon, his life as a covert CIA operative taught him what it feels like to be programmed. I wonder if having his memory of me erased from his mind has helped him learn what it was like to be separated from his other half. Atalon erased the memory of Xanos from Shalma's mind. In this life, someone did the same thing to him. They erased his memory of me and of everything we endured to stay together.

After Gunther and I were re-married in 1994 on our 5th wedding anniversary, he said to me:

"No one will EVER be able to separate us now!"

What he said on August 30th, 1994 also remind me of what he said on August 28th, 1989.

"I am Atalon, and you are my other half. I have searched the combined universes for millions of years. Now that I have found you, *no one* will *ever* be able to separate us."

Someone *did* separate us. Why did they separate us? I doubt if I will ever know the truth. You will have to draw your own conclusion. You now know almost as much about this as I do.

I invite you to join me on the Obergon Forum.
http://www.obergonchronicles.com

If you have questions, I will try to answer them there. But please remember, I don't have answers to everything. I can only tell you what I saw, heard and lived through. Most of which still doesn't make sense to me… so don't be disappointed if I can't answer your question.

Blessings,
Rayelan

Index

A

B

C

W

X

About the Author

Rayelan Allan (Russbacher) is the publisher of Rumor Mill News. She is a well-known writer and researcher on government crime and corruption and the inter-connected network of families who own and/or control most corporations and banks throughout the world. This network is commonly known as the New World Order. Best known, before her marriage to Gunther Russbacher, as a speaker on esoteric history and secret societies, Rayelan presented workshops throughout the United States and was a regular guest lecturer at the United Nations.

Her husband, Gunther Russbacher, was the October Surprise Pilot. He was imprisoned two days after they married. For four long and dangerous years, Rayelan worked to keep herself and Gunther alive by publicizing his status as a political prisoner of the Bush Adminis-tration. She met with imprisoned CIA, FBI, and DEA agents and operatives who provided documents impli-cating Bush Administration figures in drug and arms smuggling.

Further investigations uncovered government mind control operations that are linked to assassinations, satanic cults, New Age channels and a world-wide conspiracy to change culture through media "programming" and Hegelian conditioning.

As a teacher, publisher and writer, Rayelan Allan has had a career that demonstrates her deep love for her country and for all of its people in all of their conditions. She is the author of *Diana, Queen of Heaven, The New World Religion*.